HAMMOND INNES

Maddon's Rock

VINTAGE BOOKS
London

Published by Vintage 2013

Copyright © The Estate of Hammond Innes 1948

First published in Great Britain by Collins in 1948

Vintage
Random House, 20 Vauxhall Bridge Road,
London SW1V 2SA

www.vintage-classics.info

Addresses for companies within The Random House Group Limited
can be found at: www.randomhouse.co.uk/offices.htm

The Random House Group Limited Reg. No. 954009

A CIP catalogue record for this book
is available from the British Library

ISBN 9780099577751

The Random House Group Limited supports the Forest Stewardship
Council® (FSC®), the leading international forest-certification
organisation. Our books carrying the FSC label are printed on
FSC®-certified paper. FSC is the only forest-certification scheme
supported by the leading environmental organisations, including
Greenpeace. Our paper procurement policy can be found at:
www.randomhouse.co.uk/environment

Printed and bound in Great Britain by
Clays Ltd, St Ives PLC

MADDON'S ROCK

Ralph Hammond Innes was born in Horsham, Sussex, on 15 July 1913 and educated at Cranbrook School, Kent. He left school aged eighteen, and worked successively in publishing, teaching and journalism. In 1936, in need of money in order to marry, he wrote a supernatural thriller, *The Doppelganger*, which was published in 1937 as part of a two-year, four book deal. In 1939 Innes moved to a different publisher, and began to write compulsively, continuing to publish throughout his service in the Royal Artillery during the Second World War.

Innes travelled widely to research his novels and always wrote from personal experience – his 1940s novels *The Blue Ice* and *The White South* were informed by time spent working on a whaling ship in the Antarctic, while *The Lonely Skier* came out of a post-war skiing course in the Dolomites. He was a keen and accomplished sailor, which passion inspired his 1956 bestseller *The Wreck of the Mary Deare*. The equally successful 1959 film adaptation of this novel enabled Innes to buy a large yacht, the *Mary Deare*, in which he sailed around the world for the next fifteen years, accompanied by his wife and fellow author Dorothy Lang.

Innes wrote over thirty novels, as well as several works of non-fiction and travel journalism. His thrilling stories of spies, counterfeiters, black markets and shipwreck earned him both literary acclaim and an international following, and in 1978 he was awarded a CBE. Hammond Innes died at his home in Suffolk on 10th June 1998.

OTHER NOVELS BY HAMMOND INNES

Air Bridge
Attack Alarm
Atlantic Fury
Campbell's Kingdom
Dead and Alive
Delta Connection
Golden Soak
High Stand
Isvik
Killer Mine
Levkas Man
Medusa
North Star
Solomons Seal
Target Antarctica
The Angry Mountain
The Big Footprints
The Black Tide
The Blue Ice
The Doomed Oasis
The Land God Gave to Cain
The Last Voyage
The Lonely Skier
The Strange Land
The Strode Venturer
The Trojan Horse
The White South
The Wreck of the Mary Deare
Wreckers Must Breathe

CONTENTS

CHAPTER I
WE SAILED FROM MURMANSK   PAGE **9**

CHAPTER II
THE EXPLOSION   **33**

CHAPTER III
ABANDON SHIP!   **55**

CHAPTER IV
THE COURT-MARTIAL   **78**

CHAPTER V
DARTMOOR PRISON   **107**

CHAPTER VI
ESCAPE FROM DARTMOOR   **138**

CHAPTER VII
MADDON'S ROCK   **166**

CHAPTER VIII
THE *Trikkala*   **193**

CHAPTER IX
MAROONED   **216**

CHAPTER X
DYNAMITE   **237**

To

MY WIFE

You have fed me *Treasure Island* for years as the most exciting adventure story ever written. Well, this isn't *Treasure Island*. But there is an island. And there is bullion. And it is an exciting adventure story. I hope you will like the finished book as much as you did when I outlined the story to you at Cape Cornwall.

Aldbourne.
December, 1946.

CHAPTER I

WE SAILED FROM MURMANSK

THE STORY of the *Trikkala* is a strange one. She was a Greek ship, taken over by Britain in 1941, and operated by the Kelt Steamship Company on behalf of the Ministry of War Transport until 5th March, 1945. At 0236 hours on that March morning her career officially ended. A single paragraph, in a trade paper, records her end : The *s.s. Trikkala*, a freighter of 5,000 tons, was mined and sunk on 5th March, 1945, with the loss of twenty-three lives. She was in convoy and her position at the time of the sinking was approximately 300 miles north-west of Tromso.

Yet, on the 16th of May, 1946—just over a year later— the Naval W/T station, Loch Ewe, near Oban, picked up an S O S from a vessel describing herself as the *Trikkala*. Shortly afterwards this vessel radioed information that left no doubt as to her identity. It was the *Trikkala*. In view of the importance of her cargo, an Admiralty tug was sent out to bring her in, and for two days there was hardly a person in the country who was not speculating on the mystery of her dramatic reappearance.

I suppose I know more about the *Trikkala's* story than any one still living, except perhaps Bert Cook, who was with me. I was one of the survivors of the sinking in March, 1945. And it was I who sent out the S O S from the *Trikkala* in May, 1946. Accordingly, I have set out here the full story as I saw it, beginning from the night before she sailed from Murmansk.

It was the 2nd of March, 1945. Bert and I were awaiting repatriation to England. Murmansk was bitterly cold. The wind ran shrieking through the great wooden shed of a warehouse in which we were billeted. It tore the cardboard packing from the broken window panes. It ripped in under the eaves and up through the cracks

between the floorboards. And with it came a powdery
drift of snow that sifted along the floor like sand across
a desert. The vast storage floor of the shed was packed
with Red Army men, vague doss-house shapes, huddled
in blankets that were whitened with snow.

There were eight of us awaiting repatriation and we
had been allocated a room to ourselves that had once been
an office. It had a calendar and a brazier. That was all
the furniture. Most of us were huddled around the brazier
for warmth that night. Twenty-two days were marked
off on the calendar. We had been waiting for a ship all
that time. I remember thinking how in England the
blackthorn would be out and there would be a smell of
spring in the air. But in Murmansk the trees were black
and the world was still in the grip of winter. There was
ice everywhere, and a heavy blanket of snow muffled all
sound, so that even the great Red Army supply wagons,
with their iron-shod wheels, moved through the streets
without a sound. Murmansk will always be to me a
memory of intense cold, of men's faces ruddy in the glow
of a brazier and of the never-ceasing noise of the wind
above the clatter and whistle of the trains and the singing
of the Russian soldiers.

An extra heavy gust of wind beat against the windows.
One of the cardboard panes blew out and an icy blast
shivered through the room. "Cor stone the crows!"
Bert Cook muttered. " 'Ark at that awful wind. As if
life ain't miserable enough, but it 'as ter blow a blizzard.
An' it's me berfday tomorrer. Nice berfday I'm goin'
ter 'ave, I don't fink." He looked round the bare wooden
room, cluttered with kit, and then leaned closer to the
brazier. He had a little monkey-like face. It was creased
by laughter, and the lined, almost leathery skin was
reddened by the glow of the hot coals. He had had all
his teeth out just before leaving England and his cheeks
had fallen in around the empty gums like the cheeks of
an old crone. "S'pose the Ruskies ain't got no glass,
poor devils," he went on. "But they might board the
winders up—cardboard ain't no good in this sort of
wevver." He got up then and fitted the bit of cardboard

back into the window. He leaned a rifle against it to keep it in place. Then he came back to the fire. " Reminds me of the Free Fevvers da'n St. Pancras way, this place does. Always was a draughty pub." He grinned at the others and spread his dirt-stained hands to the blaze."

I liked Bert. He was the sort of man that makes four years in the ranks seem worth while. Nothing ever really got him down. He was a Cockney. His home was in Islington. But Islington or Murmansk, it didn't worry him. I'd met up with him at a Russian Ordnance depot near Leningrad. I had been sent over to assist in the maintenance of certain predictors and Bert was there with a gunnery team, demonstrating the drill for a new gun Britain had recently sent to Russia.

Bert was gazing round the group of faces huddled close to the brazier. " Help! What a country ! " he muttered. " No wonder Jerry couldn't stick it." His face brightened to a grin. " I got 'arf a bottle of vodka in me kitbag. I was savin' it fer termorrer. But we'll knock it back when we're in the ol' scratcher. That'll help liven up the cockles." And he rubbed his hands over the blaze. Then his face clouded. " But when I fink of the Ol' Woman all alone wiv the kids in Islington," he added, " it fair makes me blood boil. A munf's disembarkation leave we got waitin' fer us when we land. An' we're stuck in this dump. Look at that calendar ! Free whole weeks we bin hincarcerated in this ware'ase—the job finished, guns all ready ter bang away at Berlin an' a nice word o' praise from a Rusky colonel. An' wot do we get ? Free weeks in this 'ell 'ole. Dartmoor ain't got nuffink on this place. Got any fags left, Corp ? "

I opened my case. " Gawd ! " he said. " Only four left—an' Rossian at that. Better save 'em ter smoke wiv the firewater. Where's Mister Bloomin' Warrant Officer ternight ? "

Warrant Officer Rankin was the senior occupant of the room. He was large and fat with a smooth face and a soft voice. Blue eyes peered at you over little pouches of white flesh and his hands, which pawed eagerly at the shoulder of any subordinate who was sufficiently servile, were podgy and neatly manicured. When angry his soft voice became high-pitched. He stood very much on the dignity of his rank. And one felt that without that advantage of rank, his voice might easily deteriorate into a whine. He had been sent over to do a technical job for the Navy and was temporarily in charge of some Naval stores.

"The same place as he was last night," I told Bert in answer to his question, "and the night before and every night since we've been here."

He gave an evil cackle, displaying his toothless gums. "Calls it learnin' Roosian. That's a joke, that is. When 'e's in China, 'e learns Chinese, an' when 'e's in Sigypore, he learns whatever the native lingo is there. I bet it's the same words 'e learns everywhere 'e goes." The faces round the brazier cracked with laughter. They all hated Rankin's guts. "Where's 'e get the dough from, anyway?" Bert demanded.

"Oh," I said, "he's in some racket or other. Started with watches—you know how crazy the Russians are for anything that ticks. He managed to smuggle some out with him. Told me so the other night. And then he's in charge of stores. That's always a help to a man like Rankin. And he's chummed up with that little political commissar who speaks English."

"D'yer mean the fresh-faced boy wot's s'pposed ter keep tabs on the local commandant?" Bert scowled into the fire. "I seen 'im yesterday, struttin' alongside of 'is boss fit ter burst a ligyment. Smart as a new pin, 'e looked. A sly little chit, if you ask me. Ever bin in that place da'n on Molotov Street, Corp?"

"No," I told him.

"Wish I 'ad as much dough as Rankin's got," he went on. I was only half-listening. "I s'ppose 'e'll be drunk again ternight when 'e comes back—chuckin' 'is weight aba't as usual, gettin' poor little Sills ter make 'is bed fer 'im. 'E's a fair swine."

And at that moment we heard Rankin's voice in the corridor outside. It was angry and slurred. "Why the hell can't we go aboard in the morning?" we heard him ask. And another voice replied, " Special duty. Lt.-Commander Selby insisted that you'd got to be there by 2200 hours. That's why I had to rout you out."

Then the door opened and Rankin stood there with a piece of paper in his hand. He wasn't drunk. But there were two hectic spots in the smooth white of his cheeks and his eyes were bright. With him was a Naval writer from NOIC's office—that was the office of the Naval Officer in Charge, Murmansk. Rankin leaned his bulk against the doorpost, pushed his cap on to the back of his head and said, " Who want's to go home ? " He had a sadistic little smile on his lips as he watched our faces. He knew that we were all fed to the teeth with Murmansk. He watched the rustle of expectation that ran through the faces round the brazier.

" Thinks 'e's rafflin tickets for a passage 'ome in the *Queen Mary*," muttered Bert, and the others grinned.

Rankin heard the remark, but the smile didn't leave his face. " I see you and I are going to get on well together, Cook." Then he turned to the clerk. " What's the time ? " he asked.

" Seven-thirty," was the reply.

" If I have 'em paraded at eight-thirty and get down to the quay about nine—that all right ? "

" As long as you're on board before ten, Mr. Rankin," was the reply.

" Good." Then he turned to me. " Corporal Vardy ! "

" Yes ? " I said.

" You'll parade with the others detailed on this list at eight-thirty sharp, outside. And see that it's a smart turn-out. Sills, get my kit packed and ready." With that he handed me the paper and went out.

An eager crowd of faces peered at it over my shoulder. We read it by the light of the brazier :

The following personnel awaiting repatriation will embark on the s.s. Trikkala, No. 4 berth, Lenin Quay, not later than 2200 hours, 2nd March, 1945 :

Warrant Officer L. R. Rankin, Corporal J. L. Vardy, Private P. Sills, Gunner H. B. Cook.

*Dress for Army personnel: F. S. M. O. Kitbags will
be carried. Warrant Officer Rankin will be in charge of
the party throughout the voyage. He will report to Captain
Halsey, master of the "Trikkala," on arrival on board. He
will hold himself and his party at Captain Halsey's
disposal for special duties during the voyage.*

We drank Bert's vodka then and there, and two hours
later were trudging through the snow-carpeted streets
towards the river and the lights of the docks. The *Trikkala*
was not a beautiful ship. She hadn't even the utility
lines of the American liberty boat berthed astern of her.
She was like an angular old spinster with her single tall
funnel, high bridge and clutter of deckhousings. She had
a three-inch gun perched on her high bows and another
aft. Boats hung in their davits either side of the bridge
and there was a third at the stern. Rafts clung precari-
ously to their fittings above the after deckhousing. But
we weren't worrying about her looks as we climbed the
gangway. We'd have cheerfully embarked in a North
Sea trawler if it had been going to England.

The *Trikkala* was loading as we went aboard. Her holds
were open and into them was being poured load after load
of iron-ore. She had her derricks working and the clatter
of the donkey engines and the roar of the ore pouring
into the ship was deafening. Fore and aft the holds smoked
like volcanoes as the ore dust billowed up into the dazzle
of the loading lights. The thick mantle of snow that
covered her decks was no longer white, but a dirty, reddish
brown.

" Halt your men there, Corporal," Rankin ordered.
" I'll go and see the Captain."

We halted at the top of the gangway and stood waiting
whilst the bitter wind blew choking clouds of ore dust
in our faces.

Had we known then what Fate had in store for us,
no military order ever devised would have sent us across
that gangway on to the deck of the *Trikkala*. But we
didn't know. We just stood there, numbed and cold,
watching without curiosity as Rankin climbed the ladder

to the bridge where Captain Halsey paced to and fro. We knew nothing then of the nature of the man or of the thoughts that were racing through his mind as he walked the bridge of his ship.

Captain Halsey's dead now. But he still haunts me in my dreams—a little, violent man with a black beard and black hair and black little button eyes to match, eyes that were wild and greedy and cruel. A madman full of dramatic gestures and long Shakespearean speeches that he plucked from his memory to suit his mood. A madman ? But there was method in his madness. My God, yes—there was method in it. The devil himself in a peaked cap and a blue serge uniform with little gilt buttons couldn't have plotted the damnation of a platoon of human souls with an easier conscience than Halsey planned the cold-blooded murder of a like number of human beings.

And whilst we stood on that frozen deck, the Rock was waiting for us out there in the Barents Sea. Maddon's Rock. I shall never forget that place. Milton's blind eyes had never seen the desolation of those seas when he described his Hell. Torrent fire, dire hail, perpetual storms and parching air, yes—but out there, lit through the eternal night by the cold, groping fingers of the Nothern Lights, is my idea of Hell ; a restless tumult of waves tumbling in thunderous cascades across the reefs, climbing the cliffs of the Rock and pouring green along its flanks. And the Rock itself—living rock, as much a part of our earth as a green hill or a moss-grown bank, but here an island, thrust up out of the wrack of ocean— grey, bleak, sheened with ice and polished by the waters so that it is as smooth as the skull of a dead man.

But we knew nothing of all this as we waited for Rankin on the *Trikkala's* frozen deck. In five minutes he was back with the first mate, a dour, lanky Scot named Hendrik, with restless eyes and a scar that ran from the tip of his left ear to the point of his jaw. " Come along, Corporal," Rankin said, " and I'll show you your quarters." I followed them to the after-deckhousing. Just aft of the engine-room hatches on the port side was

a wide steel door. The mate threw off the clips and slid
it back. Then he switched on the lights to reveal a bare
room about twenty feet by ten. There were no portholes
and no fittings of any sort. The walls and roof were of
steel and steel deck plates formed the floor. It smelt of
stale grease.

"There ye are, Mr. Rankin," said the mate. "They'll
live here wi' the cargo."

Rankin turned to me. "Get your men settled in,
Corporal," he said. "A special cargo will be coming on
board to-night. It will be stowed here. You and your
men will act as guard." Then to the mate : "Any idea
what this cargo is, Mr. Hendrik ? "

The mate's eyes flicked to Rankin's face and he said,
"No." But it was said a little too emphatically.

Rankin looked at the empty space of the room. "Can't
be a very big cargo if it's to go in here," he murmured.
"What was the place used for, Mr. Hendrik ? "

"Mess-room for the after-deck," Hendrik replied.
"We shifted 'em oot this morning."

"Queer, having a mess-room right on deck," said
Rankin.

"Aye. But it wasna designed for a mess-room. The
Trikkala's Clydeside built to Greek specifications. I
fancy the Greeks used this as a handy place for stowing
passenger's baggage and odd bits of cargo that couldna
be stowed away in the hold of her."

Rankin seemed to have lost interest. He turned to me
and said, "Get your men settled in now, Corporal. Mr.
Hendrik here will have blankets and hammocks sent up.
I'll let you have your guard orders as soon as the cargo
arrives."

As I turned I heard him say to the mate, "The
Captain mentioned that there was a spare cabin I could
use."

"Aye," Hendrik replied.

"Well, chum, wot's the griff ? " Bert asked as I returned
to the two figures standing forlornly by the gangway.

"You'll see," I said, and took them aft to our new
quarters.

Even Sills, a little uncomplaining north countryman, said, " It's goin' ter be beastly cold laike oop 'ere." Bert looked at me and said, " Wot's the idea, Corp ? I was speakin' ter one of the seamen an' 'e said there was bunks to spare da'n in the foc'stle. I s'ppose because we're in the darned Army, they fink we'll be 'appy ter kip da'n in a perishin' spot like this."

I said, " We're here because there's some sort of a special cargo coming on board and we're detailed for guard duties throughout the voyage."

" Guard dooties ! " Bert flung his kit into one corner. " They would fink up somefink like that. Why can't we be repatriated peaceful-like, same as if we was decent citizens. Where's that Mr. Rankin ? Don't see his kit around. S'ppose 'e'll be feedin' wiv the officers da'n in a nice cosy mess-room while we're freezin' ter death up 'ere. I can just 'ear 'im saying to the capting, 'Hi'm a Warrant Officer of the Royal Navy. Hi'm not accustomed ter feedin' wiv the men.' " He slipped his pack on to the floor and his tin hat clattered on the steel deck-plating. " Nice trip this is goin' ter be ! Didn't you raise a squeal for better quarters, Corp ? "

" Couldn't very well," I said. " You saw the movement order. Detailed for special duties during the voyage."

" Gawd ! " he said and sat himself down morosely on his kitbag.

Half an hour later as I stood on deck watching the loading of the ship, four Russian lorries came lumbering along the dockside and stopped opposite the *Trikkala*. They were open trucks and they were loaded with big square packing cases. There were three Red Army guards on each truck.

A British Naval Officer came on board and went up to the bridge. Shortly afterwards one of the derricks was swung out towards the leading truck and the work of swinging the packing cases on board began. It was our special cargo. The cases were marked " Hurricane Engines for Replacement."

" First time I ever heard of a special guard being placed on dud aero engines," Bert grumbled. I'd never

seen him in this sort of mood before. He was usually
so cheerful.

When all were stowed safely, the Naval Officer with
Rankin and the skipper of the *Trikkala* and a Russian
official of some sort came in and counted the cases. Then
a sheaf of papers was produced and everybody signed.
When that was done the Naval Officer turned to the
Trikkala's skipper and said, " Well, it's your responsibility
now, Captain Halsey." Then to Rankin, " See that you
keep a strict guard, Mr. Rankin." Then they went out, all
but Rankin, who called me over and handed me a type-
written sheet. " Those are your guard orders, Corporal,"
he said. " Two hours on, four hours off night and day.
Guard on duty will be properly dressed and armed.
He'll stand or march up and down outside this door."
He leaned closer to me and his breath reeked of drink as
he added, " And if I find any slackness—the guard not
on duty or not dressed correctly—you'll be in trouble,
Corporal, and so will the man on duty."

Bert stood up and came towards us. " Two on an'
four off," he said. " Ain't yer goin' ter do guard dooty
wiv us then, Mr. Rankin ? "

For a moment Rankin appeared too surprised to speak.
He gave a little intake of breath and then said stiffly and
with suave menace, " A Warrant Officer of the Royal
Navy, Cook, doesn't do guard duties."

" So we 'as ter do it for you, eh ? That ain't fair,
yer know. We're all in the same boat, in a manner o'
speakin'. If we 'ad a sergeant wiv us nah instead of a
ruddy Warrant Officer, he'd muck in like any decent
bloke would."

Rankin literally shook with anger. " A Warrant Officer
is not a sergeant," he said and his voice was pitched a
shade higher than usual. " Any more lip from you, Cook,
and I'll have you up before the Captain."

Bert gave a toothless grin. " An' do me guard dooty
for me whilst I'm in irons—I don't fink."

" I'm not as simple as that," replied Rankin smoothly.
" You're expecting some leave when you get in, aren't
you ? "

"Gosh! I should 'ope so," Bert answered. "Four munfs in Roosia—ain't I earned it?"

Rankin's voice suddenly sharpened. "Whether you've earned it or not, my lad, you just watch your step. All of you," he added, his eyes glancing quickly from one to the other of us, "or you won't get any leave." Then he turned to me with a little sneering smile. "I hear you're going for a commission, Corporal?" And when I didn't say anything, he said, "Well, are you or aren't you?"

"Yes," I said.

"Good!" He smiled and turned to go. At the door he stopped. "You see this guard runs smoothly then, Corporal, or I'll give you a report that'll send you running back to your unit with your tail between your legs. Now get your sentry posted."

When he had gone, Bert turned to me. "Why don't yer stand up to 'im?" he said. "It's you wot's got the stripes, not me." And when I said nothing he turned away with a look of disgust and I heard him mutter to Sills, "Going for a commission—fine feeble awficer he'll make."

I posted him as sentry and then went for'ard for a stroll round the ship. Loading appeared to have ceased. The derricks were still and the holds were just dark craters in the ship's decks. The arc lights for our berth had been switched off. The Liberty boat behind us was still loading. The clatter of her donkey-engines split the nights like pneumatic drills. And across the river the arc lights blazed above the wharfs and the temporary wooden sheds where roofs were weighed down with snow. The sound of loading came loud and clear through the frozen night.

But the *Trikkala* seemed to have settled to sleep in her little pool of shadow. Only the deck lights swung their dim yellow globes in the wind, casting dark moving shadows across the deck. On the bridge the muffled figure of the watch paced to and fro. The wind was from the east. It came roaring over the huddle of dockside sheds and made strange noises in the *Trikkala's* superstructure. It was bitterly cold and already the snow had a crisp crust of ice that crunched beneath my feet. I got

to windward of the bridge on the starboard side and
leaned my back against the sheltering ironwork.

The noise of the docks was now no more than a distant
clatter. There were no arc lights to dazzle the night. I
had a clear view down the black waters of the Tuloma
River to Kola Bay. Distant buoy lights danced with
their reflections like will-o'-the-wisps. Down the estuary,
far, far to the north, the horizon showed as a black line
against the cold, changing colours of the Northern Lights.

I lit a cigarette. I felt depressed. I cursed Rankin for
letting slip that I was going for a commission. And I
was angry with Betty for forcing my hand. Instead
of a month's disembarkation leave, I was due to report
immediately to Deepcut for pre-OCTU training. Besides,
I wasn't cut out for an Army Officer's job. The Navy—
yes. I've been sailing very nearly since I could walk. At
sea I've plenty of confidence. But the Navy had turned
me down on eyesight. And in the Army I'd always felt
like a fish out of water.

A light suddenly shone out from a porthole just to the
left of where I was standing. The porthole was open. A
voice said, "Come in, Mr. Hendrik, come in." It was a
soft, gentle voice with a strangely vibrant quality : A
door closed and there was the sound of a cork being drawn
out of a bottle. "Now, what about this guard ? "

Hendrik's voice answered, "Well, it's nae more than
we expected."

"A guard—no. But we expected soldiers, not a Naval
Warrant Officer. That might make it awkward. Know
anything about this fellow Rankin, Mr. Hendrik ? "

"Aye. I met him in—weel, I met him the other
nicht. I've an idea that if there's any deeficulty wi' him
he could be made to see reason. He's no short o' cash.
If ye like I'll away and see Kalinsky in the mornin'.
It'd be Kalinsky he'd be dealing wi'—they all do. As
for the corporal and the other two soldiers, we'll no have
any trouble——"

And that was all I heard of the conversation for the
porthole suddenly closed and the little circle of light was
blotted out as it was battened down from inside. I stood

there for a moment, watching the glowing tip of my cigarette and trying to make sense out of the fragment of conversation I had heard. Hendrik had been speaking to the captain. I realised that. But just what the significance of it was I could not determine.

Puzzled, I walked slowly back to our quarters. Bert was pacing up and down outside the door. He had his rifle slung on his shoulder and he swung his arms to keep himself warm. His face looked pinched and cold in the light that swung above the engine-room hatches. " Any luck, Corp ? " he asked as I came up.

" About what ? " I asked.

" Why the blankets and 'ammocks. Thort that was wot you'd gawn off ter see aba't."

" Haven't they been sent up ? " I asked.

" Not a sign of 'em," he replied.

" I'll go down and see Rankin about them," I said.

" Good. An' when yer see 'im, Corp, give 'im my love and tell 'im I'd like ter ring 'is stupid neck. I can just see 'im sticking it fer two long hours a't in this beastly wind. Ask 'im why we can't do our guard dooties inside."

" All right, Bert," I said. There was a companionway in the after-deckhousing. I went down this and found myself in a long corridor. It was warm and smelt of engine oil and stale food grease. The only sound in that empty steel-lined corridor was the steady hum of the dynamos. I hesitated and at that moment a door opened and a man in gum-boots went aft. The sound of men's voices drifted through the lighted doorway. I went down the corridor, knocked and entered. It was the crew's mess room. Three men were seated at one of the scrubbed deal tables. They took no notice of me. One of them, a Welshman, was saying, " But I tell you, man, he's not sane. This very morning, it was, up for'ard where the Russians were fixing that plate. The door of Number Two bulkhead was open and I went through to see what was going on. The Captain was there, with Mr. Hendrik. Watching the Russians, they were. And as soon as he sees me, he says, ' Davies,' he says, ' what are you doing here ? ' So I tells him I just stepped through to

see what all the racket was about. ' Well, get out, man,'
he says. And then 'Out, damned spot! Out, I say!'
And with that he starts roaring with laughter. ' Go on,
Davies,' he says, ' back to your work, man.' "

The other two men laughed, and one of them said, " You
don't want to worry about that, mate. He's always like
that, Captain Halsey is. You're new to the ship. But we
bin with him four trips now, ain't we, Ernie ? Shakespeare, Shakespeare, Shakespeare. He'll stand on the
bridge and spout Shakespeare by the hour. And when you
pass his cabin, you'll often hear 'im ranting and raving
inside. Ain't that so, Ernie ? "

The man referred to as Ernie nodded and took his pipe
out of his mouth. " Aye, that's right," he said. " An'
when you take a message to him up on the bridge you
never know whether it's the ghost of Banquo or one of
King Richard's bastards you're talking to. Gave me the
willies at first. But I got used to it now. And there's
some fine speeches he makes, too. You'll find half the
crew've got pocket editions of Shakespeare in their ditty
boxes just for the fun of imitatin' the Old Man." He
looked up then and saw me standing in the doorway.
" Hullo, chum," he said. " What do you want ? "

" Can you tell me which is Mr. Rankin's cabin ? " I
asked.

" The Navy feller, eh ? Reck'n he's got the one next
door to Mr. Cousins. Here, I'll show you." He got to his
feet and led me along the corridor. But when we found
Rankin's cabin, it was empty. " Does he drink ? " the
man called Ernie asked me in a whisper. I nodded. " Oh
well, then he'll be in the Chief's cabin." He knocked at
the door of a cabin farther for'ard and a slurred voice
mumbled " Come in ! " He opened the door and peered
in. " Okay, chum, there you are," he said.

I thanked him and went in. The Chief Engineer was
lying on his bunk. Bloodshot little eyes peered at me
above florrid cheeks. The naked electric light bulb beat
down upon his bald head. Bottles of beer lay about the
floor and on a chest of drawers stood two opened bottles
of whisky. The room was thick with smoke and the stale

smell of drink. Rankin sat on the foot of the Chief's bunk. He was in his shirt sleeves and his collar was undone. They were playing cribbage. The cards were laid out on the blankets of the bed. " Wot d'you want ? " asked Rankin.

" We've no blankets and no hammocks," I said.

He gave a sneering laugh and turned to the Chief. " Did you hear him, Chief ? " he said. " No blankets and no hammocks ! " He belched and scratched his head. " You're a corporal, aren't you ? Going to be an officer ? Where's your initiative, man ? Go and find the ship's storeman. He's the man to give you blankets and hammocks, not me." And then as I did not move, he said, " Well, what are you waiting for ? "

" There's another thing," I said. But I stopped then. His little pale blue eyes, like baby oysters swimming in their own mucus, were watching me closely. He knew what I was going to say. He knew that it was unnecessary for the guard to be outside. And he was waiting for me to say it, so that he could sneer at my ability to carry out orders. This was the sort of man for whom the protection of rank meant the pleasures of despotism. " It doesn't matter," I said and closed the door.

It was the sailors in the crew's mess-room who produced blankets and hammocks for me. Bert met me at the top of the companionway and relieved me of some of my burden. " Did yer see Rankin ? " he asked.

" Yes," I said.

" Any chance of us doing the guards inside ? "

" No."

His little monkey face peered up at me from his balaclava. " Yer did ast 'im, didn't yer ? "

" No," I said. " He was drunk and he was just waiting for the opportunity to get at me. It wasn't any use."

Bert slid the door of the storage room back with his shoulder and flung the handful of blankets he had taken from me on to the floor between the packing cases. " Blimey ! " he said, " if you was a rooky yer couldn't be more spineless." And he turned away to continue his guard.

I hesitated. But I only said, " I'll relieve you at one."
Then I went inside and slid the door to. Sills and I slung
the hammocks between the packing cases. It was past
midnight before we'd got them fixed. I climbed into mine
and tried to get some sleep before I went out to do my
turn. But I couldn't sleep. I felt angry with myself and
depressed about the present and the future. Even the
thought of being back in England didn't cheer me. But
for the fact that it would be the end of things between
Betty and myself. I knew I should have thrown up the
idea of going for a commission.

When I went out to relieve Bert an hour later, loading
seemed to have stopped throughout the docks. The arc
lights had all been switched off and a peace had descended
on the place. The snow-covered roofs of the dock sheds
glimmered faintly in the light from the deck lights.
Beyond lay a vague huddle of ships and sheds. The
Northern Lights lay right across the northern sky,
pulsing coldly. In their light the snow-muffled town
looked chill as ice. " Wind's droppin' a bit," Bert said.

I offered him a cigarette. There were only two left.
He looked up at me quickly and then took one. We lit
up and stood leaning against the rail for a while without
speaking. Suddenly Bert said, " Sorry I lost me temper
this evenin', Corp. Must a' bin the wevver. I felt fair
bra'ned off, I did."

" It's all right, Bert," I said.

We stood there in silence for a time and then he said,
" Goodnight," and left me alone to the cold and my
thoughts.

It was seven o'clock when I came out on deck for my
second spell of duty and in the dull morning light there
was an air of bustle about the ship. The hatches were
being battened down over the holds, fore and aft, and
billows of black smoke pouring out of the funnel showed
that we were getting up steam. As the light strengthened,
the port seemed to come to life. Tugs hurried back and
forth across the river, hooting ; and occasionally the deep
note of a ship's siren sounded. A destroyer lay farther
down the estuary, a dirty white ensign just visible in the

drifting smoke of her funnels. Shortly after Sills relieved me, two corvettes slipped down to join her and the three steamed slowly out of sight round a bend. " Think we'll sail this morning, Corp ? " Sills asked. There was a strange longing in his voice. He was not more than twenty. Probably this was the first time he'd been out of England.

" Looks as though there's a convoy forming," I said. " There's two boats over there being towed out from their moorings."

Ten minutes later the Liberty boat in the next berth to us slipped her moorings and with much hooting was hauled out into the open river by a diminutive tug that fussed around, churning the cold slate surface of the water to a muddy brown. I took a stroll round the ship. There was no doubt about it, we were getting ready to sail, and I began to feel that sense of excitement that is inevitable with the thought of putting to sea.

As I came abreast of the gangway I saw the figure of the first mate hurrying across the quayside. He walked quickly up the gangway and disappeared below the bridge in the direction of the Captain's cabin. I was reminded then of the conversation I had overheard the previous night. I leaned against the rail staring down unseeingly at the bustle of the docks, trying to figure out what had been meant, when Rankin's voice interrupted my thoughts, " Get your bedding all right, Corporal Vardy ? " he asked.

I turned. His face looked grey above the blue-clothed bulk of his body and the little oyster eyes were bloodshot. " Yes," I said, " I got them all right." And then without stopping to think, I said, " Does the name Kalinsky mean anything to you, Rankin ? "

He took a little breath and his eyes narrowed. " You trying to be funny, Corporal ? " he asked, endeavouring to cover that momentary shock.

" No," I said. " I just happened to hear two people mention your name in connection with Kalinsky."

" Who were they ? " he asked.

I turned to go. But he caught me by the shoulder and spun me round. " Who were they ? " he hissed angrily.

The bloodshot little eyes were staring at me over their pouches of flesh and there was a flicker of something I couldn't make out for a moment. And then I realised that he was frightened. " Who were they ! " he repeated.

" The Captain and the first mate," I said.

He let me go then and I left him standing slightly dazed at the top of the gangway. It was warmer now and the heat of the boilers was melting the snow round the engine-room hatches. Several ships had moved out into the harbour and there was an air of expectancy over the ship and the port that it was impossible to ignore.

I went below for a shave. The crew's washrooms were primitive. But there was plenty of hot water. The cook was standing in the open doorway of the galley, a fat, greasy man with a wart on his lower lip and little twinkling brown eyes. He produced a tin mug full of steaming cocoa for me with the conspiratorial air of an amateur producing a rabbit out of a hat.

I stood chatting with him as I drank, gratefully sweating in the warmth of his roaring galley fires. He'd been in almost every port on the globe. This was his fourth visit to Murmansk. " Ever heard of a man called Kalinsky in Murmansk ? " I asked.

" On Molotov Street—wot used to be St. Peter's Street ? " he asked.

" Maybe," I said. " What sort of a bloke is he ? "

" Well, he ain't a Slav and he ain't a Jew and he ain't a Turk neither, nor a Greek," he said. " But I guess he's a mixture of every race that ever set up shop to barter the pants off of an honest seaman. He's wot we'd call in England a fence. Why, you ain't in trouble with him, are you ? "

" No," I said. " I've got nothing to barter except my rifle."

His round little tummy heaved with laughter. " Kalinsky ain't above buying rifles," he said. " He's doing a good trade just at the moment in rifles and sabres with the Yanks as souvenirs of Russia. Swears they're Cossack, but they range from Lee Enfields to Italian *carabinieri* carbines."

The whole thing fell into place now. Rankin had been in charge of some Naval stores and Kalinsky was a receiver. No wonder Rankin had had plenty of money. But what puzzled me was why the Captain and his first mate wanted a hold over Rankin.

It was past eleven when I went up on deck again and Bert was on duty. " Any signs of our pushing off ? " I asked him.

" Not a sign."

The gangway was still down. But the Captain was up on the bridge, pacing to and fro, his black, pointed beard darting aggressively about him as he surveyed his ship. The quayside was practically empty. A solitary girl walked through the churned-up snow. She was dressed in a khaki greatcoat. A black beret was pulled over her dark curls and she carried a kitbag. She was looking up at the name of the ship, her face white in the dull light. Then she made for the gangway and began to struggle up it, trailing the kitbag behind her.

" Blimey ! there's a girl comin' on board," Bert said, catching hold of my sleeve. " Don't look all that strong neither. Why don't yer go an' give her a 'and wiv 'er kit ? " Then as I didn't say anything, he pushed his rifle into my hand. " 'Ere 'ang on to that, mate, an' pretend yer on guard. If you ain't goin' ter be a little gentleman I s'ppose I'll 'ave ter show yer that's it's a board school eddication wot's the best."

It's incredible to think that I let Bert go and help her up the gangway, instead of going myself. Was it because I was too busy gazing at that white, strained face ? It was a sad face and yet it looked as though it should have been gay. I wondered about her nationality and why she was coming aboard a ship bound for England. Some stray emerging from war-shattered Europe—a Pole perhaps, or a Czech, or possibly a Frenchwoman ?

I watched Bert shoulder her kitbag, saw the sudden flash of a smile on that wan face and then a voice at my elbow said, " Have ye seen Warrant Officer Rankin, Corporal ? "

It was Hendrik. "Not for the last hour," I told him.
"Why?"

"The Old Man wants him. If ye see him, tell him to
be gude enough to step up to the bridge."

He went for'ard and I stood there looking down at
the empty quayside. The ice in the snow ruts ruled black
lines beside the sheds. A tug hooted close by and a voice
from the bridge—Hendrik's voice—called through a
megaphone, "Stand by to catch that line, Jukes."

Bert suddenly materialised from the companionway,
his leathery little face puckered in a grin. "Well," I said
as he took his rifle, "what was she like?"

"As nice a kid as I met in me natural," he replied.
"An' believe it or not, mate, she's English. Name of
Jennifer Sorrel. Seen it on the label of 'er kitbag. Gawd
knows wot she's doin' in this dump. Didn't ast 'er. But
she looks as though she's 'ad a pretty thin time of it.
Face as white as the snow on that roof over there and the
skin sort of transparent-like and dark rings under the eyes.
But a lady, I could tell that." He began whistling *Daisy,
Daisy*, or trying to, for he'd lost the art with his teeth.
"That Mr. Cousins, wot's second officer, he took charge
of 'er. The bleedin' officers always 'as all the luck. An'
me wiv no teeth in me 'ead. The missis ain't 'alf goin'
ter kid me aba't that. 'Ope the new'ns 'ave come through.
They should 'ave by now, shouldn't they? 'Ullo, they're
gettin' the gangway up. That means we're on our way,
don't it?"

As if in answer to his question the *Trikkala's* siren
blared forth. A feather of white steam blew at the funnel
head. The tug gave a single answering hoot. Captain
Halsey appeared on the bridge, a megaphone in his hand.
"Let go for'ard," he called. The second officer, Mr.
Cousins, waved his arm from the bows. A Russian on
the quayside lifted the heavy loop of the line from its
bollard. It splashed in the water as the bows began to
swing away from the quay. The gap between the ship's
side and the quay steadily widened. The black, refuse-
scattered water lapped at the piers. "Let go aft." And
as the line hit the water, the engine-room telegraph rang

twice. The engines suddenly sprang to life under the
hatches close beside us. The ship shuddered. The filth
of the river bottom was churned to the surface. Then,
as we slipped our tow, the *Trikkala*, under her own
steam, swung in a great arc across the river and made
down-stream, round the bend and out into Kola Bay,
where the convoy was forming.

It was one o'clock before all the ships of the convoy
were gathered in the mouth of the estuary. And at one-
fifteen we sailed. When I came off duty at three the
Murman Coast was just a dirty white smudge between the
leaden grey of the sky and the restless grey of the sea.

According to the gossip of the ship we were bound for
Leith in the Firth of Forth. And I reckoned that it would
take us about five days. I mentioned this to Bert when
I relieved him again at seven that evening. He said,
" Christ ! Have we got five days of this." The wind was
getting up and it was freezing cold out there on the
blacked-out deck. " I'd like ter know what the 'ell's in
them cases. You'd fink it was the Bank of England we
was guarding. If it's aero engines, I reck'n it's a ruddy
disgrace. Why should we 'ave ter stand abart 'ere catching
our death for nuffink. Them cases ain't goin' ter get up
an' walk overboard."

" I can't help it," I said. " The orders are that a guard
has to be mounted on them, and that's all there is to it."

" It ain't your fault, Corp. But it do seem ruddy silly,
don't it ? Well, s'ppose I may as well turn into the ol'
scratcher an' git a bit o' shut-eye before I come on dooty
again. Goo'night, Corp."

" Goodnight," I said.

He disappeared and I was left alone in the dark. By
leaning over the rail I could make out the white line of
our wake. And for'ard were the dimmed navigation lights
of the ship ahead riding above the white path she carved
through the sea. An occasional burst of sparks trailed
from our funnel. The superstructure of the deck was
a vague dark silhouette against luminous clouds behind
which flickered the Northern Lights. The steady throbbing
of the engines and the sound of water swirling back from

the *Trikkala's* bows filled the night with sound. I was alone there save for the officer of the watch on the bridge and my blood thrilled to the feel of the ship live under my feet as she trod the dark waters, skirting the top of Norway.

At ten to nine by my watch I slid back the door a fraction to call Bert. " What the hell are you two up to ? " I cried, and stepped quickly inside, pulling the door to, for they had the lights on and there was only a piece of sacking for blackout. Bert and Sills both had their bayonets in their hands and the fools were busy ripping the top off one of the packing cases.

" We ain't doin' no 'arm, Corp," Bert said. " Just 'avin' a look-see to find a't just wot it is we spend all day out there in the miserable cold guardin'. Sorry, mate —we planned to 'ave everything put back nice and tidy like before you came orf guard. But these cases is stronger than we expected."

" Well, get to work right away hammering it down again," I said. " If anyone sees they've been tampered with there'll be trouble."

" 'Ere nark it, Corp. Look, we just aba't got this one open. Put yer baynit in there, Sills," he said, pointing to a corner of the case they had been working on. " Now —up she comes."

With a squeak of nails being drawn out of wood they prised the lid up. Inside were smaller boxes packed tight together. " Well, whatever it is, it ain't aero engines like it says on the a'tside," Bert said.

" You fools ! " I said. " For all you know this may be some sort of a secret weapon, a dangerous chemical— anything. How do you expect me to explain that case being opened."

" Orl right, Corp, orl right." Bert said, taking out one of the smaller boxes which measured about eighteen inches by nine. " Keep yer shirt on. We'll fix it so as nobody won't notice." He got the box between his knees and I heard the top of it come open. Then Bert whistled softly through his gums. " Cor, knock me for a row of little green apples ! " he exclaimed. " Take a look at

this, Corp." He thrust the box towards me. " Silver !
That's wot it is, mate. Tons and tons of it. No wonder
they put a guard on it."

It was silver all right. Four bars, snug in their little
wooden box, winked brightly in the light of the naked
electric light bulb.

" Gawd ! Wot couldn't I do wiv one o' them," Bert
muttered. " I'd like ter see the Ol' Woman's face when
I dumped one of 'em on the kitchen table, casual like,
as though it were a bar of soap." He stopped then for
there was the sound of boots on the deck outside. " Look
a't—someone's comin' ! " He and Sills whipped the
box out of sight as the door swung back and Rankin
entered.

" Why's there no guard outside ? " Rankin asked.
His face was flushed with drink and his little eyes blinked
in the glare of the light.

" I just came in to call my relief," I said.

" You should train your men to relieve you automatically," he said. " Get to your post. Just because it's
dark, I suppose you think you won't be seen sneaking
in out of the wind. Fine officer you'll make ! I came to
tell you that if we have boat-drill, our boat is Number
Two, on the port side." Then he saw the bayonet in
Bert's hand. " What are you up to, Cook ? " he asked.

" I ain't doin' nuffink, Mr. Rankin—honest." Bert's
expression was one of injured innocence.

" Why've you got that bayonet in your hand ? "
Rankin persisted.

" I was just cleaning it."

" Cleaning it ! " Rankin sneered. " You've never
cleaned anything in your life that you weren't to ordered
to clean. Let's see what you've been up to ? " He moved
farther into the room and then he saw the opened packing
case. " So, you've been opening one of these cases, have
you ? When we dock, Cook, you'll find yourself——"

" 'Ere 'alf a mo', Mr. Warrant Officer," Bert interrupted
him. " Ain't yer got no curiosity ? We wasn't doin' no
'arm. We was just curious, that's all. Do you know wot's
in them boxes ? "

" Of course, I do," Rankin replied. " Now get that case done up again."

Bert chuckled. " Bet you fink it's aero engines, same as wot it says on the a'tside. Well, 'ave a decco at this." And he kicked the box of silver bars across the floor.

Rankin's eyelids opened in surprise. " My God ! " he said in an awed voice. " Silver ! " Then he turned to Bert and his voice was angry and a little scared. " You fool, Cook ! This is bullion. See, there was a seal on that box. You've broken it. My God—there'll be trouble over this. As soon as we dock, you'll be under arrest. So will you, Corporal," he added, turning to me. " And get back to your post."

I was moving to the door when Bert's voice stopped me. " Nah look 'ere, Mister Rankin," he said. " I ain't goin' on no fizzer, see. Soon as we dock I'm going on leave ter see the missis an' kids. If there's any fizzin' ter be done, it won't be me wot fries."

" What do you mean ? " Rankin asked.

" I mean that it's you wot's in charge o' this guard," he said. " An' it's you wot's responsible for the correct be'aviour of your guard—get me ? The best thing for all of us is ter pack this little treasure box up an' no more said. Wot you say, Mr. Rankin ? "

Rankin hesitated. " All right," he said at length. " Pack it up. I'll have to make a report to the Captain and it'll be up to him whether any action is taken or not. You can't hide that broken seal and the Treasury officials at the other end will want to know how it happened."

I went back to my post then. And a few minutes later Rankin came out. " That man Cook needs watching, Corporal," he said and disappeared into the dark bulk of the bridge structure.

CHAPTER II

THE EXPLOSION

THE DISCOVERY that we were guarding a cargo of silver bullion made a profound impression on me. But I can't say that I felt in any way uneasy. As I paced alone in the gloom of the deck, listening to the throb of the engines and the swish of the water swirling along the ship's sides, I had none of that sense of suspicion and doubt that developed later. But I suspect that it was the sense of responsibility that sharpened my wits. And then again, I was at sea now. I was in an element I understood. All the frustration and acceptance of authority engendered by four years in the Army was blown away. With the deck alive under my feet and the sting of the salt spray in my face, I felt more assured, more confident than I had felt for four years.

As I stood there in the dark against the port rails with the icy east wind cutting my face, the mechanical voice of a distant loud-hailer blared at us across the water. "Ahoy, *Trikkala* ! Ahoy ! " it called. " *Scorpion* calling *Trikkala*."

The bridge answered, the voice muffled by a megaphone. "Ahoy, *Scorpion. Trikkala* answering. Go ahead."

At first I could see nothing. Then the white of a bow wave showed in the darkness off our port quarter. And as the loud-hailer blared out again, I made out the sleek shadow of a destroyer coming up alongside us. " Gale warning, *Trikkala* !" said the loud-hailer. " Gale warning ! Close *American Merchant*. Close *American Merchant*, and keep closed."

"Okay, *Scorpion*," the bridge answered. The engine-room telegraph rang and the beat of the engine took up a faster rhythm. The destroyer's bow wave creamed to a white plume and the vague shadow of the warship sheered away from us and was swallowed in the darkness.

Sills came out to relieve me. "We nailed oop cases, Corporal," he said. "But we couldn't do ought about seals."

Inside the guardroom I found Bert sitting on one of the cases rolling a cigarette. We had got an issue of tobacco out of the ship's canteen. For such a cocky little man he looked almost crestfallen. "Sorry, mate," he said. "Reck'n I put me foot in it proper this time, but I didn't see them seals. Anyway, 'ow was I ter know we was sitting on the blessed Bank of England."

"It'll sort itself out, Bert," I said. And I went below for a mug of cocoa. The cook was seated in front of the red glow of his fire, his hands clasped across his stomach and a pair of steel-rimmed spectacles on the end of his nose. A book lay open on a pile of chopped-up meat on the table at his elbow and a tortoise-shell cat lay curled up in his lap. He had been dozing. He took off his glasses as I entered the galley and rubbed his eyes. "Help yourself," he said.

The dixie of cocoa stood in its usual place. I dipped my mug into it. My body absorbed gratefully the warmth of the galley and the thick liquid scalded my throat as I drank. He began gently stroking the cat. It woke, blinked its green eyes and stretched. Then it began to purr, the sound blending into the roar of the galley stove and the distant pulsing of the ship's engines.

The cook tilted his chair back and fetched down a bottle of whisky from a shelf. "There's a couple of tooth glasses over there, Corporal," he said. He poured out two stiff tots and began to talk. He had a deep, rich voice, and its mellow tones took me on a cook's tour of the world. He'd been twenty-two years at sea, always cooking, shifting from ship to ship as the fancy took him. He'd a wife in Sydney and another in Hull and claimed a nodding acquaintance with the population of practically every port in the Seven Seas. Half an hour of listening to him left me with the impression of a dirty-minded old rapscallion who'd gone his own way through life and had got a lot of fun out of it. When he paused for a time staring into the fire, his thick fleshy fingers automatically stroking the back of the purring cat, I said, " Have you done many trips with Captain Halsey ? What's he like ? " I was still thinking of Rankin's decision to report the opening of that case to the Captain.

" Five trips I've done with him," he replied, still staring into the fire. " But I wouldn't say I know much about him. I never seen him before I shipped on the *Trikkala* in '42. The only men on this ship who really know 'im are Hendrik, the first mate, a seaman called Jukes and a little Welsh stoker by the name of Evans. They were all with him when he skippered the old *Penang* in the China Sea. But they don't talk much. An' I don't blame 'em."

" Why ? " I asked.

" Well, it's only hearsay, so don't you go opening yer trap saying I bin telling you things." He turned his sharp little brown eyes on me. " But I heard things. So've others who bin out in China ports. Mind you, I ain't sayin' they're true. But I never known port gossip that hadn't some truth in it."

" Well, what was the gossip ? " I asked as he fell to staring at the fire again."

" Oh, it's a long story," he said. " But to put it briefly— it was piracy." And then he swung quickly round on me again. " Look here, me lad," he said, " you keep your mouth shut, see. I'm a garrulous old fool to be telling you anything at all. But I don't talk to me shipmates about it. I ain't aimin' to start any trouble. But you're different. You're only a visitor so to speak." He turned to the fire again then and, after a moment, he said, " It was in Shangai I first heard of Captain Halsey, and I never thought then to be serving on a ship of which he was Captain. Piracy, did I say ? Piracy and murder, that's what I heard of him in Shanghai. Have you ever heard him rantin' and ravin' ? No, I don't reckon you bin on board long enough. But you will—you will."

" I've heard he declaims long speeches from Shakespeare," I said. " Is that what you mean ? "

" That's it—Shakespeare. It's 'is Bible. He's at it all day long, rantin' and ravin'—up on the bridge, down in

his cabin. Flings quotations at his crew all mixed up with
the orders so that a newcomer to the ship don't know
whether he's coming or going. But you listen to the
passages he picks. I've read Shakespeare. I take one
around with me 'cos it's a good, fat, meaty book to read
when the company's dull an' the voyage a long one.
Well, you just listen and you'll find it's always the bits
about murders and wrong 'uns that he quotes. And
another thing, he picks his passages to suit 'is moods.
Now this morning he was Hamlet. You know what
Hamlet was—a ditherer. Well, when he's Hamlet you
don't need to worry. And when he's in a merry mood,
he'll quote Falstaff at you. But you watch your step
when he's Macbeth or Falconbridge or one of those men
of action. Like as not he'll heave anything that comes
handy at you. A maniac, that's wot he is—a rantin',
ravin' lunatic. But a fine sailor and a man that knows
how to run a ship. Never had any complaints about the
grub since I joined this ship. The men takes wot they're
given an' no Bolshie nonsense."

He leaned forward and raked at the fire. " They say
he was an actor once and grew his beard to hide his
identity. I don't know about that. But what I heard in
Shanghai was that he picked up the old *Penang* in a
typhoon off the Marianas, which were Jap islands in
the Pacific. He had a trading schooner in those days and
finding the *Penang* deserted went aboard and got the
pumps working and sailed her back to Shanghai. She
wasn't insured and the owners couldn't pay salvage and
by some wangle he got her for nothing. That was how he
started and accordin' to the gossip it were about 1925.
It was all in the papers, I'm told. But wot followed ain't
in the papers. He patched her up and began sailing her
for a firm of Chinese merchants with as pretty a bunch
of scallywags for crew as you could meet in them parts.
It was legitimate trade all right, though I won't say there
wasn't some smuggling on the side. There's few doing
coastal trade in the South China Sea that don't indulge
in a little smuggling. But it weren't smuggling wot got
the old *Penang* her reputation. No, it were the fact that

she was too often in the neighbourhood of ships wot went
down with all hands in a storm. It were piracy that they
began to talk about in the ports. That strikes you as
pretty incredible, don't it ? But out there, it ain't the
same as England. To begin with the ships concerned
hadn't got no wireless. And then again there's lot's of
queer things happen out there. And when the Japs
invaded China—well, there was plenty of scope for a man
without scruples who was in with the right people. At
all events, old Blackbeard—that's wot they called him—
sold the *Penang* to the Japs for a tidy sum around '36
and retired to the Philippines where he'd bought himself
a nice little property. But there, it's all gossip. Ain't
a shadow of evidence. An' don't you tell nobody wot I
been saying."

"I certainly won't," I said. "But why did you tell
me ?"

He laughed and poured more whisky. "When you been
at sea as long as I have, me lad, you come to be a bit of
a gossip. When a new shipmate comes aboard, first thing
I does if I likes the look of 'im is to ask 'im into the galley
for a yarn. Not many ports left that I ain't visited an'
it's nice to hear news of them. There's plenty of wot you
might call characters knocking around up an' down the
ports and it sort of gives you an interest in life to hear
about 'em, the skippers partic'larly. They most of 'em
get a bit queer one way and another. It's a lonely life
a skipper's and it takes 'em different ways. With some
it's drink, with others it's religion—and with Cap'n
Halsey it's Shakespeare. I bin on the *Trikkala* now five
voyages—a total of twenty-six months ; one of 'em was
to Tewfik by way of the Cape, see. An' all the time I bin
bottlin' this bit o' gossip up inside o' me till I were fair
bustin' to tell someone. It was you mentioning Kalinsky
wot started me off. Now Kalinsky's the only man so
far as I know that the *Penang* ever rescued out of a dozen
or more ships that went down in her vicinity. And he
set up business in Canton and they say he was pretty
thick with the crew of the *Penang*. But there, as I say,
it's all gossip. But the way I look at it, there ain't no

smoke haze round a man's name without there's a fire
burning somewhere. This cat now—you wouldn't reckon
there to be gossip about a cat, would you ? But she's
thought to be a lucky cat and the story goes that she
saved a ship. Well, I'll tell you how that story got
around. . . ."

I don't know to this day what the cook's name was.
He was drowned with the rest of them. But talk—he
could talk for hours so long as he'd got a drink and someone
to listen. But I'm afraid I was a disappointing audience
for the story about the cat. My mind was puzzling over
the conversation I had heard between the Captain and
his first mate and what the reference to Kalinsky and
Rankin had meant.

I was still thinking about this when I went up on deck
again. I strolled for'ard, filling my pipe as I went. I
passed the bridge, skirted the donkey-engines and the
hatch covers of Number One hold, and then, stepping
over the anchor chains, went right up past the three-inch
gun to the bows. The wind had shifted to the nor'-west
and was beginning to blow. The clouds had thickened so
that they were no longer luminous with the cold glare of
the Northern Lights. The night was thick with a snow-
haze so that, though we were close in the wake of the
ship ahead—the *American Merchant*—I could barely make
her out. The sea was getting up. I could feel the pitch of
the bows under my feet and each time they bit into a
wave a cascade of spray whipped away on either side of
her like a ghostly veil blown through the darkness of
the night.

I bent down in the lea of the bulwarks to light my pipe.
As I struck the match a girl's voice said, " Oh, you
frightened me."

I shaded the match and saw the white oval of a girl's
face above a khaki greatcoat. She was seated on a coil
of rope, her back to the iron plates of the bows. The
match flickered and died. " Sorry," I said, " I didn't
know anyone was here. I just dived down to light my
pipe. Are you Miss Sorrel ? "

" Yes," she said.

She had a soft, pleasant voice with just the trace of an accent which was difficult to place.

" It's so dark," I said, " I can't see you at all."

" I shouldn't have seen you if you hadn't struck that match. Now you're just the glow of a pipe. How did you know my name ? "

" I'm the Corporal of the guard they put on board," I said. " One of my men helped you with your kit when you came on board."

" Oh, that nice little Cockney." She laughed. " You've no idea how homely it was to hear his voice. What are you guarding ? "

The suddenness of her question took me by surprise. I hesitated. Then I said, " Oh, just some stores."

" Sorry," she said, " I shouldn't have asked that, should I ? "

We were silent then. Crouched there I could feel the dip and swoop of the bows, the shudder of the plates as they took the shock of the next wave and the live throb of the engines. It was bitterly cold even under the lea of the bulwarks. " You ought to be in your cabin on a night like this." I said.

But she said, " No—it's so small. I don't like being shut in."

" But aren't you cold ? " I asked.

" Yes, I suppose I am," she answered. " But I'm used to the cold. Besides, I like to hear the sea. I've sailed all my life. I've got my own boat at home. My brother and I were always sailing——" Her voice trailed off then. " He was killed at St. Nazaire," she said.

" I'm sorry," I said, " I love sailing, too." Again a short silence fell between us. But I sensed that she wanted to talk, so I asked her where her home was.

" Scotland," she replied. " The Western Highlands—near Oban."

" There's good sailing there," I murmured. And then as she had fallen silent again I said, " You mentioned that you were used to the cold. Does that mean you've been in Russia a long time ? "

" No," she said. " In Germany—or rather Poland."

I was staggered at her answer. " Poland ! " I exclaimed. " You mean you were a prisoner ? "

" Yes. Nearly three years."

It seemed incredible that this frail slip of a girl should have come alive out of Poland to finish up at Murmansk. " But how ? " I asked. " I mean—three years—you couldn't have been there when war broke out."

" No." Her voice was toneless, flat. " They caught me in France. I used to go over to contact people. My mother was French, you see. I knew a lot of useful people. It was my third trip that they caught me. I was in Rouen. After a time they sent me to a concentration camp near Warsaw." She gave a little dry, mirthless laugh. " That is why I don't feel the cold." Her voice changed to a lighter tone. " But don't let's talk about me. I am so tired of myself." She was speaking English very correctly as though she were not sure of the language. " Tell me what you have been doing with yourself during the war and what you're going to do and all about yourself."

I felt embarrassed. " I've done nothing much," I said. " I understand the mechanism of predictors. That's about all. They sent us over to Russia to get some gunnery equipment of ours ready for action. Now I'm on my way back to England."

" And when you reach England, what will you do ? " She sighed almost luxuriously. " Oh, isn't it lovely to be saying ' England ' and feel that with every beat of the ship's engines, we're getting nearer. England ! England ! Isn't it a lovely sounding word ? " There was a fierce longing in her voice that gave it a strange quality. " They used to talk about England in that camp," she went on quietly. " All those people whose countries had been over-run—they spoke of it the way an Arab might speak of Mecca." Her voice changed again as she leaned towards me and said, " And when you get to England you'll have leave, I suppose—you'll go off to your home and your wife will be waiting for you. You've no idea what a wonderful thing it is to think of families still in existence, not broken up, but whole and real—it's something solid that I thought was lost for ever."

"Yes—but I'm not married, you know," I said with a laugh.

"Well, your family. The things that make up a home. People clustered about the fire at Christmas." She hesitated, a faraway look in her eyes as she remembered the things she had missed for so long. "To go home ! It's so wonderful just to be able to say to myself—I'm going home."

As she turned away to hide her tears I heard Sill's voice calling my name. "What is it ? " I called back.

He came forward then. "Mr. Rankin wants you, Corporal. You're to see the Captain right away."

I felt suddenly like I did as a small boy when called to the headmaster's study. It sounded like trouble. "I'm afraid I'll have to go," I said to my invisible companion. "Will you be here when I come back ? "

"No," she said. "I think it's getting too cold."

And then, without thinking, I found myself saying, "Meet me on the deck sometime to-morrow, will you ? "

"All right," she said. "Goodnight."

"Goodnight," I said and went aft with Sills, my mind strangely disturbed at the thought of meeting the man the old cook had gossiped about.

Rankin was waiting for me in the guardroom. He was seated on one of the cases of bullion, his white fingers methodically breaking a match into a geometric pattern. He started up as I entered. His face looked puffy in the hard electric light. He was undoubtedly nervous, but I got the impression that he was frightened too.

We went for'ard to the officers' quarters. Rankin left me in the passage and went into the mess-room. I heard him say, " I've got the Corporal with me." And then Hendrik's voice replied, " Gude. Capt'n Halsey's waitin' for ye." There was the sound of a chair being pushed back and then Rankin came out followed by the mate. We cut across by the wash place to the starboard side and stopped outside the Captain's door. A voice was speaking inside the cabin. Faintly through the door I caught Hamlet's words, ". . . . *and my two schoolfellows, whom I will trust as I will adders fang'd, they bear the mandate ; they must sweep my way, and marshal me to knavery.*"

"Och, it's Hamlet he is again the nicht," said Hendrik and knocked on the door.

The drone of the voice ceased. "Come in." This sharp and decisive. When I went in, I found myself looking at a pair of black, sharp, little eyes set in sockets that were yellowed and lined with the sun of the tropics. The features were difficult to determine beneath the thick beard which had been black, but was now showing streaks of grey. Wiry hair, thick and inclined to curl, was brushed straight back from the broad, deeply-lined forehead. It matched the beard and so did the thick, beetling eyebrows. Captain Halsey was quite short in stature and very neat in appearance. But I scarcely noticed anything of this at that first meeting. My impression was of a man of violent personality and restless energy and all I noticed about him were his eyes—they were almost unnaturally bright and hard like onyx.

"Shut the door, Mr. Hendrik." His voice was soft, almost gentle. He was standing by a desk and his dark, lean fingers drummed on the leather top of it. "Are you the corporal of the guard ? " he asked me.

"Yes, sir," I replied.

"I understand your men have opened one of the cases and now know the nature of the cargo they are guarding ?" His voice was still soft and gentle, but his little black eyes watched me without blinking.

"Yes, sir," I replied. "You see they'd no idea——"

"I don't require your views on their action, Corporal." Still the soft voice, but there was a strange quality about it that made it almost menacing. It had the patient softness of a cat purring after its prey. "I find it most disturbing that you should have allowed this to happen. Those cases contain just over half a million in silver bullion. It represents some payment by the Russian Government for arms we have sent them. The cargo has to be delivered to Treasury officials when we dock at Leith and they will not be pleased to find some of the seals broken. The nature of my report on the matter will depend on the behaviour of you and your guard during the remainder of the voyage. The only people who know the nature of that cargo are the four of us here in this cabin and your two soldiers." He leaned suddenly and swiftly forward across the desk. " It is imperative, Corporal, that they do not talk." His voice was no longer soft. It was hard and crisp. " Is there any likelihood of their having mentioned it to any of the crew ? "

" I'm sure they haven't," I said.

" Good. In wartime you can't pick and choose your crews. I've nearly a dozen men on board who've never sailed with me before this trip. I don't want them to know that we carry bullion. Understand ? I'm holding you responsible, Corporal, that it doesn't get around the after-deck. Upon that one thing will depend what sort of a report I make to the authorities on the matter. Is that clearly understood ? "

" Yes, sir," I said.

He grunted and his eyes shifted to Rankin. The interview was over. The others at his invitation stayed. I went aft and communicated the result to Bert and Sills. They both gave me their solemn word that they would not mention it to a soul. But I wondered about Rankin. Ever since he came on board he had been drinking and playing cards with the Chief Engineer.

It was just after eleven then and I turned in to get some sleep before relieving Bert at one. It is difficult now, after all this time, to remember exactly what I felt about things at that moment. I remember I could not sleep. My mind was a kaleidoscope of impressions—impressions of personalities, I think, more than of events. There was the Captain, with his quiet voice and magnetic eyes, his dour mate with the livid white of that scar running down his weather-beaten cheek, that rascally old gossip of a cook—and Jennifer Sorrel with her pleasant, rather sad voice and strange history. And as background to my thoughts the steady throb of the ship's engines as she rolled slowly along the southern edge of the Barents Sea towards Leith.

I don't think even then I had any real sense of uneasiness. The reason I could not sleep was just that my mind was full of so many things. My hammock swung with the movement of the ship. My stomach recorded each swoop. I felt the slight shudder as the bows struck the next wave and then my back pressed hard on the canvas of my hammock as we rose. Sills suddenly tumbled out of his hammock and was sick in a bucket behind one of the cases. His face was green and shining with sweat as he sat with his head in his hands on one of the cases, moaning slightly. The air became foully sweet and nauseating. At twelve-thirty I got up and went outside. " Just going for a stroll round before I relieve you," I told Bert. " Sills has been sick."

I went for'ard and stood for a moment in the lea of the bridge structure. The wind was nearing gale force and a biggish sea was running. White-caps went hissing past in the dark, dimly seen blurs of white that gave a frightening picture of black, angry water. Footsteps sounded on the iron plating of the bridge over my head. I heard the Captain's voice say, " The glass is still falling."

And Hendrik replied, " Aye. It'll be a dirty day to-morrow."

" Suits us, eh ? "

They spoke quietly and only the fact that I was standing directly beneath them as they leaned on the canvas windbreaker of the bridge enabled me to overhear their conversation.

" We'll make it to-morrow night," Halsey went on. " Have you switched the watches ? "

" Aye, Jukes will be at the wheel from two till four to-morrow night," Hendrik replied.

" Good. Then we'll make——" Halsey's voice was lost to me as he turned away. Their footsteps faded slowly over my head as they paced back to the other wing of the bridge.

I did not move. My mind had fastened on one point in that scrap of conversation—they had switched the watches and Jukes would be at the wheel between two and four the next night. Jukes! According to the cook's gossip, he was a seaman who had been with Halsey on the *Penang*. They'd a right to switch watches. Jukes was a seaman ; no reason why he shouldn't be on duty at the wheel. But why had Halsey said that it suited them to have a dirty day to-morrow. Had there been a U-boat warning ? There were a dozen explanations for the scrap of conversation I had overheard. Yet it is from that moment that I can definitely say I had a sense of uneasiness.

I don't know how long I stood there under the port wing of the bridge. It must have been some time, for when I became conscious of my surroundings again, I felt wretchedly cold. I walked briskly round the deck and the flying white-caps hissing past us through the darkness seemed to surround the ship with vague menaces.

When I relieved Bert, he said, " You bin for a long stroll, Corp. Thort you'd fallen overboard." He leaned his rifle against the after-deckhousing and lit a cigarette, hiding the glowing tip of it in his cupped palm the way you learn to in the Army. He leaned against the rail watching the great whale-backed waves slide under our keel. We didn't speak for a while. But at length he said, " Yer very silent ternight, Corp. Not worried aba't them seals being broke on that case, are yer ? "

" Not particularly," I said.

" Gosh ! You don't 'alf sound miserable. Wot's on yer mind ? "

For a moment I was tempted to tell him all the little bits of gossip and scraps of conversation and half-toned suspicions that were wandering in a tangled mêlée through my mind. I wanted to talk it over with somebody and have them reassure me that it was all nonsense. But in the end I said nothing.

" Thinkin' of yer girl, are yer ? " Bert persisted. Then he asked, " You 'ave got a girl, ain't yer, Corp ? Never seen no photograph up over yer bed."

" Yes. I've got a girl," I told him.

" Well, cheer up, for Gawd's sake," he encouraged. " We ain't doin' time." Then after a moment's hesi-

tation he said, " You ain't in trouble wiv yer girl, are
you ? I mean, she ain't got tired o' waitin' or anyfink
like that ? "

My mind switched to Betty. She was so sane and practical. She would have cleared my mind of uneasiness in
a moment. " No, not exactly," I said, glad of the opportunity to talk about something else. " But it's she who
insisted on my going for this commission. I don't want
to. The truth is, Bert, I'm not cut out for it—not in
the Army. If I'd been able to get into the Navy it would
have been different. But not in the Army. But her
family is Regular Army and she's been badgering me
to go for a commission ever since I was called up. A
few weeks back she wrote saying either I took a
commission or she'd break off our engagement."

" Well, so you oughter take a commission—eddicated
bloke like you." Bert gave vent to a cackle of laughter.

" Cheer up, mate," he said. " It ain't as bad as you
fink being a jolly awficer. Wish I could shout a't in
the morning—' Private 'Iggins. Where's me boots ? ' "

But my mind had gone back to the conversation I
had so recently overheard. " Bert," I said, " have you had
a chat with any of the crew since we've been on board ? "

" 'Corse I 'ave," he replied. " Don't we mess wiv 'em ?
I'm practically a life member. Why ? "

" Know a seaman called Jukes ? " I asked.

" Jukes ? Can't say I remember the name. But then
I knows 'em mostly as Jim or Ernie or Bob."

" Or Evans ? " I asked.

" Evans. A little Welshman wot never stops talking ?
There's two of 'em da'n there—Evans an' a bloke called
Davies. Talk aba't laugh ! They're like a couple of
comics. Why do you ask ? "

" Point Jukes out to me next time he's on deck, will
you," I said.

" Okay."

He drifted off to bed shortly afterwards. At three
o'clock I called Sills. He looked weak and ill. But I
thought the fresh air would do him good and left him
vomiting over the rail.

Next morning, the 4th of March, dawned grey and cold. The cloud was practically down to sea level and a thin, driving sleet reduced visibility to a few hundred yards. The wind was at gale strength out of the nor'-nor'-west and the ship staggered and corkscrewed her way through giant waves, burrowing her bows into their green bellies and tossing the stinging spray across her decks from end to end. Just ahead of us, and yet on the edge of visibility, the blunt stern of the *American Merchant*, a Liberty ship, wallowed through a welter of shaggy white-caps, an ugly slug of a ship, half hidden in spray. Two vague shapes pitched in the sleet-grey void to the south of us and across the starboard rail, just visible, was the sleek outline of the destroyer, *Scorpion*, rolling crazily with the sea washing in a smother of foam across her decks. Behind us was nothing but the white path of our wake, obliterated almost instantly by the raging waters. We were the last ship in the northern line of the convoy. I remember feeling thankful as I went on duty that we were no longer at the height of the U-boat campaign and that there was little likelihood of our having to take to the boats. . . . It was a vicious sea, with the wind whipping the spume off the breaking wave tops like white curtains of steam.

Twice during the morning the destroyer came alongside to order us to close the *American Merchant*. Each time she thrashed off into the grey sleet to speak to other ships like a fussy little hen overburdened with a brood of ugly ducklings. About two o'clock in the afternoon Jennifer Sorrel came and chatted to me. She looked wan and cold. Her skin had an ivory transparency that made her look as though she had the beginnings of jaundice. She talked of her home near Oban, her yacht, the *Eilean Mor*, which had been requisitioned by the Navy in '42, of her father. Her dark hair blew about her face and her teeth flashed gaily in the dull daylit misery of our surroundings. Her lips were almost bloodless and she bemoaned her inability to obtain any lipstick in Murmansk as though that were the greatest of all the misfortunes that had befallen her.

I asked her if she was comfortable. She made a wry
face. " The cabin's all right," she said. " But I don't
like the officers. Oh, Cousins is all right—he's the young
second officer. But Captain Halsey terrifies me and that
drunken beast of a Chief Engineer—I'm having my meals
served in my cabin now."

" Why ? " I asked.

" It was the Chief Engineer. I couldn't stand him
ogling me across the table. He was drunk, of course,
as usual. I thought I'd got used to that sort of thing.
But somehow you don't expect it in your own race."

" What about Rankin ? " I said, feeling unaccountably
angry. " He's always with the Chief. Does he annoy
you ? "

" Oh, no," she said with a little laugh. " He's not
interested in women. Surely you realised that ? "

We then got on to the subject of sailing. We exchanged
notes on all the various types of boats we'd sailed. About
two-thirty she said she felt cold and went below. Sills
relieved me at three. His face was dead white, but he
swore he felt better. I went below for a mug of cocoa
and took it into the crew's mess-room. Bert was in there,
cracking jokes with five or six of the crew. I sat down
beside him and after a moment, he leaned towards me and
whispered, " You was mentioning Evans last night—
well, that's 'im, 'long at the end o' the table there."

The man Bert pointed out to me was a little fellow in
dirty blue overalls with a thin, crafty face and dark oily
hair. He was talking to the man next to him who had a
broken nose and the lobe of his right ear missing. As I
sat there drinking my cocoa and watching his crafty
little face, I began to wonder how he would react if I
mentioned the name *Penang*. The man next to Bert
suddenly pulled out his watch. " Four o'clock," he said.
" Come on, me lads." Two others scrambled to their
feet. When they had gone it left only Evans, the man
with the broken nose and a pint-sized old fellow with a
tubercular cough.

Evans was telling the man with the broken nose about
a tanker he'd sailed in that had run hashish for an

Alexandrian Greek. He spoke very fast in an excitable
Welsh sing-song and he had a queer way of moving his
arms to emphasise a point. " I tell you, man," he said
at the end, " that was the daftest ship I ever sailed in."

I couldn't resist it. " What about the *Penang* ? "
I said.

His head jerked round in my direction, eyes narrowed.
" What did you say ? " he asked. His companion was
staring at me too.

" The *Penang*," I said. " You were talking about
queer ships. I should have thought she was the
queerest——"

" What do you know about *Penang* ? " growled the
man with the broken nose.

" Just gossip," I said quickly. They were both
watching me closely, bodies taut as though about to
spring on me. " I live in Falmouth," I added. " Sailors
back from the China Seas used to talk about her."

Evans leaned towards me. " And what makes you
think I was ever on the *Penang* ? " he asked.

" Captain Halsey was the skipper and Hendrik first
mate," I explained. " I heard that you and a man named
Jukes——"

" My name's Jukes," growled the man with the broken
nose.

" Go on," snapped Evans.

I didn't like the look of it. Juke's brown hand had
slowly clenched as it lay there on the table. The index
finger was missing, but even so his fist looked like a
sledge-hammer. " I heard you had sailed with Halsey
before and naturally I though you must have been with
him on the *Penang*."

" Well, we wasn't, see," snarled Jukes.

" My mistake," I said. And then to Bert, " Come on,
time Sills was relieved." Jukes thrust his chair back and
started to his feet as we began to move. But Evans
restrained him.

" Wot's up wiv 'em ? " Bert asked as we got outside.
" You mentionin' that ship seemed to get 'em proper
scared."

M.R. D

" I don't know—yet." I said.

Another thing happened that evening. Bert relieved Sills an hour before midnight. I was in my hammock, half asleep, when Sills came in. " You awake, Corporal ? " he asked.

" What is it ? " I said.

" Is it all right if I go and kip down in one of the boats ?" he asked. " Bit stooffy laike in here an' I'd feel more comfortable in't fresh air."

" It's against regulations to get into the boats," I said, " But it's none of my business where you sleep."

He went off then and I settled myself to sleep. In less then ten minutes he was back again and jerking at my shoulder to wake me. " What is it now ? " I asked.

" Have you got a torch ? " he whispered. He was excited and a bit scared.

" No," I said. " Why ? What's up ? "

" Well, it's laike this, Corp," he said, " I got in't boat and was just settlin' down naice an' comfy when I felt boards give under me. I felt around with me 'and and I could move 'em. You come an' have a look."

I climbed out of my hammock, got my boots on and went for'ard with him. The boat he'd climbed into was the one on the port side, Number Two boat. He climbed underneath and felt around on the seaward side of the keel. " There," he said, " feel that."

The wood was wet with spray. I felt the ribs of the planks under my fingers. I pressed against them. They were solid enough. I moved my hand further out, up the port side of the boat, and suddenly one of the planks moved. The next one moved and the next. Altogether five of them were loose. It was only a slight movement. One or two of the screws had probably rusted. Without a torch it was impossible to estimate the extent of the damage. But it was the boat to which we had been assigned if anything happened and I didn't like the thought of those loose planks. " I'll go down and have a word with Mr. Rankin," I said.

Rankin was in the Chief Engineer's cabin as usual. The place looked just the same as that first night we'd come on board. The Chief was lying on his bunk, Rankin sitting on the end of it and the cards between them. The place was littered with bottles and thick with cigarette smoke. " Well, what is it, Corporal ? " Rankin asked.

" I've come to report Number Two boat unseaworthy," I said. " I think Captain Halsey should be informed."

" What the devil are you talking about ? " he cried. " Your job is to run a guard, not to go nosing round the ship."

" Nevertheless," I said, " some of the planks are loose in the boat and the Captain should know about it."

" How do you know about it ? "

" Sills discovered it," I told him. " He climbed into the boat to get some sleep in the fresh air. He reported to me that——"

" Good God ! " Rankin interrupted me, flinging his cards down on the bed. " Haven't you more sense than to let your men go sleeping in the boats."

" That's not the point," I said. I was beginning to feel angry. " I went and had a look at the boat myself. Five planks are loose and my view is that she's in no fit state to take the sea if the necessity arose."

" Your view ! " he sneered. " My God ! anybody'd think you were one of their Lordships instead of a bloody little corporal. What the hell do you know about boats ! You wouldn't know the difference between a cutter and a sieve. Now get back to your guard."

" I've been sailing all my life," I told him sharply, " and I know as much about small craft as any man on this ship. That boat is the one allocated to us in the event of boat stations and I'm reporting to you the fact that it's not seaworthy. I insist that you pass on my report."

Rankin looked at me for a minute. He wasn't sure of himself. He turned to the Chief Engineer. " How often are the boats inspected ? " he asked.

" Oh, about every week," the other replied. " In fact Hendrik and one of the men were working on 'em while we were in Murmansk."

" I thought so." He turned back to me. " Did you

hear that, Vardy? Now perhaps you'll stop getting panicky."

"I don't care when Mr. Hendrik was working on them," I said. "The boat's unseaworthy at the moment. Come up and see for yourself."

He hesitated. Then he said, "I'll have a look at in it the morning. If there's anything in what you say, I'll report it to Captain Halsey. There, will that satisfy you?"

"I'd rather you came and looked at it now," I told him.

"That's out of the question," he said. "The ship's blacked out. Anyway, if there were anything the matter with the boat nothing could be done about it till daylight." And with that I had to be content. Almost I was convinced that Sills and I must have been mistaken. Down here in the solid bowels of the ship the slight movement I had felt in the planks of the boat seemed unreal and not very important. But one little fact rattled uneasily round my mind. *Hendrik and one of the men had been working on the boats in Murmansk.* I turned into the galley for a chat with the cook and casually, in the course of conversation, I said, "Did you notice Mr. Hendrik and one of the men working on the boats when the *Trikkala* was in Murmansk?"

"I believe they were doing something to them," he said, sleepily stroking the cat which purred contentedly on his lap.

"What was wrong with them?" I asked.

"No idea," he replied.

"Who was working with him?" There was no suspicion in my mind as I put the question. I asked simply because I thought it might be one of the crew I knew and I could then find out what work they had been doing on the boat.

But the cook's reply shattered my peace of mind. "Jukes," he said and the cat purred.

Jukes! Jukes at the wheel in the small hours of the morning. Jukes working on the boats with Hendrik. Jukes sullen and suspicious at the mention of the *Penang*.

I went up on deck and paced the ship in the mad flurry of wind and driving spray, my mind a turmoil of half-formed suspicions, doubts and uncertainty.

At one o'clock I relieved Bert ; at one o'clock on the 5th of March, 1945. He was cold and tired. " Turned a't nice again," he said with an effort at cheeriness. The door of our quarters slid to on the muttered " Goodnight " and I was alone with my uneasy thoughts in the menacing darkness. Even when my eyes got accustomed to the darkness, I could see nothing, not a glimmer of light, not even the shadowy bulk of the after-deckhousing behind me. I was alone in utter darkness and the only thing my eyes could see was the glimmer of foaming wave tops as they thundered past the ship. Occasionally I leaned over the rail and looked for'ard along the ship's side. Far away in the black turmoil of the sea two little pin-points of light glimmered faintly ; the *American Merchant* not properly blacked out. They seemed the only friendly things in that nightmare darkness.

Under my feet the steel deck plates vibrated steadily to the roar of the engines that percolated through the closed hatches. But louder than the engines was the sound of the wind howling through the *Trikkala's* superstructure and the intermittent thump of the bows as they buried themselves in a wave followed by the inevitable splatter of spray as it hit the decks. I was partly protected by the bridge for the wind was off the starboard bow. By walking for'ard a little I could see a white glimmer of surf pouring across the forepeak and against it the dim outline of the port wing of the bridge. On the extreme end of the bridge wing I could just discern the faint red glow cast by the port navigation light.

The time slipped slowly by and my thoughts revolved endlessly around all the little things that in themselves were insignificant, but the sum of which had left me uneasy. Two o'clock came and went. Jukes would be at the wheel by now. Why had the watches been switched ? What had Halsey meant when he had said, " *It suits us* " ? I paced up and down. Each time I turned into the wind, spray stung my face, salting my lips. Two-fifteen. I

went to the rail and leaned out to look for the friendly
pin-points of light from the *American Merchant*. I gazed
for'ard along the line of the ship. There was not a sign
of them. All around us was empty darkness shot here
and there by the hissing white of the broken wave tops.
I went for'ard towards the bridge. I saw the black bulk
of it against the ghostly glimmer of the surf pouring
across her bows. But there was no sign of the warm
glow of the port navigation light. And then a great sheet
of heavy spray struck me, stinging the *left* side of my face.
I knew then that we had altered course. That was why
I could no longer see the navigation lights of the *American
Merchant*. A U-boat warning? It was common for
convoys to zigzag if there was warning of a U-boat in
the neighbourhood. But I'd heard no depth charges being
dropped. In any case, for the Navy to order the whole
convoy to alter course at night would mean breaking
radio silence.

Footsteps clattered down the iron bridge ladder. I
saw the figure of a man standing below the port wing of
the bridge. He was outlined against the surf breaking
across the bows. He was joined by the man from the
bridge and they both disappeared into the black bulk of
the bridge accommodation.

I looked at the luminous dial of my wrist watch.
Two-twenty. Forty minutes to go before Sills relieved
me. I paced up and down, conscious of the position of
the wind. waiting for the ship to swing on to the next
leg of the zigzag. Probably they had orders to change
course at certain times. It hadn't happened the night
before, but perhaps the skipper had received orders to
that effect during the day.

At two-thirty I noticed that the port navigation light
was again visible against the steel plates of the bridge.

Six minutes later the ship staggered under a terrific
explosion.

CHAPTER III

ABANDON SHIP!

I WAS STANDING almost exactly amidships when the explosion occurred. I remember I had just looked up. A chink of light from the door to the bridge accommodation shone out on the vague bulk of the funnel beside me. I had looked up to see a trailer of sparks float aft in a billow of smoke. Then I looked for'ard again, watching for the two figures I had seen emerge. I saw the bows dip and the water cream across them as she wallowed into the next wave. I saw them lift and the surf begin to cascade over the side.

Then it happened.

Shock, sound, sight—all seemed to come on the instant. The shock threw the ship sideways and I was flung against the rail. The sound was heavy and muffled—like the sound of a depth charge, and yet less solid, as though the explosion had been at no great depth. As I hit the rail the top of a wave that was boiling white and seemed almost level with the deck close under the bridge, blossomed like a great white mushroom and then flung itself in a roaring curtain of water at the clouds. At the instant my body hit the rail and I grasped the cold wet iron in my fingers, the white blur of upflung water hovered motionless over the ship. Then it came down. It hit the deck with a crash. The weight of the water was crushing. I fought upwards through it as though I were being smothered. Then suddenly it was over. Save for the sluicing of the water in the scuppers it was as though nothing had happened. The pulsing of the engines continued. The wind howled through the superstructure. The waves went hissing past us in the night.

For a whole minute it seemed the ship held its breath in stunned surprise. There was a sort of shocked normality. Then somebody shouted. The engine-room telegraph rang twice, the bell sharp and urgent in the gale-ridden night. It rang again. The sound of the engines died. And from below decks a murmur of voices rose louder and louder—shouts, queries, the rush of feet, orders. As though the engine-room telegraph had rung the curtain up the *Trikkala* shook off her instant's stupefaction and came to life.

I found myself still gripping the rail as the crew tumbled on to the deck, vague shadows that ran and collided with each other and swore and asked the world what the hell had happened. I found my rifle which I had dropped. Halsey's voice thundered out from the bridge. He used a megaphone, but even so I remember thinking what a terrific compass his voice had. "Boat stations!" he shouted. "Get to your boat stations and then stand by."

The deck lights were suddenly switched on. Men stopped in their rush towards the boats, blinking sleepily. Some were only half dressed. Others had forgotten their life jackets. I saw one man limping along a boot on his left foot, the other in his hand dangling by its laces. A man called out to him, "Where did it hit us, George?" And he replied, "Number One hold. You can hear the water pouring in amongst that iron-ore cargo."

"Lucky it ain't rice, like we was carrying last time," somebody said.

"Threw me right a't o' me hammick, it did."

"Torpedo, that's wot it was."

"Get away wi' ye. How would a U-boat be after torpedoing us on a night like this? It's a mine, I tell ye."

Scraps of excited talk were flung in my ears by the wind. And the ship looked strangely normal in the bright glare of her deck lights. There was no sign of damage to her superstructure. She had no list. But with her engines stopped she was swinging broadside to the wind and rolling drunkenly. Hendrik appeared out of the bridge accommodation. With him was the little Welshman, Evans. Halsey's voice boomed out again through his megaphone. "Quiet!" he shouted. "There's no need to panic. Go quickly to your boat stations. Mr. Cousins! Get Number

Two boat swung out and then stand by. Chief ! Get Number One swung out. Mr. Hendrik ! Go below and ascertain the damage. Take Evans with you. He's right beside you."

The normal appearance of the ship had calmed the men. They went quietly to their stations. Some dived back down below for clothes or forgotten life jackets. They clawed their way along the decks as the ship rolled drunkenly. The engines began pulsing again and below the sound of the wind and the seas breaking aboard I heard the roar of the pumps working.

I clawed my way back to our quarters, clutching the rail. Each time the ship rolled into a trough, the next wave broke inboard. At times I was up to my waist in water. As I reached our quarters, the door was slid back and Bert and Sills pitched out against the rail. Their faces looked very white. " Wot's up, guvner ? " Bert gasped as he got his breath.

" Hit a mine for'ard," I said. " Get your life jackets on." I dived into our quarters and struggled into mine. I helped the other two on with theirs. When I went out on deck again the starboard boat had been swung out. Some of the men were getting into them. " That's our boat—Number Two on the port side," I said.

Bert grabbed my arm. " That's the one wot's got those loose planks, ain't it ? Sills told me." His voice sounded scared. I'd forgotten all about it until he mentioned it. I felt a sudden surge of panic grip me by the guts. I made no comment. " Get to your boat stations," I said.

As we started off along the deck I fancied she was already getting heavy in the bows. Hendrik suddenly materialised almost at my elbow. Evans was with him. They both hurried for'ard. Somebody called out to the Welshman, " Hey, Evans—didn't you go down with Mr. Hendrik ? "

" Yes, I did," he called back.

" How bad is it ? "

" Bad as it could be, man," he called back. " It caught that weak plate we had strengthened at Murmansk.

There's a hole about a mile wide in Number One and the water's pouring through like Niagara Falls." His excitable high-pitched voice carried round the deck.

Hendrik ran up the bridge ladder. Everyone was watching as he reported to the Captain. Then Halsey turned with the megaphone to his lips. " Mr Cousins! Get the men embarked in the boats. Call a roll. Report when each boat's complement is complete. The ship's settling by the head. We've got about ten minutes before she goes down."

A shocked murmur ran through the crew. " Cor lumme ! " Bert said in my ear. " Bang goes 'alf a million quid's worf o' the old bright an' shinin'."

We were just under the bridge now, by our boat station. I heard Captain Halsey call to Hendrik to see that all hands were out of the engine-room. " Mr. Cousins ! " he shouted, cupping his hands and leaning over the side of the bridge, " get Number Two boat swung out. Look sharp there ! "

" Are the bulkheads holding, sir ? " Cousins asked.

" Number Two bulkhead's gone," the Captain shouted down at him. " Mr. Hendrik expects Number Three to go any minute. Come on, jump to it."

" Aye, aye, sir," Cousins answered.

A sailor standing near me said, " That's funny. Number Two were still 'olding when I come up."

" Ain't yer goin' ter do nuffink, Corp ? " Bert asked me. " I mean, them poor devils oughter be told ab't that boat."

" What's the use, Bert ? " I answered. " It's the boat or nothing for them now."

" Wot aba't them rafts,? " he asked.

" There are only two," I pointed out. " They'd hold about four men apiece."

" They could 'ang on to 'em."

" And die in an hour from the cold," I said. " This is the Arctic, you know. Those planks may hold."

" You three soldiers," Cousins called out to us," come and help swing this boat out."

We stumbled forward to where several of the crew

were trying to force the boat out on its davits. The *Trikkala* rolled and we were flung in amongst them. Rankin was there. So was my friend the cook. I remember he had the tortoise-shell cat in his arms. The ship rolled, the davits creaked and the boat swung out. A broken wave top thundered against the ship's side, blinding us with spray. For an instant we seemed almost submerged in water. Then the side of the ship shook clear of the wave. The sea spouted outboard, dragging at our feet, as she rolled away to starboard. And in all this din of wind and roaring water, I heard Halsey's voice ; " *Blow, winds, and crack your cheeks ! rage ! blow ! You cateracts and hurricanoes, spout till you have drench'd our steeples, drown'd the cocks !* " He laughed wildly in the teeth of the gale and then shouted down at us, " Come on—man that boat. Mr. Rankin ! You and your men in Number Two boat."

" Aye, aye, sir," said Rankin.

" All clear below, Mr. Hendrik ? "

" All clear, sir," Hendrik replied.

" Put Miss Sorrel in Number Two, Mr. Hendrik."

" Aye, aye, sir."

Rankin gripped me by the arm. " In you get, Corporal. Sills, Cook—up you go."

I hesitated. The crew were piling into the boat. Oars were being unshipped. It looked crowded and frail. I thought of the planks that had shifted under the pressure of my fingers. I looked aft to where the two rafts still hung in their fixtures above the after-deckhousing. " I'll take a chance on one of the rafts," I told Rankin.

" You'll do as you're told, Corporal," he replied sharply. Give him his due, he didn't seem scared.

And almost I obeyed. The habit of obedience was not easily shaken off. But the sound of the sea was all about me. And suddenly my mind was made up. " Remember what I told you about the state of that boat ? " I said. " I'm taking one of the rafts. I advise you to do the same."

" I'm wiv yer, Corp," Bert said. " I ain't hembarking in a ruddy sieve."

Rankin hesitated. But at that moment Halsey's voice shouted down at us, " Mr. Rankin—get yourself and your men into that boat."

" Aye, aye, sir." Rankin's Naval training reasserted itself. " Now in you get, both of you," he said. " That's an order. Sills ! "

Sills moved towards the boat. " Now you, Cook," Rankin ordered.

" I'm going wiv the Corp," Bert said, and there was an obstinate expression in his face.

" Coom on, lad," Sills said to him. " You'll only get yourself in trouble for nothing. Maybe the planks ain't as bad as they seemed."

" Corporal ! " Rankin ordered.

" I'm taking a raft," I reiterated.

Rankin's hand gripped my arm. His voice was excited. " Corporal Vardy—I'll give you one last chance. Get into that boat ! "

I shook him off. " I'm taking a raft," I shouted at him. " Why the hell didn't you pass on my report to the Captain ? "

Captain Halsey's voice sounded from just above us. I looked up. He was leaning over the bridge. His beard glistened with salt spray. His eyes were excited and wild looking. " Mr. Rankin ! " he roared. ' I'm ordering you to get yourself and those two men into that boat. What's the trouble ? "

" They refuse to embark, sir " Rankin replied.

" Refuse to embark ! " he screamed. " Report to me on the bridge." He disappeared from view and from the other end of the bridge I heard him ordering Number One boat away. There was a confused medley of orders. Then the boat disappeared from view. In a lull in the wind I heard the falls whistle as they slid through the blocks. At that moment Jennifer Sorrel was escorted on to the deck. She looked white and almost fragile in her khaki greatcoat and the cumbersome bulk of her cork life-jacket. Hendrik was with her. He handed her over to Cousins. The second officer had got all the men embarked. Sills was up there too. His thin, damp face looked white in the lights. He was scared. The cook was hugging his cat, which was struggling and clawing at him in a frenzy.

I suddenly found Jennifer Sorrel standing beside me. Cousins was about to help her into the boat. The *Trikkala* rolled heavily. Once again the port rail disappeared in a welter of swirling water. Then we were clear. The girl was right beside me at the rail. " Miss Sorrel," I said, " Don't go in that boat. I'm convinced it's not safe."

" How do you mean ? " she said.

" The planks are loose in her," I said.

Cousins overheard me. " Stop that nonsense, soldier," he said, angrily. " Hurry, please, Miss Sorrel. We ought to be clear by now."

Suddenly I felt at all costs I must stop her going on that boat. " Please," I said. " Take one of the rafts. It'll be cold. But it'll float."

" What the hell are you talking about ? " Cousins' hand gripped my shoulder and spun me round. " The boat's all right. I went over it only a week ago myself." His right fist was clenched.

" Yes, but you didn't inspect it last night," I told him, watching for his fist. " I did. Miss Sorrel," I said pleadingly over my shoulder, " please believe me—you'd be safer on the raft."

" Listen, you," Cousins shouted. " If you're scared to get into a boat in a rough sea, I'll have to make you." There was an ugly glint in his eye and his youthful face was set hard.

Bert suddenly stepped forward and gripped the wrist of his clenched hand. " The Corp's right, mister," he said. " I felt them planks meself. They're loose. An' don't you start nuffink, see." Then he turned to the girl. " You take my tip, Miss, an' do as the Corp says. You'll be safer wiv us."

The men were murmuring at the delay. The *Trikkala* was beginning to feel sluggish at the bows and though it was impossible to be sure in that turmoil, she seemed to have a definite slant for'ard. Halsey's voice suddenly shouted above our heads. " Mr. Cousins ! Clear that boat, will you."

" Aye, aye, sir," Cousins answered. He threw Bert off. " Come on, Miss Sorrel, please. We've got to get clear."

I saw her hesitate. Her eyes searched mine. Suddenly she turned to Cousins and said, " I'll take a chance on one of the rafts."

" My instructions are to take you in this boat," was Cousins' reply. " Come on now. I've no more time to waste." And he made as though to pick her up.

" Leave go of me," she cried and wriggled away from him.

" Clear that boat, will you, Mr. Cousins," Halsey screamed. He sounded beside himself with rage.

" For the last time, Miss, are you coming ? " Cousins asked.

" No, I'll take a raft," was her reply.

At that he shrugged his shoulders and climbed into the boat. He gave an order as the *Trikkala* rolled to port. They let go the falls when the wave top was almost touching her keel. As she hit the water something jumped out of the boat and an instant later I saw the cook's tortoise-shell cat clinging to the trailing falls. The water swirled away from us and the boat slid out of sight into the inky trough. I went to the rail. The *Trikkala* reached the height of her roll and then I felt myself swinging down into the sea again. Cousins' boat came up to meet me. The oars were out and they were fending off for dear life. She looked dry enough. " Mr. Cousins ! " I yelled as the boat came almost level with the rail to which I clung. " I'm cutting the port raft into the water. Have your boat stand by it till you know whether it's seaworthy or not." He gave no sign of acknowledgment. I don't know whether he heard me. But it was all I could do. " Bert," I called. " Give me a hand with that raft. We'll use the starboard one."

We scrambled aft as fast as we could. And as I slithered along the deck, the tortoise-shell cat shot ahead of me and disappeared down the after-companionway towards the galley. I was to see that cat again—but in very different

circumstances. I reached the raft and began hacking at
the lower ropes with my clasp knife. Bert swarmed up
on to the deckhousing and begun slashing at the upper
ties.

Suddenly Halsey's voice cut through the almost
deserted ship. " Mr. Hendrik ! Mr. Rankin ! " he roared
through his megaphone. " Stop those men cutting that
raft clear."

I heard them coming at us along the deck as I cut the
last of the lower ropes. They were shouting to us. I stood
back. The mate was leading. He had picked up an iron
bar and his eyes gleamed viciously. The scar on his
cheek showed white in the swinging lights. The ship
rolled. I saw Jennifer Sorrel clutch a rail by the bridge.
Halsey was hurrying down the bridge ladder. The tall
shaft of the funnel, the mast, the rusty bulk of the bridge—
all swung in a dizzy arc. Hendrik clutched at a storm
rope. Then as the ship rolled back he came on again.
There was murder in his eyes. I slipped my rifle from my
shoulder. Why didn't they want the raft cut clear ? The
question flashed through my brain to justify my action.
" Stand back ! " I ordered, and gripped my rifle in both
hands. The mate still came on. I thumbed forward the
safety catch and worked the bolt. " Halt—or I fire ! "
I ordered.

He stopped then. So did Rankin. There was a
frightened look on his white face. Surely he had reported
the condition of that boat to the Captain ? " Go on, Bert,"
I called, " Cut her away."

" Okay," Corp," he answered. " I'm on the last rope.
Here she comes."

There was a grating sound over my head. I looked up.
The raft had begun to move. And then, with a roar, it
was away. A heavy burst of spray told us that it was in
the sea. As the *Trikkala* dipped to port I saw it floating
like a dark platform in the boiling crest of a wave. Then
it vanished. There was no sign of the boat.

Halsey was level with his mate now. He stopped.
" Corporal—you realise this ship is sinking," he said.
" You're endangering the lives——"

" Clearing that raft wasn't endangering lives, Captain
Halsey," I said. " Number Two boat was unseaworthy.
Surely Rankin told you that ? "

" The boat was all right," Halsey said. " Mr. Hendrik
went over all the boats whilst we were in Murmansk."

" There were five planks loose," I said.

" That's a lie," Hendrik shouted. But his eyes were
shifty and his face was as white in the deck lights as the
scar that ran from his ear to his chin.

Evans had come up and was standing beside Hendrik.
Jukes I could see over by the starboard rail. Suddenly
it was clear to me, the whole monstrous plot. I was
staggered by the horror of it.

" Come on, put your gun up," Halsey said. " You
have committed an act of mutiny, Corporal. Try to
understand what that means."

" And what have you done ? " I answered. I don't
think until that moment that I had quite appreciated
the significance of my action. But now I didn't care.
I saw poor little Sills' frightened face and the cook with
his cat clawing desperately free of him. The cat had
known. " Those men in the boats," I cried. My voice
was hoarse, I hardly recognised it. " You meant those
planks to be loose. That's what Hendrik was doing to them
in Murmansk."

The mate started to come at me then, the iron bar
swinging in his hand. I raised my rifle. I would have
shot him dead. He knew that and he stopped. He was
scared.

" You must be mad, Corporal," Halsey said.

" Mad ! " I cried. " Who was working on the boats in
Murmansk—Hendrik and Jukes. Both men who served
with you on the *Penang*." I saw Halsey start. " Who's
left on the ship now ? Just the four of you—just the
four who ran the *Penang* in the China Sea. What's your
game, Halsey ? " I asked. " Why have you murdered
the crew of the *Trikkala* ? Is this another act of piracy ? "

Halsey gave a little quick nod of the head. And at the
same moment Bert shouted, " Look a't."

I swung round. Jukes was close behind me. As I turned

he had his fist drawn back. I saw his thick, powerful body lean towards me. The face, with its broken nose and small eyes, was set and hard. Then he hit me.

The next thing I knew was a dizzy sensation of rising and falling in infinite darkness and the sound of water all about me. Very faint I heard Bert's voice say, " 'E's comin' ra'nd, miss." Then, nearer, " You orl right, Corp ? "

I felt sick and my head hurt. I lay still, my eyes closed, and all the time I had that horrible, dizzy feeling of being lifted up high as a church steeple and then shot down again as though in an express lift. I struggled with a dark nausea. I was soaked to the skin and shivering. The sound of water persisted, the angry hiss and roar of waves breaking. I struggled to sit upright. Somebody supported my back. " What happened ? " I mumbled. My jaw was almost too painful to open. " Something hit me."

" I'll say it did," Bert's voice answered. " That fellow Jukes, it was. Crep' up behind yer an' then, when the Capting nodded, 'e 'auled off an' socked yer. 'Ow yer feeling ? "

" Bit dizzy, that's all," I said. I opened my eyes. I could see nothing. All was inky darkness. For a moment I panicked at the thought that I had been blinded. Then as we shot skyward I saw a blur of white all round us— the white of breaking waves. Then we plummeted down again.

Somebody's hand was stroking my head gently. " Who's that ? " I asked. " I can't see a thing."

" It's me," replied a girl's voice, and I realised with a shock that they had put Jennifer Sorrel on to the raft after all. " Oh, God ! " I said, " I'm sorry."

" You ain't got nuffink to be sorry aba't, Corp," Bert said. " She's safer 'ere than wot she would be in that boat."

I sat up and looked about me. There were just the three of us on the raft, vague shadows only visible against the boiling white of a wave crest. " Where's Rankin ? " I asked.

" He stayed be'ind. Capting's orders. 'Alsey was most apologetic to Miss Sorrel, but said 'e couldn't risk 'er stayin' on board the *Trikkala* till 'e left in 'is boat. Promised to pick 'er up in the mornin' when it was light."

On the top of a wave I saw a line of lights. " Is that the *Trikkala* ? " I asked.

" That's 'er, mate," Bert answered. " Capting told us to shove orf. 'E was afraid we wouldn't be clear when she went da'n. The wind's carried us well clear of 'er."

Jennifer Sorrel suddenly spoke. We were in the trough of a wave and it was strangely silent. " Funny ! " she said. " Our whole world has dwindled to a dark, cold, seething mass of water. And yet over there, there are cabins and hot water and food and lights."

" That's right, miss," Bert put in. " An 'alf a million quid's worf of silver—all ba'nd for the ruddy bottom."

We rose, the raft slanting crazily. Then the water boiled all about us, the wind cut through our wet clothes and out there in the darkness were the lights of the *Trikkala*. The raft tilted. We raced down the back of the wave. All was quiet for a moment. There was no wind. Then suddenly we seemed lifted skyward by unseen hands and we were on top again of a raging torrent of water. The lights of the *Trikkala* showed for an instant and then were suddenly gone, leaving just a blank, empty darkness. For a moment I thought we had dropped to a trough again. But the water still boiled all round us and then the raft tilted and raced down the back of the wave. When we rose again, there was no flicker of light.

" Listen ! " I said, " I thought I heard the sound of her engines."

" Just a trick of the wind, mate," Bert said. " She's gone."

And I was convinced he was right. The *Trikkala* had gone to the bottom. We were alone on a raft in the Barents Sea.

" The Captain said he'd pick us up in the morning," Jennifer Sorrel said.

I lay back and closed my eyes, trying to think. All those accusations I had made. I had been so sure of them in the heat of the moment. But what reason could they possibly have had for tampering with the boats ? They couldn't have known they would hit a mine. And if it was the silver they were after, they wouldn't get much of it away in an open boat. I felt I'd made a fool of myself and yet . . .

There followed hours of terrible darkness. On the wave crests the wind cut through our soaked clothing like a knife. The water surged around the raft. Sometimes it broke right over us. The rolled canvas-covered bulwarks became coated with ice. We hung on to the ropes with frozen fingers. In the troughs it was comparatively warm. It was a dizzy nightmare of violent movement. I was shivering violently. I felt ill and dazed. We huddled close against each other for warmth. As though by common consent we didn't talk of what had happened. Bert began to sing. And for what seemed hours we sang old Army favourites, going over and over again our limited repertoire. And when we could think of nothing more, Jennifer suddenly began to sing arias from operas— Boheme, Rigoletto, Tosca, the Barber and others that I did not know. She had a clear, sweet voice. The gayer songs sounded strange in that wretched welter of foam and wind and dizzy movement.

So we passed the time, waiting for dawn. We dared not sleep though we were all half dead with tiredness and cold. We were none of us sick. The movement was too violent. It numbed our frozen guts. The time went slowly by in a leaden daze.

And when at last a faint light crept into the sky it made the wretchedness of our state more apparent. It is difficult to imagine what it is like on a raft in a gale in those northern waters—the awful sense of loneliness, the deadly fear that you are simply waiting for the end in a living death. In twenty-four hours we should be dead from the cold. We could not possibly survive another night. We were soaked and shivering and frozen. And all around us was that grey, mercilessly wind-torn sea.

Not a sign of the *Trikkala*. No boats—nothing but storm-tossed water, surging restlessly, and the sky leaden with the promise of snow. Bert voiced my thoughts. "Gawd!" he said. "Fair beast of a mornin', ain't it? Yer know, Corp, I was 'appier in the dark. Couldn't see them waves then. Fair vicious they look. This one, for instance. You can't hardly believe we'll make the top of it, can yer?" We were in a trough at the moment and high above us towered a green mountain of a wave, its crest curling wickedly in a surge of wind-whipped spray. It looked as though it were tumbling down on top of us, bent on crushing our frail craft. It didn't seem possible that we could survive. Yet the raft tilted quickly and was born aloft in an instant to be almost submerged in that foaming surf. And so it went on until we took it for granted that we should make it each time.

I tried standing up for the instant that we were poised on the crest, Bert gripping my legs at the knees. But I could see nothing—no sign of the *Trikkala's* boats, nothing. Visibility was barely a mile. A cold haze hung over that desolate sea.

Jennifer was shivering. Her face was dead white with strain and there were dark rings under her eyes. I thought of all she must have been through. And now this. And only a few hours ago she had been talking rapturously of England! She no longer sang. She just sat there, patient, exhausted—resigned to the inevitable. The spirit which showed in the strong formation of her face was crushed out of her with this final blow.

Once, when I stood up, I caught sight of something dark in the sea near us. The wind drove us quite close to it. A wave crest hit it so that it turned over and swooped down into a trough with us. It was a wooden seat. For a moment the word TRIKKALA stared at us from the water. Then it was gone, swept away in the break of another wave. It was one of the seats that had been fixed below the *Trikkala's* bridge.

Shortly afterwards an oar drifted alongside. Bert leaned out and made a grab for it. He missed and only the united efforts of Jennifer and myself saved him from

going in. Next instant the oar was thrown right against
the raft and we took it on board. There was nothing to
tell us definitely that it was an oar from one of the
Trikkala's boats. But Bert and I exchanged a glance and
he said, " Poor devils ! "

Strangely enough my watch, though soaked with water,
still continued to function. At nine-forty, standing up
for a quick look round as the raft steadied itself on a wave
top, I saw the dim shadow of what looked like a ship on
the edge of visibility. I tried again on the top of the next
wave, but I could see nothing. I kept on trying—though
fearing that my eyes had deceived me—and the fourth
time I really saw it, a corvette, rolling drunkenly on the
top of a wave and half-hidden in spray. I reckoned she'd
pass within about half a mile of us.

I told the others and when we hit the next wave top we
could all see it quite plainly, half drowned in water which
streamed off her as she rose from the trough.

" We must wave something," Bert said, " on this oar.
Got anyfink coloured, Corp ? Khaki ain't no good."

I shook my head. Then Jennifer said, " I've got a red
jumper on. If you two boys will just turn the other
way."

" No," I said. " You'll get cold."

She suddenly smiled. It was the first time I'd seen
her smile that morning. It lit her whole face—it was
like a ray of sunlight. " I can't be colder," she said.
" Anyway, I don't mind if it means a hot drink and bed
afterwards."

Bert said, " Go on, miss—'urry up. If that ship don't
see us we've 'ad it. She's 'eadin' up into the wind, back
towards the convoy."

A moment later a red jumper swung from the top of the
upraised oar. It hung limp for a moment in the trough
and then bellied out as the wind tore through it so that
it looked like the trunk of some strange scarlet spectre,
its arms outstretched in mute appeal. Each time we hit
a wave top we swung the oar back and forth, our eyes
watching the sleek, half-smothered outline of the warship.
She was abreast of us now. There was no doubt about it,

she was headed back to the convoy. The water creamed
from her dripping bows as she made what speed she
could in the teeth of the wind.

Our hearts sank. A squall of sleet came down and for
a time she was blotted out. When we saw her again she
was passed us. We could begin to see her stern. We looked
at each other as we lay for a second in a trough. Bert's
lined, monkey-like face was set in desperation. Jennifer's
was blank, hopeless. The next wave top showed the
corvette farther off. It was the end. Soon she would
vanish into the curtain of the mist.

And yet when we rose again, she still seemed just as
near. She presented no more of her stern. It was as though
time had stood still. Up again and there she was still, but
broadside on to us. And when we rose again, it dawned
on us. We cheered wildly—a thin ragged sound in that
waste of water. She was turning in a wide circle towards
us.

A few moments later and her small, knife-sharp bows
were pointed straight at us. She looked like a toy, the
slim hull of her pitching violently, her mast and funnel
like matchsticks waving in the wind.

Within half an hour Bert and I lay in bunks in borrowed
pyjamas in the corvette's little sick-bay, each of us with
two hot-water bottles pressed against us and a tot of rum
in hot cocoa inside us. I never slept so solidly in all my
life.

Next morning the skipper came to see us. He was a
lieutenant, a youngster of about twenty-three. His voice
had the fatherly tone of a man who had been brought up
to treat all men as his children. It was from him I learned
that we were the only survivors of the *Trikkala*. The
Trikkala's wireless operator had contacted the escort
ships of the convoy and the corvette *Bravado* had been
ordered to stand by till dawn to pick up survivors. She
had seen a good deal of wreckage which had been identified
as belonging to the *Trikkala*. But there was no sign of
the boats. I was staggered. All the wild thoughts I had
had about the *Trikkala* and her skipper crumbled away.
The accusations I had hurled at him seemed like the

ravings of a delirium. The third boat—Halsey's boat—
had gone down with the rest.

A medical orderly treated my jaw, which was swollen
and painful. My temperature was normal. I felt tired and
stiff, otherwise all right. But Bert was running a bit of a
fever and starting to cough. His face was unnaturally
flushed and his eyes bright. The orderly told him he'd
have to stay in bed. I could get up when I liked. I asked
him how Miss Sorrel was. He told me she was fine.

Shortly after eleven there was a cry of " Up spirits."
The orderly brought us each our tot of rum. He was a
pleasant, long faced, rather serious boy with carroty hair
and ears that flaired out from either side of his head.
" Looks as though 'e's goin' ter take off any minute,"
Bert said in an effort at cheeriness.

I lay in bed all morning. Bert's breathing became
heavy and the cough more noticeable. I didn't like the
sound of it. I tried to read. But it wasn't easy. The cabin
swayed and tossed. The sea thundered against the closed
ports, the noise of it drowning the rhythmic roar of the
engines which vibrated through the whole ship. We were
making good speed in a heavy sea and it sounded like it.

After lunch I got up, dressed and went on deck. When
I say I went on deck, all I mean is that I slipped up a wet
companionway and took a quick look round. It was a
grey, dingy sight. The sea was just as it had been the
previous morning. The corvette was awash from stem
to stern. The mast, with a torn white ensign flying,
swayed alarmingly. The ship was flinging herself through
the waves.

I went below again. The orderly was in the sick bay.
I asked him whether it would be all right for me to see
Miss Sorrel. He took me for'ard along a narrow steel
passageway that swayed and dipped wildly. He indicated
the door of a cabin and left me. I knocked. I found myself
strangely nervous as she called, " Come in ! "

I found her propped up in a bunk wearing a man's
white sweater with the colours of some team knitted into
it. Her face still looked tired, but it lit up with a smile
when she saw who it was.

I sat with her for quite a while. I don't know what we talked about. I only know that I enjoyed talking with her. She was natural, friendly—easy to talk to. We had the love of the sea in common.

Shortly after midday the corvette rejoined the convoy. The gale had blown itself out and the sea was falling. When I went on deck after lunch a watery gleam of sunshine picked out the white flecks of the wind-broken sea. We were passing along the southern fringe of the convoy. The merchant ships wallowed slowly in the remnants of the gale like a flotilla of ungainly ducks. Ahead of us the slim grey lines of the destroyer *Scorpion* patrolled in a smother of spray. I returned to the sick-bay. Shortly afterwards came the faint sound of the loud-hailer. The skipper of the *Bravado* was reporting to the Commander of the *Scorpion*. I wondered how he felt, poor devil, losing the one ship in the convoy that carried a valuable cargo for the British Treasury.

Bert got steadily worse during the day. He didn't cough much, but fever burned in his eyes and by the evening his temperature was up to 104. He still tried to crack an occasional joke, but his voice was weak and he lay in a semi-coma. The medical orderly suspected pneumonia.

I had tried to comfort him with the thought that in about thirty-six hours we would be in Leith and a doctor would come on board. But when I went up on deck the next morning for a blow before breakfast, there was no sign of the convoy and the corvette was hurrying north. I asked one of the crew why this was—were we making for Scapa ? He said, " No, Iceland. The Old Man's had orders to pick up a couple of Yankee freighters at Reykjavik and escort them down to meet a westbound Atlantic convoy."

Back in the sick-bay Bert's fever-bright eyes looked up at me over the bedclothes. " Are we nearly there, Corp ? " he whispered.

" No, Bert," I replied. " We've left the convoy. We're bound for Iceland."

He gave a little grunt and closed his eyes. I thought he

had gone off to sleep again. But in a moment he said,
" Just the job, Iceland—get me silly temperature da'n."
And his face cracked into a tired grin.

Jennifer came to visit him in the afternoon. Her red
jumper, freshly washed, was a gay splash of colour in
the little sick-bay. Her face looked bright and cheerful.
The dark rings under her eyes had gone and her skin
had more colour in it. There was even a gleam of laughter
in her grey eyes. It wasn't until she had been in the
room several minutes that it dawned on me why she
looked so gay. " You've got hold of some lipstick," I
said. " Wherever did you find that on a warship ? "

She laughed. " The skipper. He's a dear. When he
lent me that sweater of his he rather shyly produced some
powder and lipstick. Last port he was in was Calais and
he'd bought cosmetics for his girl friends and his sister.
He said he was sure his sister wouldn't mind."

For some reason I felt sullen and angry. When the
medical orderly came in, she took him on one side and
questioned him. It seems she knew all about pneumonia.
I suppose there was plenty of it in the concentration
camps. Anyway, she was constantly in and out of the
sick-bay after that in the capacity of self-appointed
nurse. She confirmed that Bert had pneumonia, but she
said he'd be all right. He hadn't got it badly. The next
night he was over the worst. By the time we reached
Reykjavik he was sitting up in bed, cracking jokes and
demanding his arrears of rum ration. " Pity the Army
don't cotton on ter this 'ere rum 'abit, ain't it, mate ? "
was his comment.

Altogether we were nearly three weeks on board the
Bravado. I'll always remember that as one of the happiest
times I spent in the Army. The weather turned fine.
We were given very little to do. And as nobody fell sick,
the skipper left us quartered in the sick-bay, which was
a good deal more comfortable than the after-deck. And
every day I saw Jennifer. Mostly we talked of sailing. I'd
done a month's sailing among some of the islands off the
west coast of Scotland. I knew Oban and Mull and the
Kyle of Lochalsh. She told me the story of the Lady's

Rock and about the race that runs between the rock and
the lighthouse on Eilean Musdile, of the seals on the
islands off Lismore, of lobster breeding, of the story of
Duart Castle. She told me of the trips she had done with
her brother on her 25-ton ketch, the *Eilean Mor*, and I
in my turn told her of voyages made from my home town
of Falmouth. I was with a firm of architects and the
junior partner, a fairly wealthy young man, had owned
a gaff-rigged cutter. With another fellow and myself
as crew we'd done trips to France and even Spain. We'd
taken her into most of the ports of Britain's west coast
at one time or another.

So the time passed in a timeless haze of chatting, reading
and lazing. We were a week at Reykjavik and left in
glorious sunshine with two American Liberty boats.
We tacked them on to their convoy some twelve hundred
miles from New York and then turned homeward. The
rumour got around the ship that we would dock at
Falmouth. I stopped the skipper one day and asked
him whether it was true. " You see, it's my home
town," I said, " and it's nearly a year now since I saw my
family."

He smiled and nodded. " Quite true," he said. " We'll
dock at Falmouth on the 30th, all being well."

At ten o'clock on the 30th we steamed past Zose Point
and slid into the anchorage beyond the Ferry. A line
of Naval patrol boats—ML's and MTB's—were moored
close to the foreshore and there was a destroyer and two
corvettes at anchor. All about me were old familiar things
that I had not seen for a long time. The little pier where
I'd fallen into the water as a kid was still there just as it
had always been in my lifetime. It was as though I'd
never been away. Bert and I stood against the rail looking
out on to the town. I was so busy pointing out places
to him that I didn't hear Jenny come up—I'd been calling
her that for several days now. " Well, Jim," she said,
" I'm afraid it's goodbye now."

She was wearing the khaki greatcoat and little black
beret that I had seen her in that first time when she
struggled up the gangway of the *Trikkala*. I hadn't given

this moment a thought and I felt a sudden emptiness.

" Are you going ashore now ? " I asked.

" Yes," she said. " They're just lowering a boat for me."

I stared at her. She was going ashore. She was walking right out of my life when I'd come to take her presence almost for granted. I suddenly felt I was losing hold of something precious to me. " I'll—I'll see you ashore, won't I ? "

But she shook her head. " I'm leaving right away for Scotland," she said. " I haven't seen Daddy for over three years. I expect he thinks I'm dead—you see, we couldn't write. I'm not going to 'phone him. I'm just going to walk right in on him and give him the surprise of his life."

A rating came up. " Boat's alongside, Miss Sorrel."

" Goodbye then, Jim."

She held out her hand. I took it. I thought her face looked sad. I hoped the parting meant as much to her as it did to me. Then she removed her hand and shook Bert's. " Goodbye, Bert. Don't do too much. You'll feel a bit depressed if you do."

" Goodbye, Miss Sorrel," he said. " You must come for annuvver trip wiv us sometime. The Corp an' I is thinking of startin' a little company to run trips ter Davy Jones an' back fer people like you wot 'asn't 'ad enought hexcitement in their lives."

She laughed. And then with a little wave she was gone. She never looked back. I leaned over the side watching the boat pull away for the shore. She sat staring straight in front of her. She never once turned her head. It was as though she had turned her back on all that section of her life. She was going home.

The coxswain touched me on the arm. " Captain's orders, Corporal, and you an' Cook is to report to the sick-bay and remain there until you're sent for."

That brought me back to earth with a jolt. The trip was over. Jenny had gone. We were back in the Army again.

We went below. For two hours we remained in that

little sick-bay. Nobody came. Twice I got up with the
intention of trying to see the skipper. It was infuriating
to be sitting there with my home just across the anchorage,
held up by some wretched little bit of red tape. But
each time I sat down again. The skipper was bound
to be busy. He'd been very decent to us. He knew my
home was in Falmouth. He'd send us ashore as soon as he
could.

We were called for food. And finally at two-thirty a
rating poked his head round the door. " Wanted on deck,
Corporal," he said. " You an' yer mate."

" Shall we bring our kit ? " I asked.

He said we'd better. He stood in the doorway watching
us curiously as we gathered our things together.

My eyes blinked in the sunlight as we came out on
deck. A launch was lying alongside. And standing by
the rail, close under the bridge, was a military police
sergeant.

" 'Ullo, 'ullo—wot's this ? " Bert said. " Beastly Red
Cap—an' a sergeant too. Looks like trouble, mate."

" You Corporal Vardy ? " the sergeant asked as we
came up. He looked down at a piece of paper he had in
his hand. " Corporal J. L. Vardy ? "

" Yes," I said.

" Gunner H. B. Cook ? " he asked Bert.

" That's me, Sarge."

The sergeant folded the piece of paper up and put it
in his pocket. " I have orders to place you both under
close arrest," he said.

For a moment I think I just gaped at him. I couldn't
believe I'd heard correctly. " Place us under arrest ? "
I said.

" Blimey ! " muttered Bert. " Fine 'ome-coming this
is." Then he looked up belligerently. " 'Ere, wot are
we supposed to 'ave done ? " he asked.

" Yes," I said. " What's the charge, Sergeant ? "

" Mutiny," he replied. " Come on now. Get into the
boat and look sharp about it."

I never saw my family. And Bert never got up to
London to see his missis. We were driven straight from

the docks at Falmouth to a military camp near Plymouth, occupied by Number 345 Holding Company. There we were locked in a small room, at the rear of the guard post, which we shared with a frightened little medical fellow waiting to go before a civilian court for assault. This room acted as a temporary cell, the permanent cells being all occupied, and here we spent wretched weeks of waiting.

CHAPTER IV

THE COURT-MARTIAL

THE MORNING after our arrival at the camp we were
taken before the Adjutant and remanded. The charge
was confirmed as one of mutiny. I asked who had made
the charge. The answer was, "A Warrant Officer of the
Royal Navy—Rankin." The Adjutant then informed us
that a summary of evidence would be taken and the Camp
Commandant would then decide whether he would send
us for Court-Martial.

That the charge had been made by Rankin was the
first indication we had that we were not the only survivors
of the *Trikkala*. And if Rankin had survived, then Halsey
and the others in the Captain's boat had probably survived
as well. I remember as I stood at attention in that drab
wooden office, with the spring sunshine cutting a broad
shaft through the curling tobacco smoke, I was troubled
again by all the doubts and uneasiness that had been in
my mind during those last few hours on board the *Trikkala*.
The loose planks, the scraps of overheard conversation,
the cook's story of the *Penang*, Jukes' clenched fist when
I mentioned the ship's name, Captain Halsey's sharp,
black eyes, his whispered—*it suits us*, the ship's alteration
of course, Jukes at the wheel when the explosion took
place—it all flooded back into my mind as I stood there
staring stiffly at the three polished brass pips on the
Adjutant's service dress. And I cursed myself for not
having mentioned any of these things in my report to
the skipper of the *Bravado*. The whole structure of my
suspicions had collapsed like a pack of cards as soon as
I had heard that we were the only survivors. There had
been no point in voicing suspicions that I no longer
believed to have any foundation. Now they were all
revived.

Back in our quarters I talked it over with Bert. " You'd

78

think the silly fool would 'ave bin willin' ter let bygones be bygones, wouldn't yer ? " Bert said. " Just you wait till I get me 'ands on that rotten warrant awficer ! "

I went over the whole thing with Bert time and time again—the conversations, the feel of those planks shifting under our fingers, the events of that night which had ended with the three of us on the raft. We listed everything we'd heard about Halsey and Hendrik and Jukes and Evans. But we got no further. Vague suspicions, that was all. Nobody to corroborate our evidence, except Jenny. And she knew very little but what I had told her. We needed some supporting evidence of a member of the crew. Perhaps there had been other survivors ? If Cousin's boat had gone, Number One boat might still have been picked up. Even so, we were in a spot. There was no question of our guilt. We had refused to obey the orders of our superior officer, and I, at any rate, had threatened him and a ship's officer with my rifle. What we had to prove was justification and my heart sank at the thought of trying to put across my frail suspicions as justification to a bench of hard-bitten Regulars sitting in judgment at a Court-Martial.

I suppose I had been pacing the room a long time when Bert said, " Fer Gawd's sake, why don't yer sit da'n, mate ? Ain't no use worryin'." And then on a sudden note of anger : " These guardrooms—they give me the willies. If we was civvies na', they'd allow us out on bail —then we could at least dra'n our sorrows in a drop of the ol' pig's ear."

I sat down then. I felt depressed and utterly wretched. " I can't forgive myself for getting you into this mess, Bert," I said.

He suddenly grinned. " Come on, nark it," he said. " If you 'adn't done wot yer did, I'd 've got into that boat. An' where should I 'ave bin na'—feedin' the little fishes, that's where, like poor little Sills. D'yer reck'n the planks was loose in both the boats, Jim ? "

I shrugged my shoulders. Speculation seemed so hopeless now. " I don't know," I replied. " I don't know what to think. One thing I'm certain of now—that is that the planks were loose in the one we examined. Remember? It was Sills who discovered it. Then he did what he was told and got into the boat—poor devil!" I remembered his pinched, frightened little face as he sat there in the bows. I remembered the cat clawing free of the cook and jumping on to the deck. Had the cat known what was going to happen? "If only that second officer, Cousins, had stood by the raft after we had cut it into the water." I was thinking aloud—going over in my mind all the circumstances as I had been doing all that morning. "Some of them might have been saved then. I suppose they couldn't see it. It was dark as pitch." I looked across at Bert. "What I don't understand," I said, "is why the Captain didn't want that raft cleared. I suppose I shouldn't have insisted. It was his responsibility. I just acted on the spur of the moment. But I don't understand that. Rankin had reported to the bridge. He must have told Halsey the reason we wouldn't get into the boat. Yet he ordered Hendrik to stop us cutting the raft clear."

"Mebbe he wanted the boats to sink," Bert said. He said it casually—not jokingly, but without thinking. His words echoed my thoughts. For an instant I think I actually believed that that was the truth of it. Then my thoughts came down to earth. It wasn't possible. It just wasn't possible. What had he to gain anyway? The *Trikkala* was sunk.

At that moment the sergeant of the guard came in. "Here you are," he said. "Letter for each of you. Registered one for you, Corporal." He held out a book for me to sign.

"Blimey!" said Bert. "A letter from me ol' trouble. Thanks, Sarge."

I put the registered envelope down on the scrubbed deal table top. The neat linen paper with the blue lines of its registration was as impersonal as a legal document. I did not need to open it. I knew what would be inside. The address was in Betty's neat, precise writing. I sat there, staring at it in dumb misery.

Bert had opened his letter. " Gosh ! " he said. " Listen to the Ol' Woman ! This is wot she says : ' Just like you, Bert, ter get yerself in trouble when yer doo for a munf's leave an' I was reckoning on you ter do the washing up an' look after the kids. However, as you says, better alive an' in trouble than at the bottom of the sea like that other poor fellow. Though I don't know wot the neighbours will fink.' " He looked up angrily. " Who on earth cares wot the neighbours fink ? " he cried. " That's the trouble wiv the Ol' Woman—always worryin' wot the stupid neighbours fink."

I had opened the envelope now. The little platinum circle with the rubies and diamonds had rolled out on to the table. It lay there, glittering brightly, accusingly. I read the letter and then tore it up. I couldn't blame her.

" Wot's that you got there ! " Bert asked suddenly. " Blimey ! A ring ! Does that mean yer girl's bin an' thrown you over on account o' this ? "

I nodded. " It was her father ; made her do it," I said. I wasn't angry. Just wretchedly depressed. " Remember, I told you it was her idea that I went for a commission ? Well—instead of going for a commission, I'm under arrest. Her family is Regular Army. To her, it's as bad as if I'd been jailed as a common thief."

" But strewf ! " Bert exclaimed. " She don't know whether you're guilty or not yet. She don't know the circumstances."

" Oh, yes she does," I replied. " Look at it from her point of view. Her family's friends are all retired Service people. It was bad enough when she had to admit to being engaged to a corporal. This places her in an impossible position." He didn't say a word and I just sat, staring down at the ring, wondering what to do with it. " Wish I had a girl that wrote to me like your missis does, Bert." I hesitated. A sense of desperate loneliness was closing in on me. " Would you—read me some more of your letter, Bert ? " I asked. " It sounded so—so friendly."

He didn't answer for a moment—just sat there, his

brown eyes watching me sympathetically. I was suddenly
very glad Bert was with me. " Okay," he said. He gave
a little forced grin. " But the ol' girl ain't very 'ot at
expressing 'erself," he said. " She ain't got the gram-
maktical flair wot I 'as." He turned to the letter again.
" Where was I ? Oh, yes . . . Wot the neighbours will
fink. 'If you let me know when the trial is an' where,
I'd like ter come along so as I can give their Lordships a
piece of me mind if they don't acquit you, Bert. I could
park the brats wiv Mrs. Jackson—that's the ol' lady
wot's moved into the rooms up above us. But would
they let me in the court ? I 'ad a word wiv young Alf
wot assists in the grocer's shop da'n below—'e's the one
I told yer copped a packet at Salerno an' got 'is ticket
'cos 'e was minus an arm—an' 'e said 'e didn't fink
civilians was allowed in military courts. Not that 'e's
ever bin court-martialled—'e made that point very plain.
Whereupon 'e said . . .'"

There were several pages of it, written in a straggling,
ill-educated scrawl—but friendly, sympathetic, practical.
He finished and I sat for a moment staring at that ridiculous ring. The red and white stones sparkled as though
with devilish laughter. I suddenly picked up the bauble
in a fury. I don't know what I was going to do with
it. I only knew I wanted to be rid of it. I think I was going
to throw it through the barred window. But instead
I turned to Bert. " Will you do something for me ? " I
asked.

" 'Course," he said . " Wot is it, mate ? "

" I want you to send this ring to your missis, Bert," I
said. " Tell her—no, don't tell her anything. Say you
picked it up. Say anything you like about it. But send
it to her. Here—catch ! "

The stones twinkled. He caught it and stared down
at the glittering stones as they lay in his dirty, wrinkled
palm. " 'Ere, wot's the idea ? " His tone was offended,
suspicious.

" I don't want it, Bert," I said. " I'd like your missis
to have it."

" But—look 'ere, mate," he said. " I can't do that.

Wouldn't be right. Worf quite a bit these days. An' wot'd she do wiv it ? She ain't never 'ad nothing like this before."

" That's why I'd like her to have it," I said.

" 'Ere, take it," he said. His voice seemed almost scared. " I don't want it. I ain't never taken nuffink from nobody."

I flared up angrily. " Can't you understand ? " I cried. " I don't want it. I never want to see that wretched ring again. But I can't just throw it out of the window." The outburst was over. " I'd like her to have it, Bert," I said quietly. " Please send it to her. Tell her to sell it. It'll help pay her rail fare to come down and see you. I'd like to meet your wife, Bert. I think—I think she must be a lovely person.

Bert suddenly laughed. " Blimey ! I'll tell 'er that. It'll tickle 'er no end." He looked down at the ring. " As fer this, we'll talk ab'at that later," he said and slipped it into a little notecase in which he kept photographs of his wife and kids.

That afternoon my family came over. It was an awkward meeting. I was their only child. The people they knew were mostly connected with the Navy. My father had been in the Diplomatic Service before he returned to Falmouth to take over the management of the family's quarry business at his father's death. Mutiny was a charge more startling to them than murder. They were kind. But I saw that all their hopes, which had been centred on me, were shattered.

After that time drifted by slowly, timelessly. I had written to Jenny, just to warn her that I might have to call on her as a witness for the defence. She filled my thoughts more and more. But the days drifted by and no word came. Our routine was easy. Bert and I helped the medical fellow clean out the guardroom in the mornings. We had half an hour's exercise each day. Otherwise we were left to ourselves. There were two smaller cell rooms attached to the guardroom. The assault case was moved into one of these. I persuaded them to leave Bert and I together. Bert's companionship became more and more my only hold on life. I persuaded him after long arguments to send the ring to his wife. I still have the letter she wrote me. The hours of thought it had taken her to compose it were painfully obvious in every line. And yet through it, I got a glimpse of a woman whose bitter struggle through life had given her a wonderful sense of sympathy. She said she wouldn't accept it, but she'd keep it until I had recovered from the blow and she could hand it back without upsetting me.

When we had been in the guardroom a week, a summary of evidence was taken. A Lieutenant Soames took it. The delay had been caused by the necessity of waiting for statements to arrive supporting the charges. He read me a statement by Rankin and another by Captain Halsey. They were quite correct in their facts. In my statement I explained all the cumulation of little things that had gone to build up my sense of uneasiness. I stressed the discovery of the loose planks in Number Two boat, Rankin's refusal to report the matter to the Captain that night and Captain Halsey's inexplicable attitude over the clearing of the raft *after* Rankin had reported to him the reason we had refused to enter the boat. The lieutenant wrote it all down laboriously in longhand. I read it through and signed it.

The taking of the summary of evidence took all morning and part of the afternoon. We returned to our quarters shortly after three.

" Reck'n they'll send us for Court-Martial ? " Bert asked.

" They've no alternative," I said. " There's a clear case against us. But somehow we've got to convince the Court-Martial that we were justified."

" Fat chance we got o' doing that," Bert said. " I know a bit aba't Court-Martials. There ain't no such thing as justicification. You either obeyed the order or you didn't. If yer didn't, then Gawd 'elp yer. Didn't a bloke write a poem once, somefink aba't ' There's not ter reason why—there's but ter do an' die.' No amount of explaining will get us a't o' this. Oh, well, wot's it matter ? Six munfs—a year ; better'n being dead, like Sills."

That's how I felt. Our situation was hopeless.

Next morning we heard the guard outside clatter raggedly to attention. " Bit early for the orderly awficer, ain't it ? " Bert said. Boots sounded on the bare boards of the corridor outside. Then the door was flung open and the sergeant's voice bawled out, " Prisoners ! Prisoners, shun ! " We sprang to attention and a captain came in.

" All right," he said. " Sit down, both of you." We relaxed. He seated himself on the table and took off his hat. He had dark hair and a blue, determined chin. His voice was sharp, precise, but not unfriendly. " I've come to tell you," he said, " that the Camp Commandant, Colonel Ellison, has decided, on the summary of evidence taken, that your case be remanded for trial by Field General Court-Martial. You will be formally remanded by him later to-day. In the meantime there is the question of your defence. You can brief a professional lawyer. Or you can have any particular officer you wish to defend you, provided he is available. Alternatively, I am willing to act as Defending Officer. My name is Captain Jennings. I'm a solicitor in civilian life." He looked quickly from one to the other of us. " Perhaps you'd like to think it over ? "

I hesitated. I liked the look of him. His quick, precise manner of speech inspired confidence. To get a lawyer would mean calling on my family for finances. The only officer I would really have liked—a barrister who had been sailing with us several times—was overseas. " As far as I'm concerned, sir," I said, " I'd be glad if you'd act for me."

He glanced across at Bert. " An' I'd be glad if yer'd do the same fer me, sir."

" That's fine," he said. " We can get down to business right away." The tone in which he said this suggested a man mentally rolling up his sleeves. It was almost as though he were really interested in the case. Indeed, I never had any cause to regret that our case was in his

hands. " I've had a look at the summary of evidence,"
he said. " In it you both admit your guilt. What we
have to decide now is the line we are going to take for
your defence. Vardy, suppose you tell me exactly what
happened and why you took the action you did. Just
go through the whole thing as you remember it. I want
to know what your thoughts were from the time you
boarded the *Trikkala* to the time she was mined. Just
relax and give me a chance to understand the thing from
your point of view."

There was not much I could add to what I had said in
the statement to Lieutenant Soames. But I went through
it all, explaining my growing uneasiness, the discovery
that the planks were loose. I tried to make him understand why we had taken the action we did.

At the end, he turned to Bert. " Have you anything
to add to that, Cook ? "

Bert shook his head. " It's just as the Corporal said,"
he replied. " We was quite pally yer see, an' we talked
things over. I didn't 'ave no 'esitation in followin' 'is
line of action."

" Just one point," said Captain Jennings. " Did you
actually test the planks yourself or did you merely take
the Corporal's word for it ? "

" No," Bert replied. " I felt 'em meself. It was Sills
wot discovered they was loose. I was on guard at the
time. But 'e told me all aba't it and when the Corporal
relieved me I got 'im ter take me for'ard to 'ave a look for
meself. Well, we couldn't see 'em, of course. But I put
me 'and up underneath the boat an' as I recollect there
was five of 'em loose. They didn't move much. But
enough ter make me doubt wevver the boat was seaworthy.
Yer could move 'em aba't a quarter of an inch."

" I see." He sat for a moment, swinging his leg.
" Interesting case." He spoke more to himself than to us.
Then he looked at me. " It amounts to this, Corporal ;
you both intend to stick to the statements you have
already made ? "

" Well, it's the truth, sir," I said. " I acted hastily—
but what else could I do ? "

" H'm. It makes it very difficult," he murmured. Then in a coldly matter-of-fact voice, " You see, a Court-Martial always has the question of discipline at the back of its mind. You refused to obey an order. Not only that, but you took upon yourself a decision that only the Captain had a right to make, and when ordered to stop cutting the raft clear, you threatened those who tried to stop you with your rifle. To clear yourselves of such a serious charge of mutiny, you would have to prove that the boat was, in fact, unseaworthy and that, knowing this, the Captain was deliberately trying to prevent the men being given the added safety of a raft. In other words, you would have to convince the Court that the Captain had some sinister motive and was deliberately sending the boat away in an unseaworthy condition, which is clearly fantastic. We needn't bring it up, but you yourself admit that the second officer, Cousins, was convinced the boat was seaworthy having recently inspected it himself. It's going to be difficult, you know," he added. " And I must warn you right away that there's not much chance of getting an acquittal. About all I can hope to do is get you off with light sentences by emphasising your previous good record and pleading that whether you were, in fact, justified or not, you were acting in good faith in that you felt justified at the time. I'm not sure it wouldn't be best for you to plead guilty. Would you be prepared to plead guilty, Corporal ? "

" Yes," I said, " if it would look better that way. I certainly am guilty of the charges. But," I added, " I'm convinced I was justified in what I did. I know it doesn't sound like that from a disciplinary point of view. But the more I think about it, the more convinced I am that there was something wrong somewhere. My uneasiness wasn't all just imagination. I'm sure of that. But I can't prove anything. I can't even say what I suspect. I don't know. But I'm still convinced there was something wrong."

He looked at me for a moment probingly. I could see he was trying to make up his mind whether he should believe what I had said. At length he said, " You made a statement on board the *Bravado* presumably ? "

" Yes, sir."

" Did you refer to your suspicions in that ? "

" No, sir. You see, when I heard we were the only survivors I thought my suspicions had been groundless."

He nodded. " Pity," he said. " A Board of Trade enquiry might have helped your case a lot. And now that you know there were other survivors your suspicion have been revived."

" Yes, sir." And then I asked, " Just who was picked up, sir ? Have you a list of survivors ? "

" Yes," he said. " I know who the survivors are." Again that searching look. " Who would you expect to be amongst the survivors ? "

My answer was prompt. " Captain Halesy," I said. " Hendrik, the first officer, Warrant Officer Rankin, Jukes and Evans."

" Anyone else ? " he asked.

" No," I said.

" In other words all those who were left on board after the two boats had got away ? "

I nodded.

After a moment he put another question to me. " Who exactly did you know to be on board after the main body had abandoned ship ? Who did you actually see on board ? Rankin and Halsey, of course. Hendrik, who got the raft alongside. Jukes who hit you. What about Evans—did you actually see him ? "

" No," I said.

" But you think he would be one of the men to go with the Captain in his boat ? "

" Yes, sir."

" It's extraordinary," he said. " You're quite right, Vardy. The list of survivors is exactly as you said—Halsey, Hendrik, Rankin, Jukes and Evans. They were picked up by a minesweeper not far from the Faroes on the 26th of March—twenty-one days after the *Trikkala* went down."

He sat there swinging his leg for a long time. At length

he slid his body off the table and picked up his hat. "Well," he said, " I'll go and sleep on it. I'll come and see you both to-morrow evening and we'll have another talk about it. In the meantine, go over the whole thing again and see if there isn't something you've missed that we could bring out. The refusal of the Warrant Officer to pass on that report of yours about the state of the boat —that's the sort of point that tells."

He left then.

"Seems a decent sort," Bert said as the guard was brought to attention in the guardroom.

"Yes," I said. " But that won't get us out of this jam."

Boots sounded in the corridor. The door was thrown open. " Corporal Vardy ! " It was the sergeant.

"Yes ? " I said.

"There's a young lady here. Been waiting nearly an hour. She had a word with the Orderly Officer and he said she could see you."

"A young lady ? " I exclaimed.

"Yeah. Good looker too." He gave a wink. He was a friendly sort. " I'll send her in, shall I ? "

I was a little dazed. Surely Betty hadn't changed her mind ? A great hope surged through me. " Yes," I said. " Yes, send her in, would you ? "

"Fings is lookin' up," Bert said with a grin. " Reck'n she's come ter get 'er ring back." He began whistling *Daisy, Daisy, give me your answer, do* through his gums.

The sergeant's footsteps returned. Beside his heavy boots I heard the quick patter of a girl's shoes. Then the door opened and Jenny entered.

I was so amazed I just sat there, gaping, as she crossed the room towards me and the sergeant closed the door behind her. I just couldn't believe my eyes. And she seemed so different. Instead of the shapeless khaki greatcoat, she was wearing a smart tailor-made, and the beret had been replaced by some ridiculous little bit of nonsense that gave her a gay, jaunty appearance. She looked gay and sparkling and bright—and very lovely— in that drab room. I stumbled awkwardly to my feet.

She took both my hands in hers. Her eyes were looking straight into mine. I felt such a surge of desperate joy that I nearly kissed her. " Jenny ! " I cried. " Whatever brought you here ? I thought you were in Scotland."

She let go of my hands then and sat herself on the table. " So I was. But I got your letter and—well, here I am. And how's my Bert ? " she asked.

" All right, thanks, Miss," Bert replied with a shy grin.

" But—whatever made you come all the way down here ? " I asked.

" Curiosity," she said, laughing. " I wanted to find out what all this business about being arrested for mutiny was. I also wanted to see you both. And—well, I came as soon as I could."

" But you shouldn't have come all this way, Jenny," I said. " I mean, you've only just got home and your father——"

" Don't be silly, Jim," she interrupted me. " Of course, I came. And Daddy expected me to. After all the travelling I've done through Europe in the last few months, Oban to Falmouth wasn't such a very long trip. Now," she said, " what is all this nonsense ? "

" It's not nonsense, I'm afraid," I told her.

Bert began edging his way to the door. " Look, chum," he said, " I'll slip a't an' 'ave a chat wiv the boys in the guardroom."

" Don't be silly," I said. I don't know why, but I didn't want him to go.

" What's the idea, Bert ? " Jenny asked. " Come and sit over here. I want to hear all about this business."

" Orl right, miss," Bert had the door open now. " I'll be back in a jiffy. But I got an idea there's some char comin' up. Usually does ab'at this time. Bet you could do wiv a cup, couldn't you ? " And with that he went out, closing the door behind him.

Jenny suddenly laughed. It was a happy, carefree laugh. " Jim," she said, " the way Bert's behaving you'd think he regarded us as lovers, or something."

" I—I don't know," I said. " I think he just thought we'd like to talk alone for a bit."

She looked up at me and then looked quickly away. There was a moment's silence. And then she said, " He's a pet anyway. I'm glad you've got him for company. He's such a—friendly person." She looked at me then. " How's your fiancée taken this ? " she asked. " Have you heard yet ? "

I'd told her all about Betty and how she'd forced me to go for a commission.

" Yes," I said. " I've heard."

" Well ? " she said. She wasn't looking at me. She was staring down at the neatly shod little foot she was swinging to and fro.

" It's finished," I said.

" Finished ? " She looked up at me incredulously.

" Yes," I said. " She wrote to me and enclosed my ring."

" Didn't she even come to see you ? "

I shook my head. " I—I thought for a moment when the sergeant said there was a lady to see me that—well, that it might be her."

" Oh, Jim." She rested her hand lightly on my arm for a second. " And it was only me. I am sorry."

I looked at her then. The sight of her warm, friendly look made me feel suddenly happy. " Don't be," I said. " I'm so very, very glad to see you. It—it just never occurred to me that it might be you. That day when you left the ship—you never looked round or waved—I thought I should never see you again." She offered me a cigarette and we smoked in silence for a moment. Then I said, " Tell me what you've been doing since you got back."

" Oh, seeing friends," she replied. " Helping Daddy with his stamps. Doing things that needed to be done to the house. And seeing about the refitting of the *Eilean Mor*. The Navy de-requisitioned her about four months ago. She's in quite good shape. I had her out the other day. Went as far as Ardmore Point at the tip of Mull and back. Now MacPherson—he's our old boatman—has got the engine down. In a few months I'll have her in fine condition again." She got down off the table then. " Jim,"

she said, " who's defending you at the Court-Martial ?
There will be a Court-Martial, won't there ? "

" Yes," I said. " A fellow called Captain Jennings has
offered to defend us. He's a solicitor in private life and
seems quite competent."

She had fallen to pacing the room. " You know," she
said, " it's a strange thing, but I met the skipper of the
minesweeper that picked up Captain Halsey and the others.
It was at a party in Oban. As soon as he learned that I
was one of the survivors of the *Trikkala*, he said ' That's
funny. I landed the skipper of the *Trikkala* and several
other members of the *Trikkala's* crew here in Oban about
a week ago.' He'd picked them up about 50 miles north-
east of the Faroes. I think he said it was on the 26th of
last month. I know he said it was twenty-one days after
the *Trikkala* went down. He was a bit puzzled at finding
them in that position. He says that according to reports
he'd had of the weather in the area through which they
must have sailed, it was fair with a moderate sea and the
wind mainly from the north. His point was that sailing
from the point where the *Trikkala* went down he would
have expected them to have been in the neighbourhood of the Dogger Bank in a week's sailing. Instead he
found them north-east of the Faroes after twenty-one
days."

" Did he question Halsey about it ? " I asked.

" Yes. Halsey's reply was that the wind had been
changeable, as often as not blowing from almost due
south."

" And he believed what Halsey told him ? "

She shrugged her shoulders. " Naturally. His weather
reports had only been gathered from vessels he had spoken
to. After all, Halsey was hardly likely to prolong a
voyage in an open boat unnecessarily."

" What was their condition when he picked them up ? "
I asked.

" Not good," she replied. " But better than he would
have expected after twenty-one days in an open boat at
that time of the year." She suddenly stopped pacing and
looked at me, her forehead puckered in a frown. " I

can't understand it," she said. " Halsey promised he'd
pick the raft up at dawn. When I thought we were the
only survivors, I presumed he had failed to get clear of the
ship in time and that he and the others must have gone
down with it. But now that I know he got his boat clear
in time, I just can't understand why he didn't wait to
pick us up. It's almost—oh, I don't know."

" Almost what ? " I asked.

"Well——" She hesitated. " It's almost as though
he had some reason for not waiting in that area. I know
it was blowing a gale and visibility was bad. It's quite
possible for him to have missed us. But—well, I began
remembering all your suspicions and wondering whether
there was some truth in them."

" Jenny," I said, " you were in the officers' quarters
on the *Trikkala*. You must have heard them conversing.
Did anything strike you as strange—not at the time, of
course, but now."

"Ever since I got your letter to say you'd been
arrested," she replied, " I've been racking my brains for
any scrap of conversation that would help. But I'm
afraid I've not been very successful. The relations between
the various officers seemed reasonably normal. The
Chief Engineer was a detestable drunk and as far as I
could see was generally ignored, except by Rankin. The
second officer, Cousins, seemed a likeable and efficient
young man. Hendrik was little more than the Captain's
shadow. He was dour and brusque. I should say efficient,
too. He was often in the Captain's cabin. And it was
outside that cabin that I overheard the only piece of
conversation that I can remember as being at all unusual.
It was the afternoon we sailed. I was going up on deck
and I stopped to fix my greatcoat. It was outside the
Captain's cabin and I suppose the door must have been
ajar. Hendrik was just making a remark. I didn't hear
what he said, but I heard Captain Halsey's reply. It
was : ' Yes, I'll think up something to cover that.' Then
he gave a sharp chuckle and quoted : ' *Henceforth my
thoughts be bloody or be nothing worth !* ' I didn't pay
much attention to it. The first part might have referred

to anything. As for the quotation, well he was always quoting Shakespeare, as you know. You could hear him almost any time you passed the cabin." She looked across at me. " Do you think he might be a bit mental ? " she asked.

" No," I said. I didn't know what to think, but I was certain Halsey was not a mental case—or if he was there was some sort of twisted method in his madness.

There was a gentle knock at the door and I said, " Come in ! "

It was Bert. " Only me, chum," he said. " 'Ere we are —free mugs o' the ol' Rosie Lea."

He put the mugs of thick, brown liquid on the table. " Well done, Bert," I said and handed one of the mugs to Jenny. " I'm afraid it won't taste much like tea, but it's wet and warm."

Jenny stayed chatting until our lunch arrived. As she prepared to go, I said, " Will I see you again ? "

She shook her head. " No," she said. " I'm catching the afternoon train to London. There are things I've got to do there. But I'll come down for the trial. And if you need me as a witness——"

" I think we probably shall," I said. " We're going to be a bit short of witnesses for the defence by the look of it. Thank you for promising to come for the trial. It— it'll help a lot knowing you're there, even if we can't speak to each other." I hesitated. " Jenny," I said. " Will you do something for me before you leave the camp ? "

" Of course," she answered at once.

" Will you have a word with Captain Jennings ? Tell him what you can. I think he's inclined to believe my story. If you spoke to him—well——" I suddenly laughed. " With that ridiculous little hat you'd convince him of anything."

She smiled. " Is it only the hat ? " she asked in mock disappointment.

" No," I said, " you look bewitching enough to bias anyone."

" Oh, you want him bewitched, do you ? Well, I'll do

my best." She said goodbye then. As she shut the door
behind her, the drab wooden walls of the room closed in
on us again.

When I next saw Jenny three weeks had passed. It
was outside the hut in which the Court-Martial was being
held. She was standing amongst a little group of people,
some civilians, others in khaki. She smiled at us as we
were marched in. Captain Halsey was also there, so
was Hendrik and Jukes and Evans and Rankin.

The Court-Martial was held at a camp just outside
Exeter. It was due to start at nine-thirty. We left our
quarters at eight in a military police three-tonner, one
of those cumbersome trucks with a post-office grill at
the back that they use for rounding up drunks. It was
a glorious day. The sun shone out of a blue sky and the
roadside was bright with spring flowers. The primroses
were thick on the hedge banks and the woods were
carpeted with bluebells. "Makes yer wish you was a
nipper again, don't it ? " Bert said as the tyres of the
three-tonner hummed on the tarmac. I didn't say anything. I felt wretched.

But the sight of Jenny cheered me immensely. It was
so wonderful to feel that someone cared about what
happened to us—cared enough to come all the way down
from Scotland. She was standing next to an elderly,
grey-haired man with a little moustache and sharp,
bright eyes. I guessed it to be her father. She had written
to say that he would be coming down with her. We were
marched straight into the hut and put into a small room
on our own. A military police corporal remained with
us.

As the door closed on us, Bert said, " Did yer see my
missis ? " He was excited. He hadn't seen her for a long
time. " She was standin' on 'er own by that tree. No,"
he said with a grin, " I reck'n you'd only have eyes for
Miss Jennifer. Nice of 'er ter come down. Was that 'er
father wiv 'er ? "

" I think it must have been," I said.

We didn't talk much after that. It was like a dentist's
waiting-room. We heard the shuffle of people going into

the court-room. A sergeant came in and asked if we were
the prisoners. I had got accustomed to being referred
to as a prisoner. "Prisoners! Prisoners, shun!"
It had happened every day as the orderly officer came
round to make the formal request of "any complaints?"
But now it seemed to have a special significance. We
were in the grip of the military legal machine. We were
no longer individuals. We were just the day's quota of
prisoners to be tried by Court-Martial.

The sergeant read from a sheet of paper. "Number
025567342 Corporal James Landon Vardy. That's you,
is it, Corporal?"

I said, "Yes, sergeant."

He checked Bert's identity. Then he went out. A
broad shaft of spring sunlight stretched from window to
floor. Dust flecks sparkled in it every time we moved.
Lorries lumbered by on the road outside. Once a tank
clattered past. And all the time a blackbird sang in a
tree directly above the hut.

At last we were called. "Give me your hats," said the
military policeman. Bareheaded we were marched into
the court-room. We were told to sit facing the plain
trestle table at which our Judges were seated. The atmosphere of the court gripped me the moment I entered.
It was cold, impersonal—a place for the weighing of
facts. And the facts were all against us. The very
impermanence of the surroundings—the wooden benches,
the trestle tables, the blackboard on the wall behind the
judges, the plain matchboard walls—all emphasised the
emergency conditions of the country. The windows were
closed to block out the sounds of the normal world
outside. The sunlight made bright patterns on faces,
uniforms and fresh-scrubbed floor. The Judge Advocate
rose and read the convening order. When he had finished,
he turned to us. "Do you object to being tried by either
the President or any of the Court you have just heard
read?"

We said, "No."

He faced the Court again and in his cold, precise voice
said, "Everybody will stand uncovered whilst the oath is

being administered." The court-room clattered to its feet. He turned his alert eyes on the President. " Now, Sir, will you repeat after me ? " The clear, precise voice, followed by the gruffer tones of the President, patterned the hushed room with sound—" I swear by Almighty God . . . that I will well and truly try the accused before the court according to the evidence . . . and I will administer justice according to the Army Act now in force . . . without partiality, favour or affection. . . ."

After the President, the various officers of the Court and finally the witnesses were sworn in.

And whilst this was going on I had an opportunity to look around. Facing me were the five officers who sat in judgment, the President, a Guards' officer with the crown and two pips of a colonel, in the centre. He had a heavy, commanding face. The red tabs on his lapels were bright daubs of colour against the drab khaki of his service dress. His sharp eyes roved restlessly over the Court. He had a habit of massaging the left side of his jaw with the fingers of his left hand. A gold signet ring glittered on his little finger. The officers on either side of him were younger. On the table in front of them lay white, clean sheets of foolscap on fresh pads of pink blotting paper. There were five pads and a pen and an ink-pot beside each pad. To the left of us was the prose-cuting officer. There was a pile of papers and a brief-case on the table in front of him. Captain Jennings was on our right. Near him were two other officers. I gathered afterwards that they were under instruction. At the back of the court-room the witnesses stood taking the oath. Jenny was standing next to her father. She caught my eye as I turned. Just behind her were the four *Trikkala* men and Rankin. Strange—every single survivor of the *Trikkala* was gathered in this stuffy little courtroom.

The swearing-in was finished. The witnesses were ushered out. The Court settled in its seats. " Think we got a chance ? " Bert whispered as we sat down.

" God knows," I answered.

The court-room was full of nervous little coughs. A

tank rumbled by, the sound of its tracks muffled like the distant tattoo of a drum. The blackbird's song was a faint, unreal echo of spring. The Judge Advocate was on his feet again. He had a sheet of buff paper in his hands. " Number 025567342 Corporal James Landon Vardy, R.A.O.C., attached Number 345 Holding Company —is that your correct name and description ? " he asked me.

I nodded. " Yes, sir."

Then he turned to Bert. " Number 43987241 Gunner Herbert Cook, R.A., attached Number 345 Holding Company—is that your correct name and description ? "

Bert said, " Yes, sir."

The Judge Advocate put the paper down on the table and looked across at us. " You are charged with joining in a mutiny in His Majesty's Forces." His voice was cold, impersonal. " Contrary to Section 7, sub-section 3 of the Army Act. And the particulars are that you, on board the s.s. *Trikkala* on the 5th March, 1945, joined in a mutiny by combining among yourselves to resist and offer violence to your superior officers in the execution of their duty." His eyes fixed on me. " Corporal Vardy—are you Guilty or Not Guilty ? "

" Not Guilty," I replied.

He turned to Bert. " Gunner Cook ? "

" Not Guilty," Bert answered.

The Judge Advocate went on then: "Do you wish to apply for an adjournment on the ground that any of the rules relating to procedure before the trial have not been complied with and that you have been prejudiced thereby or that you have not had sufficient opportunity of preparing your defence before trial ? Corporal Vardy ? "

" No, sir."

" Gunner Cook ? "

" No, sir."

Then finally the proceedings opened. The prosecuting officer rose and began to put his case. I don't remember his speech in detail. But I shall always remember his opening words. He addressed the President and in a

sharp, vibrant voice said, " May it please the Court,
the two accused are charged with joining in a mutiny,
which is one of the most serious offences known to military
law and for which the maximum penalty is death . . ."
Those words—*the maximum penalty is death*—rang in
my ears throughout his speech. I turned to Jennings
trying to see in the lines of his face some flicker of hope.
But he sat, impassive, almost disinterested, watching the
prosecution.

Rankin was called as first witness for the prosecution.
He seemed nervous. His large, round face was white and
puffy. I noticed for the first time that his dark hair was
flecked with grey at the temples. The gilt buttons of his
navy blue uniform looked dull beside the gleaming brass
of the officers ranged behind the trestle table.

Rankin's eyes flicked once in my direction. There was
no sign of recognition. He looked at me with the cold
appraisal of a man looking at some object known by a lot
number that was up for auction. He straightened the
dark blue tie in his spotless white collar. He gave his
evidence in a dull voice, without inflection ; the sort of
official voice that policemen use when giving evidence.
My heart sank. It was so coldly factual, the way he said
it. And his facts were correct. I felt there was no more
to be said, that all the Court had to do was decide on the
length of sentence. I looked across at Captain Jennings.
He was sitting back comfortably in his chair. The paper
in front of him was white in the sunlight, unmarked. He
was watching Rankin's face.

The prosecuting officer began to emphasize the points
of the evidence by asking questions. The President took
it all down in the form of notes. The prosecuting officer
had a little ginger moustache and a freckled face out of
which blue eyes peered, as though he were in a state of
perpetual surprise. His voice was sharp and quick, not
a pleasant voice, but a voice that impressed itself on the
ear so that the points he made were easily remembered.
Now he was hammering home the point that Rankin had
given us every opportunity to obey his orders. " Mr.
Rankin," he said. " I want the Court to understand this

point clearly. You say you ordered the Corporal into the boat three times ? "

" That's correct, sir." Rankin was more assured now. He even had an air of smugness as though he were enjoying his own performance.

" And on the second occasion did you make it clear to all three soldiers that it was an order ? "

" Yes, sir." Rankin turned towards the President. " But the Corporal still insisted on taking a raft. And Cook said he'd go with him."

" Did all three of them understand that it was a military order you were giving them ? "

" Yes, sir. That was when Sills said he'd get into the boat. And he advised the other two to do the same to avoid trouble. I told the Corporal I'd give him one last chance. I then ordered him again into the boat. But he still said he'd take the raft. Cook stayed with him. I reported to the Captain on the bridge."

" Was it whilst you were on the bridge that the Corporal persuaded Miss Sorrel not to get into the boat ? "

" Yes, sir."

" The boat was cleared then and as you left the bridge you saw the two soldiers cutting the raft clear. Was that when Captain Halsey ordered you to stop them cutting the raft clear ? "

" Yes, sir. The order was given to myself and Mr. Hendrik, the first mate."

" Why did you think they were cutting the raft clear ? "

" The Corporal had said he intended taking a raft," Rankin answered. " I presumed they were clearing it for their own use."

" What did the Corporal do then ? "

" He ordered Mr. Hendrik and myself to stand back. He unslung his rifle and held it at the ready."

The prosecuting officer leaned forward. " I want you to be very careful on this point. Was the rifle cocked ? "

" Yes," Rankin answered. " I distinctly saw the Corporal work the bolt of his rifle."

There was a little murmur in the court-room. The President of the Court looked up and then made a note.

Rankin smiled. He reminded me of a fat, white cat, that has just found the cream. The swine was enjoying himself.

The prosecuting officer nodded in a satisfied way. " Thank you," he said. " That is all."

The Judge Advocate looked across at Captain Jennings. " Captain Jennings, do you desire to cross-examine ? " he asked.

Jennings rose to his feet. He had a rather bored, off-hand manner. We had talked it all over with him. He was going to try to show that we had no confidence in Rankin. But in the face of that evidence I felt he had been given an impossible task. His manner almost suggested that he felt it too. " There are just one or two points," he said in a mild, rather tired voice. Then, as the President nodded his permission he turned to Rankin. " Mr. Rankin, you were in charge of this guard ? "

" That's right, sir."

" Did you do guard duties yourself ? "

" No, sir. It's not customary for a Warrant Officer in the Royal Navy to do guard duties."

Bert nudged me. I could almost hear him imitating Rankin's voice.

" Quite so," Jennings agreed. " But this was an un-usually small guard—that made no difference as far as you were concerned ? "

" No, sir."

" I see. But naturally you slept with the cargo you were guarding and were there most of the time ? "

" No, sir." Rankin's hands fluttered up to his tie. They were very white against the dark blue of his uniform. They looked soft and well-cared for, like a woman's. " The Captain gave me a cabin. I messed with the ship's officers."

" Oh ? " Jennings' voice was mildly surprised. " You didn't think that your duties were such as to necessitate your being with the cargo—a cargo which had been described to you on your own statement as a special cargo ? "

"No, sir," Rankin answered. Jennings was clearly not pressing the point. "The Corporal was there. I had given him written orders. And I inspected the guard regularly."

"How regularly?" The question was put mildly, almost without interest.

"Well, at different times of the day, sir—so they wouldn't get slack."

And then suddenly Jennings' voice became sharp, precise. "How many times a day?"

"Well, sir—I don't know exactly." Sudden nervousness had crept into Rankin's voice.

Jennings seemed to relax. "Well, just roughly," he encouraged the witness. "About ten or twelve times a day—or more often?"

"I don't remember." Rankin answered woodenly.

"Would it be right to say that you did not visit the guard more than four times from the moment the *Trikkala* sailed until she was sunk?" Jennings asked.

Rankin saw the trap opening before his eyes. "I couldn't say, sir," he replied.

Then Jennings struck. He leaned forward. "You couldn't say?" he repeated in a tone of amazement. And then with damning emphasis. "You mean you don't want to say. I suggest that you took a very light view of your duties." He turned to the Court. "I shall later bring a witness to show that Mr. Rankin spent most of his time playing cards and drinking, and that on two occasions —two occasions in just over forty-eight hours—he was drunk." Jennings took off his glasses, polishing them abstractedly. The slight stoop of his tall, rather scholarly figure seemed more pronounced than ever. He put his glasses on again and looked at the witness. "Now," he said, and his voice was quite mild again, "I am going to put a question to you and I want you to answer it very carefully. Did you know what it was that you were guarding? You had been told, I understand, that it was a special cargo. But did you know what it actually was?"

"No, sir." Rankin had recovered himself, but his

little eyes looked at his questioner warily like a hedgehog wondering whether to curl up. " Not at the beginning," he added quickly. " Later I found Gunner Cook, in the presence of the Corporal, had prised open one of the cases."

" And that was when you realised that it was silver bullion ? "

" Yes, sir."

" And what special precautions did you take when you discovered the nature of your charge ? "

Rankin's tongue flicked across his lips. " I—I told the Corporal to ensure that his guard——"

"His guard ! " Captain Jennings' voice was sharp again. " Surely you mean—your guard ? " He turned to the Court again. " Later I am going to show that all the Warrant Officer did on discovering that he was responsible for a huge quantity of silver bullion was to go to the Chief Engineer's cabin and get drunk over a game of cards."

At that the prosecuting officer jumped to his feet. " Sir," he said, addressing the President, " I object. Mr. Rankin is giving evidence."

The President stroked the left side of his cheek. The gold of the signet ring flashed in the sunshine. He glanced at the Judge Advocate, who said, " I agree."

Jennings hurried on: " I am trying to show the background to this affair—to show the Court that the two accused had no confidence in their superior officer and felt themselves justified, therefore, in taking the action they did."

He turned back to Rankin. The Warrant Officer's face was white—white as the spotless collar he wore. His eyes were restless as though they were scared of meeting the gaze of any of those present.

" Mr. Rankin," Jennings continued, leaning forward with both hands on the table top, " I suggest that, knowing you were guarding a very valuable cargo of bullion, you still considered that the Corporal should bear full responsibility for the task you had been given ? "

" He had full instructions for his guard, sir."

"I see." Jennings looked down at some notes he had uncovered. "Now, Mr. Rankin, we come to the night of the sinking. The *Trikkala* was struck, I understand, at 0236 hours on 5th March. Did Corporal Vardy come to you at about 2030 hours on 4th March to report that Number Two boat was unseaworthy?"

Rankin hesitated. "Yes, sir." And then hurriedly: "He came to me with some story about loose planks. Sills, the third member of the guard, had apparently got into the boat for shelter. I told him that Sills had no right in the——"

"Just a minute," Jennings interrupted him. "What were you doing when the Corporal made this report to you?"

"I was playing cards, sir."

"Anything else?"

"I don't follow, sir." Rankin was nervous again.

"What I am trying to discover," Jennings said, "is whether you had been drinking?"

"Well, me and the Chief, we'd had one or two, sir. But we weren't——"

"You weren't drunk is what you were going to say, I suppose," Jennings put in. And he added quietly, "The person concerned is not always the best judge of that."

"Well, we'd only——"

He was interrupted again. "By *we*, you mean you and the Chief Engineer?"

"Yes, sir."

"Were you often with the Chief Engineer?"

"We got on well, sir, and we both liked cards."

"And drink, eh?" Jennings was wiping his glasses again and peering at him through short-sighted eyes. Then he put on his glasses and turned to the Court. "Sir, I should like to say that I shall be calling another witness, Miss Sorrel, a passenger on the *Trikkala*, to show that the Chief Engineer was known as a drunk among his fellow officers, and in fact, was the cause of Miss Sorrel requesting that her meals be served in her cabin." Then to Rankin. "Now, back to the matter of the boats," he said brusquely. "What action did you take on the Corporal's report?"

"I didn't take it very seriously," Rankin answered, but he was unsure of himself. "The Corporal was hardly likely to know as much about boats as the ship's officers," he hurried on. "The Chief told me they were inspected regularly. However, I said I'd have a look at the boat in the morning when it was light."

"Did the Chief tell you that Mr. Hendrik, the first mate, had been working on the boats with one of the seamen whilst the *Trikkala* was in Murmansk?"

"I believe he did." Rankin's voice sounded surprised.

Jennings nodded. "I shall refer to that point with another witness," he told the Court. Then to Rankin, "You didn't think it worth while reporting this matter to the Captain right away?"

"No, sir."

"Do you remember Corporal Vardy saying he'd been sailing all his life and knew as much about small craft as any man on the ship?"

"He said something of the kind."

"But you still did not think it worth while investigating his report at once?"

Rankin was twisting one of the buttons of his jacket. "It was dark," he said.

"But you had a torch." Jennings was leaning forward again. "I suggest that you were too blind to your responsibilities to pause in your card playing and your drinking. Had you taken your duties less lightly, it is possible that the lives of a dozen men—perhaps more—might have been saved—and your Corporal might have retained some vestige of confidence in you." He gave a quick nod. "That is all." He sat down.

Rankin was told he could stand down. He manœuvred his big body awkwardly through the huddle of seats to the door. He was like a whipped cur. He did not know where to look, his eyes trying desperately to avoid everyone's gaze. He passed quite close to me and I swear he was trembling. Certainly his broad, white forehead glistened with sweat. I saw it shine in a patch of sunlight. I got the impression that he was scared.

I looked at Jennings. His long face with the rather aquiline nose was bent over the table as he glanced through some notes. He had a confident air. We were lucky to have got such a good defending officer. He knew his stuff and he knew how to cross-examine. The way he had handled Rankin had impressed the whole court-room. I sensed a stir of excitement all round me. Bert nudged me and surreptitiously raised a thumb. His brown eyes gleamed and he was grinning. For the first time since we had been arrested I felt we had a chance.

CHAPTER V

DARTMOOR PRISON

ALL THAT MORNING the Court sat. I thought the case would never end as witness after witness was called by the prosecution—Halsey, Hendrik, Jukes. My mind was in a daze. I remember the details of Rankin's cross-examination because I disliked him personally and I was excited—and therefore more receptive—by Jennings' handling of him. Of the other witnesses for the prosecution, I only remember the high lights of their cross-examination. This, chiefly because it did little to help our case, though Jennings worked hard enough. He was endeavouring to build up something that was essentially insubstantial, whereas the prosecution dealt in fact all the time. And as the evidence of each fresh witness corroborated previous evidence for the prosecution I felt our chances fading.

Halsey, for instance—Jennings made little impression on the stocky, bearded Captain. The man was solid as a rock, immovable, and his personality dominated that dreary court-room. His little black eyes darted from officer to officer, not uncertainly and restlessly like Rankin's, but meeting each fresh gaze with sharp, aggressive mien. He had the confidence of a man accustomed to command. That confidence impressed itself on everyone—even, I think, on Jennings.

I remember Jennings tried to make a point out of the fact that Halsey had heard from Rankin that I had discovered loose planks in Number Two boat *before* he gave the order to stop me from having the raft cut adrift.

" Captain Halsey," Jennings said. " Would you tell the Court why you did not want that raft cleared ? "

Halsey's black eyes looked sharply at his questioner. " Certainly," he said. And then he turned and addressed his reply to the Court. " In an emergency there can only be one man in charge of an operation. Otherwise all is confusion. You, as experienced officers, will appreciate that." His voice was mild but forceful. " Those rafts were for use in emergencies. I needed them in reserve in case one or other of the boats was dashed to pieces."

" But at this particular time surely both boats had been cleared ? " Jennings said.

" They were both in the water," Halsey replied. " But not necessarily clear of the ship."

" I see." Jennings looked down at his notes. " Number Two boat had just been launched—that's correct, isn't it ? "

" Yes."

" Now supposing you had been informed that it was not seaworthy—would that have affected your action ? "

Halsey met Jennings' gaze across the court-room. " There was no question of that," he said. " One of my officers inspected the boats daily, usually Mr. Hendrik."

" Quite," Jennings said in a soothing voice. " But I am asking you for your opinion. If you had suddenly heard that Number Two boat was not seaworthy, wouldn't you have encouraged rather than tried to prevent Cook and Vardy clearing that raft ? "

" I cannot reply to that," Halsey replied shortly. " Actions in an emergency are taken on the spot. It is impossible to say what one would or would not have done had the circumstances been different."

I could see Jennings was a little nettled by Halsey's obstinacy on this point. But he persisted. " Captain Halsey, I put it to you that had you been aware of the state of that boat—as Vardy and Cook were, or thought they were—you would have encouraged them to cut the raft clear."

In an endeavour to break the Captain's confidence, Jennings said, " Perhaps your reluctance to express an opinion which would have been helpful to the prisoners' case arises out of the fact that at the time you ordered them to stop cutting the raft clear, you *did* know that the boat was unseaworthy. When you were informed by Warrant Officer Rankin that the prisoners had refused to enter the boat, you told him to report to the bridge. Correct ? "

" Yes." Captain Halsey's black eyes watched his questioner warily.

" What reason did he give for their refusal ? " was the next question.

Halsey did not hesitate. " He said they thought it was unseaworthy," he replied.

The members of the Court exchanged glances.

" But you paid no attention to that ? " Jennings went on.

" No," Halsey answered. " A lot of men not accustomed to the sea get panicky when told to get into the boats. You must remember there was a gale blowing and a fairly big sea running."

" Did the Warrant Officer say whether he believed what the Corporal had told him ? "

" I did not enquire."

" Did he tell you they preferred a raft ? "

" I believe so."

Jennings leaned forward. " Did you stop to consider that if those boys were afraid to embark in a boat, it was strange that they should be willing to take a raft ? Surely that must have struck you as strange ? "

" I didn't consider it." Halsey glanced at the Court. " You must remember," he said, and his voice was quiet and reasonable, " that the ship was settling and I had a lot on my mind. I had no time to worry about two men who were getting panicky. I told the Warrant Officer that, boat or raft, he was to get them off the ship."

Jennings left it at that. To Halsey we were just a couple of soldiers who were getting panicky. His view was impressing itself on the Court. He was, after all, the master of the *Trikkala*. He had appealed to the Court as experienced officers and they could understand his point of view.

Jennings asked him why he had taken Rankin in his boat and made Miss Sorrel go in the raft. Again his answer was reasonable. " It was her choice, not mine. There were things to be done before I could leave the

ship. I saw no reason to endanger her life by having her
wait for me. I knew she would be perfectly safe on the
raft, though perhaps not very comfortable. I expected
to be able to pick her up in the morning when it was
light." As regards Rankin, he pointed out that as he was
a Naval Warrant Officer, he had no hesitation in having
him wait on board.

Jennings then asked him why it was that he had failed
to pick Miss Sorrel up in the morniug. "It's hard to
say," Halsey replied. "Some freak of the gale, maybe.
We were being driven in a notherly direction for a time.
I believe the raft was being blown in a south-easterly
direction. That happens sometimes. Also, visibility that
morning was bad. We could have been within a mile
or two of the raft and not seen either it or the corvette
that picked it up."

"I have reports here from the Admiralty," Jennings
went on, "that suggest that the wind to the south of
the Barents Sea between the time you took to your boat
and the time you were picked up off the Faroes three
weeks later was mainly northerly. This would suggest
that by using your sails you could have been in the
neighbourhood of the Dogger Bank within a week of the
Trikkala being sunk."

Halsey shrugged his shoulders. "Whatever the Admiralty may say about the winds at that time, all I can
say is that we experienced varied winds. At one time we
were as far south as latitude 68 and then we were blown
as far north as the seventies. You are surely not sug-
gesting that we enjoyed staying in an open boat half
frozen and with insufficient food ? "

I saw that the President of the court was no longer
taking notes. Once or twice he looked at his watch. He
was getting restive. Jennings put a question about the
Chief Engineer. "Warrant Officer Rankin spent a lot
of time in his cabin playing cards—would you describe
your Chief Engineer as a drunk ? "

Halsey replied, "A lot of sailors drink. All I can say
is that he was an efficient officer." And he muttered,
"God rest his soul."

That was the first time in the course of the evidence that I knew that Halsey was lying. But lying to save the reputation of a dead officer. If Jennings had proved that point it would not have helped us.

"I have only two more questions," Jennings said. "At about midnight on the first day out you were on the bridge with your first officer, Mr. Hendrik. Hendrik said it would be dirty the following day. Do you remember what you replied?"

"No," Halsey answered. "Conversations about the weather occur too frequently on board a ship for one to remember them."

"I will refresh your memory then. You said, 'It suits us.' Would you explain why dirty weather suited you?"

Halsey leaned a little forward. "I don't understand the point of this question. One of the prisoners I suppose has been listening with too much interest to conversations which have nothing to do with him. However, I can answer your question easily enough. The Russian convoy route passes a little too close for comfort to the northern tip of Norway where Germany has bases. Dirty weather is quite a good protection against U-boat attacks."

"You said, 'We'll make it to-morrow night,'" Jennings went on. "And you then asked Mr. Hendrik whether he had switched the watches so that Jukes was at the wheel between two and four—it was between those times and on that night that the *Trikkala* was mined."

"The suggestion behind your question is offensive, sir," Halsey said sharply. He turned to the Court. "Have I got to explain every scrap of conversation overheard by people who could not understand what I was talking about? The watches were switched because we were short-handed. My remark about making it the next night referred, if I remember rightly, to the necessity for switching over duties so that the men would not be unduly taxed."

"I am merely trying to show the effect of a scrap of conversation upon the mind of Corporal Vardy, knowing that he was in charge of a very important cargo,"

Jennings pointed out. "I have one other point I would like cleared up. And let me say in advance that this conversation was overheard by Miss Sorrel, and not by either of the prisoners. Shortly after you sailed from Murmansk, Captain Halsey, you said to Mr. Hendrik : 'I'll think up some reason to cover that.' What did you mean by that ?"

"I can't say I remember the conversation," Halsey replied. "But if that is what I said, I was no doubt referring to some stores we'd wangled from a Naval vessel." And he gave a slight chuckle. The Court also chuckled. They understood the point.

"Immediately afterwards," Jennings continued, "you quoted a passage from Shakespeare—from Hamlet. You said : '*Henceforth my thoughts be bloody or be nothing worth.*' Why ?"

"I often quote Shakespeare," Halsey replied shortly, two little spots of colour appearing in his sallow cheeks.

"So I understand," Jennings answered quickly. "I am also given to understand that you choose your characters to fit your mood : that morning you were Hamlet—and Hamlet in a mood contemplating violent action. And that, I submit, is an important point when you consider that had you known about the loose planks in Number Two boat a lot of lives might have been saved. One more question," Jennings hurried on before Halsey could protest. "Were you by any chance the owner and master of a ship called the *Penang* in the China Sea before the war ?"

It was then that Halsey's black eyes flashed with unmistakable anger—anger and something else. That something else I realised later was fear. But I didn't know him so well then as I came to know him later.

And whilst Halsey hesitated uncertainly, the prosecuting officer came belatedly to his rescue. "I protest," he cried. "These questions have no bearing on the case."

"I agree," the Judge Advocate said.

"I will show that they have—later," was Jennings' reply and he sat down.

With Hendrik, who was the prosecution's next witness,

Jennings had more success. He questioned him about the same scraps of conversation. Hendrik with his shifty eyes and white scar was not the type of man to impress the Court. But he was not easily put out, and though his replies differed from his Captain's the difference was not great. And then Jennings sprang on him the question about the *Penang* and the scar became a livid streak in his ashen face. " Is it true," Jennings rapped out, " that in the China Sea the *Penang* had a reputation for being in the neighbourhood of several ships that sank with the loss of all hands ? " Whilst Hendrik was still searching confusedly for an answer and before anyone had time to protest, he said, " I understand, Mr. Hendrik, that you were working on Number Two boat with one of the crew whilst the *Trikkala* was in Murmansk. What was the work that had to be done to the boat ? "

" On the Captain's instructions I was carrying out a general overhaul of all boats," was the answer.

" There was nothing definite that needed repairing ? "

" No. Just a general overhaul."

" Who was the member of the crew who was working with you ? "

" Jukes, sir."

That was all he asked Hendrik. The next witness was Jukes. As soon as Jennings came to cross-examine him, he said, " You worked on the boats with Mr. Hendrik whilst you were in Murmansk, didn't you ? "

" That's right," Jukes replied.

" Was your watch switched so that you were at the wheel at the time the explosion took place ? "

" Yes," Jukes said. But he was beginning to look worried.

Then Jennings suddenly leaned towards him. " Were you a member of the crew of the *Penang* by any chance ? "

There was no doubt about it this time—Jukes was scared. He was the type of man that is scared in any court of law. His broken nose, tough features with missing ear lobe, were not calculated to impress a court. He was clearly a man who gravitated by nature to the shadier quarters of the ports he shipped in and out of.

He had not expected to be questioned about the *Penang*
and he was frightened.

But Jennings had made his point. He had too little to
go on to press it home. He let it go at that. Evans was
never called. The case for the prosecution, being closed,
Jennings opened for the defence. After a short speech,
he had me give evidence on oath. Under his guidance I
took the court through the whole story of those two days
from my point of view. I kept nothing back. I told of
my suspicions, my growing sense of uneasiness, what
the cook had told me of the *Penang*, how I had actually
felt the looseness of the planks of that boat. Here the
Judge Advocate interrupted me to ask whether it was
dark and if I had inspected them with a torch. When I
had finished, Jennings called Bert to corroborate my
story. And finally he called Jenny to show that my
attitude to embarking in the boat had been so strong that
she had felt convinced that a raft was safer.

That concluded the case for the defence. There followed
the final speeches of defence and prosecution. And then
the Judge Advocate gave his summing up.

Finally, at twelve-fifteen, the Court was closed for
consideration of the finding. The only people who were
allowed to remain in the court-room whilst this was
happening were the two officers under instruction.

Back in the little waiting-room, Bert rubbed his hands
together and grinned at me. " Cor ! I wouldn't've
missed that for anyfink. Did yer see their faces each time
Capting Jennings mentioned the *Penang* ? Bet yer it was
piracy they was up ter. And Miss Jennifer—she impressed
'em."

I nodded. It had been exciting whilst Jennings had
been cross-examining the witnesses for the prosecution.
But all I could think of was the cold, factual summing up
of the Judge Advocate. And now back in this dreary
waiting-room with the military policeman at the door,
all elation was stripped from me. Jennings had done his
best. He'd tried to show the state of suspicion and
uneasiness that had prompted our actions. But this
wasn't a civil court. There was no jury to impress. The

men who were sitting in judgment on us were Army
officers, concerned primarily with the maintenance of
discipline in a civilian army at the end of a long war.
And against our frail case was the solid, factual statements
of witnesses reporting what had actually occurred.
Jennings had warned us not to expect an acquittal. And
now that the case had been presented and we were out
of the court-room, I realised how thin were our chances.

"Come'n, mate—'ave a fag," Bert said in a chirpy
voice. "You look as though we was hincarcerated in
the beastly Glass'a'se already. I know the ruddy prosecution didn't mince 'is words in 'is final speech. An'
the summing up of that Judge Advycate bloke—that
won't 'ave 'elped us much."

"Oh, it was fair enough," I said.

"Well, I reckon we got a chance, see. Jennings made
Rankin look pretty cheap. Wot d'you fink?"

He was holding a packet of cigarettes out. I took one.
I didn't want to damp his cheerfulness, so I said nothing.
"Oh, well," he said, "maybe they'll 'ave ter find us
Guilty fer the sake of appearances. But I reck'n the
sentences'll be light."

"Well," I said, "we won't know what the sentences
are for some time. If we're found Not Guilty they tell
us right away. But if we're Guilty we're not told anything
now."

We smoked in silence for a moment. Then the door
opened and Jenny and her father came in. With them was
Bert's missis. I don't know what we talked about—
anything but the trial. Jenny's father was a gentle-
voiced man with bright twinkling blue eyes and white
hair. He was a Scot. He had great charm. Though they
were not in the least like each other physically, he and
Jenny had much in common; the same trick of looking
constantly surprised with the world, the same easy almost
childish delight in things, the same soft, musical voice.
But where her father's enthusiasm for life merely twinkled,
hers sparkled gaily.

They were an odd contrast to Mrs. Bert, who was a
solidly built, angular woman with a rollicking sense of

humour that shook the walls of that wood-lined room. She might have been a barmaid or kept a winkle stall in her youth. But now there was only the faintest trace of the buxom Cockney beauty she had once been. She was worn with work and cares. But beneath the wrinkled skin and faded clothes was a warmth that did me good. It was the warmth of a friendly nature that seemed to expect the worst from a hard world, accepted it and triumphed over it so that you felt in her that flood of good-neighbourliness that is the spring of happiness.

Time passed slowly. Conversation was not easy. It was like waiting for a train to go out. At a quarter to one our visitors were ushered out and we were marched back into the court-room. Nothing seemed to have changed. Everyone was seated in the same places. But there was a subtle difference. And the difference was in the attitude of the five officers of the Court. Their faces were no longer receptive. They had made up their minds. Their eyes watched impersonally as the court-room settled itself. I suspect they were impatient for their lunch. No doubt there were more cases to be dealt with and ours had taken longer than they expected. I felt a chill void inside me as we were ordered to stand to hear the sentence of the court.

Tobacco smoke drifted in a splash of sunlight. They had relaxed, smoking, whilst deciding our fate.

The voice of the President was cold and impersonal as he addressed us. " The Court has no announcement to make." The signet ring flashed in the sunlight as he massaged his jaw. " The findings of the Court, being subject to confirmation, will be promulgated in due course."

The court-room stirred restlessly. I felt cold and numb as though nothing could hurt me any more. The Judge Advocate turned to the prosecuting officer and asked, " Have you any statement to make with regard to the accused ? "

The prosecuting officer produced our Army records. Jennings made a speech of mitigation, stressing our excellent record and the fact that our actions had been prompted by good intentions. Once again the Court was closed, this time for consideration of sentence.

Ten minutes later we were taken in again. This time we were told, " The sentence of the Court, being subject for confirmation, will be promulgated later." And then the President glanced round the room. " And, therefore, the proceedings now in Open Court are accordingly terminated."

A buzz of conversation swept through the room. Chairs scraped. I found myself being marched out. I remember a brief glimpse of Jenny, smiling brightly, and then we were behind the wire cage of the three-tonner and roaring back along the road we had come.

Two weeks later the sentences were promulgated. I shall never forget the shock I experienced when I stood before the Camp Commandant and heard him say: " Corporal Vardy. At your trial, which took place at Exeter on 28th April, 1945, when you were charged with mutiny, you were found Guilty and sentenced to be discharged the Service with ignominy and to serve four years penal servitude. That sentence has been confirmed by the confirming authority, and findings and sentence are accordingly promulgated."

Bert got three years.

I don't think we really believed our ears for the moment. It took time for the harsh reality of it to sink in. But during the evening we went through a process of mental readjustment which was frighteningly humiliating. We had to accustom ourselves to the idea that we should be cut off from the world as we knew it for three and four years. It seemed like eternity.

Next morning we were packed into the same three-tonner with the wire-caged back and driven off. " Where d'yer reckon we'll serve our time ? " Bert asked. All the cheerfulness had been beaten out of him.

" God knows," I said.

We skirted Plymouth and drove inland through Yelverton. We turned right there and began climbing. It was sunny with cotton wool clouds and the plain below us a patchwork of cloud and sun. The earth looked warm and

glowing. A tor with an RDF mast on the top of it appeared
away to our left as we sat looking down the winding
road to the flat country of the Tamar. And suddenly
an awful fear gripped me. For I knew where I was. I
knew this part of the country. Several times I had stayed
with a friend of mine at his family's place at Dartmeet.
This was the Moor. And the road we were on led to
Princetown.

I had heard some talk about long-term military prisoners being imprisoned there. I hadn't thought much about
it. But now that rumour gripped at me like a stomach
ulcer. I looked at Bert, blissfully unconscious of his
whereabouts. He caught my eye and grinned wanly.
" Turned a't nice again, ain't it," he said. Then he shook
his head. " The kids'd like this sort of country. D'yer
know they ain't never seen the country ? Bin in ruddy
Islington all their lives. The eldest is only four. The
missus was kind o' lonely an' I reck'ned I'd soon be going
overseas. That's why we started raisin' a family. Poor
little chaps ! All they seen o' the world is bombs an'
rubble an' dirty tenements. They ain't never seen street
lights after dark, nor eaten bananas—but the eldest,
already 'e knows the difference between a Spitfire and
a P38, can tell a bomb from a V-1 an' knows the barrage
balloons by 'is own pet names. An' now, when the stupid
war's nearly over an' I reckoned ter be able ter show 'em
the sea an' a spot o' country like this on me demobilisation
leave, this 'appens. It's just damnable ! " he added
savagely.

I put my hand on his shoulder. There was nothing I
could say. Thank God I had no family. But I felt I'd
let him down. I ought not to have acted so hastily—I
ought to have thought of the consequences. And yet if
we'd obeyed Rankin, we should have got into that boat
and we should not have been alive now. I thought then
what irony of fate it was that Rankin, who had brought
the charges against us, owed his life to me. He, too, would
have been in that boat if I hadn't refused to obey his
orders.

The truck had reached the top of the long climb out

of the plain. We were in the moors now and all about us were fire-blackend hills. Here and there patches of gorse that had escaped the flames blazed golden in the sunlight. The road snaked out behind our humming wheels, curving like a white ribbon over the shoulder of a rock-crested tor. Behind the tor the sky was dark with smoke. Away to our left the moors rolled endlessly to the sky-line, and everywhere smoke curled up from the warm, peaty earth. In a valley close below the road men with flaming brands were setting fire to grass and gorse, the flames crackling merrily in a great curve that the wind had made. They were burning the moors over to improve the grazing— swaling, they call it. They do it every spring. They were not supposed to do it during the war because of the blackout. But they did it all the same, beating the flames out at night.

We picked up the railway and a few minutes later drove into Princetown. I waited with my heart in my mouth. If we turned left in the market square ... The truck slowed and then turned. I suddenly felt frightened. To suspect the worst is one thing. To see your suspicions confirmed is another. This meant solitary cells and the coldest, dampest, most horrible prison in the whole of Britain. Cold little stone houses bristled at the road edge. They were warders' houses. Then a high, bleak wall beat back the sound of our engine. The truck stopped and the horn was blown. Voices and then the heavy sound of bolts being withdrawn. I looked quickly at Bert, sur- prising a dumb, hurt look in his eyes as he stared with horror at that blank wall. I looked away. A voice called out, " Okay ! " The truck ground forward in bottom gear and bumped noisily between great iron-studded gates that had been thrown back. As we went down the slope into the prison, the gap in the wall through which we had entered closed on us as the two great doors were swung to and bolted.

The truck stopped. Our escort came and unlocked the wire cage. There was a warder with him. " Come on, you two—out you get," the warder ordered. And then added automatically. " Come on, look sharp now."

Bert and I jumped out. We were in a kind of V
formed by two of the many wings of the prison. The
wings were ugly rectangular blocks built of solid granite
from the nearby quarries. The roofs were of grey slate
rising to a shallow crest. Each prison block was punctured
by rows of neat little barred squares. Cell windows!
Rows and rows of them like square portholes in grim,
age-old prison hulks. A round brick chimney dominated
the prison, belching smoke in the sunlight. Bert looked
about him, dismayed and awed by those sombre granite
blocks. He turned to the warder. His voice sounded
husky as he said, " What's this place, mate ? " The
warder grinned. " For goodness' sake where are we ? "
Bert repeated.

" Dartmoor," the warder answered.

It took a moment for this to sink in. The warder
didn't hustle us. Bert gazed about him, an expression
of surprise and horror on his face. Then he turned to the
warder again, " Come orf it, chum. You're kiddin'.
That's the place they used ter send the ol' lags to, the
ones wot were sentenced ter long stretches." He turned
quickly on me. " 'E's kiddin', ain't 'e, Jim ? "

" No, Bert," I said. " This is Dartmoor all right.
I've often seen it—from the outside."

" Dartmoor ! " Bert's tone was one of utter disgust.
" Blimey !—give me the merry Glass'a'se any day."

" Come on—stop that talking ! " the warder bawled out
with sudden impatience. Then he marched us away out
of the sunlit compound between the granite blocks into
the cold, dark interior of the prison with its clanging
doors and the sound of iron-shod boots ringing hollow
on stone-floored passages. We were inspected, inter-
viewed, docketed, clothed and finally marched to our
cells. As the iron door clanged shut and I was alone,
I realised at last that we had been absorbed into the
soul-destroying machinery of the prison. The walls
closed in on me, the ceiling clamped down on my head,
the barred square of light that was the window seemed to
recede until it was barely wide enough to put my hand
through. A sudden panic seized me. I felt crushed by the

smallness of that rectangular cubicle. Six paces long four wide. Steel bars at the door. Steel bars at the window Pencil scribbles on the walls. Initials and dates cut deep into the stone. The dingy carbolic cleanliness of it clamped down against my brain so that I wanted to scream. And ahead of me streamed the years I was to spend there. Four years—say, just over three if I got full remission for good conduct. One thousand, one hundred and twenty-six days! No—I should still be here in 1948, and 1948 was a leap year—one thousand, one hundred and twenty-seven! Twenty-seven thousand and twenty-four hours! One million, six hundred and twenty-one thousand, four hundred and forty minutes! And I had calculated all that in a minute. Just one minute! And more than a million and a half minutes to go. I suddenly felt I wanted to scream. Footsteps sounded in the empty corridor, keys jangled. I sat down on the bed. I must get a grip on myself.

Then somebody began tapping on the wall. I replied. Thank God for my basic training. I knew morse and realised suddenly that even in the confines of my cell I was not alone. I could talk. The jail telegraph was morse. The message tapped on the wall above my bed was passed on from Bert and told me that he was in the next cell but one. The knowledge that Bert was there, even if I couldn't see him or talk to him, was a great comfort to me.

I am not going to dwell on the time I spent in Dartmoor. It is only an interlude in the story and has no real bearing on what happened later, save that it toughened me mentally and physically. I doubt whether, without that period in Dartmoor, I should ever have had the guts or desperation to do what I eventually did. It was sheer desperation that drove me to Maddon's Rock on one of the wildest sea enterprises it is possible to conjure up even in a dream. It was Dartmoor—the damp, grim, granite awfulness of Dartmoor—that gave me the courage. Now, as I look back on the year I spent in that wretched prison, it seems like some frightful nightmare, so faded and veiled are its memories by more recent happenings.

The dread of solitude, however, has never really left
me. I hated that cell with a bitter loathing. It crowded
in on me, it symbolised my isolation from the rest of the
world, it was the thing above all that seemed bent on
destroying me utterly—crushing my spirit and warping
my brain to madness. I have always had a tendency to
claustrophobia—a dread of being alone in small, enclosed
spaces and a morbid curiosity in any cave or shaft that
took me into the bowels of the earth. The result was that
I was happiest sweating my guts out in that damned
quarry which had provided the stone to build the prison
or labouring on the prison farm. I didn't mind the cleaning, the discipline, the work—so long as I was in the
company of other human beings. Even now I cannot
read accounts of men who suffered solitary confinement
in German concentration camps without feeling panic
seizing at me. I think if that had happened to me I should
have gone mad. But as long as I had plenty of hard work
during the day and a book to read at night, I managed
to stave off the feeling of loneliness that I dreaded more
than anything else.

There were about three hundred military prisoners in
Dartmoor at the time. Of these only about a third were
in for military crimes for which they had been sentenced,
like Bert and myself, by court-martial. The rest were
soldiers who had committed civil offences for which they
had been tried and sentenced by civilian courts. Their
crimes covered the whole gamut of civil offences—
assault, theft, arson, burglary, manslaughter, looting.
Some of them were pretty tough ; hard-bitten die-hard
criminals from London's East End, sly characters from
the race-courses, tough little men from the Gorbals
district of Glasgow, men to whom razors came more
readily to their hands than a rifle, men without any
social conscience, bullies, liars, cheats, habitual criminals,
murderers, men with minds so warped by their up-
bringing that they took it for granted that the world
and every one they met in it was against them. All the
riff-raff, hooliganism, abnormality that the Army had
swept up in the maw of conscription and had been unable

to digest. And a few, like Bert and myself, who seemed to have landed up there by mistake.

I'll never have a better schooling in world misfits than I had there. Sometimes it made me hate my own kind I was so disgusted. And sometimes I wanted to burst into tears at some example of kindliness exhibited by a man who looked tough enough to kick his best friend to death if he should so much as trip over a curb and be temporarily at his mercy.

All the time I was in Dartmoor I never really ceased to be conscious of the grim history of the place. You couldn't escape it. There were initials everywhere. *J.B.N. July 28, 1915—1930.* I always remember that. It was deeply etched into the wall above my bed. I often wondered about J.B.N., for I had been born on the day he entered Dartmoor and by the time he was out I was a boy of fourteen. The cells, the prison yards, the workshops, the kitchens, the laundry—everywhere the ghosts of these men who had been forced to live out long stretches of their life in this place clung to walls and tables and benches in the form of initials and dates. But these ghosts of the past were not obtrusive. They were too numerous. The walls had seen too much misery and wretchedness and hopelessness to retain any impression of individual cases—only there was a general atmosphere of wretchedness imprisoned on those damp-streaming walls.

It's a strange irony that this prison, which had been built for French and American prisoners of war at the beginning of the nineteenth century and had been a horrible Home Office ash-can for the country's human refuse for almost a century should now hold British soldiers. But we weren't the only occupants of Dartmoor. Ours was a world apart, an almost military world with prison discipline. But there was another world within those walls—the world of Borstal. Why the authorities turned over part of this most disreputable of all our prisons to be a home for Borstal Boys, God knows. But they did, and the boys shared the Moor with us. It was not an easy marriage. Their world was a softer, pleasanter

world than ours. They were divided into houses like a
school. They were allowed a number of little privileges
which made our own lot harder to bear. And the easier
discipline gave rise to riotous outbreaks for which there
was no cure. For these boys were only boys in the eyes
of the authorities. Their ages were anything up to twenty-
three or so, and many of them were hardened criminals.

All these impressions came slowly. At first I was too
dazed and too absorbed in the task of adjusting myself
to the life to absorb much of the atmospere. But gradually
I came to take the background for granted and then,
when I had time to think and take stock—that was when
I began to feel frightened. But I got over it. I established
a routine for myself so that I would never have time to
think. I always made certain I had something to busy
myself with in the evenings in my cell. I caught up with
the days and kept a calendar, but I never allowed myself
to think of the months stretching endlessly ahead of me.
I tried not to think of what had brought me here. To
kick against the pricks and to count the days to release
—that would bring no satisfaction. I no longer tried to
sort out the mystery of whether there really had been
something wrong with the *Trikkala's* boats or what
Captain Halsey had been up to during the twenty-one
days he had been sailing in an open boat in the Barents
Sea. I accepted it all and that way got some peace of
mind. I tried not to think about myself at all, but abstract
things—geography, history, cross-word puzzles. Anything but myself. I wrote to my family to tell them where
I was. It was not an easy letter to write. I knew how hard
they would be hit by the news that their son was in
Dartmoor. But after that my correspondence with them
was easier, for it became entirely impersonal.

But letters to Jenny were more difficult. We fell into
a regular correspondence. And whilst I looked forward
with the excitement of a school kid to a letter from her,
keeping it in my pocket unopened for days, trying to make
it bridge the gap to the next, they were a weakness in the
armour of acceptance and indifference I was building to
my condition. For she wrote to me of the Highlands, of

hunting, of sailing in the lochs, she sent me plans of the *Eilean Mor*, took me all through her reconditioning almost plank by plank. It was hard, because she wrote of things I loved which were out of my reach. But her letters were a real contact with the outside world. They were my one form of dissipation in the routine of forgetfulness that I had planned. They made me think of the future, of what I should do at the end of my three years. They made me unhappy. And yet I loved them as the one bright thing to look forward to from day to day.

So the spring warmed into summer. VE Day came and went. Then VJ Day. The leaves turned on the trees behind the church and blew in gay clusters around our marching feet as we turned in at the prison gates. Then winter clamped down, hard and black. The moors became thick with mists. In November a drift of powdery snow stung our faces on an early parade. The walls of our cells streamed with damp. Our clothes never seemed dry. The moors, so pleasant to summer visitors stopping for tea in their cars, became a mysterious, frightening void. The mists closed down on the prison for days at a time so that the great rocky battlements of the surrounding tors were seen as dim glimpses through fleeting gaps in the murk.

All this time Bert and I were in constant contact. Messages passed back and forth between us through the intermediary of a burglar who occupied the cell between us. This burglar had been on the Moor before. He was a hardened criminal, a mixture of Scot and Irish with a small bullet head and a wicked temper. He had been in R.E.M.E. till he burgled the till of a Naafi canteen in a big military camp near Carlisle. He was always planning escape. He never did anything about it. But he'd work it out to the last detail and then pass it on to Bert and myself. It was his way of passing the time. He might just as well have done cross-word puzzles.

Sometimes Bert and I managed to talk to each other. I remember one day he was in a great state of excitement. We were in the same work party and he kept on catching my eye, his face all a-grin. As we fell in to march back

to the cells he pushed his way alongside and whispered,
" I seen the dentist, mate. They're goin' ter give me me
denchers." I looked at him quickly. I'd got so used to
him without them that I couldn't visualise him with
teeth. The screw in charge of the party told us to stop
talking.

Then one day about a month later I met Bert on our
cell landing while on the way to empty some slops and
barely recognised him. The wizened little monkey face
was gone. His mouth was full of teeth. They grinned at
me like horse's teeth. It was as though he had filled his
mouth with some white pebbles and was afraid of swallow-
ing them. It made him look grotesquely young. I'd never
thought about his age before. But now I realised suddenly
that he could not be more than thirty-five. The teeth
moved up and down as he spoke.

However, I think I got used to them quicker than he
did. Scotty, our burglar chum, spent hours relaying to
me Bert's comments on those teeth. Bert came in for a
lot of chaff, but he gave as good as he got. He was popular
with everybody. With or without his teeth he continued
to grin and crack jokes.

Christmas came and the snow began to pile up on the
Moors. For a week in January we seemed to do nothing
but clear the snow, shovelling a way through the drifts
to keep the roads open. " Huming snowploughs, that's
all we is," Bert grumbled. But I enjoyed those days out
in the snow. It was warm working and if we made good
progress discipline was relaxed and we were able to talk
and sing.

Then suddenly the snow was gone and the moors
glowed a warm golden brown in crisp sunshine. Life
began to stir even up on those bleak hills. An occasional
bird began to sing. The men became restive. They
smashed up their cells. Fights became more frequent.
The Borstal Boys started organised rioting. I was infected
by the general spring malaise. The limitations of my cell
began to irk me more and more. I wanted to smash it
up. But I was scared—scared of chokey. I couldn't face
solitary confinement. I had fits of terrible depression,

violent longings to get out and walk in freedom across the moors. I found my thoughts becoming dominated by memories of shady walks in summer woods, meadows of buttercups beside a river and the sparkle of water in sunlight as my sailing dinghy trod the wavelets in Cornish estuaries. And all these longings began to focus on Jenny. I started counting the days to each letter, getting miserable and angry when they were late, or what I chose to consider as late. I found myself upbraiding her in my letters and then tearing them up. And then one day I woke up to the realisation that I had fallen in love with her. I cursed myself for a fool. I was a prisoner in Dartmoor, disowned by my fiancée, a failure to my parents. What future could I possibly have ? What could I possibly offer her ? In a fiendish debauch of mental masochism I didn't write to her for three weeks, so that she wrote to me asking why I hadn't written, was I sick, should she come down and see me ? I hated myself then, hated myself even more when I wrote a dull, impersonal letter in reply.

And then suddenly the world changed and my cloak of misery and frustration fell away from me in the eager burst of enthusiasm with which I concentrated all my thoughts on one single idea.

It happened this way. I got hold of papers whenever I could. One of the screws, a jailer named Sandy, was a decent sort and used to slip me one now and then. I read them avidly. They gave me great satisfaction. It was an impersonal contact with the outside world. They produced the illusory feeling that I was sitting by my own fireside. On the 7th of March, it was—7th March, 1946. I managed to see a copy of the previous day's issue of one of the London dailies. I was glancing through it with the pleasant absorption that went with the illusion that I was part of the world about which I was reading, when my eye was caught by the single word *Trikkala*. It was in the second head to a down-column story on the front page. It was quite short, a paragraph or two, but it started my brain racing with a thousand half-digested thoughts and suspicions.

I tore the story out and the worn fragment of newsprint
lies on my desk as I write. This is what it said :

**FIRST POST-WAR UNDERWATER
TREASURE HUNT**

Trikkala's Master to Salvage Bullion

NEWCASTLE, TUESDAY—Captain Theodore Halsey, master
of the Kelt Steamship Company's 5,000 ton freighter,
Trikkala, at the time she was sunk, plans to salvage the
half-million pounds worth of silver bullion that went
down with the ship some 300 miles north west of Tromso.
He and several other survivors of the *Trikkala* have
pooled their resources to form a limited company called
Trikkala Recovery. They have purchased an ex-Admiralty
tug and are equipping it in a Tyneside dock-yard with
all the latest deep-sea diving equipment. It is already
fitted with azdec which will be used to locate the wreck.

When I met Captain Halsey on the bridge of the tug,
which has been christened the *Tempest*, he said, " I'm
glad you've come along to-day, for it is exactly a year
now since the *Trikkala* was mined and sunk." Captain
Halsey is short and stocky with a neat black beard and
sharp, restless eyes. His movements are quick and
decisive. His manner is confident. " I don't think there
is any secret now in the fact that the *Trikkala* carried a
valuable cargo of silver bullion. I intend to lift that
bullion. I know where she went down. It happens to
be in an area where the depth is reduced by a wide shelf
of rock. I believe she lies on that shelf. If I am right
then I am convinced that with the help of the improve-
ments in diving equipment and methods achieved during
the war, we shall be able to raise the bullion." He
described the expedition as the first post-war underwater
treasure hunt.

He introduced me to his officers, both *Trikkala*
survivors. Pat Hendrik, a Scot, had been first officer.
He looked tough and competent. Lionel Rankin had just
come out of the Navy after fourteen years. He was a

Warrant Officer. Two other *Trikkala* survivors are among the crew. All are in the syndicate. "We feel that those who had the misfortune to be on board the *Trikkala* when she was hit and who survived a three weeks' voyage in an open boat in winter should be the ones to claim salvage on the recovery of the bullion," Captain Halsey said to me. "And I think we'll do it. We aim to leave on 22nd April,. all being well." He refused to reveal who was backing the expedition, merely repeating that the five survivors had a financial interest.

God knows how many times I read that story through. I went over it word by word. And all the time something at the back of my mind kept fidgeting my brain with the thought that there was something phoney about it. For the first time since I had been in prison I let my mind roam over the events and conversations on board the *Trikkala*. And all the time the thought rattling round my mind was, *why are all these survivors still together ?* Halsey, Hendrik, Rankin, Jukes and Evans—they were together on the deck of the *Trikkala* when we were put on to the raft, they were together in the open boat that was twenty-one days afloat in the Barents Sea before being picked up, they were together at our Court-Martial, and here they were together again on board a tug going in search of the *Trikkala's* bullion. Rankin had even got out of the Navy to be on that tug. They must be very sure of recovering the bullion. And why hadn't some of them got jobs ? That Halsey and Hendrik should be together in the venture was reasonable. But Jukes and Evans might have been expected to ship on other boats and be at the other end of the world. Was it chance that brought them all to England at the same time to ship with Halsey ? Or was it something else ? Suppose they were afraid of each other ? Suppose they shared some awful knowledge ? Suppose the boats had been tampered with ?

Thoughts like these shot like electrons through my brain. And out of the chaos emerged one decisive view— there was some compelling force, outside of the natural

I

desire to hunt for treasure, that kept these five men bound irrevocably to each other. Of that I became convinced. And all my subsequent reasoning was based on that assumption. The name *Penang* began to stand out in my mind as large as *Trikkala*. I began to recall the details of that story. The old cook drifted into my cell, his apron floating in water, his hair like short strings of seaweed, and his lips framing the word PIRACY. Then he was gone and my mind grasped at the straw my imagination had produced. The money for the purchase of the tug—where had that come from? What would it cost to purchase and equip a salvage tug—£20,000, £30,000? Halsey had refused to say who his backer was. Suppose it was Captain Halsey of the *Penang* who was backing it? Jewels fetch high prices now. Jewels are a cash transaction in many places in London. Jewels might well have financed this expedition.

I communicated the contents of the paragraph to Bert. We spent the rest of the evening discussing it through the medium of our burglar chum. Next day, I remember, it was bright and clear. The moors lay all about the prison, warm and brown and friendly. The tors were no longer black, mysterious battlements, but sun-warmed rock cresting the hills. The sky was blue.

It was on that day I decided to escape.

At what moment I made the decision I cannot recall. It was an idea that grew within me. And the focal point of my idea was Rankin. I don't think I had any feeling about Halsey or Hendrik, certainly not about Jukes or Evans. But Rankin had grown in my imagination to the size of an ogre. The long winter of captivity had taught me to hate. And though by my effort of will, I had suppressed all conscious thought of these men or the events on the *Trikkala*, yet when the flood tide of recollection was released from my pent-up brain by the story of the salvage attempt, I found myself with a violent hatred for Rankin. His heavy body, soft hands, white face and little eyes seemed stamped in my memory, together with every action, every gesture so that I felt him to be the embodiment of everything unhealthy.

He wandered in and out of my brain like a big, white maggot. And because I knew he would be afraid of me if I suddenly accosted him when he thought me safe in Dartmoor, I became feverishly excited with the idea of doing just that. From him I would get the truth. And I would get it before the *Tempest* sailed, if I had to smash every bone in his body. Dartmoor had done that for me. It had toughened me mentally as well as physically. I felt there was nothing I would not dare, nothing I would not do to come at the truth which had forced me to spend almost a year in that dismal place.

It was typical of my frame of mind that at first I thought only of what I would do after I had escaped, not of how I was going to escape. All that evening I planned. I would make for Newcastle. I would find the tug. Rankin would be on board, or if he had not yet taken up his quarters on board, he would be in the vicinity, probably at one of the hotels in Newcastle. I would lay in wait for him. And then, when he gave me the chance of a lonely spot, I'd wring the truth out of him. I visualised it all so clearly. I never stopped in my dreaming to consider the snags that might arise to prevent my reaching him, or to wonder if the truth might not be just as they had stated and all my suspicions and uneasiness the imaginings of an over-wrought mind.

But next morning dawned cold and chill, with the moors hidden in a thick mist. The cold damp of the grim, stone blocks pressed upon my spirits and I suddenly began to have doubts. How was I going to get out? I'd need money and clothes. As we went out on the parade ground the great prison wall seemed to mock at my plans. How was I going to get over it? How was I to get clear of the moors? I knew the prison routine for escapes too well—the tolling of the great prison bell, the patrol cars, the warders out beating across the moors, and the dogs. There had been several Borstal escapes quite recently. They'd got caught in the end. And I knew what happened outside. I'd seen it on holidays before the war. All the towns around Dartmoor warned. The few roads through it patrolled. Police checks at every road exit. An escaped prisoner had to walk off the moors and at night. I knew enough about the moors to reckon the chances of succeeding pretty slim. I began to feel depressed.

And then something happened that made me feel as though fate were on my side. Half a dozen of us were detailed for a painting job. We were taken to a shed on the east side of the prison. Inside it were paint pots, brushes, carpentry tools, and ladders. I walked out of that shed supporting one end of a long green ladder and the prison wall was right above me. When we brought the ladders back in the evening, I managed to slip some putty into my pocket. This I transferred to a tobacco tin I happened to have in my cell to keep it moist. That night I tapped a message to Scotty in the next cell. Being a RÉME engineer he was employed in one of the workshops. If I gave him a putty impression of a key could he cut it for me in the workshops ? Back came the answer—Yes. Two days later I got my opportunity. We were painting the outside of one of the blocks and the screw in charge suddenly discovered that we had no turps. I should say perhaps that I was regarded quite favourably by most of the staff. Anyway, the warder turned to me and told me to run over to the shed for the turps. And he tossed the key across to me. I remember staring down at it in my hand hardly daring to believe my eyes. " Come on, look sharp, Vardy," he said. I made off then before he changed my mind.

Next morning when we were cleaning out our cells I slipped Scotty the tin with the putty impression of the key. Bert was close beside me at the time. " Wot you bribing 'im for, Jim ? " he asked. He thought I had handed over a tin of tobacco. I told him then what I planned to do. He'd a right to know, for if I succeeded in getting anything out of Rankin it might well lead to a revision of our sentences.

I've never seen a man come to life with excitement the way Bert did. I realised then that below all his cheerfulness and wise-cracking, he was pretty wretched. " You'll let me come wiv yer, Jim," he whispered. " You'd never make it on yer own like."

I said, " Don't be a fool, Bert. You've served at least
a third of your sentence allowing for good conduct
remission."

" Nark it," he said. " That ain't got nuffink ter do wiv
it. If you're makin' a break I'm comin' wiv yer. I know
wot you're up to. It's on account o' that story in the
paper aba't those brutes going after the *Trikkala's*
bullion. You fink there's somefink phoney, an' so do I.
You'll make for Newcastle, won't yer ? "

I nodded.

" Well," he said. " I don't aim ter be in stir while you're
beating the living daylights a't o' that little tyke, Rankin.
Yer can count me in. Wot aba't makin' it Friday ?
There's a rumour goin' ara'nd that the Borstal Boys is
goin' ter stage another riot on Friday. Zero hour is
planned for eight o'clock in the evening."

" Look, Bert," I said. And then I stopped, for one of
the jailers was approaching us.

That evening Bert was telegraphing to me madly. I
was surprised at his insistence. I thought at first that he
wanted to come out of sheer good nature. I was already
feeling a little scared at the thought of doing the whole
thing on my own with no one to brace up my spirits.
But as message after message was relayed to me demanding
to come with me, I began to realise that it was something
more. Bert wanted to come, wanted to come for the sake
of the chance in a million of getting clean away. I warned
him again and again what it meant if we discovered there
was nothing phoney about the *Trikkala* salvage attempt.
If Halsey and the rest of his gang were on the level he
would be a fugitive for the rest of his life unable to live
with his wife and kids, unable to have any sort of a normal
job. That was, if we got clear. If we were caught, it
meant a severe increase in his sentence just when he was
getting to the time when he could begin to think of the
future. To all his pleadings I replied No. Finally his
messages ceased and I thought he had accepted the
situation.

But next day he reopened the matter over a bin of
potatoes. We were on spud peeling. It was one of those

wretched jobs that crop up from time to time. He
manœuvred himself next to me and I found myself
alone with him in a corner of the shed, our heads close
together across the bin. "When d'you aim to make the
break, Jim?" he asked.

"I don't know," I said. "First opportunity I get when
Scotty gives me the key. If opportunity offered, I think
I'd choose just before eight on Friday, as you suggested.
If the Borstal Boys start rioting everything will be so
confused it may mean longer before they find out I've
escaped."

He nodded, his hands working busily at the potatoes.
"'Ow d'yer aim ter get up ter Newcastle?" he asked
then. "There's money and clothes ter be got, the police
checks ter be avoided. An' don't ferget them beastly
dawgs. You don't want ter be lying a't on the moors
this time o' the year fer long. Look wot 'appened ter
them two Borstal kids wot got away Christmas time.
Free days a't on the moors an' sufferin' from frostbite
when they was brought in."

"Well, it's warmer now," I whispered. "As for
clothes and money—remember I told you I'd stayed with
a friend of mine at his people's place at Dartmeet when
I was a kid? Well, they still live there. He's dead—killed
at Alamein. I wrote to him some months back. Thought
he might come up and see me. It was his father who
replied. A nice, kindly letter. I think I might be able
to get clothes and money there. As for getting off the
moors, well that'll depend on luck as much as anything
else."

He said nothing for a moment and we went on peeling
potatoes in silence. Suddenly he stopped and looked up
at me. "Listen, Jim," he said. "We bin pals ain't
we? You an' me—we bin through all this business
together. We ain't done nuffink wrong. We ain't crooked
or rotten or anyfink. We ain't deserted or got scared in
a scrap an' run a't on our pals. We don't belong in this
dump. An' if you're goin' ter take a chance on gettin'
a't, well I aim ter come wiv yer."

His brown eyes were watching me anxiously. He wasn't

pleading now. He was stating his decision. I thought of his missis and the kids he hadn't seen much of and the fact that he'd probably little over two years to go. "Don't be a fool," I said. "We've been over all this last night. In just over a year you'll be out."

"I'm comin' wiv yer," he repeated obstinately. "We bin in on this together from the start. We'll see it fru tergether."

"You fool!" I said. "Look—the odds are I never get as far as Newcastle. It's not easy getting off the moors. If you're caught, there's a nice little sentence added on."

"Well, wot aba't you?" he said. "You're takin' the risk, ain't yer."

"In my case it's different," I told him. "Even allowing for good conduct I've got at least two years more to serve. And that's a hell of a slice out of one's life. Besides, unless I can get evidence that'll reverse the decision of that Court, what sort of future do you think I've got?"

"Well, wot aba't me? Ain't I got no pride? D'yer think I want people sayin'—'Oh, Bert Cook, 'e's the bloke wot done three years on the Moor fer mutiny'? I got me self-respec'. No. If you makes a break, you takes me along wiv yer. An' if we gets caught, well, we gets caught, that's all. Now I knows where Rankin is I aims ter be ara'nd when 'e gets 'is horrid dial bashed in. 'E ain't the type ter take a thrashin' an' 'old 'is tongue. If there anyfink ter spill, 'e'll spill it."

I was beginning to argue, when he caught my arm suddenly in a fierce grip. His hand was trembling. He was wrought up to a sudden nervous pitch. "Listen, Jim," he said. "I wouldn't 'ave stuck this place if it 'adn't bin fer you. As long as you were in it wiv me, it was all right. I saw you stickin' it an' I thought if 'e can stick it a't, Bert, then so can you. But don't leave me, Jim. Fer goodness' sakes don't leave me. I wouldn't stand it, honest, I wouldn't." He was all worked up and his eyes had no laughter in them now—they were wide and scared. "You saved my life," he went on in a quick flood of words. " But you done more than that. You've kep' me from doin' somefink foolish. I couldn't stand it 'ere on me own. I got some good pals ara'nd, but they're crooks an' scum—they ain't my type o' crony. Nah jist you resign yerself ter the fact that I'm comin' wiv yer. Okay ? "

I started to tell him it was impossible, stupid. But he stopped me with a fierce gesture. I was watching his face. It was a-twitch with anxiety. He was so tensed up that I was convinced he meant what he said. It seemed stupid for him to run the risk. But—I held out my hand. " If that's the way you feel about it, Bert," I said, " I'll be glad to have your company. We'll make it somehow."

He gripped my hand eagerly. His face was suddenly full of a bright grin. " We'll 'ave a jolly good try any-way, mate," he said.

So it was agreed. Next morning Scotty slipped me the key he had made to fit my putty impression. " A'm no guaranteeing it'll work," he said. " But onyway, gude luck to ye."

That was on the Thursday. That evening we were able to confirm that the Borstal riot was scheduled to begin at eight o'clock the following night. It would be dark then. We decided to make the attempt at 7.45, a quarter of an hour before the riot. The one problem was how to be legitimately out of our cells at that hour.

And it was here that Scotty, who knew all about our plans, gave us a hand. He'd made so many escape plans that the organisation of a small detail like this came quite easily to him. He tapped through to me that he and a pal of his were detailed for a coal fatigue the following day after the evening meal. He reckoned the fatigue would take about one and a half to two hours. His idea was that we went on that fatigue and answered to their names when the roll was called. If we kept in the back-ground the screw in charge wouldn't notice that we'd changed places. He and his pal would return to their cells, feign sickness and say they couldn't do the fatigue, but that we had replaced them. That would account for our being absent from our cells. The rest was up to us.

It was the best plan we could hit on. Accordingly we reported with about twenty other men for coal fatigue at 6 oclock on the Friday evening. We kept in the background and the warder calling the work party roll never glanced up from the list of the detail as he called the names.

Five minutes later Bert and I and the rest of the work party were loading coal into sacks. " Got the key, mate ? " he whispered as I shovelled coal into the mouth of the sack which he held open for me.

" Yes," I said.

We didn't talk after that. I think we were both too busy with our own thoughts. There was a slight drizzle falling. The light slowly faded from the leaden sky. The clouds were very low. Every now and then grey wisps curled about the eaves of the ugly prison blocks. The weather was with us. In half an hour it would be pitch dark. I looked at my watch. It was just past seven. Three quarters of an hour to go.

CHAPTER VI

ESCAPE FROM DARTMOOR

I THINK that must have been the longest three quarters of
an hour I have ever lived through. When we had filled the
sacks we loaded them on to a lorry and began distributing
them round the blocks. I kept on glancing at my watch.
Slowly the light faded. The drizzle showed like a thin
silver veil against the light of an open doorway. For
five minutes I was busy stacking coal in a bunker beside
one of the furnaces. When I came out to the truck again
it was dark. The mist seemed to have come down like
an impenetrable blanket. I suddenly felt panicky that
we should lose our way. The truck moved slowly out into
the parade ground. The lights of the prison showed all
about us. The mist was not as thick as it had seemed.
I got my bearings again.

Bert plucked at my sleeve. " Ain't it time yet, mate ? "
he asked.

I showed him my watch. The luminous dial showed
twenty to eight. " Keep close by me now," I whispered.
" First opportunity we get, we'll slide off."

The truck turned up beside another block. We piled
out and began unloading more sacks. The warder in
charge went inside the boiler house to supervise the
stacking of the coal.

" Okay, Bert," I whispered, " slip your boots off."

A minute later we were gliding along under the shadow
of the towering bulk of the block. At the end we paused.
Behind us the headlights of the lorry blazed against a
granite wall. Above us cell windows glimmered faintly.
Ahead, there was nothing but impenetrable darkness.
The ground struck cold through my prison socks. My
knees were trembling. We listened. No sound of footsteps disturbed the silence of the darkness.

" Come on," I said.

I took Bert's arm and we plunged out into the open.
Our stockinged feet made no sound. Twice I paused to
glance back at the lights of the prison. I had tried to
memorise the position of the blocks in relation to the
paint shed. But it was the wall we struck and not the
shed. We turned left, feeling our way along. I was
hoping to get the building in which the ladders were
housed in silhouette against the lights of the prison
blocks. We went fifty yards before we hit up against
an entirely different building and I realised we had come
the wrong way. We hurried back. It was ten to eight.
Incredible how fast the time went now. I was scared
that the Borstal riot might start early. Once that
started the authorities might train searchlights on to the
walls.

My heart was racing as I saw the sheds we were looking
for. I took the key out of my pocket as we felt our way
along the side of the building and found the paint shed
door. Everything depended on whether the key fitted.
I fumbled for the key-hole. My hand was trembling
violently. The key slipped in. I tried to turn it. Panic
seized at me as I found it would not turn. I pulled the
key out and inserted it again. It was sticking somewhere.
It would not go right home.

"Wot's up?" Bert asked.

"Key doesn't fit," I said. I pressed hard against it and
tried again. It wouldn't move. I tried to pull it out, but
it wouldn't budge. It was jammed. Bert tried. At
length he whispered, "We'll 'ave to 'ammer it in, chum.
Okay?"

"Yes," I said.

We listened. There was not a sound. I glanced at
my watch. Five to eight. I could just see Bert grasp
one of his boots. Then he was hammering at the end of
the key. The sound seemed to shatter the stillness. I
felt they must hear it. I thought they'd come running
from all directions. The hammering stopped. Bert gave
a grunt. The key rasped in the lock and we were in the
shed.

It was the work of a moment to get the long green

ladder out. We shut the door. But the key was firmly wedged. We had to leave it there, a dumb witness to our escape. It seemed an age that we walked with that ladder between us. But at last we were at the wall. We put our boots on and then up-ended the ladder. A moment later we were standing on the top of wall and pulling the ladder up after us. The lights of the prison stood out so clearly that I felt we must be seen. But the dark back-cloth of the moors hid us. We tipped the ladder over the wall and set it up on the far side. In an instant we were down. We carried the ladder well clear of the wall and set it down in longish grass. And then we began to run.

We'd no compass unfortunately. But I knew the district too well to go wrong at this stage. We made downhill to the road that joins the Tavistock road to the Exeter road at Two Bridges, by-passing Princetown. And as we ran all hell let loose behind us. The silent prison seemed to flare into a mushroom of sound. It was a deep angry roar that grew in volume till it seemed to fill the night air.

The Borstal riot had started.

We made the road, crossed it and plunged up the slope beyond, bearing away to the right. Glancing back over my shoulder I saw an orange glow near the roof of one of the blocks. " Looks like they set fire to somefink," Bert panted.

" Well, I hope to goodness they don't need the ladders from that paint-shed to get the hoses up there," I said.

" Gawd, I hope not."

As if in answer, the great prison bell began to toll, drowning the roar of the riot with its deep tongue. " D'yer reckon that's fer us or on acca'nt o' the riot ? "

" I don't know," I said.

The going became rougher now. We were no longer running. We were stumbling along. Once I pitched forward on my face. I scrambled to my feet without waiting to see what it was I'd fallen over.

" Can't we let up a minute, Jim ? " Bert said. " I got the stitch."

" Not until we're on the far side of the Exeter-Princetown road," I told him.

" Wot's them lights da'n there ? " he gasped.

" That'll be Two Bridges," I answered. " There's a pub there. The road to Dartmeet branches off on the hill right above it."

" Don't 'alf look nice da'n there," he grunted. " I could jist do wiv a nice pint o' wallop right nah. Don't reck'n I can go much furver, chum."

" Well, save your breath," I said.

The headlights of a car lit the hill crest ahead of us. Then they swung in an arc and the car roared down the hill, the beam of the lights illuminating the hotel and the bridges. The water gleamed silver for an instant and then the car was a red light soaring up towards Princetown.

Bert suddenly stopped. " Let me get me bref a moment," he gasped.

I looked back towards the prison. Lights were blazing. The headlights of several cars swung out of the main gates and turned towards Princetown. " Come on, Bert," I said. " Give me your arm. We've got to get across that road before those patrol cars get through Princetown and down to Two Bridges."

" Okay," he said. Then, as we stumbled forward again, " D'yer reckon we got a chance, Jim ? "

I didn't reply. I had counted on an hour or two at least before our break was discovered. But now I thought our chances very slender. But we weren't far from the road now. If we could cross that we might still have a chance.

" Wot say we pinch one o' them cars a'tside that pub ? " Bert said. " There's free of 'em. You can see their sidelights."

" People don't leave their ignition keys in their cars these days," I said.

Bert suddenly stopped again. " Listen ! " he said. " Wot's that ? D'yer hear it ? " His voice was scared. Faint behind us came the baying of dogs. " Oh, my Gawd ! " Bert cried. And he started to run again, his breath coming in sobs.

The baying followed us as we ran, audible above the uproar from the prison. It was a horrible sound. We reached the crest of the hill. The going became easier. The lights of another car beat back the night as it drove towards Princetown. We were quite close to the road now. "When we're across the road," I panted, "we'll make for the river. That'll put the dogs off." And then I stopped, clutching Bert's arm. The headlights of the car were swinging across the face of the hotel and a man was coming out of the entrance. He was making straight for one of the parked cars. "Bert," I said, "are you willing to take a risk?"

"Wot d'yer fink I'm doin' a't 'ere?" he demanded with a flash of his old humour.

"Okay," I said. "Watch that car. He's on his own. If he turns up this way, get out in the road and lie down— just where it tops the rise there. He won't have time to notice your prison clothes then. Lie as though you'd been hit by a car. If he stops call out to him for assistance. I'll look after the rest. Watch there's nothing coming the other way."

"Okay," he said. "Look—he's movin' off nah."

The car, still with only its sidelights on, was beginning to move. It climbed slowly up to the road and hesitated. The headlights were switched on. Then they swung in a great arc of light till they were blazing straight up at us. The car began to gather way up the hill towards us.

Bert dived for the road. I crossed it and plunged down in the wet grass at the verge. The headlights blazed in the night as the car ground up the hill. Bert was half lying, half crouching in the road. I no longer heard the baying of the dogs, or the tolling of the bell or the uproar in the prison. All I heard was the engine of the car propelling it up the hill towards us. I felt quite cool.

The lights topped the rise, pointing skywards. Then, as the car reached the top of the hill, the headlights dropped to show Bert sprawled in the road, the fork with the sign-post that pointed to Dartmeet behind him. Bert waved his arm feebly. The car slowed and stopped. Bert called. The door opened and the driver got out.

He was within a few feet of me as I rose from the grass verge. He only saw me in time to turn his head so that my fist hit him right on the chin.

" Okay, Bert," I said as I staggered under the weight of the dazed man. Bert was already up. I glanced back towards the hotel at the bridge. All was quiet. But beyond the bridge the hill crest was ablaze with the lights of cars. Our margin of time was as narrow as that.

We bundled the driver into the back of the car. Bert dived in with him. I jumped into the driving seat and we were off. I took the right hand fork. The car was old, but she could do fifty all right. I kept the accelerator pedal right down all the time. In ten minutes we were pelting down the long hill into Dartmeet. I crossed the little hump-backed bridge and swung on to a track to the left that ran beside the babbling waters. I parked the car on the greensward among some tall gorse bushes.

Bert had already got the driver's hands bound and his mouth gagged. He was busy tying the poor fellow's feet. " I'll try not to be long," I said. " Fifteen minutes at the outside."

Actually I was less than that. It was a long time since Henry Manton's father had seen me. But he recognised me at once. I felt horribly ill-at-ease as I told him what I wanted. He shook his head sadly. But he made no comment, simply asking about my friend's size. He left me standing in the hall. I heard a car roar past. In a few minutes he was back with a pile of clothes and some shoes. There was a suit of Henry's—his son I knew was about my size. For Bert he had included an old suit of his own. Shirts, collars, ties, hats and raincoats—he'd missed out nothing. And as I bundled the clothes over my arm, he pressed a roll of notes into my hand. " There's eighteeen pounds there," he said. " I'm sorry it's not more. But that's all I have in the house."

I tried to thank him. But he pushed me towards the door. " Henry was fond of you," he said quietly. " And I would not like Henry to feel that his was a fair-weather friendship." He put his hand on my shoulder. " Good luck, my boy," he said. " But I fear it's a hard road you've

started out on. Don't worry about returning either the
clothes of the money."

And whilst I was still trying to thank him, he pushed
me gently out into the night and closed the door. He
understood my need of haste. That gesture of trust
from a man I had not seen for several years warmed me.
I hurried back to the car and we changed down there
by the Dart, sinking our prison clothes with a stone in
the dark, swift-flowing waters of the river.

Then I got the car back on to the road and continued
south towards Totnes. But I didn't go far. Below the
village of Postgate the road crosses the Dart again by a
narrow hump-backed bridge. That marked virtually the
southern limit of Dartmoor and I guessed that if the police
had yet set up check points, it would be on that bridge.
Just beyond Postgate, therefore, at the top of the hill
leading down to the bridge, I parked the car out of sight
among the bushes. The poor wretched owner had been
too scared, I think, to struggle at any time during the
drive. His eyes stared widely up at me as I bent over him
to apologise for the rough handling he'd had.

We left him then, firmly trussed up on the back seat
of his car and hurried down the slope of the hill towards
the river we could hear talking to the stones in the valley
bottom.

The slope was steep and strewn with rocks. The night
was unutterably black. There was no sound save the
babble of the Dart hurrying over the rocks of the river
bed. Our feet seemed to make a great deal of noise
scrambling against the rocks or brushing through the
dry heather twigs. Gradually we approached the river.
But we could not see it. We could see nothing beyond a
few yards. A light drizzle damped our faces and out of it
bush and rock would suddenly materialise as a vague
shadowy bulk in the night. An unearthly scream suddenly
disturbed the peaceful pattern of sound made by the
water. It was high pitched, shrill as a bat. We stopped.
I listened, imagination galloping wildly. The outline of
a bush showed like a crouching woman just in front of us.
It seemed to move. There was a scuffling sound at its

feet. Then something slid away quietly into the night.
" Gor, love old iron," Bert muttered. " Didn't half give
me a fright. Wot d'yer reckon it was, Jim ? "

" Fox, maybe," I said, and we went on.

We were close to the river now. The water slipped
noisily among the rocks, drowning all other sounds. We
entered a little belt of dwarfed trees. And as soon as we
were among them, they closed about us as though there
were no such thing as open moorland. Dead vegetation
collapsed beneath our feet. Below this decayed carpet
was rock—no earth, or grass, just a jumbled heap of
moss-grown rocks, tumbled there by the river when this
had been its bed. They were smooth and round. They
moved under our feet. It was a dangerous spot to come
scrambling in the dark.

It took us nearly twenty minutes to reach the water
through that devilish patch of wood. But at last we
reached a slab of rock and the air was cold and damp
with the smell of water. We clambered down this slab
and then we were in a jumble of black rocks with the
water pouring past our feet, loud and insistent, whispering
perpetually with a voice that seemed as slight as the
rustle of wind through a patch of reeds, yet it drowned
all other sound. We stood there for a moment looking
down at that rush of water. We could just see it. It
creamed white round the vague shapes of the rocks.
Between these white, chattering frills, we sensed rather
than saw the sleek black swirl of the water as it slid
between the rocks.

" I don't like the look of it," Bert said. " Why don't
we go up and 'av a look at the bridge. Didn't see no
sign o' lights as we came da'n. Mebbe there ain't no
police check there. Even if we get through this, we're
goin' ter look pretty peculiar specimens till we dry."

I hesitated. With the water swirling wickedly among
the rocks in front of me, I was greatly tempted. And yet
it was a risk. If we were caught that way we'd kick
ourselves. " At any rate we could go up near the bridge
and when a car comes down we could see whether there
was a check ? " Bert added. That seemed reasonable.

M.R.   K

" All right," I said. And we turned along a path that
ran close beside the river.

Soon we were out of the wood. The path was no longer
rock and mud, but grass. We were in the open and though
we could see nothing, yet it seemed vaguely lighter. I
began to be worried lest we should come upon the bridge
without knowing it. The river was not so noisy here and
I had the impression that it was wider and consequently
less deep. I suddenly stopped. I didn't like being out in
the open like this. Beyond the river I knew there were
woods. Once among the trees we would be clear of the
moors and on our way to Ashburton and Totnes. " We'll
cross here," I told Bert.

He accepted my decision without question. I think he
was getting worried too. We grasped each others hands
and stepped off the bank into the swift flowing river.
The water was icy cold. It came just above our knees,
sweeping against our legs with a steady pressure. Pebbles
and small rocks moved under our feet. We waded out,
keeping the flow of the water on our right. Gradually
it deepened until the water was up to our loins, making
us gasp with the shock of its cold touch. We must have
been about halfway across when Bert's hand tightened
on mine and he half swung me round so that I was facing
upstream. The hills were a black hump in silhouette
against the lights of a car coming from Postgate. In a
moment, they would top the crest and as the car started
on the descent into the valley, the headlights would
swing across us. Without a word we plunged forward.

But before we had reached the further bank, the car
had reached the top of the hills. The twin beams of the
headlights dipped towards us. I suddenly ducked my
body into the water, pulling Bert with me. We crouched
there in the middle of the stream with the water swirling
round our necks, gasping for breath as the icy current
seeped through our clothes. The headlights dipped. We
saw the wood we had padded through as a huddle of
brightly-lit trees and deep shadows, leaning towards the
river as though charging pell mell into the rock-torn
stream. The lights swept across the further bank. It

was bare of cover, a pleasant greensward running up to the line of woods that clothed the further hillside. They illumined for an instant the dark, smooth surface of the water where we crouched. The branch of a tree swept passed my face. I saw the shadow of my head move across the surface of the water. I turned to look at Bert and caught a glimpse of his teeth chattering with the cold. And then the headlights swept on and the bridge stood clear before my eyes. It was an old hump-backed bridge of mellow lichen-covered stone. Two black recesses marked the spans as they bridged the river. And standing by the parapet was a man in a blue peaked cap. That bridge was scarcely forty paces upstream from where we crouched in the water.

It was only a momentary glimpse I had. Then the headlights swung away and all was darkness again. I glanced at the hillside behind us. It streamed with light as the car came diagonally down it on the road to the bridge.

" Quick," I whispered in Bert's ear. And we began scrambling for the bank. We reached it and pulled ourselves out on to the short turf. Our clothes were heavy with water. It was wretchedly cold. For the first time I realised that there was a breeze—it cut like a knife through our soggy clothes. I looked back as we lay gasping for breath. As I did so, the car swung on a bend. " Keep still," I whispered to Bert. The headlights were full on us. Our shadows lay on the grass—two black and shapeless humps. The shadows moved and lengthened. The car's headlights swung away. The bridge stood out again clear as in an etching. The man in the peaked cap was waving a torch. The car halted on the bridge. We could hear voices, a vague sound just topping the smooth hustle of the river. All about us was a diffused light. A pony's droppings looked like a huge dunghill so close was my face buried to the ground. Here and there were low bushes of gorse and bramble. And fifty yards up the slope of the hill the fringe of the woods mocked us.

The car moved on. Its headlights were swallowed up

in the woods. The red tail-light disappeared. All was black again. A torch flashed by the bridge. Footsteps sounded sharp and frosty on the macadam of the roadway. We got up then and made for the woods. A voice suddenly called out. Headlights instantly flashed on, bathing all the open space in which we ran with a bright artificial light. We flung ourselves to the ground, scarcely daring to breathe.

Surely they must have seen us. Why the shout ? Had they been waiting for us ? We lay motionless, two frightened, wretched heaps of sodden clothing in a prickle of gorse that went unnoticed in our sudden scare. A car engine purred. The headlights swung away from us and the police car disappeared up the road through the woods.

Darkness again and silence.

Cautiously we got to our feet. My face and hands were scratched with gorse and bramble. But we were out of trouble for the moment. We hurried then into the shelter of the woods.

Ten minutes later we were standing in a clearing high up on the wooded hillside. We were panting and our clothes clung to us like wood pulp. The heat of our exertions rose in a thick steam. But I don't think in that moment we gave a thought to our dilapidated condition. We were looking downhill, across the clearing, to where the tree tops on the further side stood etched against an orange glow that flared up into the night. It shone on the low bellies of the drizzle-laden clouds so that they glared redly like a backcloth in Berlioz's *Damnation of Faust*.

" It's a fire, that's wot it is," Bert said. He suddenly gave a cackling laugh. " Strewf ! " he chuckled. " That's two fires in one day, ca'nting the one the Borstal fellers started in the prison. I ain't 'ad such a riotous evenin' since I was a nipper an' saw a pub in Islington, a shop in the Gray's Inn Road an' a tram-car at King's Cross, all free of 'em on fire the same night. Gosh ! I wouldn't mind warmin' meself at that blaze. Wot d'yer reckon it is, a rick ? "

" I don't know," I said. " It's quite a blaze by the

look of it." And then a sudden idea swept through my mind. " Bert," I said, " I believe it's an hotel on fire. I remember there's one in these woods somewhere. Listen! If it is an hotel, there'll be a fire engine there. Now suppose we go down and mingle with the fire-fighters. That would account for our being soaked through. A few black smudges on our necks would cover up our prison haircut. We'd get warm and with a bit of luck we might get a lift. Anyway, the police Would never think of looking for us amongst a crowd of people helping to put out a fire. Come on," I said, suddenly excited by the idea.

He clapped his hand on my shoulder. " Blimey! " he said. " You oughter've bin in the Resistance Movement, you ought." And I suddenly felt light-hearted, almost confident.

The woods ran right down to the blaze. It was the hotel all right. We came out of the trees amongst some outbuildings. The fire had not extended to these. But the main building appeared to be a sheet of flame. The red paintwork and gleaming brass of a fire engine shone in the light of the flames. Twenty yards from the blaze we felt the heat of it. Two silver jets of water hissed into the crackling mass of flame. Steam hung over the wrecked building like a cloud. Some men were removing furniture from a side of the building that had not yet been engulfed. We joined them. We got as close to the flames as we dared. I have never been so glad about somebody else's misfortune. The heat of the fire had our clothes steaming as though they were in a quick-service cleaners. Our grateful bodies absorbed the warmth. I could feel my clothes drying on me, stiffening and getting hot. Now and then sparks fell and the pungent smell of singed cloth filled the air.

I suppose the fire lasted about an hour from the time we arrived. Gradually the weight of water subdued the flames. And then, quite suddenly it seemed, the glow and heat was gone and all that remained was the brick shell of the building crammed with a twisted heap of broken and blackened timber.

All this time we had kept out of the way. Parked close beside the fire engine was a squad car. Two policemen in blue peaked caps, one a sergeant, stood by the fire chief. I wondered whether this was the police car that had given us such a scare at the bridge below Postgate. Probably the driver of the car they had stopped had told them he could see the glow of a fire from the top of the opposite hill. It would certainly have been visible from there.

The fire was out now. The firemen were packing up. The only light was the spotlights of the fire engine. "Bert," I whispered, "what about getting a lift on the fire engine?"

"Nark it, guvner," he said quickly. "They'd want to know why we was 'ere. An' s'ppose they asked us for our hidentity cards?"

I hesitated. But I was convinced this was our chance. I was too excited by the idea to be warned off it. "Listen, Bert," I said in his ear. "That's a Totnes engine. I asked one of the firemen just now. And Totnes is on the main line to London. Once in Totnes we'd be clear. It's too far from the moors for them to have a police check on the railway station, not on the night of the escape at any rate. If we could get a lift on that engine we'd be clear. No police check would think of stopping a fire engine to search for escaped prisoners."

"Okay," said Bert a little doubtfully. "D'yer really fink they'll give us a lift?" Then suddenly he gripped my arm. "Wot aba't waitin' till that patrol car moves off? The firemen wouldn't 'ave 'eard aba't us, but them coppers 'ave. They only came da'n ter look at the fire. It's us they're after really."

"No, we'll do it now," I said. "And just to make certain they do give us a lift we'll ask the police sergeant."

"Here, nark it," Bert exclaimed in alarm. "I ain't talkin' ter no coppers."

"You don't have to," I answered. "Just keep in the background. I'll do the talking." I crossed the gravel drive, Bert following reluctantly at my heels. "Excuse me, officer," I said. The police sergeant turned. He was a

big bull of a man with sharp eyes sunk deep in a ruddy face
and a little clipped moustache. " I wonder if you could
help us," I said quickly. I tried to control the nervousness in my voice. " My friend and I are in a bit of a jam.
We were waiting for the bus up on the road when we saw
the flames and came down to give a hand. Now we're in
a pretty filthy state and we've missed the bus. I was
wondering if it would be possible for us to ride back on
the fire engine. It is the Totnes engine, isn't it ? "

" That's right, sir." His sharp eyes inspected us
critically.

" Well, I know it's against regulations and all that,"
I hurried on, " but I thought perhaps in the circumstances
—you see, we're staying in Totnes and I don't know
how we'll get back otherwise. I thought if you were to
have a word with the fire chief——"

He nodded. " I will that, sir. I'd give 'ee a lift meself
only we're going up on to the moors. Two of 'em blasted
prisoners 'as broken out. Hang on a minute, sir. I'll
'ave a word with Mr. Mason 'ere."

He went over to the officer in charge of the firemen.
They were looking at us all the time they were talking.
The fire engine suddenly switched on its headlights. I
felt sure they would see what we were in that bright glare.
Bert coughed nervously and began to back out of the
glare. My knees felt weak. I cursed myself for this bit
of bravado. I wanted to run. But instead I found myself
saying to Bert, " Stand still and pretend to be talking
to me as though you didn't mind being in the glare of the
headlights."

" Okay," he said. " Wot shall we talk about." His
eyes were wide in the lamplit glare.

" About the weather—anything," I said. " But for
God's sake don't look so scared."

" I can't 'elp it, mate," he answered. " I feel like a doll
wot's got a 'ole in the knee joints fru which the sawdust
is seepin' a't."

The police sergeant suddenly nodded. Then he came
deliberately towards me. I braced myself for the grip of
his hand on my shoulder. " That's all right, sir," he said

in his friendly Devonian voice. " Just 'op in the back. You'd best look sharp 'cos they're just leaving."

" Thank you very much indeed, officer." It was an effort to get it out. " Goodnight ! " I added as we moved towards the fire engine.

" Goodnight," he replied and began talking again with the constable.

" You got a good nerve," Bert whispered. The tone of admiration in his voice was like a tonic to my weak legs.

" I nearly did an over-reach," I whispered back. " If they'd been going the other way we'd have been riding into Totnes in that patrol car."

A figure emerged from behind the glare of the head-lights. " You the two gentlemen that want a lift ? " a voice asked.

" That's right," I replied.

" Jump up on the back then. We're just off."

A fireman gave us a hand up on to the platform beside the escape ladder. The two policemen got into their car and drove off. We could see their headlights dancing through the trees that bordered the drive, climbing up to the road high in the woods above the hotel. Their lights showed like a fast-moving lantern as they turned back towards the bridge below Postgate. The motor of the fire engine suddenly revved, the bell clanged and we moved off into the sweet-smelling night, away from the acrid smoke of smouldering wood.

Our clothes, I discovered, were still damp. It was a bitterly cold drive. But I didn't really notice it. My heart was singing within me. For with each minute of that biting wind, the humming wheels of the engine were carrying us farther from Dartmoor.

It was shortly after one that the fire engine dropped us outside our hotel in Totnes, or what we said was our hotel. We stood on the pavement until the red tail-light of the engine had disappeared and then cut down a side alley. The alley led into another street. It was dark and deserted. Our footsteps clattered noisily on the pave-ments. We were as conspicuous at that hour of the night as we should have been with a spotlight trained on us. We stopped in the shadow of a shop doorway to consider our next move. There was no question of going to a hotel. The story of the fire would explain the state of our clothes and our late arrival, but the porter would almost certainly ask for our identity cards. The hotels would most probably be full anyway. To hang about either in the town or the station would be suicide. " Remember passin' a pull-in as we came into the town ? " Bert asked. " It was a petrol station and there was a couple o' lorries there. We might get a lift, or a bite to eat. I could just do wiv a bite."

I remembered the place. It was about a mile out of the town. We did not meet a soul as we walked through the unlighted streets. We kept out of sight when cars passed us. There were three lorries in the pull-in. We had sandwiches and thick coffee essence. We told how we'd helped to put out a fire and ridden in on the fire engine. " Trouble is we missed our train," Bert said.

" Where yer makin' fer," asked the man behind the coffee counter. When I told him London, he said, " Stick ara'nd. One of the regular London boys will be in. I'll get you a lift."

At that a little fellow in the corner coughed self-consciously and said in a croaking voice, " I'm goin' ter London. Give yer a lift if yer like. But it's fish."

We didn't stop to think what it would be like lying on a load of mackerel for 200 miles so anxious were we to get on our way. I'll never regret that we took that lift. But I wouldn't want to do it again. It was a hard bed and the smell seemed to impregnate itself into our clothes.

But we got to London. It was just after eight as we dropped off outside Charing Cross station. I bought a morning paper. It was full of the Borstal riot at Dartmoor and two prisoners that had escaped. Our names and descriptions stared back at us from the printed page. Fortunately there was no picture.

We got ourselves cleaned up, bought a few things we needed, had a slap-up feed and caught the first train to

Newcastle. I had the devil of a job to restrain Bert from
going up to Islington to see his missis. He knew I was
right, but he looked wretched about it.

I had no plan when I got on to that train. I was dazed
with the desire for sleep and there's little I can remember
about the journey. And when we got off the train at
Newcastle I still had not the faintest idea how I intended
to get the information I wanted out of Rankin. It was
raining. Night was falling and the wet streets reflected
the glare of street and shop lights. I felt crumpled and
dirty. My brain was muzzy with sleep. But I was no
longer tired. We got a wash at the station and then went
to the nearest pub for a drink.

By the time we'd fed it was nearly eight and we went
down to the docks to get news of the tug. We had no
difficulty in finding her. Everybody seemed to know
about Captain Halsey's expedition to recover the
Trikkala's bullion. The tug was moored against one of
the Tyneside wharfs. Her squat funnel was dwarfed by
a litter of cranes and dingy warehouses. The wharf
looked dark and deserted. The water lapped dolefully
against the wooden piles. A clutter of crates was piled
before one of the warehouses like a child's wooden
building blocks. The air was still and full of the damp
smell of water and that strange odour of decaying
vegetation and oil that hangs about the waters of a
port.

We managed to get quite close to the *Tempest* without
fear of being seen. A short gang-plank spanned the gap
between the ship and wharf. Above the gang-plank a
naked light bulb swung on a wire. A radio blared from
somewhere in the foc'stle. "Wot's the bettin' Rankin's
a't ra'nd the boozers?" Bert whispered.

I didn't reply for at that moment Hendrik appeared
on deck. It was strange to see that tall, loose-knit,
powerful figure again. Such an infinity of time seemed to
have passed since I had watched him nervously giving
evidence against us. Evans followed close at his heels.
The little Welshman seemed arguing with him about
something. At the top of the gangway Hendrik suddenly

turned. I could see the scar on his cheek. The light of the naked bulb fell full on it. " Weel, it's the Cap'n's orders," he snapped. " Somebody's got to stay on board and see that he doesna go ashore. I stayed on board last night. The Cap'n the night before. It's your turn to-night. He can have all the drink in the world, but on board."

" But I tell you, man, I've got a date," the little Welshman cried. " Why could you not tell me I was to jolly well stay on board yesterday ? "

" Because I thought Jukes would be on board," Hendrik snarled. " But the Cap'n's sent Jukes over to Jarrow, so ye'll jist have to do wi'oot yer lassie fer the nicht." And with that he crossed the gangway and went quickly down the wharf.

Evans stood on the gangway mouthing curses at his officer. His little eyes looked quickly about him. Then he disappeared below.

" That's Halsey, Hendrik and Jukes off the tug," Bert whispered to me. " D'yer s'ppose it's Rankin they was talkin' aba't ? "

" I think so," I replied. " Hendrik said he could have all the drink in the world, but on board. It looks as though he's on the bottle in a big way and they don't trust him ashore."

" 'E always was a horrible drunk," Bert muttered vindictively.

Evans suddenly appeared on deck. He had a hat pulled rakishly over one eye and he'd put a collar and tie on. He looked neat and dapper as he glanced warily up and down the wharf. Then he crossed the gang-plank and hurried towards the lights of the town. " Blimey ! Bit o' luck that, mate," Bert whispered. " Come on— wot you waitin' for ? Ain't nobody on board 'cept Mr. Rankin."

I don't know why I hesitated. As Bert said, it was a bit of luck. But from the very first day in Dartmoor that I had begun to plan escape, I had always thought in terms of getting Rankin ashore. Once we went aboard the *Tempest* we ran the risk of being trapped there.

Bert tugged at my sleeve. "Come on, fer Gawd's sake," he said. "Nah's our chance."

The wharf was deserted. The gang-plank shone white in the wind-swung light. *Money is the root of all evil*, a girl crooned in a husky-sweet voice over the blaring radio. The water pattered loquaciously against the piles. We slid out of the shelter of the crates. The gang-plank sounded hollow under our feet. Then we were on the rusty deck-plating of the tug. We went for'ard to the bridge accommodation. I paused in the entrance to look back. The wharf was just as it had appeared when we were concealed behind the crates. It did not seem to have noticed that we had slipped on board the *Tempest*.

We made straight for the sound of the radio. I flung open the cabin door. It was Rankin all right. His heavy body lolled on the bunk, the muscles slack, the hands drooping listlessly from the wrists. The neck of his shirt was unbuttoned to the waist showing a white, hairless chest and the first folds of his stomach. His face was white save for two hectic spots on either cheek. His eyes were moist and bloodshot. His forehead glistened. The bowl of an electric heater glared redly. On a table beside the bunk stood a bottle of whisky, a cracked china jug of water and a tooth glass.

"Come in," he mumbled. "Come in. What d'you want?"

He was drunk. He didn't recognise us. I motioned Bert to close the door. "Close the porthole and switch the radio up," I told him. I picked up the jug of water and flung it in Rankin's face. The sight of him sprawled there brought a year's suppressed anger bubbling to the surface. His larded face gasped at the shock of the water and the little oyster eyes opened wide. "I know you," he squealed. His voice was pitched high and there was fear in it. Probably that's why he was on the bottle—why Halsey didn't trust him ashore. He was scared.

I seized him by the collar of his jacket and pulled him towards me. "You remember us, eh?" I cried. "Do you know where we've been? Dartmoor! We escaped last night. We've come here to get the truth out of you. The truth, do you hear? " He seemed too terrified to speak. I slapped him across the face. " Do you hear? " I shouted.

He pursed his bloodless lips. " Yes," he breathed. His breath reeked of whisky. I flung him back so that his head crashed against the wall. " Now," I said, " you're going to tell us what happened after we left the *Trikkala.*"

He moaned and his smooth pudgy hand felt the back of his head. " Nothing happened," he murmured. " We abandoned ship and got blown——"

I leaned forward then and collared hold of his jacket again. He fought me off and I hit him across the mouth with my fist. He cried out. But I seized hold of him by the wrist and, with a quick twist, brought his arm up into the small of his back. " Now then, let's have the truth," I shouted. " If you don't tell me the truth, Rankin, I'll break every bone in your body."

I'm not very proud of what followed. We beat the wretched man up pretty badly. But I wanted the truth. And I had a year in prison to incite my fists to smash that white, unhealthy face. In the end his fear of us over-rode his fear of Halsey. " Was Number Two boat seaworthy? " I demanded for the third time.

" I don't know," he moaned.

" Oh yes, you do," I insisted. " Was that boat seaworthy? Come on, tell me the truth."

" I don't know. I don't know anything about it." He struggled and then writhed as I brought the whole weight of my body on to his twisted arm. " No," he screamed. No, it wasn't."

" That's better." I relaxed.

" It wasn't anything to do with me. I only did what Captain Halsey told me. It wasn't my idea. I couldn't have done anything anyway. He'd have killed me. He was mad—mad to get at all that silver. I just did what he told me. I tell you it was nothing to do with me. It wasn't my idea."

" What wasn't your idea? "

But the sudden spate of words had dried up. He stared at me in obstinate silence.

I returned to my original line of inquiry.

"Were either of the boats seaworthy?" I asked him. His little bloodshot eyes looked up at me with a grotesque expression, half crafty, half pleading. I wrenched at his arm again and repeated my question.

"No." His reply was like a strange cry forced from his lips.

"Did Captain Halsey know they weren't seaworthy?" I still had the whole weight of my body thrusting at his twisted arm.

"Yes," he screamed.

"When did you find out?" I asked then. He struggled. I heard Bert's fist hit him again. I felt sick. But we had to get the truth out of him. I clenched my teeth. "When did you find out?"

"When I reported to the bridge," he answered thickly.

So—he knew the boats were unseaworthy. Halsey had told him. Twenty-three men had been murdered. And this stupid fool could have saved them. I saw red then. I wrenched his arm so that he was doubled up with his head to the floor. He began to scream with the terror of what he had told us. Bert silenced him with his foot. "What a beastly swine," Bert muttered. He was beside himself with anger.

I pulled Rankin back to the bunk. "Now you've told us so much," I said, "you'd better tell us the rest. And make it quick. You're as guilty of the murder of those men as if you'd slit their throats with your own hands. What did Halsey offer you to keep your rotten 'little mouth shut?"

"All right, I'll tell you," Rankin breathed. "I'll tell you everything."

"What did he offer you?" I repeated.

"Money," he replied. "A share of the silver." And then in quick succession, "It wasn't any of my business. He was the captain. It wasn't my idea, I tell you. He'd have killed me along with the rest if I hadn't done what he'd said. I couldn't do anything to save them. I couldn't help them. You must believe that. It was nothing to do with me. I——"

" Shut up ! " My voice was thick with anger and the horror of what he'd done and what he was. " You were a Warrant Officer in the Royal Navy. You could have stopped it if you'd any guts—and if you'd wanted to. You're as guilty as Halsey."

He stared at me unbelievingly, his eyes wide with fear.

" Now then," I said. " When we'd abandoned ship— what happened then ? "

" We—we got into the Captain's boat and drifted——" His voice trailed away as I caught hold of his collar. The way he spoke, the look in his eyes—I knew he wasn't speaking the truth. Then before I had hit him, he cringed away and said, " All right. I'll tell you. I knew it had to come. I've known that all along. I've been scared stiff ever since it happened."

" Well ? " I asked.

" We—we got the *Trikkala's* engines going again. There was a device for sealing off the hole in the ship's side. It was all planned."

" All planned ! " I echoed. Then all the little inexplicable things on the *Trikkala* fell into place. " You mean it wasn't a mine ? " I asked.

" No. Just cans packed with cordite."

" And then ? "

" We sailed."

" Where to ? " I asked. I was excited now. Here at last was proof. The *Trikkala* afloat and hidden in some port under another name. " Where to ? " I repeated.

" I don't know," he began. Then, as he saw me leaning towards him, he hurried on, " No—I just meant I don't know the position." I had seized his arm again. " Let go," he screamed in a panic. " Let go, for God's sake."

" Where did you sail to ? " I asked again.

" Towards Spitzbergen," he murmured. " An island called Maddon's Rock—near Bear Island. We beached her there—through a gap in the reefs—on a little patch of beach to the east of the island."

" 'E's lyin', Jim," Bert whispered. "Beached 'er on an island—that's a jolly likely tale, I don't fink. I can see that brute, 'Alsey, leavin' 'alf a million quid lyin' rottin' on an island for a year."

Rankin heard him. " It's the truth," he blubbered, half crying with fear. " I tell you it's the truth." And then as Bert leaned over him he added quickly, " We beached her on Maddon's Rock. That's the truth, I swear it. We beached her, silver and all." He was almost whimpering with fear.

I pulled Bert back. " He'd never make up a story as incredible as that," I said. " Having told us enough to hang himself, he wouldn't have lied about the rest."

Bert brow was furrowed. " It don't seem ter make sense to me," he muttered. His head jerked up. A door had banged. " Wot's that ? " he asked.

I switched the radio down. Footsteps sounded in the passageway. They stopped outside the door of the cabin. I saw the handle turn. There was no time to do anything. We just stood there. The door opened, framing the figure of a man in the dark gap. Gilt buttons gleamed and a collar showed white. The rest merged into the background. Then he stepped forward into the cabin.

It was Halsey.

He had taken in the scene at a glance. His eyes jerked to the handle of the door. And then back to Rankin. If there'd been a key in the lock he'd have slammed the door to and locked us in. But there wasn't. He stood in the doorway and for a moment he was uncertain what to do. His eyes came to rest on me. And as I met his gaze I felt all the courage drain out of me. I was scared. A year in a place like Dartmoor makes you subservient to authority. And the power of authority was vested in this man. His personality dominated the cabin the moment he entered. His uncertainty was gone in a flash. His eyes were cold, authoritative as he said, " You fool, Vardy. You've escaped from prison. That's nothing to do with me. But you come here and beat up one of my officers—that does concern me. You're a convict and you come here and beat up the man who sent you down. A Court will give you a heavy sentence for an act of revenge that——"

"I didn't come here for revenge," I interrupted him. My throat felt dry and my voice sounded unnatural.

His eyes narrowed. "Then what did you come here for?" he asked.

"I wanted the truth," I replied.

"The truth!" He looked at Rankin. "What have you been telling them?" His voice was cold and menacing.

Rankin's fat bulk seemed to wilt. "I didn't tell them anything," he whined. "I told them nothing, I tell you." He was cringing against the cabin wall, his body tucked up on his bunk.

"What did you tell them?" Halsey repeated.

"Nothing. Lies. Anything that came into my head. They were breaking my arm. I said nothing. I——"

Halsey cut him short with a gesture of disgust and turned to me. "What did he tell you?"

I found myself looking into those black eyes, and I was suddenly no longer afraid. I was thinking of Sills and the cook, of all the men crowded into that boat. And this was the man who had sent them to their deaths.

"What did he tell you?" His voice was less controlled now and in his eyes was the same expression that I had seen when Jennings had mentioned the *Penang*. And I suddenly knew that he was scared.

"He told me how you murdered twenty-three men," I said.

I saw his hands clench as he took a grip of himself. He suddenly laughed. It wasn't a pleasant sound. It seemed to cling to the walls of the cabin. It was a wild, uncontrolled laugh. "Murder?"

"Murder and piracy," I said.

"Try and prove it," he snarled.

"I will," I answered him.

"How?" His eyes were watching me like a cat.

"I know where the *Trikkala* is," I said. "A reconnaissance plane can be there——"

M.R.   L

But he wasn't listening. He had swung round on Rankin. "You lying, drunken sot," he said. "What did you tell them?"

And Rankin, his body quivering with fear, seemed to brace himself with his hands clenched to the edge of the bunk and said, "I told them the truth." Halsey stood watching him. Rankin's sudden unexpected bravado collapsed. "I didn't mean that. I don't know what I'm saying. I told them a lot of lies." He stretched a white hand out to the bottle of whisky and poured himself a drink. The neck of the bottle clattered against the rim of the glass.

Halsey turned to me. "What is truth?" he asked, smiling in his beard. "A man says one thing one minute, another thing the next. Is that truth? You think I'm a murderer and a pirate. Well, go and tell the police. Tell them what you like and see if they'll believe you. See if they'll believe the droolings of a drunk who'll tell a different story to-morrow." He laughed. "You beat Rankin up out of sheer spite. That's what they'll believe. If you go to the police, all they'll do is to give you a longer stretch."

"They may not believe me at first," I said. "But they will when they know that the *Trikkala* did not sink."

"For Gawd's sake—let's get a't of 'ere." Bert was plucking at my sleeve.

But I shook him off. I was thinking of those men in the boats. And this cold-blooded devil stood there laughing in his beard. "You can't get away with murder when the evidence of your guilt still exists. The *Trikkala* is my witness. You may get away with murder and piracy in the China Seas, but not in this country you won't."

At the mention of the China Seas his eyes glittered wildly. His hands clenched. I suddenly realised that he was wrought up to a pitch of madness. One more thrust and his brain might topple into the past. "How many men did you cold-bloodedly send to their death when you were master of the *Penang*?" I asked him.

I thought he would rush at me. If he'd had a gun in his hand he'd have shot me then. A cold madness glazed his eyes. " What do you know of that ? " he asked. And then with sudden lucidity : " You know nothing. You tried to bring it up at the trial. But you knew nothing."

" I knew nothing—then," I said.

His eyes glittered. " God ! " he cried, with an extravagant, theatrical gesture. " Does death not stop their mouths, but they must come to me in the guise of convicts ? Is nothing secret ? Can they rise up through fathoms of salt water to accuse me of what was their inevitable and pre-destined end ? " I do not know whether he was quoting from some old play or whether he had made up those words. But the next passage I recognised— Macbeth in the great banquet hall of Duncan's palace. " *The times have been*," he cried, " *that, when the brains were out, the man would die, and there an end ; but now they rise again, with twenty mortal murders on their crowns*." He stopped then, panting. I realised suddenly that reality had no substance for him. He transmitted life into words and so felt neither pity, sorrow, nor affection.

" For God's sake stop your play-acting," I said. " Does murder mean no more to you than an opportunity to rant Shakespeare ? "

" Play-acting ? " he snarled. His eyes had widened and his breathing seemed to have stopped.

I remembered then what the *Trikkala's* cook had said. " Why do you hide yourself behind a beard ? " I cried. " Are you an actor that's afraid to show his face to the world ? "

I thought he was coming at me with his bare hands. Each individual hair of his wiry beard seemed to stand out against the sudden pallor of his skin.

" For Gawd's sake," Bert whispered impatiently. " 'E gives me the creeps. Let's get cracking."

" Okay," I said.

Halsey didn't try to stop us. He seemed dazed. I don't believe he saw us go. His eyes were dull as though they saw things beyond the tiny cabin.

The cold night air was like a breath of sanity. We crossed the gang-plank and hurried along the wharf.

"That bird oughter be in a loony-bin," Bert muttered as we threaded through dark alleyways towards the lights of Newcastle. "Wot's the next move, guvner? Reckon the police would swallow a tale like that? I s'ppose Rankin was tellin' the truth?"

"Yes," I said. "He'd never have made up a story like that. But Halsey's sane enough in his reasoning. The police won't believe a word of it. And Rankin would deny the whole story. We've got to get proof," I added.

"Proof!" Bert laughed derisively. "The only proof we got is beached on a rock near Spitzbergen."

"If only Halsey hadn't turned up when he did," I said. "I was planning to get a written confession out of Rankin. As it is, he'd say we'd beaten him up for revenge. We'd be in a hell of a spot."

"They might send a plane to investigate, like you said," Bert suggested hopefully.

"What, with Halsey making an open bid to salvage the bullion," I said. "They'd laugh at us. That's what's so devilishly clever about the whole thing. This isn't a hole-in-the-corner business. Halsey has organised it in a blaze of publicity. Even if we'd got a signed statement out of Rankin, I doubt whether the police would have paid much attention to it. Rankin would say we'd forced him to write the nonsense in order to try and clear ourselves. No, the only way we'll be able to convince the authorities is by going out to Maddon's Rock and bringing back a bar or two of the bullion."

"An' 'ow the 'ell d'yer fink we're going ter do that, chum? Spitzbergen, 'e said. An' even I know where that is—way up in the ruddy Harctic, that's where. We'd 'ave ter 'ave a boat." He suddenly seized my arm. "A boat! Blimey—I wonder if Miss Jennifer——"

"Just what I was wondering, Bert," I said. It was just a chance. A 25-ton ketch with an auxiliary engine—it might make it. "We'll go to Oban," I said.

"'Ere, 'old on a minute, guvner," Bert said. "Yer just kiddin' yerself, that's all. We'd never make it. I ain't a sailor. We'd need two more for crew. And—well, I reck'n we'd be a lot safer in Dartmoor."

"Safer," I agreed. "But not so happy. There's just a chance we might make it. And it's the only chance that I can see. Let's go up, anyway. I'd like to see Jenny again."

"Okay," he said gloomily. "The ruddy Harctic, it is. But don't say I didn't warn yer. Gawd! Why wasn't I in a reservated occipation?"

At that moment we came out into a busy thoroughfare full of lights. We took a bus to the outskirts of the town and at a roadside café we found a lorry going north to Edinburgh.

CHAPTER VII

MADDON'S ROCK

WE REACHED Oban shortly after midday on Sunday, 17th March. The sun shone and the water between the town and the island of Kerrera looked almost blue. Beyond Kerrera, the mountains of Mull stood out clear and brown in the rain-washed atmosphere. We hitched a ride to Connel Ferry and there we were directed to the Sorrels' house. It stood back from the road on a sloping hillside surrounded by pines. From the drive we could see past the iron girders of the railway bridge that spanned the narrow, racing waters of Loch Etive out to the Morvern hills. And eastward, through a gap in the first we got a glimpse of the lofty mass of Ben Cruachan. The tip of it gleamed white in the sunlight with the remains of the winter's snow.

An old woman opened the door to us. I told her my name and she disappeared. " Reck'n you oughter've telephoned," Bert said. " S'ppose she don't want ter see us. I mean it ain't as if we was respec'able. Don't ferget we're a couple o' escaped convic's."

Until he spoke of it, I don't think it had occurred to me that our presence might be an embarrassment. I had no claims on Jenny and yet I had turned to her naturally, taking it for granted that she would assist us as though she were my own kin. I had been so excited at the thought of seeing her again that I had not considered it from her point of view. But standing there on the doorstep of what was obviously a respectable Scottish home, I felt like a trespasser. For all I knew her father might be a local Justice of the Peace.

The old woman returned and led us down a long carpeted passage. She opened a door and we found ourselves in a big book-lined study with french windows leading out on to lawns sloping away towards the loch. A fire blazed cheerfully in a big open hearth. It was Jenny's father who came forward to meet us. "We have been expecting you," he said, shaking me by the hand.

"Expecting us?" I echoed in astonishment.

"Yes," he said, smiling and leading us to the fire. "You see I've little else to do these days but read the papers. As soon as I showed her the paragraph about your escape, she was sure that if you succeeded you'd come here. She'll be sorry she's not here to welcome you. She's away to Mull about some fowl the MacLeods have promised her." And he went on talking quietly in his soft Highland voice until I felt as though I'd arrived home after a long journey.

I don't know what we said or how much we told him then. Looking back on it, all I can remember is that he gave us the nicest welcome any man could give to two tired wanderers. The warmth of his personality, like the warmth of the fire, gave us a delightful sense of ease and relaxation. Peace stole over my taut nerves and I became drowsy with the luxury of feeling that I was amongst friends, no longer on the run with every man's hand turned against me.

He gave us tea—a real Scots tea with all sorts of home-made scones and girdle cakes, home-made jam and farm butter. And when we had finished he said, " Jim, if you're not feeling too weary and would care for a walk, you'd just about be in time to meet Jenny coming up from the village. She said she'd be back by four. Bert and I will have a wee chat whilst you're gone." And his blue eyes twinkled at me from beneath the shaggy white brows.

He came with me to the door. " We anchor the *Eilean Mor* down under Dunstaffnage Castle," he said. " You can't miss it. Go through Connel and you'll see it amongst some trees on a promontory across a little inlet of water. She'll be coming ashore in the dinghy at Dunbeg." He paused in the open doorway and put his hand on my shoulder. " She'll be glad to know you're safe," he said. "And don't be worryin' yourself about staying here. We'll be glad to have you. And you'll be safe here. We'll consider what's be to done about you later."

I didn't know what to say. I tried to thank him. But
he pushed me gently out into the drive and closed the
door.

As I walked down to the cold waters of the loch I could
not believe there was such a place as Dartmoor.

I reached the road and followed it through Connel
till I was clear of the houses and had a view across a little
inlet of water. The wavelets sparkled in the westering
sun. The pebble beach shone yellow. And there was
Dunstaffnage Castle, its mellow stone merging into the
trees that half hid it from view. And out beyond the tip
of the little promontory a small ship stood in towards
the shore under a press of white canvas, heeling gracefully
to the wind that blew down the loch.

It luffed easily and came round on to the starb'd tack,
making for the inlet. Then the sails dropped gently from
her mast, the anchor clattered and she swung round,
pointing her bows to the ebbing tide that raced under
Connel Bridge. I could see Jenny, dressed in jersey and
slacks, helping an elderly man to stow the sails. Then
the dinghy was pulled up alongside and he began to
row her ashore. I didn't wave. I was excited and
wretched all in the same moment. If only things had been
different.

She saw me when she was halfway to the shore. She
was shading her eyes from the dazzle of the water with
her hand. Behind her the *Eilean Mor* rode gracefully at
anchor, her reflection dancing in the water. Suddenly
Jenny waved. I waved back.

I went down to the water's edge and grasped the bow
of the dinghy as it beached. She jumped out and took
both my hands in hers. " Oh, Jim," she said. " Is it
really you ? " Her face, all white with salt, was alight
with excitement. " How did you get here ? Was it
difficult ? " And then she laughed. " I've got so many
questions to ask you." She turned to the man who was
pulling the dinghy ashore. " Mac," she said, " I want
you to meet an old friend of mine. Jim. This is MacPherson, our boatman. He's my water shadow. He goes
everywhere the *Eilean Mor* and I go."

The old man touched his cap. He was gnarled and bent with very blue eyes in a dour, weather-beaten face.

She sent him off then and as soon as he was out of earshot, she said, " Jim—did you go to Newcastle ? "

I was startled by her question. " Why do you ask that ? " I said.

" Daddy said you would," she replied. " He's convinced that you escaped because of that ? " She looked up at me quickly, her grey eyes enquiring. " You did know that Halsey was fitting out a salvage tug at Newcastle to lift the *Trikkala's* bullion, didn't you ? "

" Yes," I said.

" Was that why you escaped ? "

I nodded.

" So Daddy was right." Her eyes danced with excitement. " Did you go to Newcastle ? Did you find anything out ? Oh, do tell me—what did you discover ? "

" That the *Trikkala* never sank," I told her.

Her mouth fell open with astonishment. " Never sank." Then she laughed. " Oh, Jim, you're fooling." Then she gazed at me seriously. " You meant what you said, didn't you ? " She was puzzled, groping for the truth. " The *Trikkala* never sank," she repeated slowly, unbelievingly to herself. " Who told you that ? "

" Rankin," I said. " We beat him up and got the truth out of him."

Nothing would content her then but I must sit down with her on that pebble beach and tell her the whole story.

When I had finished, she sat silent for a moment. It was then I discovered that all the time I had been talking I had been holding her hand in mine. " It's unbelievable," she whispered. " To send those men to their death like that. I can't believe it, Jim. It's as though you'd told me he made them walk the plank. And yet it explains all those little things we couldn't understand. Even so, I can't believe a man would really do a thing like that."

" It's true enough," I said. " No good my going to the police with the story, is it ? "

She shook her head. " No," she said. " I believe you

because I know you and know the circumstances. But
the police wouldn't believe you. It's too fantastic."

"The truth is often fantastic," I said.

"Yes," she said. "But not that fantastic. The authorities would say you'd made it up. Rankin would swear he
said the first thing that came into his head to save himself
from being killed. You'll see—to-morrow the papers will
have a full story of how he was beaten up by two escaped
prisoners in revenge for bringing the charges. All the
evidence would be against you. The *Trikkala* crowd
would hang together just as they did at the Court-Martial."
She looked at me suddenly, her grey eyes level and serious.
"Jim," she said, "we've got to get proof."

I could have kissed her for saying "we" as though
the problem were hers as much as mine. And as though
she guessed what was in my mind she gently withdrew
her hand.

"There's only one way I can get proof," I said.

"Yes," she said. "Only one way. Where is Maddon's
Rock ?" she asked.

"Near Bear Island, Rankin said," I replied. "That's
just south of Spitzbergen."

She sat thoughtfully sifting pebbles through her
fingers for a moment. "It's a bad sea area up there,"
she said. And then : "When's Halsey due to sail ? "

"The 22nd of April," I replied. "But he may get
nervous and advance his sailing date."

"And to-day's the 17th of March," she murmured.
"If you could bring back some of the bullion, that would
be proof that even the dimmest-witted official would
understand." She turned to me and said hesitantly,
"Jim, was that why you came here ? "

"How do you mean ? " I asked.

"Because you wanted me to lend you the *Eilean
Mor*."

I stared at her. "I—I am afraid I had some idea like
that," I said hesitantly. "You see, Jenny, I didn't know
anyone else who had a boat who'd stand by me. But I
thought——" I stopped them. Her eyes were veiled
and she turned away.

" Yes," she said. " I'll let you have the *Eilean Mor*."
Her voice was flat and she was staring out to where the
bare masts nodded gently against the setting sun.

I thought she was thinking of the terrible seas through
which the little ship would have to batter her way. I
knew she loved the boat. She suddenly scrambled to
her feet. " Come on," she said. " We'll go and have a
look at the charts. The Admiralty very kindly left me
with a complete set for this area. I'd like to see exactly
where Maddon's Rock is."

She was tugging at the dinghy. I got up and together
we pulled it down to the water. Then I rowed her across
to the *Eilean Mor*. It was a sturdy little vessel, very neat
and well cared-for with white paintwork and gleaming
brass. As I followed her across the deck I experienced
that wonderful sense of freedom that a ship of whatever
size gives.

She took me aft to the little wheelhouse. From a
locker under the chart table she produced a stack of
Admiralty charts. " There you are," she said. " You
look through those. I'll see if I can find a book that
gives the danger spots of the north. I've got one here
somewhere."

I began to run quickly through the dusty charts. At
length I found the one I wanted. Bear Island. Jenny
suddenly interrupted my search for Maddon's Rock.
" Here we are," she said. " I've found it." She had a
book open in her hands. " Latitude 73.56 north, longitude
03.03 east," she read. " Would you like to hear what
it says about the Rock ? "

" Yes, read it," I said. " And I'll try to locate it on
the chart."

" 'Fraid you're not going to like it," she said. " Maddon's Rock," she read. " A lonely, rocky island inhabited
at certain times of the year by a variety of seabirds.
Little is known about it. Landings have been made on
it on less than a dozen recorded occasions. Ships will do
well to avoid this area. Heavy seas run here throughout
the year and the island and the reefs round it are mostly
hidden in spray. The extent of the reefs is not known.

The area has only been superficially charted. Drift ice can be expected in the winter. That's all. Sounds a pleasant spot, doesn't it ? "

" Not too good," I agreed. " That's probably why they chose it. Here we are," I said. " I've found it on the chart. It's just in the Barents Sea and a good 300 miles inside the southern limit of drift ice." She leaned over my shoulder as I marked the spot with a pencil. " Thank God it's spring, not winter," I said. Then I straightened up. " And you'll really let me have the boat, Jenny ? " I asked. I thought the account of the place might have made her change her mind. " I mean, you do realise that—you may never see her again ? " I added.

She was looking at me with a strange expression in her eyes. " Yes," she said. " I realise that." She hesitated, and then said quickly, " You can have her, Jim. But on one condition."

She loved the boat. I knew that. And when she gave it to me like that, I felt staggered at her trust in me. I took her hand in mine. " You really are a pal, Jenny," I said. " I don't know when I'll be able to repay you. But I will. And if we find the *Trikkala*, I'll claim salvage —then I really will be able to repay you."

She took her hand away. " You haven't heard my condition yet, Jim," she said.

" I'll accept any conditions—you know that." I was so excited by the prospect of actually having the chance to beat Halsey to Maddon's Rock that I would have agreed to anything.

" I hope so, "she said doubtfully.

" Well, what is your condition ? " I asked.

" You'll go in charge of the expedition, of course," she said. " But I want to put in my own skipper and crew."

" Your own skipper and crew ? " I echoed. " But where will you find anyone to go on a madcap expedition like this ? Besides, how will we explain—I mean they'll want to know who Bert and I are and——"

" Not my skipper," she interrupted.

"Well, who is he?" I asked. "A local man?"

She shook her head. "No," she said. And then suddenly looking straight at me—"I'm going to skipper her myself, Jim," she said. Her tone was flat, decisive. She hurried on: "MacPherson will come in charge of the engine. He's been a ship's engineer since he was a boy."

I was staggered. "But—Jenny, you're not serious?"

She was though. I could see it in the set of her firm jaw, the level look of her grey eyes. She was serious all right. I tried to argue her out of it. But all she said was, "You need a crew of four on the *Eilean Mor*. You know that. Anyway, that's my condition."

"But, Jenny," I said, "you can't come on a trip like this. There's your father——"

"I'll settle it with my father," she interrupted. I started to argue again, but she cut me short: "Either I come as skipper—or you don't get the boat," she said.

"You mean that?" I asked. I felt dispirited.

"Yes," she replied.

"Then there's no alternative," I said. "I'll have to give myself up and just hope that the authorities will believe what I tell them."

"You know they won't," she said.

"Yes, but what else can I do?"

She put her hand on my arm. "Jim, I'm offering you a boat and a crew," she said.

"Oh, don't be silly," I said. I felt exasperated. To be offered the means I needed and then for the offer to be coupled with a condition I could not accept.

She said, "If you give yourself up I shall sail for Maddon's Rock myself."

I looked at her quickly. That expression was back in her eyes. Something I could not understand—could not be sure of. "Why?" I asked.

"Why?" She shrugged her shoulders.

I caught her hand. "Yes—tell me why. Why would you do that?"

She took her hand away and bent over the chart. "Just for the hell of it, I suppose."

I caught her shoulder then. " That's not the reason."
My voice sounded harsh.

" Yes, it is," she said. " I like taking risks. If you're
scared to take me to Maddon's Rock, I'll go myself."

I stared at her. " I believe you would, too," I said.

She pushed the hair out of her eyes and looked at me.
" Yes," she said, " I would. Now, are you accepting my
condition ? "

I said, " All right—if your father agrees."

She seemed satisfied with this and we went back to
the house. It never occurred to me that her father would
agree to her going on such a dangerous expedition. But
that night when Jenny had gone to bed he produced a
bottle of old liqueur whisky. He sat over his glass for a
while, staring into the fire. At length he turned to me.
" You've heard Jenny's condition ? "

" Yes," I said. " I told her I'd accept—provided you
agreed."

" Aye." He nodded. " Well, I agree," he said
suddenly.

" But, good God ! " I said. " You don't realise the
danger."

He chuckled. " Och, yes I do," he said. " But there's
no holdin' Jenny when she's the bit between her teeth.
She intends to come with you and there's an end of it.
She always was a headstrong lass. She's as wild as her
mother was." He turned back to the fire and began to
chuckle to himself. " I mind the first time her mother
and I worried about her. She'd smuggled herself on to the
MacLeod's boat when they were away to the fishing.
Gone more than thirty hours she was and her only seven
years old. After that it was just one thing after another
until we ceased worrying about her. Yes, she was always
a madcap." He looked up again. " But then you see, the
way I look at it is you can be as careful of yourself as you
like and then get killed crossing the road. And there's
no fun in life if you're always worrying about whether
it's safe or not." He got up to refill our glasses. As he
handed me mine he suddenly put his hand on my shoulder
as he'd done that afternoon. " I like you, my boy," he

said. "You've got guts and you're no fool. What's more,
I believe your story. I don't pretend to understand the
nature of this man, Halsey. But I know this, I'll do what
I can to help you come out the winner. And I'll even
trust Jenny to you." He chuckled as he sat down. "But
for you she wouldn't be alive now, anyway."

And so the matter was settled for me. Jenny came as
skipper. At breakfast next morning she had a smug
little grin on her face. I still didn't like it. It was bad
enough going up there myself in a 25-ton ketch. But to
be responsible for her life as well. However, her enthusiasm was infectious. She and her father went at the
preparations like a couple of children planning an outing.
There was plenty to do—stores to be acquired for three
months, a second suit of sails, storm sails, Diesel oil for
the engine, spare rigging, ropes, tools, fishing tackle,
oilskins, sheepskin duffle coats. Her father financed us,
but it wasn't easy to get these things in restricted,
regulated, rationed Britain.

It took us nearly three weeks to acquire all the things
that we regarded as absolute essentials for a voyage of
this nature in such a small boat. Bert and I could do
little, for we dared not risk being questioned. Most of
the stores and equipment were acquired by Jenny and her
father. Jenny knew her way about Oban and Tobermory.
She wheedled some of the stuff out of the Navy. The
thing that really stumped us for a time was Diesel
oil. But we got it in the end from a Dutch freighter
that put into Oban during a storm.

Those three weeks were as happy as I could remember
for a long time. I took the *Eilean Mor* out most days to
get the feel of her and to teach Bert the rudiments of
sailing. She was easy to handle and rode a rough patch
well. The more I saw of her, the more confident I felt
that we had at least a chance. Even Bert, a landlubber
if ever there was one, began to regard her with respect.
In the evenings we'd discuss the successes and failures
of the day. But always there was something good to
report ; Jenny had managed to get some tinned meat or
her father had persuaded some firm to let us have the

clothing we needed. Till finally the day came when we'd everything that we could reasonably want. I could have wished for a radio transmitter, but since none of us knew anything about it, perhaps it was just as well.

On the afternoon of Friday the 14th of April we took the *Eilean Mor* into Oban and filled up her tanks with Diesel oil. Two great 40-gallon drums were lashed to her decks. Below, everything was stowed and packed. Even our quarters were cramped because they had been invaded by our provisions. God knows where it had all come from. But there it was. And now the final snag had been overcome. We had got our Diesel oil.

That evening Jenny and I strolled down to the loch and along the road under Connel bridge till we could see the *Eilean Mor* lying under Dunstaffnage Castle. " There, doesn't she look lovely ? " she murmured. She had her arm in mine and her face looked dreamy as she gazed out to her boat.

" Yes," I said, " she looks lovely."

Everything was very still. There was no sound except for the weird cry of an oyster catcher down by the shingle strand. The water was flat and silvery. The *Eilean Mor* looked like a toy ship on a sheet of glass. She had her bows pointed to the north as though she were eager for the adventure. Out beyond Dunstaffnage Castle was the island whose name she bore. Beyond, the hills had all gone purple in the evening light. They seemed remote, but friendly—the hills of Mull, Morven, Ardgour, Moidart and in the far distance, the hills of Skye. To-morrow, early, we should glide out from the shelter of those hills, through the Sound of Mull, up past Skye, through the Little Minch to the Hebrides. Then we should turn nor'-nor'-east past Cape Wrath and the Shetlands and the Faroes, out into the unknown. I wondered whether we should ever see those friendly, sheltered lochs again.

" Isn't it wonderfully still," Jenny murmured. " I love to come here and look at Dunstaffnage when it's so still you can see the castle's reflection clear in the water. The world seems so at peace then." She suddenly turned her

face to me. " I feel—you know—like one does when one
is very happy—afraid it won't last."

I was looking down into her eyes. I felt tenderness and
longing fused in my blood. " Are you happy, Jenny ? "
I asked and my voice sounded hoarse and strange.

" Yes, Jim," she answered, meeting my gaze. " Very
happy." Then she looked away towards the *Eilean Mor*
again. " But——" She hesitated.

" Scared ? " I said.

She shook her head, laughing. " Just a funny feeling
inside." She was still looking out across the loch. " I
wish the Barents Sea was calm and still like this," she
said.

" If it were, they wouldn't have beached the *Trikkala*
there," I said. "They chose Maddon's Rock because
there was little likelihood of anyone landing on it." I
was looking at the little vessel lying so quiet and at home
in that backwater. " She looks sturdy enough down
there," I said. " But out beyond the Faroes we'll hit
some pretty big seas. I hope she'll seem as sturdy then."

" The forecast is for fine weather," Jenny said. " And
she'll stand up to anything within reason."

" Within reason—yes," I agreed. " But we may meet
storms out there that are not within reason. And when
we get to Maddon's Rock we may have to hang around
for days before we can get in through the reefs. And by
that time Halsey and his tug may have arrived. Anything
could happen then." My imagination pictured it all so
clearly—the giant seas, the barrier of wicked reefs with a
narrow, foam-filled gap and the black, frozen rocks. It
was frightening enough to face it on one's own, but with
Jenny—" Why don't you drop the idea of coming with
us ? " I asked. And then I had an idea. " Suppose we
don't come back—if you were here you could get in
touch with the police and get some sort of an investigation
going."

She looked up at me with an almost boyish smile,
" No good, Jim," she said. " That's already taken care
of. Daddy will see to it. I've left a letter with him explaining all the circumstances. He's to let the police, the Board

M.R.   M of Trade and the press have it if we're not back within three months or if Halsey's tug gets in before us. Don't you see," she added, " the mere fact that I've gone on such a trip will make the press, at any rate, interested."

" I see," I said. " You've thought of everything, haven't you ? But I still wish you'd stay——"

" Don't let's go into all that again," she pleaded. " Not to-night. It's so lovely out here. Let's pretend just for now that we've not a care in the world. I'm saying goodbye again to places I love. Just for to-night I want to feel happy and at peace with the world."

" Yes, but——"

She interrupted me with a sudden flash of anger in her eyes. " MacPherson and I are coming, and that's all there is to it." Her voice was strained, almost violent. " I can handle the *Eilean Mor* better than anyone. And Mac's been a sailor all his life. I know he's getting on— he must be nearly sixty. But he's tough and he's no family to worry about. Just leave it at that, will you, Jim." Her voice had dropped to a pleading note again. We stood silent for a moment, staring out to the fading line of the hills. Her hand was still on my arm. I could feel the warmth of her body as she stood close against me. " I want to go up to the top of the hill behind here," she said suddenly. " Up there, through the pines, there's a grassy knoll. You can see Ben Cruachan from the top of it." As we turned and climbed slowly through the tall pines, she said, " Ben Cruachan's my Old Man of the Mountains. I always feel that if I say goodbye to him nicely he'll look after me and see me home safely."

So we said goodbye to that distant, snow-capped mountain and came down to our farewell dinner. Mac was there and Bert, and the old man was drinking hot rum punch with Jenny's father when we came in. Jenny disappeared and came down later radiant in a long black evening gown with a silver girdle. The table groaned with the best that the farm could offer. And afterwards there was old port and liqueur whisky. The only reminder of the dangers ahead was when Jenny's father proposed the toast of the *Eilean Mor*. " When I gave you the boat,

Jenny, she was the best I could find. I hope she proves worthy of her trust." And then he added, " The Lord bless you all and go with you." There were tears in Jenny's eyes as she drank to the *Eilean Mor*.

It was late that night when her father lighted me to my room. We were warm with drink. He paused at my door and said, " Don't let her do anything foolish, Jim. She's a wild lass and she'll be trying to play the man. Her mother is dead and her brother was killed at St. Nazaire. She's all I've got left. At the same time she must not be a hindrance to you. I'm trusting you to do what you think is right."

He took my hand. The skin of his fingers was dry and old. But the warmth and friendliness of that handshake brought a lump to my throat. " I like being old," he said, his eyes twinkling in the lamplight. " But there are times when it's irksome. If I were just a few years younger I'd be coming with you."

I thought I should never go to sleep, so many thoughts were chasing themselves through my mind as I climbed between the cold sheets. But the warmth of the drink closed my eyes almost at once and the next thing I knew it was morning and Maggie, their old servant, was shaking me.

It was a cold, crisp morning. The sky was blue. The sun sparkled on the waters of the loch. The hills were hidden in white, trailing mists. Jenny's father came down to the lochside to see us off. His tall, erect figure stood alone on the yellow beach as we rowed out to the *Eilean Mor*. Mac went below and started the engine. The decks throbbed gently as we weighed anchor. Jenny stood in the wheelhouse. I felt the little ship shudder slightly as the screw bit into the water and we slid quietly out into the tideway and made the tip of the promontory. Jenny left the wheel for a moment and stood on the deck looking back to the beach where her father stood. His figure looked very small and solitary, alone there on the beach. We waved. He waved back and then turned and walked resolutely up towards the road. He never looked back. Through the pines we caught a glimpse of the house,

the brick mellow in the morning sunlight. Then the
promontory shut us off. Jenny went back into the
wheelhouse. I think she was crying. I went for'ard.
Our bows were pointed towards the white pinnacle of
the lighthouse on Eilean Musdile. Beyond lay the Sound
of Mull. The water was oily calm with a long, flat swell
running.

After a while I went into the wheelhouse. Jenny had
the log out. I watched over her shoulder as she wrote—
*Saturday, 13th April, 1946—6.43 a.m. Weighed anchor
and left mooring under Dunstaffnage Castle outward bound
for Maddon's Rock. Weather fair.*

The voyage had begun.

In the Firth of Lorne we picked up a steady sou'-easterly
breeze and set our sails. As the mains'l filled Jenny
ordered Mac to switch the engine off. Every drop of
fuel was precious. Shortly after eight we passed between
the half-submerged Lady's Rock and Eilean Musdile.
The race that runs below the lighthouse frothed with
broken wave caps on our starb'd beam. The Sound of
Mull opened out before us. The veil of mist was drawing
back from the hills now and we could see their lower
slopes. As we came under the lea of Mull, the sails flapped
idly and we ran on our engine through the Sound.

Midday found us clear of the Sound with Tobermory
astern, and leaning under full canvas to a steady sou'-
easterly breeze, we rounded Ardnamurchan Point and
with the wind on our starboard quarter we made a steady
six knots in a long easy swell. By nightfall we were abreast
of Skye and running into the Little Minch between Skye
and the Hebrides. And when morning came, cold and
grey with a damp drizzle, Cape Wrath was astern of
us. There were no friendly hills around us now. The
sea stretched in a desolate, restless waste to the horizon
in every direction. And our bows were headed some
15 degrees east of magnetic north.

The third day out we ran between the Shetlands and
Faroes without sighting either of the island groups. The
thin drizzle that we had picked up off Cape Wrath stayed
with us, reducing visibility to a few miles. The wind had

gone round to the sou'-west. RAF weather forecasts, which we were able to pick up easily on the long waveband of our radio in the wheelhouse, remained fair. With the wind practically dead astern we were being hurried north with the long lines of the waves that heaved themselves regularly, monotonously, under our keel. We had no need of the engine. We sailed under full canvas and the *Eilean Mor* went like a bird.

An incident occurred that Monday which had a bearing on a decision we made later. It was just after two in the afternoon. I was for'ard repairing a cleat that had come adrift. Jenny, who was at the helm, suddenly hailed me into the wheelhouse. Her voice was urgent, excited. When I joined her I found her listening to the radio. Two men were talking. " It's the B.B.C.'s broadcast to schools," she said. " See if you recognise anyone ? "

I listened. A B.B.C. reporter said, "*And how do you propose to locate it ?*"

A voice answered, "*We're using azdec. That is the instrument used during the war to locate U-boats. This vessel was fitted with azdec when we bought her.*" There was something about that voice that stirred a memory. It was clear, distinct—it was as clear a voice as the reporter's. It might have been an actor's voice.

He was speaking again. "*As soon as we have located the wreck we shall send a diver down to investigate. We are equipped with the very latest in diving gear. If, as I believe, the* Trikkala *is resting on a rock shelf——*'

" My God ! " I said. " Halsey ! "

" Yes, Halsey," Jenny said. " Listen ! "

Just before the end of the broadcast we heard the information we wanted. "*And when will you sail Captain Halsey ?*" asked the reporter.

"*I was planning to leave a week to-day. But equipment has been coming through quicker than I thought and with luck I may be away the day after to-morrow.*"

"*Well, Captain Halsey, we wish you all the best in your treasure hunt and we'll look forward with interest to hearing what you bring back with you.*"

Jenny and I looked at each other. The day after to-morrow! That meant that, if he got away then, we'd only be five days ahead of him. The margin seemed all too narrow. Still, five days could be time enough if luck was with us and the weather held fair. I stared out through the glass windshield at the grey, tossing waters—not a ship, not a sign of land. And yet through that radio we had just heard Halsey talking in Newcastle from the deck of his tug. It seemed incredible that we could be linked for an instant like that, so great did the distance between us now seem.

Five days isn't much of a start for a small sailing boat against an ex-Admiralty tug capable of around twelve knots. But all that week the wind was with us, varying between sou'-west and nor'-west. The weather kept fair and the seas moderate—at any rate moderate for these waters. For five days we ran before the wind on a line almost parallel to the Norwegian coast which was about 250 miles to starboard of us. If anything our course was a little north of the line of the Norwegian coast, for Maddon's Rock lies almost mid-way between Bear Island and Jan Meyen Island. And all that time the *Eilean Mor* made between five and eight knots without our once having to make use of the engine.

On the Tuesday we ran into a long, vicious swell that had us all feeling a little uneasy in the stomach. Even Mac had a far-away look in his eyes. Bert, who was acting cook, emerged from the galley with a face that was a pallid green and glistened with sweat. " Strewf! " he said. " Me bread-basket's playin' me tricks." Then he added, " Jist my luck to click fer the job of cookin'. Me name's bin me da'nfall ever since I joined the Army. ' You—wot's yer name? Cook? Right—you fer the cookha'se.' Joke, see. Never knew a sergeant-major wot could resist it." He suddenly clutched his stomach and dived for the rail .

By nightfall the wind had freshened and the movement of the ship was more violent and consequently not so disturbing. Bert, with the adaptability of the Cockney, was becoming a passable seaman. By the end of the week he was standing his turn at the wheel, though only during the day-time.

The first week of that voyage I enjoyed. With a following wind, fair weather and a moderate sea, the work of sailing the ship was not great. I spent a lot of the time in the wheelhouse chatting to Jenny. In blue slacks, a red polo-necked jersey and her hair brushed straight back from her forehead, she looked neat and businesslike. She was a very efficient skipper and knew how to get the best out of her ship. We logged nearly 1,000 miles in that first week. And if if hadn't been for the uncertainty of what lay ahead that would have been the happiest trip of my life. But on the Sunday it began to blow hard out of the north, the glass fell and the weather forecasts spoke of nothing but depressions. Their centre was Iceland which lay on our port bow. With every day's sailing it had got colder and now an icy sleet closed about us with promise of bitter cold ahead.

But luck seemed to be with us. By Monday the wind was back in its old quarter, sou'-west, and we were running full on our course before a small gale. By the middle of the second week out the glass had risen again and we were sailing through cold, brittle sunlight with only a little over 400 miles to go. Weather forecasts were good again and the chances of arriving at Maddon's Rock in fairish weather looked reasonably bright. One thing only was really worrying me. Halsey, in that broadcast, had spoken of advancing his sailing date to the 17th of April. If he had, in fact, got away on that day, and if he had set a course direct for Maddon's Rock, I figured that at an average of ten knots he couldn't be more than two days behind us. I wished to God we had definite information as to the date of his departure. Another thing, would he dare set his course direct for Maddon's Rock? Surely he would play safe and at least make a show of going to the supposed wreck of the *Trikkala*? I kept my counsel to myself, but I realised that it was a point that was worrying Jenny for on the Wednesday she suddenly said, "I wonder where Halsey is, Jim? I think he'd

make for the position at which the *Trikkala* is supposed
to have been sunk before running north to Maddon's
Rock, don't you ? "

" I hope so," I said.

" He must do," she added. " He'd want a ship or
two to be able to say they had seen his tug on the right
course. He'd never make direct for the Rock. Unless
he's worried about you getting there first." She gave me
a quick glance. " You didn't give him any indication
that you were planning to go after the *Trikkala* yourself,
did you ? "

" Of course not," I said.

Her brows were wrinkled. " Still, he'd naturally be
worried. If you were capable of escaping from Dartmoor,
he wouldn't rule out the posssibility of your making an
attempt to get to Maddon's Rock. That's probably why
he advanced his sailing date. I wish we knew when he
actually sailed. Since that broadcast, I've listened to
every news bulletin in the hopes of hearing some
announcement about it. But there's been nothing."

The weather was very cold now. We struck a lot of
sleet and visibility generally was poor. But the wind held,
varying as before between sou'-west and nor'-west, so that
we made good progress. On Sunday, the 28th of April,
I managed to shoot the sun through a gap in the clouds.
I was thus able to confirm our position. It checked up
pretty well with our estimate for with the wind mainly
astern we'd not been blown off our course at all. " We're
approximately 85 miles sou'-sou'-west of the Rock," I
told Jenny who was at the wheel.

" When do you reckon we'll make it ? " she asked.

I glanced at my watch. It was three-thirty. We were
logging just over four knots in a rather steep sea. " About
midday to-morrow," I said, " if we keep our present
speed."

She nodded. " Good," she said. " We may just make
it in time. I've just heard a meteorological bulletin.
It's not so good. There's dirty weather coming up behind
us. The glass is falling too. I'm afraid we're about due
for a blow."

"Well, we've been lucky enough so far," I said.

She turned suddenly towards me. "You know, Jim, even with the sea like this we may not be able to reach the *Trikkala*. We don't know what the place is like. Rankin said they'd beached the *Trikkala*. That means *inside* the reefs, doesn't it ?"

"Yes," I said. "He spoke of going in through a gap."

"And that gap may only be navigable on a really calm day. Don't forget what that book of mine said— *there are less that a dozen known instances of landings being made on the island*. This is probably quite a calm day for these waters, but the seas are big enough. Right now Maddon's Rock is probably hidden in a mist of spray and the gap in the reefs made unapproachable by a mad tumble of waves."

"Don't forget," I pointed out, "that they managed to beach the *Trikkala* and get out again through the gap in an open boat that was smaller than this. And from the time we abandoned ship to the time they were picked up near the Faroes was only 21 days. They must have taken the *Trikkala* straight in and come straight out again in their boat."

"They may have struck lucky with the weather," she said. "Pray God we strike lucky with it. At best we'll only have a few days to spare before Halsey arrives with his tug. If we don't get in before then, well—we might just as well not have come. We'll get no proof. And if he catches us inside——"

She didn't complete the sentence. "Luck's been with us so far," I said. "We'll manage somehow."

She faced me then. "Jim," she said, "you're sure Rankin was telling the truth ? I mean, it seems so fantastic, beaching a ship right up here and leaving it packed with silver bullion for over a year. It sounded all right when you told me about it. But that was in Oban. Right up here, in this waste of sea, it seems—well it seems daft."

"Your guess is as good as mine, Jenny," I answered. "But at the time I certainly felt it was the truth. It was too fantastic a story for him to have made up." I shrugged my shoulders. "Oh, well," I added, "we'll know to-morrow—if the weather holds."

As if in answer, our conversation was interrupted by another meteorological announcement. My heart sank as I listened to it. A gale warning was now in operation in sea areas Hebrides and Irish Sea. From mid-Atlantic to the North of Scotland the weather was uniformly bad with the wind strong to gale force according to the locality. That night the glass began to fall in earnest.

Next morning the sea was about the same, but the wind had risen and was coming in gusts so that the *Eilean Mor* would suddenly heel over and thrust her bowsprit deep into the back of a wave. All that morning the wind was erratic in both direction and strength. The *Eilean Mor* took it all in good part, but it was not easy keeping her on her course. There was no sleet, but the clouds were low and visibility poor, not above two or three miles. The glass continued to fall. Weather forecasts were uniformly bad. I tried to appear unconcerned, but deep down inside me I was scared. The bad weather must be right behind us now and we were approaching an island surrounded by reefs that were only superficially charted. My chief worry was that we should fail to locate Maddon's Rock before nightfall. By then the gale would be upon us and the idea of running before a storm in these seas with no certainty that the island was behind us, was a frightening thought.

Midday came. Visibility was still not above three miles at the outside. The wind was beginning to whine in the shrouds and the gusts were angry buffets of air that whisked the broken tops off the waves and flung them in great curtains of spray across the ship. We were reefed down, but even so the little ship was inclined to bury her bows under the weight of the wind.

Bert staggered into the wheelhouse with a couple of mugs. " 'Ere we are," he said, " cup o' char fer the skipper an' one fer you, mate." He put the mugs down on the chart table. " Nearly there ? " he asked me.

"Any minute now," I said, trying to appear confident.

"An' aba't high time too," he said with a grin that

failed to hide his nervousness. "Me guts is fair dizzy wiv all this pitchin' an' tossin'. An' Mac—'e says there's bad wevver blowin' up. Claims 'e can smell it."

"He can, too," Jenny said as she reached for her mug. "I've never known Mac wrong about the weather. If he can't smell it, his rheumatism tells him."

I drank my tea and went out on to the heaving deck. Visibility was getting worse. I strained my eyes through the leaden murk. There was nothing—absolutely nothing but the grey, gust-torn sea heaving and breaking all about us. Every now and then the break of a wave crest caught us at the gun'l and bathed the ship in spray. Bert came out and joined me. "Fink we're runnin' past it ? " he asked.

"I don't know." I glanced at my watch. It was getting on for one. "It's possible. Difficult to correct accurately for drift up here."

"Any sign of the Rock yet, Jim ? " Jenny called from the wheelhouse.

"No," I shouted back. "Not a sign."

"Gawd luv us, it's cold a't 'ere," Bert said. "Got a nice drop o' stew on when yer want it. 'Ullo, Mac, yer old misery." The Scot lifted his nose to the weather as he emerged from below and sniffed at it like a bloodhound coming out of its kennel. "Come up ter 'ave anuvver sniff at the wevver," Bert went on. "'E's bin belly-aching aba't is rheumatics all this mornin'."

"Aye, there's dirrty weather on our backsides." The Scot gave a cackle. "Ye'll see. Ye'll no be worrit aboot yer stew then."

"Nice cheerful bloke you are, I don't fink," Bert answered back. Then suddenly he seized my arm. "Hey, Jim ! Wot's that ? Straight ahead. Come 'ere. Yer can't see it fer the jib." He pulled me a few paces to the side so that I had a clear view for'ard. "There yer are. Looks like a bad patch, don't it ? "

Straight ahead of us, about a mile distant, the sea was all broken up and thrown about as though it were in the grip of a tidal race. I yelled to Jenny. But she had seen it. "Ready about ! " she shouted.

"Gawd!" exclaimed Bert. "Look at that sea breaking."

The broken water was hidden in a great patch of white foam from which the wind whipped a grey curtain of spray. I knew what it was then—submerged rocks. "Come on, jump to it," I shouted at Bert. A moment later the *Eilean Mor* came round, canvas slatting violently in a gust and we were running due east with our port gun'ls awash and the wind on our starboard quarter. The submerged rocks were away to port now, a flurry of foam-flecked water in the grey misery of the sea. And then, beyond that patch of foam, something showed for a second, black and wicked in a gap in the curtain of driven spray. "Did yer see that?" Bert asked.

"Yes," I shouted back, as I fixed the jib. "Rock."

"It's gone now," Bert said. "'Idden in a beastly great sheet of spray. No, there it is again—look!"

I straightened up and followed the line of his outflung arm. For a second the veil of spray was drawn back. A great rock with sheer cliffs several hundred feet high stood out of the water which writhed and foamed at its base. Then a wave curled high and flung itself at the rock face. A great burst of white water billowed up the cliffs like the explosion of a depth charge. The next instant the wind had carried the spray of it across the rock and there was nothing there but a leaden curtain of mist.

"It's gone again," Bert cried. His voice was pitched high with excitement and awe. "Did yer see that wave 'it it? Seemed ter break right over it. Reck'n we bin led up the garding pa'f. Nobody wouldn't beach a ship there."

The shock of that sight was like a blow below the belt. It took all the strength out of me. "Doesn't look like it," I said. No ship could live in a place like that. And this was a relatively quiet day. What in God's name was it like in a storm? I thought of the gale that was mounting behind us. "You two stay here," I told Mac and Bert. "And watch out for reefs. I'm going to relieve Jenny at the wheel."

" Aye," said Mac, " an' ye'd best tell Miss Jenny to
shorten sail an' rin clear of the area whilst we can still
see what we're running into."

" Bloomin' pessimist, you are," Bert shouted. But his
face looked small and scared.

I went into the wheelhouse. Jenny stood close against
the wheel, her legs braced, her body taut. Her head was
lifted slightly as she watched the sails. " I'll take over
for a bit, shall I ? " I said.

She handed me the wheel and took up the log book.
" I suppose that is Maddon's Rock ? " she asked
doubtfully.

" I think it must be," I said.

She nodded and wrote : *Monday, 29th April. 1.26 p.m.
Sighted Maddon's Rock. Wind rising. Expecting gale.*
She closed the book and straightened herself, peering
out through the glass windshield. " Do you think there's
any chance of a ship existing there for a whole year? "
she asked.

I glanced away to port where the Rock showed momen-
tarily through a gap in the spray. " Well," I answered,
" if they did beach her there, they must have had a
reason to think it was safe." Again a glimpse of the Rock.
It was smooth and black like the back of a seal. It was
shaped like a wedge ; high cliffs to the west rising straight
out of the sea and then sloping away to the east. We
were running along the southern flank of it. I should
say it was about three miles away. The nearest reefs
at any rate were a good mile, probably two. " What
about getting in a bit closer ? " I said. " Mac's worried
about the weather. Says we ought to get clear of those
reefs before it closes in and begins to blow. He's right,
too. I suggest we edge in as close as we dare to the reefs,
run the length of them and if we can't find the gap, or
if it's impassable, drive east before the wind."

" Okay." She took the wheel again whilst we went
about and stood in towards the reefs. When we had
closed to within half a mile of the boiling surf, we turned
east again and began to run down the line of the surf
eastwards. When we were fully abreast of the island

we could see it quite plainly. Why it was called Maddon's Rock, heaven knows. It should have been called Whale Island, for it was shaped just like a whale—a hammer-head with its blunt nose facing to the west. Above the sound of the wind, we could hear the perpetual thunderous roar of the surf along the reefs. Visibility had improved a bit and we could see them stretching in a line parallel to the island and far beyond it to the east. It was as wicked a patch of sea as I have ever seen. The rocks that formed the reef seemed much of a height, as though they were formed by a ledge that had been tilted back by some disturbance of the earth's surface. They were practically submerged, but now and then we caught a glimpse of black, surf-worn rock from which the water poured only to be lifted back by the next wave. I picked up the glasses and searched the Rock itself. It was absolutely smooth, as though worn by a million years of ice and sea.

Bert came into the wheelhouse then. " Fair awful, ain't it ? " he said. " Mind if I 'ave a look fru them glasses ? " I handed them to him. " It'll be dark in two or free hours," he muttered. " Don't yer reck'n we oughter do as Mac says ? I mean, this spot ain't the Ra'nd Pond. Yer can't just anchor up for the night." He was looking through the glasses now and I suddenly saw him stiffen. " Hey," he cried excitedly. " Wot's that on the far side—a rock ? It's sort o' square, like a shelter or summat. Square an' black. 'Ere, you 'ave a look." He passed me the glasses. " Just where it slopes into the water."

I picked it up at once, low down to the east of the island as though it were the tail fin of the whale. " I've got it," I said. " It's not a rock. It would have been worn smooth like the rest of the island if it were." And then I realised what it was. " By God ! " I cried. " It's the top of a funnel." I thrust the glasses into Jenny's hand and took the wheel. " It's the top of the *Trikkala's* funnel. She's beached on the other side of that shoulder that slopes down into the sea."

All thought of the impending gale and of the danger

of our position was lost for the time being in the excitement of watching that distant square lengthen into a funnel as we ran down the reefs. Soon we could see one of her masts and a bit of the superstructure. It was incredible, but there she was, no doubt of that.

The reefs stretched eastward in a strip, like a long fore-finger. It took us half an hour to double the tip and then, close-hauled, we drove northward. We were about two miles to the east of the tail-end of Maddon's Rock. We could see the whole of the *Trikkala*. Through the glasses we could see her, lying high and dry on a little shelving beach like a stranded fish. She was heeled over at a crazy angle and red with rust. Two shoulders of black, sleek rock enclosed that little beach, sheltering her from the prevailing winds. Curtains of spray poured across the back of the island, spume thrown up by the waves dashing against the high cliffs at the western end. Every now and then this curtain blotted out ship and island.

It was less than two miles away now—an anchorage under a lee shore, a 5,000 ton freighter and half a million in silver bullion. And no sign of Halsey's tug. There was the evidence we wanted, almost within our grasp. But between us and that sheltered beach was a band of raging surf. The reefs seemed to encircle all but the sheer western side of the island. But here to the east they were not a regular, half-submerged line, but a jumble of jagged, blackened teeth amongst which the waves tumbled in a riot of unholy violence.

When we were within perhaps half a mile of this mad chaos of water we saw the gap. Perhaps I should say that we saw what we thought to be the gap, for it was so smothered in foam that it was impossible to be certain. It was then shortly after three. To the east of us the sea looked clear of reefs and we decided to press on to the north to check whether there was any other break in the reefs. By four we were heading nor'-west following the line of the reefs round the island. We had seen nothing that looked like a gap and the *Trikkala* was slowly being hidden from view by the northern shoulder of the Rock. We went about then and struggled back with our head

almost in the teeth of the wind along the vicious line of
tumbled surf. No doubt about it, that was the gap right
opposite the little beach on which the *Trikkala* rested.

It took us nearly an hour to beat back to the gap.
We didn't talk much. I think we were all of us over-awed
by the decision that had to be made. The wind was
rising now and the glass was as low as I'd ever seen it.
But as yet the seas were not much bigger than they had
been during the past few days, especially in the lee of the
island. The waves had no weight behind them—yet.
There was none of the heavy deep-sea swell of the kind
that might run in this area for weeks at a time after bad
weather. The decision that lay before us was whether
or not to go straight in and risk being overwhelmed in
the mad tumble of surf that smothered the gap.

CHAPTER VIII

THE "TRIKKALA"

AT LENGTH we were abreast of the gap. Jenny was at the wheel. She had edged the *Eilean Mor* in close so that we could have a good look at it. It was barely a quarter of a mile away on our starboard beam. There was no doubt about it being a gap. A pinnacle of rock stood on a ledge to the left of the entrance. It was like a lighthouse, but bigger, more solid. It was against this that the waves broke. Each wave seemed to pile up to a great height on a submerged ledge, crash against this pinnacle and then fling itself in a great wall of foam across the gap which was a good fifty yards wide. On the farther side the wave seemed to re-form, pile up and break against a solid mass of broken, jagged rocks. From these it would fall back and its backwash would meet the next wave spilling across the gap and the sea would toss itself upward in a giant leap as though it were trying to reach up to the low-hanging cloud. It was a most frightening patch of water. Just occasionally there would be a momentary lull. It was then that we could see that it was a clear gap. And beyond, where the *Trikkala* lay beached, the water seemed reasonably quiet, protected as it was on all sides by the reefs.

" Do you think there's any chance of getting through there ? " Jenny asked me. We were alone in the wheelhouse.

" God knows," I replied. " All I know is that Halsey took the *Trikkala* in through that gap and there she lies, apparently intact. And he came out again in an open boat with five men in it."

" What shall we do then ? " Jenny asked. " We've got to decide now. The wind's getting up. It'll be dark soon. We've got to make up our minds." Her voice was uncertain. She was staring at the gap. The *Eilean Mor* lurched violently. Jenny turned to me as she tightened her grip on the wheel. " Shall we stand away and run for it ? Or shall we chance it and go in ? "

I didn't know what to answer. There lay the *Trikkala* within our grasp. And yet the thought of Jenny being flung into the boiling surf if the *Eilean Mor* broke up going through the gap scared me. " You're the skipper, Jenny," I said at length.

" Oh, be reasonable, Jim," she cried. " I can't decide a thing like this on my own. I've no idea what the reef looks like in fine weather. We've had it fair for the better part of two weeks now. This may be calm for Maddon's Rock. If we wait till the storm has blown itself out, it may be weeks before we can approach as near the island at this. And Halsey would be here by then. You've got to help me decide. What would you do if you and Bert and Mac were here on your own.? "

" I don't know," I said. I hadn't considered it. " You must make the decision yourself. You're the skipper and it's your boat. The decision has to be yours."

She was looking straight at me, her grey eyes very steady, her brow slightly puckered. The salt glistened in her hair. " You'd go right in, wouldn't you ? " she said.

I looked towards the gap. A great comber piled up against the ledge and broke in a seething mass of foam across the entrance, met the backwash of the previous wave and tossed itself in the air like a giant sea horse tossing its mane. " I don't know," I said.

I felt her watching me. Then suddenly in a tight little voice she said, " Tell Mac to start the engine up."

" You're going to go in ? " I asked.

" Yes." Her voice was strained, but I knew by the tone of it that she had made her mind up.

" You aren't trying to be pig-headed, are you ? " I asked. " You do realise what it's going to be like ? It'll be worse than any sea you've ever been through— and the odds are against our making it."

" Tell Mac to get the engine going," she repeated.

I did not try to dissuade her further. "When the engine is going, get the sails stowed," she added, as I opened the door of the wheelhouse. "And have them put their life jackets on. I've got mine here. And we'll need to trail a sea anchor astern to hold her steady in that surf."

"Okay," I said. "I'll give it a tripping line and veer out about four fathoms. It'll need to be a pretty short tow with all those rocks."

Mac got the engine started. The steady throb of the decks was a comfortable feeling. Bert and I dropped the sails and Jenny swung the *Eilean Mor's* bows towards the gap. We stowed the sails and battened everything down. We got the sea anchor over the stern. Then I went back to the wheelhouse. Straight ahead of us through the windshield was the gap. It was now about two hundred yards ahead of us. From that distance the waves looked mountains high as they piled against the pinnacle on the left. Their shaggy heads would suddenly rear up, curl over and then dash themselves against the great square slab of granite that formed the pedestal. The sound of it was like a clap of thunder above the general tide of battle that stormed along the length of the reefs.

Jenny stood slim and erect against the wheel. Her eyes looked straight ahead. A sudden longing welled up in me. It was all mixed up with a feeling of pride and tenderness. She looked such a slip of a girl. But she faced that ghastly surge of water without a tremor. I went up behind her and took her by the elbows. " Jenny," I said, " if we don't—make it, I'd like you—I'd like you to know—I love you."

" Jim ! " That was all she said. I could barely hear it above the thunder of the surf. She didn't turn her head.

" Does that mean you—love me ? " I asked.

" Of course, darling." She leaned her head back so that our cheeks touched. "Why do you think I'm here ? " She was half-laughing, half-crying. Then she straightened up and became practical. " Have Mac come out of the engine-room," she said. " I don't want him trapped down there—for all we know we may turn turtle. It looks frightful." I felt her shudder. I let go of her elbows then and called to Mac. "Tell him to leave the engine running at full ahead," she called out to me.

Mac came up from below and I gave him the tripping line of the drogue. I called Bert into the wheelhouse too. There was at any rate some protection here. Then I went back to the wheel. It would need two to hold her running through that smother.

"Gawd!" Bert exclaimed as he came in and shut the door. "You ain't goin' through that, are you, Miss Jenny? You can't see nuffink beyond that surf—there may be a 'ole 'eap o' rocks there."

"We've been all along the reefs and back," I told him. "That's the gap all right. And if the *Trikkala* could go through without hitting any rocks, then a boat this size can." We were very near now. The thunder of the waves breaking was almost drowned in the constant seething hiss of that monstrous surf. "Ever seen anything like this before?" I called out to Mac.

"A've seen as bad," he replied sourly. "But a didna go through it—not in a wee boat like this. Ye'll no do me engine any gude, Miss Jenny."

"I don't care a damn about your engine, Mac," Jenny shouted, "so long as the *Eilean Mor* doesn't fall apart when she hits those breakers." Her voice sounded a bit wild. I glanced round the wheelhouse. We all had our life jackets on. Our faces looked pale and strained.

"You've got that tripping line, have you, Mac?" Jenny asked. "Well let it out as soon as we begin to swing in the surf. We'll need the weight of that sea anchor when we get into it." I don't think Mac needed any telling. The line was gripped in his gnarled hands and his eyes were creased into a thousand wrinkles as he gazed steadily ahead.

The light was pale and grey. Great sheets of spray were flung against the windshield so that it ran with water. With the engine flat out the *Eilean Mor* was making about seven knots and driving straight for the centre of the gap. The rocks on either side of the entrance were closing in on us. A great spout of water shot into the air some twenty yards ahead of us. It subsided and in a moment of slack I had a clear view of the *Trikkala* lying red and rusty between the smooth rock shoulders of the island.

The *Eilean Mor* suddenly caught the backwash of a wave. For a moment she seemed to slide backwards in a crazy mill-race of surf. Then she was driving forward again straight into the gap. Running on her engine at full speed Jenny could not pick her moment for going in. Not that it mattered. There was no chance of escaping that raging surf. "Hold tight," Jenny suddenly called. "Here we go." I gripped the wheel, one of my hands over hers. The *Eilean Mor* was lifted up and driven forward at a great rate on the seething crest of a wave.

I glanced to the left. The pinnacle of rock towered above us like a colossus. Its great black pedestal was exposed an instant in the trough of a wave, water cascading from it. The wave that was carrying us forward was piling up on the pedestal, curling, crashing against the rock. We dropped down the back of the wave, our bows pointing to the leaden sky. A great wall of surf was thundering across our bows. The wheel jerked under my hand. The bows swung. We lay in the trough of the wave almost broadside on in the gap.

Jenny spun the wheel. Slowly the *Eilean Mor* began to come round, the sea anchor dragging at her stern. She was shying like a frightened mare. "Look a't!" Bert screamed. "Right be'ind yer."

I turned my head. We were inside the entrance now, right in the path of the spilling surf. And beyond the granite base of that pinnacle a wave was piling up. Mountains high it seemed to rise. Water streamed from its broken crest like white hair in the wind. It was yellow with foam. The top curled. Then it toppled forward. It seemed it must crush our little boat. But the rock pedestal was between us. It hit the rock with a growling crash like thunder. It split into a sheet of foam and came at us like an avalanche. The noise of it drowned our cries as it hit the *Eilean Mor*. The glass windshield smashed in like the shell of an egg. The sea poured white into the wheelhouse. The ship heeled, rolled over, was utterly buried under the weight of water. I could not see. I could not breathe. I felt myself drowning. There was a terrific weight on my chest. I thought my arms would break as I clung desperately to the wheel. We were being flung forward at a terrible rate as though plunging down a giant fall.

Then the *Eilean Mor* righted herself with a jerk that shook her to the keel. She was flung skywards. The water poured off her. It drained from the wheelhouse, dragging at my legs. Through the torn glass of the windshield I seemed poised for an instant high above the yellow froth of the sea. The screw raced as it was lifted clear of the water. Then we dropped back with a crash into the sea.

By the grace of God our bows were still headed towards the *Trikkala*. I felt the screw begin to drive her forward again. The sea anchor tow had parted. There was nothing to hold her. The wheel bucked in my hand, but I held her on her course. Out of the tail of my eye I saw the next wave pile up beyond the pinnacle. The surf roared down on us. Again we were buried deep in a giant race. But this time the *Eilean Mor* did not heel so far. I felt her rushing forward at a great rate. Gradually the foam slackened, the water drained off her. Ahead the water was comparatively calm. We were through. That second wave had spilled us right through the gap as though the ship were a surf board.

"Jenny—we're through," I cried.

She was lying on the floor, her hair damp across her face. Bert was sprawled across her legs, an ugly cut down the side of his head. Only Mac was still standing. "The engine-room, Mac," I shouted. "Cut her down to slow."

"Aye, aye," he said.

Jenny stirred. Then she opened her eyes and stared wildly up at me. Her mouth opened wide. I think she was going to scream. But she suddenly got a grip of herself. She swallowed, then said, " Are we—are we through, Jim ? "

" Yes," I said. " We're through. Are you all right ? "

She put her hand up to her head. " Yes—yes, I think so. I must have hit up against something when I fell."

She sat up, pushing the dank hair out of her eyes. Bert groaned. " What about you, Bert ? " she asked.

" It's me arm," he groaned. " Help ! Feels like it's broke. It's all right, Miss," he added as she knelt beside him. " I'll be all right."

The engine slowed. The wind cut at my face through the open windshield. Huge flakes of scud floated through the air like scraps of paper in a gale. The water was chopped up, but here under the lee of the island the waves had no strength in them. I ran slowly in to the beach. Close under the rusty stern of the *Trikkala*, which lay partly in the water, I ordered Mac to cut the engine. Then I scrambled for'ard and let go the anchor.

The *Eilean Mor* was a shambles. She looked as though she'd been hit by a typhoon. But her masts still stood. The dinghy lashed aft appeared to be intact. The only serious damage seemed to be the wheelhouse, which was stove in on the port side and all its windows smashed. Blood was dripping from my arm where I had been cut by the glass. I went aft again. " How's the arm, Bert ? " I asked. He was standing up, leaning against the broken chart table. " Can you move it ? "

" Yes—it's all right, guvner. Caught it on the beastly binnacle, that's all." He suddenly grinned. " Blimey, that was a bit of a rough sea, weren't it ? "

Jenny was smiling. She seemed all right. " I think we've been pretty lucky," she said. She suddenly leaned forward and kissed me on the mouth. Her lips were warm and soft, and very salt. " You're the best sailor I've ever met, darling," she said. And then added quickly, " Now let's go below and see if we can find some dry clothes. And I'll bind that cut of yours up. I think we all want a little patching up." I saw then that there was blood on her neck.

Below decks everything was chaos. Everything that could had broken loose. Bunks had been wrenched from the wall, lamps smashed, crockery broken, lockers thrown open. Clothes and books lay strewn on the floor, all mixed up with provisions, tins, broken bottles, smashed crockery. But it was dry. The hatches had held and the *Eilean Mor's* stout timbers had stood the strain. We were afloat and dry. Only the engine-room was half flooded with water that had come in down the companion ladder from the wheelhouse.

We none of us seemed much the worse for our experience. Our cuts attended to and dry clothed, we left Mac to clean up his engine-room and got the dinghy over the side. By a miracle it had not been damaged. First we took a second anchor out, thus securing the *Eilean Mor* fore and aft. Then we rowed over to the *Trikkala*.

The stern was only just in the water. The waves broke against the lower blades of the twin screws. The rudder was red with rust. So was the hull. She had bedded firmly down in the shingle beach and had a list of about fifteen degrees to starb'd. The incredible thing was that she hadn't broken her back nor did any of her plates appear to be damaged. She might have been laid up on a slipway. From her bows two hawsers anchored her to the low cliffs that edged the beach. Aft, two more hawsers gripped her by the stern ; one was fixed to the rocks of a small reef that curved out like a breakwater from the southern shoulder of the island, the other ran into the sea to an anchor.

We rowed round the stern. The sides were sheer. No ropes hung down. To go into the beach meant risking the dinghy. We went back to the *Eilean Mor* for a light line. With this over the stern rails by the rusty three-inch gun I clambered up on to the deck. There was rust everywhere. It came away in flakes under my feet. Nevertheless, the deck plates seemed solid enough below the rust. Just by the bridge on the starb'd side I found a Jacob's ladder heaped up and fixed to the rail. I took this aft and soon we were all on deck.

" Wonder if the silver's still there ? " Bert said as he clambered over the rail.

That's what I was wondering. We went for'ard to the after-deckhousing.

" Never fort I'd see this beastly guardroom again," Bert said. There was no padlock on the door. We put our weight against it and to my surprise it moved. We strained at the rusty edge of it and gradually it slid back. Inside were the cases of bullion just as we had left them. Our hammocks were still slung from case to case. Bits of our clothing were scattered about. " Doesn't look as though anyone's been here," Jenny said.

" 'Ullo, 'ullo," exclaimed Bert, who had gone right in. " Somebody's bin muckin' aba't wiv these 'ere cases. Look at this one, Jim. Top ripped right off. An' that wasn't the one me an' Sills opened." He flung the top off. " That's queer," he said. " They ain't taken nuffink. Look—there's one o' the smaller boxes opened and the bars still there. You'd 'ave fort old 'Alsey would 'ave 'ad the door sealed up before they left, wouldn't you, Jim ? I mean, 'ere's the ol' bright an' shinin' all on its lonesome an' not even a padlock on the jolly door."

" There aren't many burglars operating in these latitudes, Bert," I reminded him.

" Oh, you know wot I mean," he said. " Sailors might land 'ere an' 'ave 'a look ra'nd the ship fer wot they could pinch—food an' clothes an' things. If the door were fastened they wouldn't bother aba't it. But left open like this—why, hits an open hinvitation ter loot, that's wot it is."

I must say I agreed. It seemed incredible that Halsey should be so careless. I went out and had another look at the door. There were two catches on the outside made for padlocks. But there were no padlocks. And then I saw clean metal showing here and there at the edge below the rust. I rubbed the brown flakes away. Below the red powder I saw distinctly the marks of a cold chisel. " Come and look at this, Bert," I said. Those marks ran all round the door. The metal at the edge seemed blistered and lumpy.

"Weldin'," Bert said. "That's wot it is."

"You mean Halsey had the door welded before he left?" Jenny asked.

"You bet 'e did, Miss."

"Then who's broken it open?"

"Yes," I added. "Who's broken it open and not taken a single bar of silver?" It puzzled me. However, the silver was there. That was the main thing. "Not much use worrying about it now," I added. "Anything might have happened whilst those five crooks were on board."

"Yes, but to weld it up and then laboriously chisel it open. It doesn't make sense." Jenny was staring at the door with a puzzled frown.

"Come on," I said. "It'll be dark soon. Let's take a look round the rest of the ship while it's still light. That door's a mystery we shall probably never solve."

We went for'ard then to the bridge accommodation. It was strange walking along the *Trikkala's* deck all red with rust and tilted at an angle. I climbed up on to the bridge itself. Everything was orderly as though the ship were still afloat, only time had left its mark in rust and a thick rime of salt. There was even a pair of binoculars in the cubby-hole where the charts were kept. I looked for'ard to the bows and the derelict-looking three-inch gun perched there like a relic of a long-forgotten war. An old tarpaulin was slung from the derricks. It undulated in the wind. Beyond those high bows, the island sloped up from the fringe of shallow cliffs. There was no sign of vegetation. It was all rock, furrowed, but smooth as though the stone were precious and it had been polished on an emery wheel. It was as black and sleek and wet as it had looked through the glasses when we first sighted it. A shiver ran down my spine. It was the most desolate place I'd ever seen. Suppose we couldn't get out through the gap again? To be marooned in this unspeakable desolation—it would be a living hell.

Down in the cabins everything seemed neat and orderly. There were no signs of a hurried departure. I went into Halsey's cabin and rummaged through the drawers. Papers, books, old periodicals, a litter of charts and atlases,

dividers, rulers, two shelves of plays including a copy of
Shakespeare and Bradley's *Shakespearean Tragedies*—
but not a letter, not a photograph, not a single object
that might give a clue to the man's history.

Jenny called out to me. I went to the door. " Come
here, Jim," she said. " I want to show you something."

She and Bert were in the officers' mess room. " Look,"
she said as I entered. She was pointing to the table. It
was still laid—just for one. There were tea things on a
tray, an open tin of oleo margarine, ship's biscuits on
a plate, a pot of paste and a hurricane lamp. " Almost
as though somebody were living here," she said. " And
look, there's an oil stove, and a duffle coat hung over the
back of the chair. I—I don't think it's very pleasant
wandering around a deserted ship. It always seems as
though there must be life on board. I remember going
over one of the freighters laid up in the Clyde when I
was a kid. It—scared me quite a bit. As though I oughtn't
to be there, prying into the secret life of a ship with all
its old memories."

I went over to the table. There was milk in the jug.
It looked all right. But then it was cold enough in these
latitudes for things to keep indefinitely. The paste was
all right too. And then I saw the watch and stopped
with the pot of paste still in my hand. " Jim ! What are
you staring at ? " Jenny's voice was startled, almost
scared.

" That watch," I said.

" Wot aba't it ? " Bert asked. " Blimey ! Ain't yer
never seen a pocket watch before ? "

" Yes," I said. " But I never saw one that ran for
over a year without being wound." It was an ordinary
service watch. Rankin's perhaps. The little second hand
jerked steadily round. The others peered at it. Nobody
spoke whilst the watch ticked off a whole minute.

" You're right," said Bert at length. " It's as though
somebody had just left it there. Fair gives yer the creeps,
don't it. D'yer fink the free of us clumpin' ra'nd the room
could 'ave started it off ? "

" No, I don't," I replied. My voice sounded unnaturally

sharp. "This ship has been battered by waves all the winter."

"Then, how can it——" Jenny's voice trailed away. "For God's sake, Jim," she added, suddenly clutching my arm, "let's find out whether there is someone on this ship. This table—laid for one like that—as soon as I saw it, I felt——" She hesitated. "Well, I felt a cold shiver run down my spine."

"Come on then," I said. "Let's go and have a look at the galley. If there is anyone on board, he's clearly someone who needs to eat. The galley will tell us."

We went down the long passageway. This was the way I had come for cocoa and my chats with the cook. The passageway had always been hot and pulsing with the throb of engines. But now it was cold and dank. The gratings that let on to the engine-room were dark and lifeless. The galley door was open. The air seemed warmer and there was a smell of food. Something moved on the cook's bed.

"What's that?" Jenny cried.

"I swear I saw somefink move then," Bert said.

Our nerves reacted on each other. Twenty-three men —the crew of this ship—had been murdered. I told myself not to be a fool. Jenny's fingers dug into my arm. Two pin points of luminous light stared at us from the dark recess beneath the bunk—two green eyes.

We stood petrified, staring at those eyes. They moved. And then out from underneath the bunk walked the cook's cat—the tortoise-shell that had jumped out of the boat just before it was launched. It came stalking across the room towards us, its soft pads making no sound, tail stiff and waving gently from side to side, its green eyes fixed unwinkingly upon us. I felt the hair creep along my scalp. I remembered how the cat had struggled and clawed at the cook. It had *known* that boat was going to sink. Then the thing was rubbing itself against my legs, purring as it had done when the cook had sat in that chair over there, stroking it with his thick, fleshy fingers.

I took a grip on myself. The cat couldn't wind up a

watch. It might eat fish paste, but not ship's biscuits. I went over to the galley stove and felt the top of it. The iron was still warm and when I raked at it, cinders glowed red in the grate.

"Somebody's still on board," I said.

"Still on board," Jenny echoed. "But, Jim, for over a year?"

"It's the same person that burst open the bullion room door. Don't you see—that's why none of the silver's missing. He couldn't take it away because he's still here."

"It's almost incredible that anyone should be living on this derelict," she said.

"Yes, but not impossible," I pointed out. "There's food and shelter here. And water—that's why that tarpaulin is slung from the derricks, to catch rain water."

"D'yer fink they left 'im be'ind as a sort of caretaker," Bert suggested. He made a face. "Blimey! Nice sort o' job that is. I wouldn't stay a't 'ere on me Jack Jones —no jolly fear I wouldn't."

"He's probably some poor devil who's been ship-wrecked," I said. "Managed to get in through the reef and been here ever since. At any rate, that explains why the cat's still alive."

"It's—horrible," Jenny murmured.

"Yes, it's not very nice," I agreed. I saw she was worried. I took her arm. "An abandoned ship always seems a bit uncanny—especially when there's someone on it and you don't know who. Come on, the sooner we find him the better." I turned to Bert. "You go aft," I said. "We'll search for'ard."

Bert's eyes looked startled. "Wot—go aft by meself?" he cried. "Why 'e may 'ave gone barmy. A year alone wiv 'alf a million in silver—'nuff ter make anyone go screwy."

I laughed. But it wasn't a very assured laugh. "Well, just call to him," I suggested. "Make friendly noises."

"Oh, orl right," he grumbled. "But if I start 'ollering, you come quick. I ain't a 'trick-cyclist' an' I ain't got a strait-waistc't wiv me."

Jenny and I searched from the engine-room for'ard through the crew's quarters and the bridge accommodation to the peak. It was a dismal business. To light us we had a hurricane lamp. Strange shadows flitted in the dark recesses of the silent engine-room, along the deserted passageways and in the corners of the cabins.

We were just emerging from Number One hold when Bert hailed us from the after deck. " I found 'im, Jim," he shouted.

Dusk was beginning to close in around the ship. The wind was rising fast and the noise of it whining through the superstructure of the ship was audible above the everlasting roar of the waves along the reefs. Spray drifted against our faces, carried right across the island from the waves breaking against the cliffs to the west of it. Bert came hurrying forward. Behind him was a short, dark-haired man in blue serge trousers and a seaman's jersey. He hung back. He seemed scared of us, like a wild thing that is shy and yet driven forward by curiosity. " 'Ere we are," said Bert as he came up to us. " Man Friday 'isself, on'y he's white. Found 'im 'idin' amongst the rudder gear."

" Poor fellow," Jenny said. " He looks scared—like a badger I once saw trapped in a pig stye."

" How do you come to be on this ship ? " I asked. And then when he did not reply, I said, " What's your name ? "

" Yer want ter talk slow," Bert put in. " 'E understands English orl right, but 'e don't speak it very well. 'E's a furriner, if yer ask me."

" What is your name ? " I asked again, slowly this time.

His lips moved, but the only sound that came was a sort of grunt. He was not tall, about Bert's height. His face was lined and leathery. It had that tired, grey colour that goes with much suffering. His mouth kept opening and shutting in a violent effort to become articulate. It was horrible to watch him fighting down his fear in that dismal half light. " Zelinski," he said suddenly. " Zelinski—that is my name."

"How is it that you are on the *Trikkala*?" I asked trying to phrase the question simply.

His eyebrows jerked up. His brows wrinkled in three tiers of deep furrows. "Plees? I not understood. It is difficult. I am alone too long. I forget my own language. I am here—oh, I have lost my memory." He searched feverishly through his pockets and brought out a small pocket diary. He flicked the pages over in nervous haste. "Ah, yes—I arrive here on 10th March, 1945. That is one year, one month, no?" He peered forward at us in sudden eagerness. "You will take me wiz you, yes? Oh, plees, you will take me wiz you?"

"Of course," I said.

And that hard, lined face creased into a quick smile. His Adam's apple jerked up and down as he swallowed.

"But why are you here?" I asked.

"Why?" He frowned and then his brow cleared. "Ah, yes—why? I am the Pole, you know. At Murmansk they say this ship is to go to England. I wish to join General Anders' Army. So—I go on this ship."

"You mean you stowed away?" I asked.

"Plees?"

"Never mind," I said.

"He must have been on this ship after every one but Halsey and his gang had abandoned it," Jenny said.

"Yes," I agreed. "We not only take back some silver as evidence, but an actual witness."

The Pole was speaking again. "Plees," he said. He was pointing to the *Eilean Mor*. "Plees—your ship. There is a big storm to come. It will be bad here. It is from the west and the water is all over the island. It will soon be dark and you must have many anchors, no?"

"Does the wind ever come from the east?" I asked.

He frowned, concentrating on his words. "No—only once. Then it was terrible. The bottom, she nearly break into this ship. The cabins all water. The waves come right up." And then he pointed to the masts.

He was exaggerating, of course. But if the wind was easterly, it was obvious that the seas would pile in over the protecting reefs and this sheltered beach would become a raging inferno of water. Thank God the prevailing wind was westerly. "Come on, then." I said. "Let's see that the *Eilean Mor* is securely anchored."

"We go, yes?" Zelinski said. "You must not sleep on your little boat. You must come here, plees. It will be very bad."

The *Eilean Mor* was lying bows-on to the beach, facing up into the wind that came roaring over the Rock. We found two small boats' anchors in the *Trikkala's* stores and with these and stout hawsers we moored the *Eilean Mor* securely—two anchors for'ard and two aft, with the long hawsers stretching seaword from the stern to hold her off the beach if the wind should change. Then we transferred to the *Trikkala* and hauled our dinghy up after us.

Zelinski insisted on cooking the meal. He had lost all his shyness. Words poured from him in an excited jumble as he hurried to and fro preparing our beds, getting us hot water, searching out the medical chest to see to our cuts. Nothing was too much trouble in his crazy delight at human companionship.

He was an excellent cook and the ship's stores had been preserved by the cold. He was three hours preparing the meal. But when he served it I can't remember a meal I enjoyed so much. When it was all on the table, he hurried out and returned with the tortoise-shell cat. "Excuse, plees," he said. "I introduce. This is my little friend. I do not know his name. But I call him Jon." He laughed nervously. "That is so that I shall not forget my own name." He poured a saucer of tinned milk for the cat and then sat down with us.

By the time the meal was over the gale was upon us. We went up on deck. It was pitch dark. The wind howled through the superstructure throwing a curtain of spray across our faces. The sound of the surf thundering across the reefs was louder now. And yet through it came a sound like distant regular gun-fire. It was like the sound of a giant battering ram, a dreadful sound that seemed to echo through the frame of the ship. It was the waves thundering against the cliffs on the other side of

the island. " It will get more bad—much more bad,"
Zelinski said.

We felt our way aft hoping to get a glimpse of the
Eilean Mor. But when we stood by the rusty three-inch
at the stern all we could see was the vague jostling white
of broken waves.

" Do you think she'll be all right ? " Jenny asked me.

" I don't know," I said. " But there's nothing we can
do about it now. We've got four anchors out. She ought
to hold. Thank God we don't have to sleep on her
though."

" But oughtn't we to take watches ? " she suggested
in a small voice.

" What could we do if she did drag her anchors ? " I
said. " Anyway, we can't even see her."

I had hold of her arm and I sensed her heaviness of
heart. " No—you're right. But it doesn't seem right
for us to sleep while she fights it out all alone."

" I know, dear," I said. " But we'll just have to wait
till morning. We'll see what it's like when it's light."

Before going to bed that night I searched for and found
the sliding plate to which Rankin had referred. It was
a neat affair operated from what had been Hendrik's
cabin—a large plate running in grooves fitted to the steel
ribs of the ship. It ran down inside the for'ard part of
Number Two hold. It had been held up by a chain
fitted to a catch under Hendrik's bunk. When this catch
was released it had slid down with its own weight and had
fairly effectually sealed the hole torn in the weak plate
by the explosion. It had later been welded.

The next morning Bert and I were up early. At seven
o'clock it was just beginning to get light. Even under
the shelter of the island the wind was so strong we had to
hold on to the rails as we struggled aft. It was near the
top of the tide and the *Trikkala* was grinding her keel
softly on the shingle beach. A perpetual curtain of spray
covered the ship. Water poured down the smooth black
flanks of the island. The air was full of wisps of scud
driven like flocks of clumsy white birds before the wind.
Aft, the turmoil was frightful. No sign of reefs now.

All around to the grey edge of visibility was a racing,
roaring, cataracting welter of foam. The sea was a giant
mill-race, all white—not white, yellow rather, and cold
and grey and wicked-looking. And just aft of the *Trikkala*
the little white-painted ship that had brought us to this
dreadful place flung herself about like a mad thing in
the broken water.

"Still there," Bert yelled in my ear. "But she don't
like it. She looks like a 'orse tossin' 'er mane and pawin'
the gra'nd wiv terror."

No, she didn't like it. But one thing was in her favour.
The little beach was sheltered from the full force of the
wind, and what wind there was just off the beach drove the
water out towards the reefs. That, I realised, was why
the *Trikkala* had not been broken up. The *Eilean Mor*
was tossing about violently enough, but the waves
weren't smashing at her and so long as the anchor held
she would weather it.

I looked back along the rusty deck of the *Trikkala*.
Jenny was fighting her way towards us. She didn't say
anything as she joined us. She stood for a moment against
the rail looking anxiously down at the *Eilean Mor*
straining at her moorings. Then she turned quickly
away.

The gale continued all that day. The sound of it was
with us throughout the ship. It tore at our nerves, so that
we became irritable. Only Zelinski kept cheerful. He
talked incessantly in his limited English—of his farm in
Poland before the war, of cavalry charges against the
Germans in 1939—he had been a cavalry officer—of the
life in Russian labour camps. It was as though words
had been dammed up inside him so long that they just
had to come out. And all the time our one hope of getting
away from Maddon's Rock lay fighting at her anchorage
at the mercy of the elements.

I spent a lot of time that day rummaging through
Captain Halsey's cabin. I felt that it must contain something of his past. But I could find nothing. I searched
through his beautifully bound copy of Shakespeare.
The pages were well thumbed but there were no letters,

no notes even. I went through all his books, but he was apparently a man who was not in the habit of using old letters as page markers. His technical books on seamanship were copiously annotated in his neat, rather angular writing. But they were just notes—there was nothing, absolutely nothing of his past.

He had several privately bound volumes of the *Theatregoer*—there were three in all covering the years 1919, 1920 and 1921. Being interested in the stage I finally gave up my abortive search and took these three volumes into the warmth of the galley to look through them. And there I made a discovery—it was in the volume for 1921, the picture of a young actor named Leo Foulds. There was something about that up-thrust chin and wide-flung arm that worried me. I knew the actor and yet I could not remember the name Leo Foulds. And I certainly had not been going to plays in 1921. I showed it to Jenny and she had the same feeling that she had seen Foulds, though she did not remember the name.

And then with sudden excitement I showed it to Bert. And he, too, felt he knew the actor. And Bert had never seen a play in his life. I took a pencil and quickly sketched in a little pointed beard and a peaked cap. And there it was—Captain Halsey declaiming Shakespeare on the bridge of the *Trikkala*. Halsey in that cabin on the salvage tug. There was no doubt about it. I tore the page out and put it in my pocket book.

At dusk Bert and I went up to have another look at the *Eilean Mor*. Jenny didn't come. She just couldn't face the sight of it when she could do nothing to help. As soon as we came out on deck we knew something had changed. For a moment I couldn't get what it was. It seemed quieter. Yet the roar of the breakers was as loud as ever and the terrible, steady booming from the other side of the island continued. Then I realised what it was. The wind—it had died away completely.

" Queer, ain't it ? " Bert said. " Not a bref."

" Yes," I said. " It is queer." The sky had a strange, unholy light in it, that foggy yellow light that goes with

snow. I didn't like the look of it. " It's the sort of thing
that happens when you're at the very centre of a storm,"
I said to Bert. " There's a lull—blue sky sometimes—
and then the wind starts blowing again from the opposite
quarter."

" The Polski said the wind 'ad only bin easterly once
the 'ole time 'e'd bin 'ere," he reminded me.

" It only needs to happen once," I said.

We went below then. I said nothing to Jenny about it.
But that night, as I lay in my bunk, I found myself
listening for that change of wind.

At what time it actually started to blow again I don't
know. It was just after four-thirty that I woke. I rolled
over in my bunk and wondered sleepily what had woken
me. The roar of the seas out on the reefs was as loud as
ever. Nothing seemed changed. Then I was suddenly
wide awake. The bunk, the whole room seemed to be
moving. The very framework of the ship quivered. There
was a deep grating sound from deep down in the bowels
of her. I lit the lamp. A little trickle of water was running
under the door. The ship quivered again as though it
had been given a terrific blow, it lifted slightly and then
settled back with that horrible grinding sound.

I knew what had happened then. I got out of my bunk,
put on sea boots and oilskins and went up on deck.
Water was pouring down the open companionway. This
companionway faced aft and the wind roared straight
in as though into the mouth of a vacuum. I fought my
way to the top of the ladder. It was pitch dark. But
foam washed the decks with a pale luminous light. I
could sense rather than see or hear the waves crashing
against *Trikkala's* stern. They must be piling in at a
great height to lift the ship like that. I thought of the
Eilean Mor lying out there on the break of them and my
heart sank. The noise of the wind and sea combined
was terrifying. But there was nothing I could do. That
was the hell of it. There was nothing any of us could
do.

I shut the door at the top of the companion ladder
and went along to the galley. There I made myself

some tea. And it was there that Jenny found me half
an hour later. Her eyes looked wild and desperate. I
put my arm round her and we stood gazing into the red
face of the stove. " I suppose there is nothing we can
do ? " she said at length.

" Nothing," I told her.

Bert came in then. Mac and the Pole joined us before
dawn. We sat there, drinking tea and staring hopelessly
into the fire. Quite frankly, I didn't think the boat had
a chance. High tide was just about first light, between
six and seven. Yet already the *Trikkala* was being lifted
bodily up at each wave and flung down again on to the
bed of the beach. If those waves could lift a 5,000 ton
freighter like that, what would they do to the little
Eilean Mor, built of wood and displacing no more than
25 tons.

Shortly after six we fought our way up on to the deck.
A grey, pallid light was filtering through the storm. The
sight that met our eyes was one of ghastly chaos. At
regular intervals great waves would pile up out of the
struggling dawn, pile up till they seemed to grin down
at the *Trikkala*, then their tops would curl and they
would fling themselves with a demoniac roar at the stern
and break into a cascade of foam that rolled, boiling,
along the deck, swirling round us till we were knee-deep
in the hissing, tugging water.

There was no question of going aft to look at the
Eilean Mor. We climbed up on to the bridge which shook
like a bamboo hut in an earthquake each time the *Trikkala*
settled on to the beach. The air was full of flying foam.
The wind-driven spray stung our eyes. We could see
nothing in that tormented half light.

Jenny had hold of my hand. " She's gone, Jim,"
she said. " She's gone."

I thought it likely and gripped her hand tight.

Then suddenly Bert shouted. I did not hear what he
was saying. It was lost in the wind. But I followed the
line of his outstretched arm and for an instant thought
I saw something white rolling on the face of a towering
wave. Then it was gone. A moment later I saw it again.

Then as the light strengthened we saw that it was the
Eilean Mor. One of the long hawsers had parted. But
the other three held her in their grip fore and aft. She'd
ride stern first up the very face of a comber like a
mountaineer scrambling over an avalanche. She'd
almost make the top, buoyant as a cork, then suddenly
all three hawsers would snap taut as bowstrings and the
wave top would hurtle over her. She had no masts, her
bowsprit was gone, so was the wheelhouse. She was
stripped of all but her deck boarding.

"Jim," Jenny screamed at me. "She's being held
down by her moorings."

It was the truth. We'd given her plenty of slack.
But it was the top of the tide and the wind was piling
the water in on to the beach. She'd have needed several
fathoms more slack to have a chance of riding those
waves.

"We've got to do something," Jenny shouted. "It's
horrible."

"There's absolutely nothing we can do," I said.

"But she's being held down. She isn't being given a
chance." She was sobbing. I could feel the breath coming
in her in great gulps.

A wave, bigger than the rest, piled in. The *Eilean
Mor* climbed gallantly halfway up the breaking comber.
Then she was pulled up short by her moorings. The wave
curled. It was like a hungry jaw opening. Then it crashed
down on top of the gallant little vessel. The moorings
snapped like bits of string. Her bows dipped ; her stern
rose. She rolled over and then came driving in on to the
beach, still struggling like a live thing. She hit the beach
stern first not twenty yards from the *Trikkala.* Her
bows thrust up into the air like the arm of a drowning
man and then she seemed to disintegrate into the original
planks and timbers. In that instant she was changed
from a ship to a heap of drift-wood.

I took Jenny below then. No use watching the remains
being battered on the beach. We had seen her death
struggle and her end. That was sufficient. "If only
I'd been with her," Jenny sobbed. "I might have been

able to do something. I brought her right up here and then I deserted her. All I did was stand by and watch her fighting for her life. Oh God, it's horrible—horrible."

Zelinski produced some brandy. We finished the bottle. Then we had breakfast. We were all of us pretty silent. With the *Eilean Mor* gone we were marooned on Maddon's Rock.

CHAPTER IX

MAROONED

As WE CLEARED up after breakfast that morning Zelinski took Mac on one side. " I dinna ken," I heard the old man say.

" Plees ? "

" I dinna ken what the hell ye're talkin' aboot."

Zelinski took his arm. Mac turned to me as the Pole led him firmly out of the galley. " A' got an idea he wants me to have a look at the engines. A'll be doon below if ye're wantin' me."

All that morning Jenny and I and Zelinski checked over the ship's stores. Bert kept us informed of the weather. With the fall of the tide the *Trikkala* ceased grinding her plates against the beach. But even at low tide the waves were still seething against her stern, so high did the wind pile the sea in over the reefs. By midday we'd checked all stores and Jenny and I sat dejectedly in the mess-room working out how long they'd last us. Zelinski had disappeared into the galley.

It must have been about one o'clock that Bert came down and told us the wind was dropping.

" It always drops with the tide," I said.

" 'Ave it yer own way," he answered. " But I say the wind's droppin'." He rubbed his hands together and grinned. " An' there's a luvly smell o' grub comin' from the galley. Decent chap, that Polski," he ran on. " First time I ever knew a bloke volunteer for the cookhouse. Peels 'is own spuds, too. Where's Mac ? "

" Still down in the engine-room," I said.

" Leave him there," Jenny said. " So long as he's got some engines to play with he's happy. It'll keep his mind off things."

" You two look pretty glum," Bert said. " Wot's up ? "

I pulled the sheet of paper on which we'd written our

stores figures towards me. "Well, Bert—we've just been doing a little profit and loss account," I said. "And there's not much on the profit side."

"Oh, it ain't as bad as all that, mate," he said, pulling up a chair. "We got 'ere. We fa'nd the *Trikkala*—complete wiv bullion an' hintact. We got ol' slinky—wot's 'is silly name ? "

Jenny looked up. "Zelinski, Bert."

"That's right—Zerlinsky. Why don't they 'ave names yer can get yer tongue ra'nd ? Well, we got 'im as witness for the prosecution. That ain't bad fer a start."

"Yes," I said, "but how the hell do we get away from here ? Look, Bert—Jenny and I have had a look at the ship's stores. There are five of us and we reckon that on a reasonable scale of rationing we've got food for just over three months."

"Well, that's better than 'aving ter live on seagulls' eggs."

His innate cheerfulness annoyed me. "You don't seem to realise that Jon Zelinski has been here over a year," I said, "and in all that time not a single ship has come near the place."

"Nah, look 'ere—free munfs is a long time. I know the *Eilean Mor's* gone. But in free munfs—well, in free munfs the five of us oughter be able ter do a lot."

"For instance ? "

"Well——" He frowned. "Get the radio going. Build a boat. There's two ideas for a start." And he smiled brightly. It was clear he'd no idea of our danger.

"To begin with," I told him, "none of us know any-thing about radio. As for a boat—all the wood on deck is splintered beyond use. The only other wood is in the cabins—matchboarding a lot of it—quite unsuitable for building a boat that'll sail through these seas. The dinghy is out of the question."

Bert shrugged his shoulders. "Wot's the Polski say ? Lumme, a bloke wot's bin marooned up 'ere on 'is own for over a year—'e's 'ad time ter fink up somefink."

Jenny sat up then. "Bert's right, Jim. Why didn't we ask him before ? "

" The man's a cavalry officer, not a sailor," I pointed
out. " And then there's the problem of Halsey."

" 'Alsey! " Bert snapped his fingers and grinned.
" That's the answer. Don't yer see. He's our return
ticket. We knows 'e coming 'ere. 'E ain't likely ter
let us down, not with all that silver here. An' when 'e
comes——" His voice trailed off. " Ain't we got no
arms, Jim ? " he asked.

" Yes," I said. " Eight rifles and a box of ammo,
four cutlasses and two Verey pistols."

" You don't reckon we got a chance of takin' the tug,
do yer ? "

I shrugged my shoulders. " We'll be hard put to it to
keep them from taking us."

" Wot—free soldiers an' a cantankerous ol' Scot ?
Wiv them eight rifles we oughter be able ter keep 'em
at bay."

" Don't forget they'll have dynamite on board," I
reminded him. " In the dark they could just blow the
ship apart. Obviously that's what they intend to do.
They won't leave a trace of the *Trikkala* when they leave
here."

" Yes, you're right there, mate," he said. " Brother
'Alsey ain't got much in the way of scruples. Like as not
'e'll dump most of 'is crew, too—all but the old gang.
An' if I was Rankin I wouldn't reck'n me chances of seein'
Blighty again very 'igh. 'Ullo, wot's that ? " he added
as a steady humming sound vibrated through the ship.
" Sounds like an engine."

The floor was vibrating under my feet. " Do you
think Mac has got the engines going ? " Jenny asked.
There was a note of excitement in her voice.

The door opened and Zelinski came in with a tray piled
with food. " Plees—dinner is sairved," he said, smiling.

" Quite the 'ead waiter, ain't he ? " said Bert with a
grin as he helped to unload the tray. " Wot's under
the cover, mate ? Smells orl right."

" Ravioli," Zelinski replied. " We 'ave so much flour,
you see—it is necessary that we eat Italian, no ? "

" Eyetalian, is it ? " Bert said and then shrugged his

shoulders. Well, I ain't perticular. Beastly starvin',
I am."

At that moment the lights came on.

We sat there blinking, too stunned to comment. Only
Zelinski did not seem surprised. " Ah, that is good,"
he said. " It is Mac, no ? He is very clever with the
machine. He will get the engines to work and then we
will go to England. I have never been. But my mother—
she was English—she tell me it is a lovely place."

Jenny leaned across the table towards him. " What
do you mean, Jon—he will get the engines going and then
we will go to England ? How can we get to England
when our boat is gone ? "

He looked up, surprised. " Why, in the *Trikkala*,"
he replied. " She will float. Her bottom has not fall out
of her yet. All the time I am here I pray for someone to
come who can work the engines. I do not understand
them. I try. But it is too complicated. And always I
was afraid I should kill them if I try. So. I wait. But
I prepare. I take—'ow do you call them ?—'awzers, out
to the reef. I make a raft of wood and carry an anchor
out. It was big work. But I do it. Now the wind is from
the east. At high tide she can be pulled into the water.
But it is not safe wizout the engines." He had finished
arranging the table. " Excuse, plees," he said. " You
must eat. It will get cold and then I shall be sorry, for it
ees good. I will call Mac." He looked quickly round at
us. " If the engines are Okay, I shall be zo 'appy. I have
given them grease. Always I have been down there wiz
the grease." He smiled and nodded his head like a happy
father speaking of his children. " I know it is good for
them. Excuse—I must go to find Mac." And then he
went out.

We stared after him in amazement. " Well, wot d'yer
know aba't that ? " Bert said. " All yer questions
answered."

" How horrible for him," Jenny said. And when Bert
asked her what she meant, she added, " Don't you see ?
He's been here alone for over a year, facing certain
death when he came to the end of the stores. And all the

time he knew he had a chance of getting away if only he'd learned less about horses and more about mechanics."

When Mac came in I asked him about the engines. "Weel," he replied, "A' wouldna say they were all reecht. There's some bearings gone on the port engine. That's all reecht. A' can replace them." He nodded dourly towards Zelinski. "Yon feller's done a gude job o' maintenance. But A'm no sure about the starb'd propeller shaft. A've a notion it's cracked. And there's the boilers, too. A'll no be sure of them till they're fired."

"Do you think we can get the port engine going?" I asked.

"Aye." He nodded slowly, his mouth full of ravioli. "Aye, A' think A' can do that."

"When?"

"Mebbe to-morrow morning—if the boiler's no rusted to pieces."

"Grand," I said. "High tide's somewhere between seven-thirty and eight to-morrow. Work straight through the night, Mac. We've got to take advantage of this east wind. It's only when the wind is easterly that the tide comes far enough up the beach to lift her stern. And if we don't take advantage of it, it may be months before we get another chance."

He raised his fork. "Aye," he said. "But what aboot the plates doon by her keel?"

"Zelinski says she's all right," Jenny put in.

"He canna be sure," the old man said severely. "Unless he can see through a cargo of iron ore."

"I don't care," I said. "It's our only chance to get clear before Halsey arrives. Whether the hull's damaged or the engines aren't going, we take her off at the high to-morrow morning. When can you let us have steam enough to work the after donkey engines?"

"Och, mebbe in two or three hours. A've got one of the small boilers fired. A' was jist testing her."

"Right," I said. "Give us steam on the after donkey-engines just as soon as you can. And keep the dynamos going. I'll need the deck lights. While you're working on the engines, we'll clear as much of the iron ore as we

can out of the after hold. And, Mac," I added, " see that
you've plenty of steam to-morrow morning. She's bound
to make water and we'll need the pumps going flat out."
I suddenly laughed. I think I was almost light-headed
with excitement. " My God, Jenny," I cried, " to think
that half an hour ago we were sitting here wondering
how we were to get back. And here was our ship all the
time. Lloyds will get a shock. She's been officially sunk
for over a year. And then we sail her into port."

" Ay, but ye're nae hame yet, Mr. Vardy," Mac said.

" Can't nuffink cheer you up ? " Bert put in with a
grin.

I got up then and went on deck to take a look at the
weather. Bert was right. The wind was dropping. But
it was still blowing half a gale and there was no change
in the direction of it. Up on the bridge the glass was
beginning to rise. A bit of planking lay high up the beach
among some driftwood. On it I saw the letters E-L-AN
MOR. I hoped Jenny would not notice it.

With Bert and Zelinski I got to work, removing the
hatch covers from Number Three hold. We got the
derricks rigged. Shortly after three Jenny came up to
say that steam was laid on to the donkey-engines. It
was wonderful to hear them clatter at the tug of a lever
and the tackle of the derricks drop into the hold. Jenny
quickly learned how to work them and with her operating
the starb'd engine and the three of us in the hold loading,
we began to clear the cargo from the hold and dump it
over the side.

We worked steadily till dusk. And then with arc lamps
rigged worked straight on into the night. In the intervals
whilst we were loading, Jenny got us bully and tea.
That was the hardest night's work I ever did. We were
shovelling almost continuously for fifteen hours in a
stifling hell of red ore dust. Each load seemed to make
little impression on the level of the cargo. But gradually,
imperceptibly, the level dropped. As we sweated we
became coated in a thick layer of the dust so that we
looked as though we were as rusty as the *Trikkala*.

At six o'clock in the morning, when the stern was just

beginning to bump on the shingle, I gave the order to pack up. " Cor luv ol' iron," Bert grinned, wiping the rusty sweat from his face, " I feel as though I done another ruddy year in Dartmoor." I was too excited to feel sleepy, but by God I felt tired. My limbs ached so that I could hardly move.

When we climbed up out of the hold it was to find that the wind had dropped to little more than a strong breeze. The waves inside the reefs were much less violent. They still broke with a shattering roar on the little beach and against the rocks on either side, but there was not the same strength in them.

I sent Zelinski off to get breakfast and Jenny and I went down to the engine-room. Mac was under one of the boilers. When he emerged he was hardly recognisable. He was covered in oil from head to foot. It was as though he'd bathed himself in sludge. " Well," I said, " how's that port engine, Mac ? "

He shook his head. " Ye'll have to gi' me anither twenty-four hours, Mr. Vardy."

I forgot that Jenny was standing beside me and swore violently. " What's the trouble ? " I asked.

" It's the feed system to the oil burners," he replied. " A'm having to take it all doon for a thorough clean. A've steam enough for the donkey-engines and the pumps —no more. The feed system of the main boilers is choked and until A've cleared it A' canna fire 'em."

There was nothing we could do about it. " Engines or not," I said, " I'm taking her off on this morning's tide. We'll just have to hope that the anchors hold. Do you agree, Jenny ? " She nodded. " You better come up and get some breakfast, Mac," I said.

Breakfast finished we all went on deck, with the exception of Mac who returned to his boilers. We went aft and got the hawsers fixed to the capstan drums of the donkey engines. The port drum took the line that ran out to the reef, the starb'd drum the line to the anchor. " Do you think that anchor will hold ? " I asked Zelinski.

He spread his hands out in a gesture of resignation.

" I have hope—that is all I can say. The bottom of the sea is rocky."

It was past seven-thirty now. The lightened stern was lifting as each successive wave spilled under it. As it came down on the beach again, the *Trikkala* shivered through her whole length and that wretched grinding noise was audible above the din of the sea. I sent Bert and Zelinski for'ard. We had already fixed the bow hawsers to the donkey-engines. Their job was to pay off for'ard as Jenny and I on the after donkey-engines endeavoured to pull the *Trikkala* into the water.

When they were all set Bert waved to me. Jenny and I took up the slack. The powerful clatter of the engines filled us with a wild sense of hope. If only we could pull her off. If only her hull was not damaged. If only the anchors held when we were clear of the beach and afloat. If only—if only—if only——

" Okay ? " I called to Jenny.

She nodded.

I signalled to Bert that we were about to commence operations. Then Jenny and I waited tense for the next big wave. We let three waves dissipate their strength, lifting the stern and crashing it down on to the beach. Then Jenny pointed. I had already seen it, a great shaggy-headed comber, that was piling in a good deal higher than the others. Its crest seethed white. It curled. Then, as it dashed itself in a great burst of spray against the stern, I nodded to Jenny. The pneumatic drill chatter of the donkey-engines drowned the sound of the wave thundering on the beach. I felt the stern lifted high. I watched my hawser stretching in a taut line out to the rocks that seethed and boiled with foam. Would the line break or would the *Trikkala* move ? The capstan drum revolved slowly. The hawser tightened, stretched to a thin line. Something had to give. The engine laboured. My heart was in my mouth. Something had to give—and I thought that thin steel strand would never stand the strain.

Then suddenly the drum was revolving faster, easier. The stern of the *Trikkala* hung on the full flood of the

wave. I stole a quick glance at the other drum. It was
revolving faster, like my own. The *Trikkala* was coming
off. I watched the ebb of the wave seeth down the beach.
I raised my hand and we stopped both our engines.
How far we had dragged the ship it was impossible to
say. There was nothing by which we could judge our
progress. But my guess was that we had wound in at
least thirty feet of cable on that wave, some of which
was stretch.

We waited, watching for the next big wave. Even
the smaller waves were lifting the stern of the *Trikkala*
easily now so that at moments I could swear we were
afloat. And each time we crashed down on the beach
with that wretched grinding noise. I didn't dare wait
long. For all I knew we might be bumping on rock now.
A reasonably big wave came rolling in. I nodded to
Jenny. The engines clattered as the three-inch gun at
the stern lifted again the background of foam-flooded
reefs. Again the hawsers tightened to thin lines. The
drums began to wind them in. The *Trikkala* was moving
again, floating on the flood of the wave.

Suddenly my engine raced. My line whipped out of
the water and came sailing towards us, snaking high
above the ship. Then it fell with a crash against the
funnel, trailing its broken end in the water. It had parted
at the reef to which it was attached. Either it had rusted
or it had chafed against the sharp edge of a rock.

Whilst it was still snaking through the air, I glanced
quickly at Jenny's line. It was very taut as it bore the
full drag of the ship. But the engine was not labouring
and the line was coming in steadily on the drum. I
signalled to her to keep going. The *Trikkala* was coming
astern quite easily now.

The wave ebbed. I signalled her to stop. But this
time the stern did not sink with a grinding thud on to
the bottom, but remained uneasily afloat. Faintly I
heard Bert call. I went to the rail and looked for'ard.
" No more slack here," he shouted through cupped
hands and then pointed to the hawsers which were
stretched taut from the bows to the black cliffs.

"Let 'em go," I yelled back and made a cutting signal with my hand. He acknowledged with a wave of his arm. A moment later I saw them fall into the water.

On the very next wave Jenny started her engine again. At first I thought she wasn't going to make it. The engine laboured, the line became tauter and tauter till it seemed as though it must part. And then at the full flood of the wave, the ship gave a little wriggle and the engine ceased labouring. A moment later and the hawser went almost slack.

We were afloat.

We took her out stern first on that single hawser till we were almost over the anchor. Then, before we dragged the anchor on too short a hawser, we let go the main anchor for'ard.

Everything depended now on whether the anchors held. As she had come off the *Trikkala* had swung a bit so that she was not quite stern-on to the wind. We let her be blown a little shoreward so that there was some length to the after anchor chain and then hoped for the best. Wind and waves were both thrusting her shoreward. It was a heavy weight that the anchors had to hold. However, silent and a little scared, we got the pumps working and then settled down to the task of trimming the ship. Our work of the previous night had so lightened the after-hold that she was floating with her stern cocked up in the air. And so, whilst Mac struggled with the engines, the four of us got to work clearing some of the cargo out of Numbers One and Two holds.

One thing, it kept our minds occupied. The hours sped by and gradually we realised that not only were the anchors holding, but that the pumps, working flat out, were able to take care of what water we were making. By dusk the wind had swung right round into the west again so that we were once more under the lee of the island. The sea dropped quickly and then there was no longer any danger of our being blown on to the shore.

We finally got the ship trimmed at three o'clock in the morning. In the galley, with the cook's cat purring round our legs, we had a little celebration party on tea

and rum. We were all practically asleep on our feet.
Mac came up from the engine-room and reported that
he'd cleared the fuel system and as soon as he'd got it
back he'd fire the boilers. There was now no doubt of
our safety. Peace of mind flooded through my aching
limbs. And with that and the warmth of the fire I fell
asleep where I sat in front of the galley stove.

I woke to find Jenny shaking me by the arm. I felt
cold and wretched. Bert was curled up on the cook's
bunk, snoring loudly. Zelinski was frying soya sausages.
" It's getting light," Jenny said. I rubbed my eyes and
stretched.

After a shave and breakfast I felt better. Mac took us
down to the engine-room. The place was hot and full
of life. One of the main boilers was fired. The flames
glowed red through the steel door. The pressure gauge
was beginning to register. " A'll have the port engine
working before midday," he said, grinning. I think that
was the first and the last time I ever saw Mac grin. He
looked like a schoolboy showing off a new toy.

Up on deck smoke rolled out of the funnel in a black
cloud. " I think I feel a bit light-headed," Jenny said.
We were standing on the bridge and I was going over in
my mind how best to handle the ship. Neither Jenny
nor I really knew anything about it. Mac was the only
one of us who had sailed in steam and he only understood
the engines.

" With luck we'll be back in a fortnight," I said, and
kissed her.

She laughed and pressed my hand. " The luck's been
with us so far," she said. " Except for the *Eilean Mor*."

We went into the wheelhouse then and began checking
equipment, testing voice pipes, examining charts. We
must have been there the better part of an hour, talking
and planning and going over things, when I heard Bert
shouting. As I stepped out of the wheelhouse on to the
bridge, his feet clattered up the bridge ladder. " Jim !"
he shouted. " Jim ! "

" What's the matter ? " I asked as he stumbled on to
the bridge.

" Look ! " he panted, pointing aft beyond the *Trikkala*
to the line of the reefs.

He pointed straight towards the gap. A wave had
just crashed against the pinnacle on the south side of the
entrance. It burst in a cloud of spray and then spilled
in a flood of surf across the gap. Everything looked the
same. The line of the reefs, the white boil of the surf,
the leaden, scud-filled sky. " What is it ? " I shouted
in his ear.

" There—in the gap," he shouted back.

The water tossed upwards as backwash hit the
oncoming surge of water. Then, as the sea settled, I
saw it. Out beyond the gap, half hidden in a curtain of
spray, was the squat funnel of a small ship. Next instant
I could see her bows, coming up black with the sea running
white off her snout like a submarine surfacing. Those
bows were headed for the gap.

I felt my nerves tense as I strained my eyes to see her
enter the gap. Jenny came out and caught my arm.
" What is it, Jim ? "

I pointed and I felt her start as the black funnel showed
for an instant in the foam. The vessel was in the gap
now. A wave broke. The funnel heeled right over.
The ship was lost in a great smother of foam. Then she
rose up, just as the *Eilean Mor* had done. For an instant
we could see her clearly—a tug—then she was down
again, smothered in surf and spray. A moment later
she spilled through the gap and was in calmer waters
not half a mile away from us.

It was Halsey's tug. No doubt of that. Unless there
were two Admiralty tugs headed for Maddon's Rock,
which was hardly likely.

" Is it—is it Halsey ? " Jenny shouted.

" Yes, that's 'im all right, Miss," Bert answered her.
" That's Cap'n blarsted 'Alsey orl right."

" Bert, get the rifles—quick," I ordered. " And the
ammo."

In a matter of minutes we were at what was for us
Action Stations. We left Mac with the engines. If only
we could get steam up before they boarded us we might

still have a chance. Jenny and I with a rifle apiece were on the bridge which had armour protected sides. Bert and Zelinski were aft. We all had revolvers as well as rifles.

The tug headed straight for us. Above the din of the reefs I distinctly heard their engine-room telegraph ring as they cut to slow ahead. Through the glasses I could see Halsey standing on the bridge. His black beard was white with salt. He had no cap on and his long dark hair hung about his face. Beside him stood the lean, long figure of Hendrik.

" Will he try and board us right away ? " Jenny asked.

" No," I said. " He'll hail us first. He won't know who's on board. He'll want to know that before he starts anything."

Jenny suddenly gripped my hand. " Jim, I've suddenly remembered something," she said. " Something Bert said. Do you remember, he said he thought that when Halsey had got the silver, he'd abandon all the crew, except the old gang. Probably Rankin, too. They must have others on board besides the five who escaped from the *Trikkala*. If we could work on their fears." She scrambled to her feet. " There's a megaphone in the wheelhouse," she said.

It was a chance. It might make them hold off for a bit. We had to have time. I seized one of the engine-room voice-pipes and blew down it. " Mac," I called.

" Is that you, Mr. Vardy ? " came his voice, faint and distant through the tube.

" Yes," I replied. " Halsey has arrived. What's the earliest moment we can get that port engine going ? "

" Weel, A' canna promise it for anither hour."

" Okay," I said. " I'm on the bridge. Let me know the instant we can use it."

Another hour ! Two hours later and we should have given Halsey the slip. Our luck seemed to have deserted us utterly. Jenny returned and handed me the megaphone. The tug's screws churned as she went astern. She had fetched up within a long stone's throw of the *Trikkala*. " Ahoy there, *Trikkala* ! " came Halsey's voice over the

loud-hailer. " Ahoy ! Who is on board ? " And then again,
" Ahoy, *Trikkala* ! This is the salvage tug, *Tempest*,
sailing under orders of the British Admiralty."

He was lying, of course. But it showed that it had not
occurred to him that Bert and I had reached the *Trikkala*.
" Ahoy, *Trikkala* ! " he called again. " Is any one on
board ? "

I put the megaphone to my lips then and, keeping well
under cover, hailed the tug : " Ahoy there, *Tempest* !
Calling the crew of the salvage tug *Tempest*. *Trikkala*
calling the crew of the *Tempest*. This is a non-commis-
sioned officer of the British Army speaking to you." I
could see the crew lining the bulwarks. " I hold the
Trikkala and the bullion on board in the King's name.
Further, I order you to deliver to me the person of Captain
Halsey, charged with the murder of twenty-three members
of the crew of the *Trikkala*. Implicated with him are
Hendrik, first officer of the *Trikkala*, and two seamen,
Jukes and Evans. These persons will be delivered on
board this ship in irons. I warn you that if you commit
an act of piracy under the orders of the prisoner, Halsey,
it is possible that you will suffer the same fate as the
crew of the *Trikkala*. Halsey is a murderer and——"

I stopped then for the tug's siren was blowing, drowning
my voice. The screws frothed at her stern and she swung
away in a wide arc, her siren still blowing a feather of
white steam at her funnel.

Jenny seized my arm. " Oh, Jim, that was terrific !
You scared him. And all that official stuff about wanted
for murder——" She was laughing.

I felt a momentary thrill of excitement—then it was
gone. Halsey would come back. The bait of half a million
in silver bullion would soon settle the anxieties of his
crew. All I had done was to tell him who we were and
gain a bit of time. I went to the engine-room voice-pipe
again. " Mac," I called, " you've got to get that engine
working."

" A' canna do anything till we've got steam up." His
voice sounded thin and peevish. Wisht ! If only Halsey
had been a few hours later.

" What do you suppose he'll do now ? " Jenny asked.

" Give his crew a pep talk and then he'll come back,"
I replied.

" Will he try and board us ? "

" God knows," I said. " If I were in his shoes I know
what I'd do. Cut the *Trikkala* adrift. We'd be on those
rocks over there in no time. Then he could deal with us
at his leisure."

The tug was hove-to now about half a mile to the north
of us inside the reefs. Through the glasses I saw the
crew assemble on the foc's'le under the bridge. I counted
about a dozen of them. Halsey was addressing them
from the bridge. Bert's voice came faintly from the stern.
I went to the port wing of the bridge and looked aft to
see what he wanted. He was standing by the three-inch.
I couldn't hear what he said, but he kept beckoning to
me and pointing to the gun. Then he went over to one
of the lockers which he had opened and pulled out a
shell. He made a motion of ramming it up the gun.

I was down that bridge ladder in an instant and running
aft. It had never occurred to me that those ancient, rust-
caked guns could be used. But then I wasn't a gunner—
Bert was. If it could be fired, then here was our answer.

Bert was fiddling with the breech mechanism as I came
up. " Is there a chance of our being able to use it ? " I
panted.

He looked round and grinned. " Don't know, guv'nor.
Barrel's pretty rusty. But I managed to lower the breech
block. She's all right on elevation. But the traverse is a
bit sticky. Wot d'yer fink ? Shall we 'ave a go ? She's
bin greased, but then that was a long time ago. The rust
just flakes off the a'tside o' the barrel. Like as not she'll
explode. But if it's our only chance, we'd better take it."

I hesitated. The thing looked rotten with rust. For
more than a year it had taken the full brunt of the waves.
" What about the one in the bows ? " I suggested.

" I ain't 'ad a look at 'er. She might be better, but I
da't it. She was facin' inter the wind all the time. Anyway, we ain't got time ter look 'er over. 'Ere comes the
ruddy tug now."

He was right. The tug was under way again. She swung in a wide arc, coming right round so that she was headed towards us again.

"Okay, Bert," I said. "We'll take a chance on it."

"Right. You take the traverse. I'll take the elevation and do the firing." He began to sing "Praise the Lord and pass the ammunition" as he lowered the breech again and rammed one of the rounds home. The breech block rose with a clang.

I told Zenliski, who was standing by, to run to the bridge and get the megaphone. "I'll give them warning," I said. "If they don't stop, we'll put a shot across her bows. Okay?"

"Right-ho, chum." Bert wriggled on to the layer's seat on the left of the gun. "The ra'nd I got up the spa't is fuzed for zero. Mind the 'awser," he added as I climbed into the other layer's seat.

It was the hawser that ran out to Zelinski's anchor. It was lying slack on the deck close by me. "It's all right," I said. "It's the bow anchor that's holding her." I didn't worry about it for the *Trikkala* was lying with her bows turned to the wind and there was no chance of the stern anchor line suddenly pulling tight.

The tug was coming up fast now. The decks were deserted. Halsey had ordered his men under cover. Through the glasses I could see Jukes and Evans with Hendrik on the bridge. Both of them were armed with rifles. They ducked down under cover as the tug neared the *Trikkala*. Zelinski handed me the megaphone. Jenny had come down with him. "Is that gun all right?" she asked anxiously.

"I hope so," I said. "You and Zelinski get under cover. And keep well away from the gun." I saw Jenny hesitate. "For God's sake get under cover," I said.

The tug was close now. She had cut down her speed. As I had thought, she was making straight for the point where the anchor cable dipped in the waves. She'd nose her bows under the cable and sheltered by the tug's hull, the crew would cut through it with a hack-saw. Then they'd do the same to the bow anchor chain.

I put the megaphone to my lips. "Ahoy, *Tempest* !"
I hailed. "Ahoy ! If you don't go about I'll open fire."

" 'E's 'oldin' to 'is course," Bert said. "Shall we let
'im 'ave it." The rusty muzzle of the gun dipped as he
depressed. I traversed right. The gearing was sticky.
But forcing the gun round with all my weight on the
traversing handle, I found the tug in my sights. "On
target," Bert reported.

I laid her off a bit ahead of the *Tempest*. "Right !"
I called out. And then with my heart in my mouth, I
ordered, "Fire ! "

There was a flash, a violent explosion that made my
ears sing deafly, and in the same instant a great fountain
of water shot up just in front of the tug's bows.

"Luvly," Bert called out excitedly. "That's put the
wind up 'em." He had jumped down from his seat and
was thrusting another round into the breech. I sat slightly
dazed with the realisation that the gun had fired and
we were still alive. Men were running about the *Tempest*'s
decks. We were sitting on top of them at point-blank
range, and they knew it. I saw somebody on the bridge
working frantically at the wheel. The engine-room telegraph rang. The screws frothed white at the stern. The
breech block clanged to. "That'll teach Capting stupid
'Alsey," Bert said. He suddenly laughed. "Look at the
poor fools, fightin' at the wheel. Blimey ! Look—they're
goin' ter foul our anchor 'awser. They're runnin' slap
into it."

In their frantic haste to bring the tug round, they
seemed to have forgotten all about the anchor hawser
they were aiming to run underneath. I thought for a
moment that it would sweep their deck of bridge, funnel,
everything. But it was the bows that hit the hawser.
The whole weight of the boat thrust at it, pushing it
out in a great loop. Jenny's voice suddenly cried, "Jim !
The hawser ! "

Then Bert's voice shouted, "Look a't ! "

In that same instant I saw the whole length of the
slack hawser rise out of the water and whip tight like
a bowstring. Something rose up from the deck like a

solid bar and crashed against my seat. A terrible pain broke through my hip and back. I felt myself flung forward. Then in a daze of pain and lost consciousness I felt myself falling, falling. Then it was dark and I was struggling. I could not breathe. I was fighting in the toils of some nightmare fabric that seemed to have no substance yet was closed all about me.

I don't remember anything after that until I found myself lying in the bottom of a boat, a man's sea boot close against my face. My clothes were soaked and I was shivering with cold. The boat pitched and tossed violently. Oars creaked rhythmically. I looked up. My head was lying between a man's feet. Two knees were hunched between me and the grey sky, framing a man's face. He looked down at me. It was Hendrik.

I closed my eyes. I thought this must be part of the nightmare. But slowly it all came back to me —the hawser whipped suddenly taut, the pain in my thigh and back, that sensation of flying through the air. I knew then that I had been flung over the stern of the *Trikkala*. The tug must have lowered a boat. Wind and tide would have carried me towards the tug. I suppose Bert had been afraid to open fire on them, or they had threatened to shoot me if he did. The boards were hard. I tried to move myself into a more comfortable position, but such a pain swept up my side that I think I lost consciousness again.

The next thing I knew I was being lifted out of the boat. More pain, but I could move my legs and I realised that nothing was broken. " Is he conscious, Mr. Hendrik ? " It was Halsey's voice.

" Aye," replied the mate. " There's nothing the matter wi' him at all. Legs and back a wee bit bruised, that's all."

I was carried down a companion ladder, a door was opened and I was dropped on to a bunk. I struggled on to one elbow and stared around me. I was in a small cabin. Hendrik was there. So was Halsey. The two men who had carried me in went out. Halsey closed the door. He pulled up a chair and sat down. " Now, dear boy, perhaps you'll tell me how you come to be on the

Trikkala?" His voice was soft, gentle as a woman's, yet without warmth, almost colourless.

I felt myself panicking. "What are you going to do with me?" I asked him, struggling to keep my voice to an even pitch.

"That depends on you and your friends," he replied smoothly. "Come, let's have your story. You and Cook came on board the *Tempest* at Newcastle. You found out where the *Trikkala* was lying from Rankin. Then what?"

"We got a boat and sailed to Maddon's Rock," I said.

"How did you get the boat? How many of you are there?"

"Several of us," I answered vaguely.

Halsey clucked his tongue. "Come, Vardy—a little more precision, please. How many of you?"

"That's up to you to find out," I replied. I was scared, but I had myself under control now.

He laughed, that jeering, mirthless laugh. "There are ways of making you talk. Or—wait a minute." He chuckled softly in his beard. "I saw a woman on board. That was just after you had fallen into the water. She was trying to persuade one of your friends to jump in after you. There was something about her—she was very like Miss Sorrel who went with you on that raft when we abandoned the *Trikkala*. Would it be Miss Sorrel?" His voice was suddenly sharp. "Would it, Vardy?" He was leaning over me, sudden excitement blazing in his eyes. I braced myself for the blow, but the violence died suddenly out of his eyes and he leaned back in his chair. "I see—it is Miss Sorrel. And she is in love with you or she would not be here." He chuckled again. "That makes it so much easier." Then he leaned forward. "Vardy," he said, "I'll give you a chance. Advise your friends to give themselves up. You are escaped convicts. The law will be against you. But if they let us come aboard the *Trikkala* peaceably, then when we get back to England——"

"I'm not a fool," I interrupted him. "You've no intention of taking your crew back to England, let alone

us. You'll abandon all but your own gang as you
abandoned the crew of the *Trikkala*."

He sighed. " Come, come, dear boy. A little morbid,
aren't you ? " He shrugged his shoulders and got to his
feet. " I'll leave you now to think over your position.
In a court of law your action in seizing the *Trikkala* and
opening fire on us would be regarded as an act of piracy."

" And what about your action in beaching the *Trikkala*
up here ? " I countered.

He laughed so that his teeth showed white in the black
frame of his beard. " Yes," he said, " I admit that I
would not like it to come to a court case. Come, I'll make
you an offer. If a little of the silver is missing when I
dock, I can always say I was unable to salvage it all.
Suppose I land you and your friends at say, Tromso in
Norway. A man with money can always disappear."
He nodded. " Think it over, my friend. Now I will go
and bring a little pressure to bear on your friends." He
shook his head, smiling. " *Oh, Romeo, Romeo, wherefore
art thou Romeo ?* " he quoted. Then with another chuckle,
he said, " Come, Mr. Hendrik. I think we will give Juliet
a hail." His evil chuckle echoed in my ears long after
he and Hendrik had gone out, locking the door after them.

I struggled off the bunk and stood up. My whole body
seemed sore as if I had fallen on to concrete paving. But
I was only bruised. Nothing worse. God ! Why did this
have to happen ? Our luck had deserted us with a
vengeance.

Up on deck the loudhailer came to life. It was Halsey's
voice, muffled and faint. " *Tempest* calling *Trikkala*.
Tempest calling *Trikkala*. Unless you surrender ship and
bullion within one hour, I intend to hang Vardy for an
act of piracy." He repeated the message and then the
loudhailer was switched off. For a wild moment I
thought he was bluffing. Bert would call his bluff and——
But then I remembered the crew of the *Trikkala* and
the cook's story of the *Penang*. Halsey meant just what
he said. In an hour's time I should either swing from a
rope's end or Jenny and Bert would hand over the
Trikkala. In either case the end would be the same—

death. Halsey would leave us marooned on Maddon's
Rock. He wouldn't kill us outright. He'd leave us to
die a natural death on that ghastly rock. Thus he would
pay lip service to his conscience.

The cabin was small, smaller than my cell in Dartmoor.
The sense of being shut in strained at my nerves. I
tried to fight down my fear. But it came at me in a mist
of terror that sent me shouting and beating on the door.
I tried to break it open with a chair. But the door was
stout and the chair broke in my hand. I searched wildly
round for some stronger weapon. But there was nothing,
and in a frenzy I beat upon it with my fists. When I
came to my senses I found myself tugging at the handle
and sobbing like a lunatic. I forced myself to be calm.
I sat down on the bunk. I must get out. I must get
clear of the ship.

CHAPTER X

DYNAMITE

GRADUALLY I calmed myself. There must be a way out. There must be something I could do. The cabin walls were of wood. But it was stout wood. No more chance of forcing a way through them than through the door. The padding of gum boots on the deck planks sounded almost over my head. I looked up. The deck planks formed part of the ceiling of the cabin. It was impossible to stand upright beneath them. But the remainder of the cabin was loftier, the increased height being obtained by a raised hatch that must rise about two feet above the deck. And then I noticed that in the side of this hatch was a small porthole about six inches in diameter. It was closed. Presumably they had battened everything down coming through the gap in the reefs. I climbed on a chair and, unscrewing the catch, opened the dead-light. I found myself looking out between a man's legs across half a mile of tossing waves to the rusty hulk of the *Trikkala*. If only that porthole had been bigger ! But I realised that it would be no use. I could not swim that distance. The water would be too cold. But the sight of the open air and the *Trikkala* raised my spirits.

And at that moment a man's voice said, " Did yer ever hear the loike of it, Will ? Oi bin at sea twenty-three years now and Oi never heard af a man being hanged for piracy. And what if it is piracy, to hang a man without trial, that's murder to my way of thinking."

The legs shifted, blocking my view of the *Trikkala*. Another voice close by said, " Murder ? " His voice sounded scared. " Well, whatever it is, man, I don't like it. The Captain must be daft. Whatever a man's done, he's a right to a trial. And Halsey now—is he a judge of what is an act of piracy ? What happened on board the *Trikkala* when all the crew were lost, just tell me that, man ? "

"Don't look round," I said quietly. I saw the legs jerk tense. "Just keep standing there," I went on quickly. "I can answer your question. The *Trikkala's* boats were tampered with so that the crew would all be lost. Twenty-three men were murdered that night. Halsey and Hendrik were chiefly responsible. They fixed it so that they had the *Trikkala* to themselves."

"How do you know?" asked the Irishman.

"I escaped on a raft," I replied. "Listen! This is the truth and your lives may depend upon it. Halsey will only take his original crew back to England. The rest will be left here on the Rock as soon as the silver has been stowed on board the tug and the *Trikkala* destroyed. Do you understand?"

They didn't answer. "Has Halsey issued arms to the crew?" I asked.

"No. He and the mate are armed and two of his old crowd, Jukes and Evans."

"So—he's got you," I said. "What about Rankin?"

"He's scared. It's only the four of them that has been issued with arms."

"Ask Rankin to come here," I said. "Tell him Vardy wants to speak to him. Say it's a matter of life and death —for him. And tell the others what I have told you. If you don't do something quickly your bones will be lying on Maddon's Rock."

"Is it true you're a convict?" one of them asked.

"Yes," I said. "I tried to warn the crew of the *Trikkala*. I was convicted of mutiny. Don't ask any more questions. But as you value your lives, take over the ship."

They did not move for a moment.

Then the Irishman said, "Come on, Will. Oi'd like a word with Jessop." And their gum boots padded off along the deck.

It was only a small ray of hope, but it gave me courage. And with that little porthole open the cabin no longer seemed to close in around me and crush my spirits. The minutes ticked slowly by. Who was Jessop? Would they believe me? And if they did, would they act before

Halsey carried out his threat ? Questions poured through my brain and fermented into all sorts of wild ideas. And the minutes dragged by slowly and inexorably.

I began to examine the cabin, more for something to do than out of any real interest. By the bunk was a small desk and over it a shelf containing books on seamanship. And among them was a Shakespeare and a complete Bernard Shaw, several of Eugene O'Neill's plays and a copy of *The Plough and the Stars*. With sudden interest I took a bunch of letters from a pigeonhole in the desk. They were addressed to Captain Theodore Halsey. I was in Halsey's cabin. After that, time slipped quickly by as I ran through the contents of the desk. I think I forgot that I'd only an hour to live in my excitement at ransacking his personal belongings for—well, I didn't know what I was looking for. But I wanted a clue to his past. And I found it.

It was a little waterproof letter case. They were all personal letters in the case—letters from his wife who signed herself Toinette in a spidery foreign hand, from lawyers, from business men in Shanghai and Canton, from ship-owners. I pulled out a half-quarto envelope and shook the contents on to the desk. They were press cuttings. And staring at me from the pile was the very picture I had seen in the copy of the *Theatregoer* I had found on the *Trikkala*. Underneath was the name Leo Foulds. It was captioned : Arson Suspect Disappears. Below the picture was the story :

The young Shakespearean actor, Leo Foulds, wanted in connection with the fire at the Lyric Theatre, Islington, on January 25, in which ten people lost their lives, has disappeared. Foulds was the owner of the Lyric, where, as actor-manager, he was running an extravagant Shakespeare season. It is believed that he was heavily in debt. The Lyric was insured for a big sum. The fire began in the orchestra pit. One of the stage hands saw Foulds coming out of the pit just before the fire started. The police have a warrant for his arrest. It is understood that he may be charged with murder as well as arson.

The other cuttings were much the same. They were from the papers of February, 1922. I pushed them back into the envelope and slipped it into my pocket. As I was replacing the letter case a voice called me softly by name. I closed the drawers and jumped on to the chair again so that I could look through the porthole. Rankin was leaning with his back against the rail. I could just see his face. It looked white and flabby. His eyes met mine for a second and then he looked away, out towards the *Trikkala.* " I was told you wanted to see me," he said quietly. His hand shook as he twisted nervously at one of the gilt buttons of his jacket.

" Yes," I said. " You're to be left on Maddon's Rock with the rest of the crew."

He turned towards me. His eyes were crazed with fear. " How do you know ? " he asked. " Did Halsey tell you ? What has he been saying about me ? "

" I accused him of intending to maroon the tug's crew on the rock," I answered him. " His reply was—You're right and I'll leave that gutless swine Rankin there to keep them company."

It was a lie. But he believed me. He believed me because it was the very thing he feared. " What do you want me to do ? " he asked. " What can I do ? " His voice was broken, pitiful. " I knew this would happen. Ever since that night in Newcastle I knew it would happen. All the way up here I knew this would be the end."

" Couldn't you have sent a radio message ? " I asked.

" No. Second day out Halsey smashed the radio equipment. Explained it by saying secrecy was essential. But I knew then—I knew why he didn't want the radio working."

" Couldn't you tell your fears to the crew ? "

" No. They don't trust me. They're treasure-crazy anyway. They're a tough lot."

" They're scared now though," I told him. " Is there a man called Jessop on board ? "

" Yes. He's an American. He's the toughest of the lot."

" Well, go and have a word with him right away," I said. " He's your man. Have you got a gun ? "

" Yes. A revolver. I hid it in my cabin. Listen, Vardy. If I had a hand in saving your neck, would you—would you give evidence on my behalf at any trial ? "

" Yes," I said. " You're not directly implicated in the murder of the *Trikkala's* crew. At worst you'd only get a very light sentence. I might be able to get you off altogether. I'd do my best, anyway."

" Mr. Rankin ! " The voice was Hendrik's. " Are you talking to yourself. Or—by God ! That's where we put Vardy."

I shut the porthole and screwed it up. Then I sat down on the bunk. Footsteps came tumbling down the companion ladder. The key turned. I buried my head in my hands as the door opened. It was Hendrik. He glanced round the cabin and then up at the porthole. He didn't say anything, but shortly afterwards Jukes came in to act as jailer. He had a rifle and there was a pistol stuck in his pocket. The door was locked after him on the outside.

So the minutes dragged by without my having a chance of any further contact with the crew. I now felt more resigned. But my brow was clammy and cold with sweat as though I had a fever. Jukes' battered nose and torn ear seemed a constant reminder of the violence I faced.

At long last the engine-room telegraph sounded faintly from the bridge and the ship vibrated gently as the screws began to turn. I could hear the water swirling past the tug's side. After a few minutes the engine-room telegraph rang again and the vibration ceased. Then Hendrik's voice ordered all men to muster for'ard. The crews' boots clattered on the deck planking above my head. Somebody was coming down the companion ladder. The key turned in the lock and the door opened. It was Hendrik. He had a length of twine in his hand. With this he bound my wrists behind my back. Then I was taken out on deck.

We were lying about four cables' length from the stern of the *Trikkala*. I could see no sign of life on the deck of the rusty derelict. I was taken along the deck and thrust up on to the bridge. Halsey was there, pacing up and

M.R.   Q down. Evans was standing by the wheel, a rifle slung over his shoulder and the butt of a pistol sticking out of his pocket. The men were clustering for'ard below the bridge. They looked a tough bunch. A rope with a noose at the end dangled from a pulley fixed to the mast.

Halsey stopped his pacing and faced me. " Now," he said, smiling gently, " if you tell your friends to hand over the ship and the bullion, I'll undertake to land you somewhere safe."

" Yes," I said loudly, " on Maddon's Rock where you're going to leave these poor fellows." And I nodded in the direction of the crew. A slight murmur ran through the crowd of up-turned faces.

" Gag him," Halsey said sharply. Jukes stuffed a dirty handkerchief into my mouth and bound it there with twine. " He'll change his mind when he feels the bite of the rope round his neck," Halsey said, and fell to pacing the bridge again. Several more men came for'ard to join the others. There were about a dozen of them now. As Halsey passed me, I heard him muttering, " *Blood hath been shed ere now, i' the olden time, ere human statute purg'd the gentle weal; Ay, and since too, murders have been perform'd too terrible for the ear.*" Then to Hendrik in a whisper, " Mr. Hendrik, keep your eyes on the men. They're getting scared and I don't trust them. And watch Rankin."

Rankin was coming aft. He walked slowly with a strangely mincing step for such a large man. His face was working and his eyes looked over-large and fever bright. He began to climb the ladder to the bridge. " Mr. Rankin," Halsey said. " I'll trouble you to stay down there with the men."

Rankin stopped. His mouth fell open. He hesitated for a moment as though fascinated by Halsey's gaze. Then he turned and went down on to the deck again and for'ard to join the men.

Halsey went to the wind-breaker of the bridge and faced the crew. All his own men were behind him on the bridge. " Men," he cried dramatically, his arm flung up as though he were Anthony calling a Roman mob to silence. " Men—I have called you for'ard to witness the execution of a man for piracy on the High Seas." The words rolled off his tongue with a violence that was accentuated by the background roar of the surf breaking along the reefs that enclosed us. " This man is a convict —a mutineer who escaped from Dartmoor and——"

But there he was interrupted by a tall, lankily-built man. " Cap'n Halsey, some of the boys and meself feel that when we shipped with you we didn't figure on being a party to murder."

" Who talks of murder ? " Halsey answered with a thrust of his beard. " This is no murder. This is an execution."

" You've no rights under international maritime law to hang a guy without trial," the fellow interrupted again.

" When I want your views, Jessop, I'll ask for them." Halsey's voice was sharp, almost a snarl.

But the American stuck to his guns and I felt a sudden hope. " See here, Cap'n, we feel this feller's a right to a trial."

Halsey's fist crashed down on the bridge rail. " If you don't keep quiet, you mutinous dog," he shouted, " I'll clap you in irons." And then in a quick undertone to Hendrik, " Keep your gun handy and watch Rankin —he's as nervous as a kitten." He turned and faced his crew again. " Men," he said, quieting the murmur that had risen, " with half a million pounds at stake, it's no time to consider the niceties of international law. We must get aboard the *Trikkala* and if it is necessary to string up an escaped mutineer to achieve our ends, then it must be done, however much we may deplore it. Either he orders his people to hand over the *Trikkala* or we string him up."

He turned to me then. " Well, Vardy ? "

I nodded my head and made noises to indicate that I wanted to speak. Several of the crew murmured, " Let him speak." Halsey came over to me and undid the gag. " Here's the loudhailer mike," he said, thrusting the little black bakelite box towards me.

" There's one question I'd like to ask first," I said

loudly so that the crew could hear. I saw his eyes
watching me narrowly and hurried on. " What are you,
going to do with these men—" I nodded towards the
crew "—when you've got the silver. Are you going to
abandon them as you abandoned——"

His fist crashed into my face and I staggered back
against Jukes. At the same moment I heard Hendrik
cry, " Look out, sir ! "

My eyes were half closed with pain, but I saw the
crowd below open out round Rankin. He had a pistol
in his hand.

" Rankin—put that gun down," Halsey ordered.

Like a man dazed with fever Rankin suddenly levelled
it at Halsey. There was a flash and an ear-splitting report
close beside me. Rankin's mouth opened. A look of
surprise crossed his face. He gave a deep, gurgling cough.
A dribble of blood flowed from the corner of his mouth.
The pistol clattered to the deck and his arm went slack.
Then slowly he sagged at the knees and slumped across
the anchor chain. Halsey stepped forward, his revolver
smoking.

He went to the bridge and looked down at the dazed
faces of his crew. " Mutiny—eh ? " he said. Then in a
wilder voice, " *Hear me, you wrangling pirates, that fall
out in sharing that which you have pill'd from me ! Which
of you trembles not that looks on me ?* " His tone suddenly
became steadier. " The first man that takes a step
forward—I'll shoot him." They were dumb with fright,
cowed. It was the madness of the man as much as the
gun in his hand that held them back. They were afraid
of him.

Hendrik plucked him by the sleeve and pointed to
the *Trikkala*. " They're training that gun of theirs on
us, Cap'n Halsey. Do ye think it wise to risk being blown
oot o' the water ? "

" So long as Vardy is alive they won't shoot," Halsey
retorted sharply. " Anyway," he added in a lower tone,
" we've got to risk it."

" We could wait till nightfall and board them under
cover of darkness," the mate reminded him.

Halsey gave a sneering laugh. "With a mutinous crew like this. The first time Vardy hailed us did the damage. And now Rankin's shot, they're scared. If I thought there was any other way, Mr. Hendrik, believe me I'd take it. Jukes, slip the noose over his head and stand him at the top of the bridge ladder. Get hold of the rope, man."

The hemp was rough and wet with sea water. I passed my tongue across my swollen lips. The blood tasted salt in my mouth. There was only one chance now. The crew wouldn't do anything. They were unarmed and he had them at his mercy. "Captain Halsey," I said. "I'll do as you want. Give me the loudhailer."

He hesitated. His black eyes fixed on me as though he would read what was in my mind. But apparently I looked sufficiently dejected, for he held the mike out to me and switched on so that I could hear the crackle of the loudhailer's amplifier on the mast above my head. "Bert !" I hailed. I could see him sitting on the elevation seat of the three-inch with Jenny on the traversing side. The muzzle of it pointed straight at us. "These are orders," I went on. "Open fire immediately."

The mike was jerked out of my hand. The noose closed like a rough vice round my neck and I gasped for breath. At the same time somebody's fist crashed into my face. I saw nothing then. I was blinded by pain and gasping for breath. Dimly I heard Halsey on the loudhailer saying, "Stop. The instant you fire, Vardy will be killed. Listen carefully ! I shall steam clear of you now and I will give you a further quarter of an hour to vacate the *Trikkala*. If you are not clear of the ship by then, Vardy will be hanged. Is that clear, *Trikkala* ?"

Then Bert's voice came floating across the water, distorted by the megaphone he held to his lips. "I got yer, Cap'n 'Alsey. But I'm warning yer, the instant Vardy's feet leave the ground, I'll blow yer a't the water. And don't yer try steamin' a't o' range or I'll open fire." And then in a louder voice, "Men of the *Tempest* —the man standin' on the bridge there is a 'omicidal maniac. If you ain't got the guts ter rush 'im, 'e'll murder you same as he done——"

" Full ahead both," ordered Halsey.

Hendrik leaped to the telegraph and clanged it sharply twice. " Full ahead, it is, sir," he reported.

The bridge trembled as the screws bit into the water. Bert had seen the water frothing at her stern. " Stop those engines," he called.

There was a murmur from the crew. I heard the American, Jessop, call out, " For God's sake stop, Cap'n."

" Get ready to use your gun, Mr. Hendrik," Halsey ordered. And then to the crew, " Keep back, all of you."

In that instant, there was an explosion and the whole scene seemed to disintegrate into a great up-thrust of water, flame and debris. I was flung against the bridge rail, slipped and fell. The first thing I remember seeing was the funnel toppling crazily against the sky. Hendrik, lying with his back across the wheel, saw it coming. I remember his mouth opening, but I could hear nothing. My ear-drums were dead. In a soundless world I saw the funnel fall leisurely forward, smash the edge of the bridge and finish up with the steam whistle embedded in the mate's stomach whilst he writhed and twisted.

Then the bridge slowly collapsed, the wind-breaker folded outwards and we were pitched amongst the crew.

When I staggered to my feet I found the rope was no longer round my neck. The tug had a great hole driven in her amidships. Flames were licking out of the centre of it. Muffled sounds penetrated my numbed ears. There were screams and shouts and a sudden roar of escaping steam. Somebody cut my hands free. I saw the American take Halsey's pistol from him as the Captain staggered to his feet. Hendrik's body lay motionless in a pool of blood. Jukes was stumbling about blindly with his hands to his eyes. Evans stood dazed and unarmed.

Jessop seemed getting some order amongst the men. They scrambled aft and got the two boats lowered. Somebody took my arm and hustled me into one of them. As we pulled away from the tug's side I saw flames leaping through the gaping rent in her side. Smoke poured from the black hole where the funnel had been. I remember looking up and seeing Halsey come running aft. He was pleading to be allowed to come in the boat. But Jessop just laughed. " Go tell your worries to the crew of the *Trikkala*," he called. And then he turned to the men at the oars. " Ain't you fellers got any sense —pull, damn you ! When the flames reach that dynamite, she's gonna blow up—an' I ain't aimin' to be in the vicinity. Come on—fellers—pull ! " he urged.

I saw Jukes and Evans were among those straining at the oars. Back on the tug Halsey was hacking feverishly at the ropes that secured the raft. He freed it and then found he couldn't lift the thing. He seemed frenzied with terror. He looked round wildly and then seized a bucket and began trying to put out the fire with it.

I turned to Jessop. " Was there much dynamite on the tug ? " I asked him.

" Why, sure," he said. " Enough to blow up the Empire State Building. Guess old man Halsey intended to leave no trace of the *Trikkala*."

" You knew that when you refused to take Halsey in the boat ? " I asked.

" See here, Mister," he said. " I got you away, didn't I ? Well, there wasn't any more room in the boat— that's my story, see. Let Halsey have a taste of his own medicine."

The rusty side of the *Trikkala* towered above us. Bert's voice called down : " You orl right, Jim ? "

" I'm okay," I said.

" Comin' da'n." A rope ladder hit the water beside the boat. I swung myself on to it and scrambled up. My legs were weak and my face felt swollen and huge. Bert helped me over the rail. Those red, flaking deck plates seemed like home. " Jim ! " Jenny was in my arms, laughing and sobbing all in the same breath.

I touched her hair. I couldn't believe it was only just over an hour that I'd been on board the *Tempest*. " Darling ! Thank God ! I thought I'd never see you again." I felt suddenly relaxed and exhausted.

" Your poor face. Come below and I'll fix it."

" No," I said. " No—there are things to do." I turned
to Bert. " Watch these men as they come up," I told him.
" Keep them covered with your rifle and fall them in on
the deck. I want a word with them."

" Okay, mate." One by one the men from the two
boats climbed over the rail. Several of them had weapons
taken from Halsey and his gang. Bert disarmed them
and lined them up against the rail. " That's the lot,
guvner," he reported. Then he went to the rail and
leaned over, looking aft. " Blimey ! " he cried. " Look
at the tug—wind's fannin' them flames a fair treat."

We all crowded to the rails, staring at the tug. She
was like a fire ship. The wind had spread the flames aft
so that she was like a blazing torch. And in the midst
of that inferno Halsey was straining frenziedly to thrust
the raft overboard. He had got it upended against the
bulwarks and his figure stood out clear and black against
flames as he struggled to thrust it overboard. With
what must have been a superhuman effort he got the
end of it under his shoulder, straightened his body and
the raft slid with a splash into the water. And in that
instant there was a series of short explosions from deep
inside the tug. Then suddenly the whole vessel opened
out like some trick firework and with a shattering
roar flung fire and debris high into the air. Slowly the
debris fell back into the water. All that remained of the
Tempest was the bows and stern. These collapsed
inwards and then very slowly slid beneath the waves.
Nothing remained then but a dark cloud of vapour
that held for a moment in the shape of a smoke ring
and then was dispersed into long trailing wisps by the
wind.

" Well, that's the end of 'Alsey," Bert said with a
shrug of his shoulders. " Can't say I'm goin' ter miss
'im." He turned his attention to the crew of the *Tempest*.
" Nah then, get fell in," he said. " Come along, you,"
he snapped at Jukes who was looking scared, " ain't
no use muttering prayers for 'is soul."

When they were lined up, I went over to the American.

" I take it you're acting as spokesman for the rest ? "
I said.

" I guess so," he replied.

I nodded. " Right. I hope you'll appreciate my
position. I'm short-handed and there's bullion on this
ship. You'll be assigned to a mess-room and locked in,
that is until we're in the shipping lanes. Two men will
be allowed out at a time for exercise. So long as you
give no trouble, I'll see that when we reach port you have
a chance to get ashore and disappear if you want to.
In any case, I'll support your plea of innocence at any
inquiry. Jukes and Evans, you'll be put in irons. Who
is the wireless operator ? " Jessop pointed out a small
man with crafty eyes and a shock of curly, fair hair.
" You'll report to the radio-room and get to work right
away on repairing the equipment. I want to contact
a shore station as soon as possible." I turned to Bert.
" Right, take 'em away. Put 'em in the crew's quarters."
Then to Jenny, " What's the engine situation."

" I don't know," she said. " We were too worried to
bother about the engines."

" Well, let's go up to the bridge and get Mac on the
blower," I said. " He should have steam up by now and
I want to get out of this place while the going is good."

It was a welcome sound to hear Mac's voice coming
up faintly from the bowels of the ship. " What's the
engine position, Mac ? " I asked.

" Ye can get going noo, Mr. Vardy," he said. " But
ye'll have to be content wi' half speed. A'll mebbe have
the other engine going by to-morrow morning."

" Okay, Mac," I said. " Good work. But with only
one engine, I'll need full ahead through the gap."

" Weel, ye can have it, Mr. Vardy," he said. " But
dinna blame me if the whole engine-room falls oot through
the bottom of her. She's no jist oot of the yards, ye ken.
Ye canna afford to take liberties wi' a ship in this
condition."

" As long as I can have full steam through the gap,"
I told him, " that's all I ask."

Five minutes later Bert came up on to the bridge.

He had Zelinski with him. They were both so festooned
around with weapons that they looked like a couple of
brigands. " Well, I got 'em all locked up—usin' the
crew's mess-room as a calaboose. Jukes an' Evans—the
ripe pair o' rotters—I gave 'em a cabin to themselves.
Fa'nd some handcuffs an' clapped those on their wrists
ter keep 'em quiet. That foxy little sparks I locked in
the wireless-room an' told 'im ter get to work."

" Good. Now you and Zelinski get the anchor up.
You can slip the after hawser. We're getting out of here
right away."

" Suits me," Bert grinned. " I 'ad aba't enough of
Maddon's Rock." He and Zelinski clattered down the
bridge ladder and hurried aft. A curtain of rain swept
over us, blotting out all sight of the beach where the
Trikkala had lain. I looked aft towards the gap in the
reef. The surf broke across it in thundering cascades.
Then my view became blurred by the driving rain. The
reef was blotted out , so was the patch of oil and floating
driftwood that marked Halsey's grave.

" I wish we could get the radio going," Jenny said.
" If there's another storm coming up, I'm not sure we
oughtn't to stay here. The *Trikkala* won't stand much
of a beating in her present condition."

" We daren't risk it," I said. " We've got to get out
of here whilst the going's good. If a storm blew up and
the wind backed round to the east again we'd be piled
up on that beach—and that would be the end."

" All right," she said. " But don't forget we've no
boats."

" I won't," I replied, as I went into the wheelhouse
and got some oilskins. As I came out, Bert and Zelinski
passed below the bridge on their way for'ard. " Okay,"
Bert called up to me. " We slipped the 'awser."

" Hang on till this squall is over," I told him.

A few minutes later the rain suddenly ceased and the
gap was visible again, a stretch of foaming white against
leaden background of sea and sky. I signalled to Bert
and an instant later the rusty anchor chain began
clattering inboard, pulling the *Trikkala* slowly towards

the beach. Suddenly the donkey-engine raced. The
ship ceased to move. I went to the starb'd wing of the
bridge and looked for'ard along the side. I caught a
glimpse of the broken end of the chain thrashing loosely
in the break of a wave. The chain was rotten with rust.
It had just snapped. It did not matter now. We shouldn't
need that anchor again until we got to England. But it
worried me. The rest of the *Trikkala* was probably as
rotten as that chain. For all we knew the engines might
do just what Mac had said—fall out through the bottom
of the ship. I glanced at Jenny. She was looking at me
and I could see that the same thoughts were in her mind
too. Well, the gap would tell us. If we got through those
seas safely with that one engine at full ahead, the pro-
bability was that the *Trikkala* would make it . . . If we
got through that gap! My stomach was a void of fear
as I stretched out my hand to the brass handle of the
engine-room telegraph. Then I had grasped it, rung it
twice and set it to full astern on the port engine.

A tremor ran through the ship. I felt the bridge vibrate
under my feet. I waited, scarcely daring to breathe.
Suppose the shaft of the port propeller was cracked. If
it broke, it might rip through the rusty bottom of the
ship. Or the bearings on the turbines might be rusty.
The engine might seize up. The vibration seemed to
increase. I could see flakes of rust breaking away from
the side of the bridge and on the deck red, rotten iron
seemed to be peeling off her.

But slowly, almost imperceptibly the *Trikkala* began
to back away from Maddon's Rock towards that patch
of oil where the *Tempest* had gone down. The vibrations
died as the ship got under way. I put the wheel over and
gradually the bows came round. When she had swung
almost broadside to the beach, I signalled Stop on the
telegraph. The vibrations ceased altogether. We were
gliding astern, softly, quietly, with a feather of smoke
from the funnel and that comforting aliveness of a ship
with its engines running.

When we had lost sufficient way for the risk to be
reasonable, I ordered Slow Ahead on the port engine.

But even at Slow Ahead the ship seemed to be shaking
its rusty plates apart. She trembled from stem to stern
as that single screw bit the water and tried to force her
ahead. At last our sternway was checked and we began
to glide slowly ahead. I spun the wheel hard over to port
and ordered Half Ahead. The long line of the reefs swung
across our bows as we turned in a wide arc and headed
for the gap.

Viewed from the bridge of a 5,000 ton freighter that gap
didn't look quite so bad. We were no longer looking up
at the waves, but down at them. Nevertheless, it was a
pretty awe-inspiring sight. A ship in good condition could
make it all right, for the wind having recently gone
completely round, the waves had less weight probably
than when we came through in the *Eilean Mor*. Nevertheless, that wall of surf cascading across the gap was
a good ten feet of solid, raging water. With only one
engine and a hull as rotten as cardboard, it looked almost
suicidal.

Jenny was standing close by me. She did not say
anything. She just kept looking straight ahead. But I
saw her knuckles white as she gripped the bridge rail
with both hands. "Better have your life jacket handy,"
I said. "And you might get mine." I yelled down to
Bert. "You and Zelinski, get your life jackets. And
stand by to let the *Tempest's* men out if we get into
difficulties."

He nodded. Then I picked up the voice-pipe and
whistled down to Mac. "Give her Full Ahead now," I
ordered. "And, Mac—stand by the voice-pipe. If we
don't make it, you'll have to look slippy getting out of
the engine-room."

"Och, ye'll make it, Mr. Vardy," he said. For once
he was optimistic.

The vibration increased. The rust danced on the rotten
deck plates. The ship slowly gathered speed like an old
steeplechaser taking a last fling at Becher's Brook. The
roar of the surf grew until it was no longer possible to
speak. The vibration of the *Trikkala's* engine ceased
to be a sound and became only a pins and needles

sensation on the soles of my feet. I hugged the southern side of the entrance as close as I dared, gripping the wheel tight in my hand, for I knew the instant the surf hit our bows the whole ship would begin to swing across the gap. Then anything might happen—the steering gear might break, the propeller shaft might snap, the whole of our bows might break away.

It was impossible to time our arrival in the gap. But we were lucky. Our bows thrust into the boiling surf just behind the break of a wave. They swung slightly, but I was able to hold the ship on her course. Away on the port bow I saw the boiling foam fling itself high into the air as it met the backwash of the previous wave. Beyond the pinnacle, with its black rock pedestal cascading water, the next wave built up. Even from the bridge it seemed like a frightful mountain ridge, piling up and foaming at its crest like a thundering avalanche. Then it broke, flung itself over the pedestal and crashed against the ship's side with a roar that was unearthly. A blinding sheet of spray rose high above the starb'd rail. The *Trikkala* started like a thrashed horse, the bows swung away to port, the deck heeled over—and then the broken spray fell in solid water on our decks as though endeavouring to beat us down into the sea. For a moment I could see nothing. I was clinging to the wheel, struggling to put it over to starb'd in an endeavour to hold the ship on her course.

Then the spray cleared, the surf went roaring past us and the next wave was piling up. The bridge still vibrated under my feet, the *Trikkala* was still moving forward. She was going through the gap now and taking it at an angle.

The full weight of the second wave was astern. The wheel was whipped out of my hand and spun wildly. Our direction was altered as the whole stern of the ship was swept round by the force of the water. The *Trikkala* virtually pivoted on her bows.

I got hold of the wheel again. We were facing south into a welter of foam. I swung the ship back on to her course through a piled-up wave that came green over the decks. And then we were clear. I couldn't realise it at first. There was the boiling turmoil of the gap full astern of us and we were headed out into the rolling furrows of a quieter sea. The *Trikkala* was rolling madly, but the engine was still running, the deck still vibrated, she was still afloat.

Jenny seized my arm. " We've done it," she shouted.

My body seemed to relax, quite suddenly, and I felt desperately tired. It was then I became conscious of the pain of my left hand. It had been caught by the spokes of the wheel and the little finger was broken. But I didn't care. We were through the gap and homeward bound.

We set our course sou'-sou'-west and before dusk closed in on us Maddon's Rock was no more than a mad tumble of surf-whitened water far astern on the edge of visibility. Ahead of us lay a grey, deep-furrowed waste of restless water. The rust-reddened bows of the *Trikkala* thrust deep into the marching waves. Great clouds of spray drove the length of the ship as we struggled forward on our one engine. Just over 1,500 miles away lay Scotland and home.

Well, that's the story of the *Trikkala*. There is not much I can add that has not been published already. Just after passing between the Shetlands and Faroes, the wind swung round and blew a gale from the nor'-east. It was the worst May gale for several years. The seas rolled green over our stern. We lost our funnel and the whole bridge structure collapsed. We began to make water faster than the pumps could deal with it. Our acting wireless operator had got some sort of a transmission working and I decided to send out an S O S The call was answered strangely enough by Loch Ewe naval station. We were then about 100 miles north of the Hebrides. There were no ships in our immediate vicinity. But when they realised who we were and had been informed that the bullion was on board, they told us that an Admiralty tug was being dispatched immediately to our assistance. That was on the 16th of May.

We then had eight feet of water in Number Three hold and were badly down by the stern.

The following day the gale slackened and by dusk the tug had us in tow.

The ether fairly buzzed with messages—from the Board of Trade, from the Kelt Steamship Company, the owners of the *Trikkala*, from the Admiralty and from practically every national newspaper. Before we docked at Oban bids for the exclusive story had risen to £3,000 and a film company had offered £2,000 just for the first option on the story.

This should have prepared us for the excitement that our arrival at Oban caused. But on a rusty hulk with the desolate wilderness of the sea all round us, it was quite impossible to realise that we were the topic of conversation of a whole nation. For three days we topped the headlines on the front page of practically every newspaper in the country.

Well, I suppose it is pretty unusual for a ship reported lost to be thrown up out of a gale over a year later. And, of course, there was that half million in silver bullion. That is what really made it a story.

When we docked we faced an absolute barrage of newspaper men, camera men and officials. Sir Philip Kelt, chairman of the Kelt Steamship Company, had flown up to meet us. And on the fringe of the crowd stood Jenny's father.

That evening, when the barrage of questions had died down and we had all of us made long statements, we were allowed to go our way. Bert was catching the train to London. With him went Jon Zelinski and the cook's cat. Zelinski was bound for Polish headquarters. Jenny and I and her father saw them off. So did about twenty newspaper men. The engine whistled. " Well, I'll say s'long fer now, mate," Bert said. ." See you at the enquiry. An' you, Miss. An' I 'opes—" he gave us a sly wink— " I 'opes you two don't go an' make a mess of it."

" We shan't," was said almost in unison. Then as the train began to move, Jenny ran forward and kissed him.

Cameras clicked. He waved his hand. " Well, s'long then," he called. " An' thanks fer the trip."

That night after dinner, Jenny and I walked down to the loch. A nearby full moon hung over Ben Cruachan. The highland hills were a vague, huddled mass. The water of the loch was like beaten pewter. We walked silently along the road beyond Connel bridge to the little inlet under Dunstaffnage Castle. There was no ship lying at anchor there now, only the little island of *Eilean Mor* stood in the placid water just off the end of the promontory.

" She was a game little boat," Jenny said. She was crying silently.

I said nothing. But I decided then that part of my salvage money would go to the building of *Eilean Mor II*. And that that would be my wedding present to Jenny.

THE END